GOODBYE MEXICO

Jack Armstrong and Gerard Finnegan Gearheardt return
in Phillip Jennings' uproarious new novel

Wall Street Heat

Available June 2018

Also by Phillip Jennings

Nam-A-Rama
The Politically Incorrect Guide to the Vietnam War

GOODBYE MEXICO

A NOVEL BY

PHILLIP JENNINGS

REGNERY FICTION

Cataloging-in-Publication Data on file with the Library of Congress

ISBN 978-1-62157-701-0
eISBN 978-1-62157-720-1

Published in the United States by
Regnery Fiction
An imprint of Regnery Publishing
A Division of Salem Media Group
300 New Jersey Ave NW
Washington, DC 20001
www.Regnery.com

Manufactured in the United States of America

10 9 8 7 6 5 4 3 2 1

Books are available in quantity for promotional or premium use. For information on discounts and terms, please visit our website: www.Regnery.com.

Distributed to the trade by
Perseus Distribution
www.perseusdistribution.com

SOUTH OF THE BORDER, BUT NORTH OF PANAMA

Gearheardt looked damned good for a dead man. Same silly grin. Same low slouch in the chair. His left foot, sockless in his penny loafer, rested on the corner of my desk and balanced him as he leaned on the two back legs of the Government Issue, standard low-level embassy employee furniture. His cigarette ash landed lightly on my inexpensive carpet, a gift from one of my Mexican assets, as he waved his arms demonstratively with his story.

"So the Nungs dragged me out, probably so they could eat fresh-cooked meat, but unfortunately for them I was alive." Gearheardt spread his arms, illustrating the point that he was living.

He had walked into my office in the embassy, pulled a chair up to my desk and said, "Jack, you look like a damn bureaucrat. Never thought I'd see the day."

I have to admit that after the shock I shed tears of joy, whooping and disturbing the embassy folks, most of whom already did not like me. (No one in the embassy liked the guys who were spooks, assuming that the

CIA was busily working against the very programs the State Department was pushing. They were mostly right.) But Gearheardt—alive! It was a miracle. Unless you knew Gearheardt.

My first reaction was to call my mother back in Kansas. She had always loved Gearheardt (did that put her in the class of bar-women around the world who also loved Gearheardt?). She had the completely unrealistic notion that Gearheardt 'protected' me as my best friend. But I knew that she would be thrilled. When I left home after a visit, departing to the hell-spots the Marines sent me, she would say "I just hope that Gearheardt will protect you. Bless his soul."

He had last been seen, or so I thought, in the middle of a pile of flaming helicopter in the Laotian jungle near the Mu Gia pass. His Air America mission had been to pick up a group of Chinese mercenaries, Nungs, who had been causing mischief on our behalf along the Ho Chi Minh trail. Letting down into the zone, Gearheardt had taken a dead-on burst from a fifty caliber and cart-wheeled in flames. The Nungs on the ground radioed there were no survivors. Three days later I held his memorial in The White Rose, our favorite Vientiane nightclub, slept with his girlfriend to comfort us both, and, not long after, left Southeast Asia. That was 1969. Now it was 1973 and the dead-man was sitting in front of me. My best friend alive and all in one piece. "You survived that fireball without a scratch?"

"Actually if you look close, these aren't *my* ears. I'll tell you about that later. I'm thirsty, Jack. Let's hit a cantina."

Gearheardt left the embassy the way he left most places when I had known him before; as if the entire staff was already mourning his departure. He spoke to all of the secretaries and the people who appeared from their offices—although he couldn't have known any of them.

Gearheardt had been presumed dead for years. After I left Asia, I had hounded the CIA to let me join the Agency partly, in some way, to continue working with his memory. They had only reluctantly let me join their ranks (The 'cover' that Air America was an independent airline might have been breached if I left it and immediately showed up as an agent, they thought). After brief training and a rapid language course, I ended up in Mexico.

The Marine at the front desk jumped to attention as we approached the exit.

"Sign Mr. Armstrong and me out, corporal," Gearheardt said, brightly. "And tell Gunnery Sergeant Wolfe I'll take him up on his offer next time." He winked at the grinning Marine and strode out into the afternoon Mexican sunlight.

I caught up with him after checking to see that the Marine actually signed the two of us out. Gearheardt's name was not on the log. Only a Pepe Woozley had signed in for admission to my floor.

"Gearheardt," I said, "You just got here this afternoon. What's all this with the Gunny? And who in the hell is Woozley?"

"The guy I thought I was when I was in Angola, Jack." He paused to let me exit the embassy gate before him. "You ask a lot of questions for a spook." He joined me and we began walking down the street. The passing Mexicans smiled at Gearheardt, who smiled back. They had always ignored me.

"Knock off the spook stuff, Gearheardt. I'm here as the embassy's economic development officer." I put my arm around his shoulders as we walked down the crowded avenue. I was so damn glad to see him. "You are one rotten bastard, you know," I said to him. "I had no idea you were alive."

Gearheardt laughed. "When the Company disappears you, Jack, no one is *supposed* to know you're alive. I've had to convince my mother I was writing her from beyond the grave. She was easier to fool than the IRS, by the way. But that's the price we pay for eternal virginitis, Jack. We're spooks for our country."

"What the hell is virginitis, Gearheardt?" I asked before I remembered he always threw in nonsense words to take your mind off of the fact that the rest of his explanation made no sense. It had worked on me again. But I didn't care. I was glad to see him. We had almost stopped the Vietnam War together and you get close to a guy when that kind of pressure is on you. We *would* have stopped the Vietnam War too, except we'd had no idea of what we were doing.

We turned into a cantina. A small, bright and cool place where I knew the proprietor was discreet (since he was on my payroll) and the beer and tortillas were cold and hot. Gearheardt headed to the back to use the cuarto de baño, and I ordered beer for us both. I was almost school-girlishly excited at seeing my old friend. My sidekick through the thick and thin of the Vietnam War and Air America in Laos. Although there was a part of me shouting *Alert! Alert! Gearheardt in the area!* since I had never been with him more than five minutes that he didn't get us both in scalding water.

"Vaya con perros, señoritas," Gearheardt was saying to the two young Mexican women he had managed to meet and get to know in the ten yards between the restroom and our table. He plopped down in the seat opposite me, raised his beer glass in a salute and drained it. "Dos mas, por favor," he yelled to the bartender. Then he leaned toward me and lowered his voice.

"I need your help, Jack. I'm taking over Mexico."

My heart sank. I knew the grinning bastard was dead serious.

CHAPTER THE DOS

EXPLODING CHIHUAHUAS

Gearheardt was well into the beer before he was half through bringing me up to date on his adventures since he narrowly escaped being a 'pork roast' on the Ho Chi Minh Trail. Beer was such a natural element for Gearheardt that I assumed he bathed and did his laundry in it. That's how he got along with beer. He never seemed to get slowly drunk. There would come a time when the next beer or the next became a catalyst and he would go from Gearheardt to raving madman; usually signaled by his taking a pistol from his shoulder holster and scaring the crap out of anyone nearby.

I watched for that signal now, but he was calm, almost mellow, in his description of his duty for the CIA in Africa. Angola to be exact.

"They slapped a gallon of Unguentine on me, Jack, and packed me off to help the folks in Angola whip the Cubans. I was the chief helicopter flight instructor for the Angolan air force." He signaled for more beer, but his hand didn't move toward the shoulder holster I could see beneath his sport coat.

"You taught helicopter flying to the Angolans?"

"I would have except they didn't have any helicopters. In fact, as far as I could tell they didn't have an air force. Typical damn CIA screw up. You would think that somebody in Washington would check these things out. How hard could it be to send someone to the airport and see if anything lands or takes off?"

"So what did you do?" I was genuinely curious. Gearheardt was not known for his veracity in the Agency, but his stories were almost always based in truth.

"I hung around the capital. Pretty boring to tell the truth. The Portuguese are obviously not going to be able to hang on. It's their last colony I think. Those guys couldn't administer a hanging in a one rope town. But guess who I ran into."

"Gearheardt, I know no one who has been to Angola, is going to Angola, or who wants to go to Angola. Just tell me who you saw." I was anxious to get him back on the subject of taking over Mexico.

"The dreaded Gon Norea."

"You're kidding. The Cuban American British Russian spy? That Gon Norea? The one the Koreans put in a barrel and ruined his back?"

"That's the man. Good guy too. We chased women around Luanda til we ran out of the CIA's living allowance. That guy is a tail hound, Jack. One night we had these three—"

"Gearheardt, could you just tell me the bare bones of what the hell you were doing in Angola and what it has to do with taking over Mexico? Which, by the way, I am not sure is in the U.S. plans for Mexico. But maybe I missed the memo."

The cantina was rocking. A number of the embassy people had stopped in and were using the happy hour prices to drink tequila and bitch about their miserable lives as embassy people. Behind the bar Mr. Chavez caught my eye, pointed to his chest and raised his eyebrows. "You need me for work?" he mouthed.

I shook my head slightly and he went back to bartending. Mr. Chavez was a reliable source of information on the Halcones (the Mexican Secret Police) and various other Mexican government officials. He owned bars and restaurants near most large embassies and across the street from the government offices. Not only did he pick up information coming from the Mexicans and others, if I wanted to plant information in the government or other embassies, I stationed an agent at a table with a bottle and let him talk to his agent companion. The next morning, the information he was 'whispering' was sure to be diffused throughout the various institutions. Mr. Chavez didn't need the small amount of money I paid him for information and an occasional small favor. He said he was happy to help the Americans because his money was all in American stocks.

Gearheardt laughed when I told him.

"You know, Jack, it's getting harder to find an honest man. The Company had me set up a shop in Luanda selling South African passports—forged of course—so that we could get guys across the border to train with UNITA. Half the damn checks I took in bounced."

I looked into Gearheardt's eyes to see if there was a twinkle of irony, pushing aside the image of African Bushmen writing checks for fake passports. There wasn't. "That *is* a sad state of affairs, Gearheardt." I moved my chair closer to the beer bottle covered table. "Gearheardt, you mentioned something about taking over Mexico. What the hell is that all about? Were you just pulling my chain? You do know that I am acting station chief in Mexico City, don't you?"

"Congratulations, Jack. Head of the agency's men in Mexico and you just a poor economic development officer. My, my, what has the agency come to?"

I stared at him. He sat, unperturbed, lightly tapping his finger against the beer bottle. He wouldn't look at me, and that worried me. I trusted Gearheardt implicitly. On the other hand, I had trusted my first dog, Roughhouse, implicitly and he had eaten my sister's rabbit. Dog's do what dog's do. And Gearheardt . . .

"You know what I like about Mexico, Jack," he finally began, "it's those Chihuahuas you fill with candy and then beat with a stick until they blow open and the candy goes everywhere. That's good clean fun, Jack."

"Piñatas, Gearheardt. Chihuahuas are little dogs."

Gearheardt didn't look up from the table, but he smiled. Then he said, "Jack, I need to tell you some things. But when I tell you, then you'll have to make some tough choices. You and I have always been honest with each other—"

"No we haven't. You have lied about every damn thing you've talked me into. Just tell me what this taking over Mexico is all about. If it's a joke, let's forget it and go get some tacos and margaritas."

Gearheardt got up from the table and pulled a wad of money from his pocket. "Let's take a walk," he said, dropping the pesos on the table without counting them.

I nodded at Mr. Chavez and followed Gearheardt out the door. The street was crowded and loud. The Zona Rosa was nearby and I suggested to Gearheardt that we head there for dinner.

"Let's walk down to the park, Jack. Chapultepec Park is one of the great strolling parks in the world." He took off down the street, smiling at the Mexicans scurrying along the crowded sidewalk.

I caught up with him. "How do you know about Chapultepec Park? I thought you said you had never been to Mexico City before."

"I told you I had just arrived in Mexico City. I meant *this* time."

"So you've been coming here and not getting in contact with me. What an asshole you are, Gearheardt. Didn't you know I was at the embassy?"

Gearheardt looked at the scores of speeding cars screaming by in front of us. He stepped into the street and was oblivious to the screeching brakes and chaotic swerving going on around him. I stuck close to his ide.

"I knew you were there, Jack," he shouted over the noise of the traffic. "But I needed to get my structure in place before I contacted you. Besides, you thought I was a standing rib roast. And don't think I don't know that you slept with Dow after I was dead."

Which was true and caught me slightly off guard. "I was just—"

"If you say you were just horny, I'll forgive you. I don't want to hear anything else. I didn't make up excuses for screwing all of your girlfriends."

I needed a minute to think through what he had said, and Gearheardt went on.

"Let's talk about Mexico, Jack. Let's talk about Mexico and Cuba," he said as we mercifully reached the curb.

We were in the park. Every night the park was lit like a festival. Bright lights underneath the giant trees. Families and lovers were the main human ingredients. The park's aura belied its existence in the heart of a frantic downtown Mexico City. At the city end of the park was the Chapultepec Castle where the U.S. Marines once fought. Not far away, on the other side of the boulevard, the National Museum of History was a crown jewel, a world class archeological exhibition palace.

Gearheardt sat on a bench beneath one of the mammoth trees and I dropped down beside him as he lit a cigarette.

"Those are the Halls of Montezuma, Jack," he said, pointing to the castle. "You know, the Shores of Tripoli and all that stuff."

"I know the Marine Corps hymn, Gearheardt."

"Don't you kind of still miss the Marine Corps, Jack? This CIA stuff is fun but there's no camaraderie or anything. Every man out for himself, know what I mean? If I'm going to try to take over a country or just kill some officials, I like to do it with a bunch of good guys. Have a few beers or something, you know? Blow something up and then run like hell. That's my style, not all this sneaking around and using some local dickhead with a burr up his ass about his own politicians."

"You haven't changed a bit, Gearheardt. A hand grenade looking for a place to explode."

Gearheardt and I had been young Marine pilots when we were asked by the president to go on a mission to Hanoi to stop the Vietnam War. We didn't do a very good job, to say the least, and were traded to Air America and the CIA after we escaped from North Vietnam. Gearheardt resented our treatment, but I thought we received better than we deserved. Gearheardt screwing Uncle Ho's girlfriend might have caused the 1968 Tet offensive. But that was behind us now.

"Got a cigarette, Jack?" Gearheardt asked.

"I gave it up. The air in Mexico City is enough to keep a good cough going."

Gearheardt waved to a young boy selling cigarettes and gum. He bought a package of each, borrowing the pesos from me and letting the boy keep the considerable change.

"I gave it up too. But I'm starting again." He lit another cigarette and blew smoke, tilting his head up and away from me. "My only hobby."

Gearheardt sat for a moment contemplating the almost carnival-like scene in what we could see of the park. When he spoke, he didn't turn his head toward me.

"This country is screwed, Jack. The new rich folks are stealing from the old rich folks. The politicians are crooked as a dog's hind leg. The peasants don't know enough to give a shit. And if they do get ahead, by some damn miracle, they just join the stealing crowd. Most of the Mexicans are just dicked." He flipped his cigarette onto the sidewalk. "The situation is so pathetic it almost makes me feel bad to screw their women."

Gearheardt didn't deal in irony and I knew that I was about to hear what he meant when he said *he* (the CIA? Gearheardt individually?) was taking over Mexico. So I kept my mouth shut.

Now he turned toward me. "Cuba has it all together, Jack. The *man* has things under control."

I assumed he meant Castro.

"You've never been to Cuba, Gearheardt. And have you forgotten the Cubans in Hanoi? The assholes torturing American pilots?"

"In Angola they're kicking ass and taking names, Jack. Toughest damn troops you ever saw. Disciplined and under control. In a fair fight, we would have a hard time knocking them on their butt. I'm not kidding you."

"What has this got to do with taking over Mexico?" I asked.

Gearheardt lowered his voice and leaned toward me. "The Russians would piss their pants if we had troops in Mexico, Jack. God knows what the Chinese would do. I would imagine they couldn't even find

Mexico with a map. But you never know. France is still pissed the Mexicans executed Maximilian. Heaven knows what Germany is cooking up. Spain hates the Mexicans because they don't want people to think Mexicans are Spanish. South America is jungle and dancing in bars. Sure, there are countries that don't have their own screwed up political agendas and axes to grind. But can you see Iceland invading Mexico? Maybe if they teamed up with Greenland they could blast their way ashore at Acapulco, but then what? So Mexico just sits here, right on our border, festering and rotting in the sun."

"I have no idea what that rambling means, Gearheardt." The concept of Icelandic troops storming Acapulco momentarily caused my mental gears to grind. "But let me explain a couple of things to you, my friend. First, there are more Russian spies in Mexico than there are Cubans in Havana. We assume they are trying to turn the country. And we're not going to let them."

"Second, I don't know what all this *festering* in the sun is about, but we're making progress here. I mean the Agency is. And we are not actually hoping some wild ass renegade hit man recently from Angola might suggest backing the Cubans in a coup, if that's what you're suggesting."

Gearheardt was maddeningly humming, his face turned away from me. I grabbed his arm. "Are you listening to me you damn wild man? No coups! If that—"

"Ix-nay on the oo-cay stuff, Jack. This Toro I see before me might speak a little English."

I had not noticed two large Mexicans standing closely in front of us. Their black suits, tight in the shoulders, and sunglasses told me they were not lovers out for a stroll. Halcones, the Mexican Secret Police. I leaned back onto the bench and knew that I should say something before Gearheardt—as he did every damn time we faced any authority—pissed them off. I never could understand how anyone could see worth a damn through those sunglasses at night.

"You boys big Ray Charles fans?" he asked, smiling the Gearheardt smile and spreading his arms across the back of the bench.

The colored lights strung along the walkways twinkled in the sunglasses. The men behind the glasses didn't seem to get the reference. In any event they were not amused.

"Get up, gringo," the closest Toro said, speaking to Gearheardt.

I started to rise, pulling my diplomatic passport (black instead of civilian green) out of my inside breast pocket. "Se ores," I began, "there might be some mistake. My friend and—"

"Creo que no," the smaller bull said. "No mistake. Your friend is coming along with us. This is no business of yours, Se or Armstrong. Go home."

"Jack," Gearheardt said, now on his feet and facing down the first Halco e, "this is not unexpected. The man asked you politely to go home. You might want to do just that. These gentlemen want to buy me a beer. They didn't invite you." He smiled and stepped between the two policemen who turned and followed him without looking back at me.

Who was standing on the sidewalk in Chapultepec Park worrying about a friend who had just been picked up by the meanest secret police in the world. I was pissed, knowing that I was now becoming part of something that Gearheardt had no doubt dreamed up and which would completely disrupt my life if it didn't kill me.

That damn Gearheardt, I thought.

The Mexican boy selling cigarettes appeared beside me. He looked at the three figures disappearing into the dark street running behind the park.

"That damn Gearheardt," he said. Then he left while I was still speechless.

CHAPTER TRES

THE ROCKET SCIENTIST'S IDIOT BROTHER

I was in my office the next morning, searching for the phone number of my contact at the Halcones, when I became 'not the acting chief of station for the CIA in Mexico City.' The announcement came in the form of my new boss sticking his head in my door and ordering me to follow him to his office. A much nicer office than mine, although harder to reach because it was hidden behind the lunch room and it was necessary to move the candy machine to open the door. Someone had penciled "Spooks Inside" on the panel beside the door and the erasing job was half-hearted.

"Major Crenshaw, Armstrong," the obviously not a major at the moment said, indicating a chair in front of his desk after we shook hands. "We'll see about the entrance here, by the way. Someone's idea of a joke, no doubt. When you leave, ask Juanita to come in and we'll get some carpenters in posthaste." He made a note to himself on his desk pad, then looked up at me and smiled. It wasn't the yellow circle face kind of smile; more like a man with stomach cramps might have if he were putting on a brave face. "And who are you?"

"Armstrong, sir. I'm the—"

"I know who you are, Armstrong. I meant *who* are *you*."

That clears that up, I thought. This was not starting out good. Crenshaw had all of the surface nomenclature of what the Marine Corps called an asshole. Introducing himself as 'Major' (no doubt a rank he had achieved in the Army some years ago); ordering me into his office like a file clerk (and me 'acting chief of station'). Before I could mellow and give Crenshaw a chance, he snatched it away.

"I'll go first, Armstrong, since you seem to be having trouble answering simple questions. My name is Major Randolph Crenshaw, not Randy and not Mr. Crenshaw, but Major Crenshaw. I have been with the Agency only eight years but have risen to the top because I run things right. (I might have debated whether the 'top' was COS in Mexico City, but he might have had a point). Just so we don't get started off on the wrong foot (too late) let me just say that I don't appreciate the fact that you obviously were not prepared for my arrival."

"Sir, I was told that you would be taking over. But no time was given. As far as I know." Defensive, but not too obsequious.

"Was my file not sent to you?"

"Yes, sir. A background file. Not knowing when you were coming or *if* you were coming, I put it in the safe and intended to read it later."

"This file?" He held up the sealed folder with his name on top. The bastard had already been in my safe. What else did I keep in there?

"The reason you didn't know I was coming now, Mr. Armstrong, was that I don't do things the ordinary way. I do them the Crenshaw way."

"The *Major* Crenshaw way, sir?"

He paused, probably not knowing if he should believe I was actually being insubordinate as it had most likely not happened often in his career. I had just reached my bullshit limit for early mornings. I needed to have coffee and needed to see if Ms. Sanchez was wearing the see-through blouse with the black lace bra.

Major Crenshaw continued. "I had the Agency drop me near San Luis Potoci last Thursday night (I was pretty sure he meant he had actually parachuted into the middle of Mexico) and then made my way down here on my own. I rode a burro over the mountains so that no one could check me at the airport."

"You rode a burro, sir?"

I probably shouldn't have done what I did next. I laughed. Maybe there was still a chance this was a joke. But Major Crenshaw somehow didn't seem the comic type, at least not in that sense of joking.

I was not feeling good about my career. First Gearheardt shows up. And now my new boss is insane. I wondered if he knew that I had flown first class on Eastern Airlines and taken a limo into the embassy when I came down for my assignment. The thought occurred to me that if no one knew he was here, I could kill him, secure the candy machine in front of the door and then I would only have Gearheardt to deal with.

"Yes, Armstrong, I rode a burro. Too many in the Company think we can run things from the ivory tower of the embassy or from some desk in Washington. (This sounded like a speech he had made many times before.) If we are to help these people, we need to know them. To experience them (like I wanted to experience Ms. Sanchez?) and become their friends and mentors." He paused and for some reason I knew he would have a pipe in his satchel. He pulled it out and went through the elaborate ministrations of the obsessed. When it was exuding industrial strength 'good old boy smell,' he looked back at me. "You can laugh if you want, Armstrong. But don't ever laugh at anything I tell you again. Do you read me?"

If I had been Gearheardt, I would have said "I thought you just said I could laugh if I want."

I smiled and tried to make it an obsequious smile. I wasn't Gearheardt and I *did* like my job in the embassy so I said, "Sorry, Major Crenshaw. I just wasn't prepared for the image of the new Chief of Station riding into town on a burro."

"It was good enough for Jesus," Major Crenshaw said. He didn't smile and for the second time in twenty-four hours my heart sank. He was serious.

We spent the next few minutes going over my mission at the embassy. Also my motivation and my commitment. This was what he had evidently meant by *who* I was. I reluctantly revealed the primary assets that I ran. My most reliable contacts. And what I felt like were the most pressing issues concerning the agency's mission in Mexico. An agent rarely disclosed everything in the first meeting, even with his boss. Secrets were currency if you got in trouble. And you were bound to get in trouble with someone sooner or later.

"That about it?" the Major finally asked. He closed the notebook that he made notes in. When he took a phone call, I was able to see that it was mostly doodles. I was happy he hadn't copied down any of the names I'd given him.

"I have a photographic memory," he said, reading my mind. "Whatever I hear, I remember. Period."

"Wouldn't that be an audiographic memory, Major?" I asked. I was still hoping he had a sense of humor. Plus I had run with Gearheardt too long not to have picked up a natural wise ass way to deal with authority. But I couldn't seem to make it work for me like Gearheardt.

"Armstrong, I'm here on a mission so secret that even the staff, including you, won't know about it," he said suddenly. He had lowered his voice and swirled his finger around the room. "Safe?"

"Yes, sir. What is the mission, sir?"

"Aren't you listening? You don't have a need to know. I have a need to know, because it's my mission. Is that clear?"

I immediately wondered if his mission had anything to do with Gearheardt. That would be good news.

"There are a number of Cuban operatives," I ventured, watching his eyes.

"I'm not surprised," he said, with no recognizable hints.

"They were very effective in Angola." Again I watched.

"I'm not here to talk about Africa, Armstrong. Anything else?"

"I guess not." I had made the decision not to discuss Gearheardt until I knew more about Major Crenshaw. And about what the hell Gearheardt was up to.

"Langley wants action, Armstrong."

"Yes, sir."

"What are we going to give them?"

"Action, sir?"

"You're damned right." He stood and didn't offer his hand, which I didn't want to shake.

At the door I had a wild thought about sticking my head back in and saying, "By the way, Major, should I buy a burro?" But I didn't.

Ms. Sanchez was wearing the see-through blouse with the black lace bra.

Back in my office I found the number of my contact at the Headquarters of the Mexican Secret Police. Eduardo was my neighbor in the apartment building where I lived. He didn't particularly like gringos, but he liked American women and when I had invited him to a few of the parties I threw for the embassy secretaries, he put aside his dislike of gringos. The best thing about Eduardo was that he sometimes had a sense of humor.

"Buenos dias."

"Eduardo, its Armstrong."

"Qual?"

"Eduardo, I know you speak English. I need to ask you something."

"El gato bebe leche."

"Knock it off, Eduardo. This is important. My Spanish isn't good enough to use."

"Entonces go eengage in eentercourse weeth your self."

I waited, breathing into the phone so he would know I hadn't hung up.

"Señor Armstrong. Jack. Is theese you?"

"Yes, Eduardo. You knew all along. I need to ask you a favor."

"Ms. Sanchez is a Catholic, Jack. She will not sleep with you unless you marry her."

"Forget that. Eduardo, can you find out if someone brought in a gringo last night. His name was . . ." I realized that Gearheardt wouldn't be using his real name. "His name was Woozely," I guessed.

A pause.

"Who would this Mr. Woozely be, Jack?"

"A friend. A social friend." He would know I meant not an official friend, I hoped.

"I don't theenk so, Jack. If I found out, I will call you." He hung up.

I checked the contents of my safe but as far as I could tell only the file on Major Crenshaw was missing. I assumed that Crenshaw had read everything else so I moved the files to my desk and began to review them. I needed to know what he knew and what he knew I had not told him.

I was running two ops that seemed to have possibilities. A contact at the University was reporting on Colombian students who had an unhealthy interest in firearms and explosive devices. Their names, the name of my contact, a student, and a copy of the inquiry sent to the COS in Bogotá made up the file. I wanted to know if the Colombians were actually students, what their background was in Colombia, and if the Agency could get a leather jacket made for me and send it up with the diplomatic pouch before next winter. Colombia had great leather goods.

I also had a file that outlined my efforts to infiltrate the intelligence service of the Mexican army. Somehow I knew that we weren't getting the kind of cooperation we should expect from the Mexican military. I wanted to know if it was sloppiness or deliberate.

The last files had profiles on various employees of the French, British, and Italian embassies in Mexico City. You never knew when you might need a favor, and the contents of these files would almost guarantee you could get a favor when you needed one. I had profiles on employees of the known anti-American agents in the city, but that was just so I could keep track of their whereabouts and contacts. Mostly Mexican whores so far.

I had to assume that Major Crenshaw had seen these files. But he wouldn't bring them up since they were marked secret and he wasn't supposed to be in my safe. So I could act like he didn't know. His ego had made him show me his file. But it was a slip and he wouldn't mention it again.

Thinking about it, I realized that it was maybe my disappointment at only being the Acting Chief of Station for less than a week that had caused me to take an instant dislike to Major Crenshaw. Maybe a number of high-ranking agents rode burros into cities all over the world. Maybe I should take burro riding lessons. Try to get along until I found out what Crenshaw was really like.

Ms. Sanchez knocked on my office door and entered. Her eyes were red and she wore a pink sweater, even in the on again off again air-conditioned comfort of the embassy. She placed a stack of messages on my desk.

"No more see-through, Señor Jack," she said.

I had been right with my first impression. The guy was a jerk.

She pointed to the flashing light on my phone. "Your friend. The nice hombre," she said and left, pulling the pink sweater together in front and closing the door behind her.

"Hello."

"Jack, ixnay on calling the Halcones about me." "How in hell did you find out I did?"

"I'll tell you later. And by the way, you can still call me Gearheardt. Or Pepe. Either one works."

"Pepe?"

"I've been called worse. But if you get any word from Pepe, it's probably me. Did you meet Crenshaw?"

"Gearheardt, how do you find out these things? Yes, I met Crenshaw. That's *Major* Crenshaw to you, by the way. Do you know him?"

"I know he's a real *book* guy. He's perfect for what we're doing. I had to pull major string to get him down here. No pun intended." *We're doing? Gearheardt and me? Gearheardt and Crenshaw?* There were a few loose ends in this budding operation.

"Jack," Gearheardt went on, "listen carefully. Get an unmarked embassy car and a driver you can trust. I'm going to give you the addresses of two people you need to pick up. Also take a thousand bucks from the 'egg money' (our emergency stash for agents and contract agents), and meet me at the El Diablo. It's on the road to Queretaro. Ask for Pepe at the desk. They'll know where to find me."

Instinctively I looked around my office as if making sure no one was listening. Lowering my voice, I said, "Look, Gearheardt or Pepe, I'm not sure what the hell this operation you've got working is all about. Involving my staff and assets without a clear plan is not a good idea. Maybe you and I should meet first. I need to know a little bit more." I didn't trust Gearheardt as far as I could throw him. Unless I needed him to save my life. That I knew he would do without hesitation.

"Operation?" he said. "What operation are you talking about? These women you're picking up are the finest in the Zona Rosa. With a thousand bucks, we'll have a suite, a boatload of tequila and the wildest naked party since training night at Madame Lulus. Get your ass in gear." He gave me the addresses and the phone went dead.

I had just decided to start smoking again, which also reminded me to track down the cigarette kid in Chapultepec Park, when Ms. Sanchez buzzed me.

"Pepe on one."

"Gearheardt, I'm glad you called back. What in—"

"Jack, I'm in a hurry. Bring a gun for me. A Walther if you can get one. Ask the Marine at the front desk if you need help. And whatever you do, don't let Crenshaw know you know me. Hasta luego."

The damn nut. I'd been more or less fat dumb and happy twenty-four hours ago. Getting the hang of the spying business. And now I'm supposed to get a pistol for a guy that is overthrowing Mexico, pick up two women with a thousand dollars of embassy money and drink tequila all night. How gullible did Gearheardt think I was?

After a quick mental check of my options, I buzzed Ms. Sanchez.

"Juanita, would you find out if Jorge is driving in the pool tonight. If he is, tell him I'll be down in half an hour. I'll be going down the fire escape. If Major Crenshaw comes looking for me, tell him I'm locked in my office. Gracias." Then, "And Juanita, I will miss the see-through very much."

AND A DOZEN DEFECTO PERFECTOS

Gearheardt's face lit up when he opened the door of Suite 200 of the El Diablo Inn. Until he noticed a lack of women standing anywhere in sight. He was nattily dressed in a smoking jacket, with an ascot of stylish purple and a gold Marine Corps emblem stickpin.

"Jack," he said, "I'm not observing any women with you. Tell me they're in the embassy car straightening their disheveled finery due to the ungentlemanly attacks on them during your journey here. Tell me that, please."

"Gearheardt," I responded, pushing past him into the room, "the women were unavoidably detained. Let's leave it at that and not get into the part where I am uncomfortable about using an embassy staff car to pick up your prostitutes."

The room was quite fancy for a Mexican motel. Suite might be a misleading term, but there was certainly plenty of gaudy decorations and two double beds, one in the room we were standing in, and one in the adjacent room. Cold cuts and various beverages, mostly beer, were carefully laid out on the built-in bar. Cut flowers, a specialty of the local market, were arranged in water glasses and milk bottles around the room.

"I can see you haven't changed your prudish attitude, Jack. Can you think of a better use of the embassy's limo than hauling women around?" He sat down heavily on the side of the bed and pulled his ascot loose around his neck. When it wouldn't slide up over his forehead, he simply reversed it and left it hanging down the back of his head like some sort of purple headdress.

"Señor," he said into the phone, "come up to the room and take all of this food. You can give it to the cleaning crew or take it home yourself. My friend forgot that he was to bring the party with him." He listened for a moment. "That's a very reasonable and much appreciated suggestion, amigo. And I'm sure the local women are every bit as beautiful as the Mexico City women. But my friend has just informed me he is now a homosexual. Gracias." He hung up the phone, looking up at me. "I won't tell you his other suggestion, Jack. But I *would* be careful passing the front desk when you leave. He thinks you're cute."

"Nice, Gearheardt," I said. "But I don't care. You and I need to talk and I knew we wouldn't get anything accomplished if there were women around."

"Define accomplished."

I took off my sport coat and threw it on the bed. "Let's talk about what you're doing in Mexico. And who the hell you're working for. Let's start with that."

"What did you think of Crenshaw?" Gearheardt asked, lighting a cigarette. "I think the guy is an Okie. You know what I think of Okies in the CIA, Jack. Remember Argo Buzzard? That low life bastard spread the clap around half of Asia before—"

"Argo Buzzard is in jail in Phnom Penh, Gearheardt. Don't start ranting to change the subject. If you know Crenshaw, and evidently you do, you already know what I think of Crenshaw. An agent's nightmare. By-the-book and with the subtlety of a zealot on acid. Is he in on your 'taking over Mexico' scheme?"

I was walking around the room checking for bugs. Not the crawling kind. Gearheardt was usually careful, but maybe he really did have partying on his mind when he called me.

"It's clean, Jack." He flapped his hand loosely at the room. "To tell the truth, I knew you would pull some kind of trick like this. Good old Jack Armstrong. All American boy." He ground out his cigarette in a Mexican flower pot. "Did you at least bring me a weapon?" He avoided the Crenshaw question. And he also knew most of my family were Okies.

I opened my briefcase and tossed the Walther PPK 9 mm pistol to him along with two clips of bullets. "I don't know how you talk me into these things, Gearheardt." I sat down in the gaily striped chair after getting a beer from the buffet.

A knock on the door and two women entered, loaded up most of the beer and food on a cart and departed. "Gracias, Pepe," they said to Gearheardt, smiling with significant molar exposure.

"Hasta luego," Gearheardt said, wagging his eyebrows. The women giggled and left. Together they must have weighed as much as the embassy car.

Gearheardt was snapping a clip in the pistol and screwing up his face as if trying to solve a painful dilemma. "Jack," he finally said, shoving the pistol into his belt, "I need you to trust me."

"No."

Gearheardt looked hurt. "Aw, Jack. You know I would never do anything that I thought would hurt you."

"Yes, you would." I paused and stared at him: my best friend through flight school, the Marine Corps and Air America. "Not intentionally, Gearheardt. I know that. But you have probably the worst judgment in the world. You're reckless and impatient. A whore monger and a renegade. You drink too much, have no respect for authority, and . . ."

"I see you've been reading my performance reports, Jack. Do they also say I'm the best damn guy they have? That if someone in the Company needs some shitty job done, they always ask me. Do the reports say that?"

They probably did. They were also probably footnoted to the effect that anyone 'running' Gearheardt needed to have life insurance and at least a good retirement plan.

No doubt Gearheardt was one amazing guy. A brilliant, fearless pilot, a dyed-in-the-wool Marine, and a friend that you had no doubt would die for you.

Tall and thin, with pale blond hair and greenish-blue eyes, he looked patrician in his smoking jacket, even with a purple ascot trailing off the back of his head. I thought of the two of us in the theater in Bangkok years ago, watching David Niven in *Casino Royale*. That's us, Gearheardt said as we walked back into the blinding Thai afternoon. If the Marine Corps doesn't want us, we'll be spies.

And now we were. In a cheap Mexican motel smelling of beer and cigarettes, cardboard filling one window, and with a toilet that ran constantly. Ostensibly on the same side, but always never totally trusting even your best friend. Bad guys seemingly everywhere, but mostly in squalorish saloons and run-down hotels. Getting further and further into the scene of 'bomb and people' smuggling, and further and further away from the reasons we signed on to this. I wasn't sure which of us was David Niven, let alone Sean Connery.

"What about Crenshaw? Is he in on your scheme or not?" I put on my 'this is serious' face. "He's my boss, you know. I can't be working in operations he knows nothing about."

"So you told him about all of your ops right now?" Gearheardt asked with a friendly smirk.

I didn't answer.

"First, Jack, this is not *my* operation. I'm just simple old Pepe doing what they ask me to do. Sure, I might act like its mine sometimes but—"

"Damn it, Pepe, I mean Gearheardt, who asked you to do this . . . this Mexico takeover thing, or what ever it is? I'm not saying I'll help you, but I sure won't do a damn thing without some authorization or something like a 'finding' document."

"The Pygmy." Gearheardt said it into his hands as he was lighting another cigarette.

I wasn't going to be taken in by the bastard. I didn't smile, laugh, frown, flinch, or react. I just stared at him. But he won the standoff after about two minutes. "The Pygmy," I repeated.

"The very one."

I stood and picked up my sport coat. As I slipped it on, I started for the door without looking at the guy who was my best friend. Before I was able to open the door, Gearheardt said, "Jack, I'm afraid I can't let you leave right now."

I looked back and the jackass was actually holding a gun on me. In fact the gun that I had supplied him. "You can't be serious, Gearheardt. Put that damn thing down before it goes off." There was an ever so slight tremor in my voice.

"Trust me, Jack. I'll shoot you in the foot. Come back and sit down. As of now, you're working for me."

"You and the Pygmy." I sat back down. I reached to the bed and helped myself to one of Gearheardt's cigarettes.

The "Pygmy" was a legendary CIA agent. A three-foot bronze man who often wore small animal skins and when stressed spoke by making clicking sounds in his throat. The smell of his cooking fires permeated CIA headquarters at Langley. He alternatively bounded and crept through the halls of the agency. As he rose up through the ranks, he developed a small but loyal following, reportedly assembling his own army of dedicated Pygmy Troops, who he used for his own black operations. And they were also a softball team.

No one knew for sure but the story was that the Pygmy arrived in CIA headquarters in the luggage of our man in a small African country. He'd hastily departed said country following an incident involving the Prime Minister's daughter and her mother, even though Agency policy clearly stated that such liaisons were to be avoided. "No tag teams in the palace" was the shorthand.

Cornered in the DCI's office that first day, the Pygmy claimed to be an Australian aborigine and demanded to be sent back there. A call to the Australian embassy quickly put the kybosh on that scheme, but the Pygmy made his escape during the phone conversation and eluded capture while somehow obtaining an Agency ID and employment documents. After a few months it became too embarrassing to admit that a Bushman of the Kalahari (another identity the Pygmy claimed) was living somewhere in CIA headquarters. The potential shame of being someone not 'in the know about things' being too great to use common sense and ask who the guy squatting in the chair gnawing on small animal bones might be. No one objected when he began sitting in on meetings and briefings

"So your project is doomed from the start."

"I didn't get the Pygmy's *Blame-o-matic*™ coverage, Jack. He really *is* involved in the deal."

Blame-o-matic™ coverage was the system the Pygmy had developed and sold inside the CIA. Basically it was his personal guarantee that he would take the blame for any mission, scheme, idea or project that failed. At first, the Project Leaders sought him out as soon as a mission began looking shaky. But the Pygmy quickly developed a new product which allowed you to obtain a statement of full responsibility—signed by the Pygmy and notarized—that you could submit along with the request for project approval. Then everyone could relax and not worry about who was going to get blamed for screwing up missions. The Pygmy became wildly popular and a 'player' around the Agency.

"He's actually running this op. And he wants you on the team."

"The softball team?"

"There is no softball team." Gearheardt sounded insulted that I wasn't taking him seriously.

"You mean the Bushmen of the Kalahari aren't really the division champs?"

"That's enough, Jack. You're just going to have to trust me."

"Or you'll shoot me?"

"Or I'll shoot you."

I leaned back in my chair, staring at insanity. "Gearheardt, I don't believe for one minute that you would shoot me. But if it's important enough for you to even act like you would, I'll listen to you."

"Now I *have* to shoot you, Jack, or you'll think I'm a pussy." He laughed, laid the pistol on the night stand and picked up the phone. "I could use some coffee. What about you?"

The coffee the desk clerk sent up wasn't bad. Gearheardt had him supply a large pot, as if we were going to be talking for quite a while.

"So what's the story, Gearheardt? No more jacking around. Tell me the mission, what the authority chain is, and what you want me to do. I'm not saying I'll do it."

Gearheardt was in shirtsleeves, shoes off and feet propped on the chair next to his bed. He looked up and saw me with a notebook. "Hey, amigo, no notes. This is stuff they need to get when they're blow-torching your nuts, not find in your pocket at the cleaners." I put the notebook away.

"I'll get to the best part and work backwards, Jack. On May Fifth, which is of course Cinco de Mayo, some kind of half-assed independence day or some shit—"

"Your cultural sensitivity is inspiring, Pepe."

"Yeah, but anyway, you're no doubt aware that this Cinco deal is special this year."

"They're also going to announce the Dallas Cowboys exhibition game. I assume that's what you're referring to."

"You got it. All eyes focused on Mexico City of course." Gearheardt was becoming more animated. He rose from the bed, brushing the cigarette ashes from his shirt front, and began pacing around the room. "That gives us only a few days to get everything in place. That's why I need your help, Jack. I need the resources of the embassy, but without the bullshit. Or in other words, without their involvement."

"So Crenshaw *doesn't* know."

"I didn't say that. Everyone knows what they need to know."

"I know hardly anything. So I must be at the bottom of the need-to-know chain. Right?"

Gearheardt stopped pacing and sat down on the bed opposite my chair. Our knees were practically touching as he leaned toward me. "Au contraire, Jack. You know next to nothing because you are one of the key people." He reached behind and grabbed the coffee pot, filling my cup and then his. "You know how we always used to think what dumb shits the higher up guys were in Air America, the Agency guys? Well, in Angola I figured it out. Gon helped me figure it out, so he deserves some credit."

"And what did you figure out? You and Gon."

"Don't you get it? Don't you see the brilliance? The higher up you go in the Agency, the less you know. Hell, near the top they only have a vague idea of what we do operationally."

"I assume this all has something to do with the Mexico mission you are supposedly on."

Gearheardt looked pensive. "Yes," he said absently. "You know, Jack, when I was in college this guy I knew went to Mexico on spring break. I was too broke to take a break, but this guy, Cecil I think, came into my room when he got back and he had a stack of pictures. Post cards, kind of. And the one on top was two Mexican girls naked and one of them was fooling with a mule's tool. The other girl was just looking at the camera and she seemed sad, you know. I thought about that for a long time and wondered what kind of a country has post cards with naked girls and mules. Every time I would mention Mexico to the guys on campus, they would roll their eyes and say 'wow, those Mexican women' or something like that. Can you imagine if we had things like that and some French guys were saying 'man, I want to go to that America on spring break. They have women who will suck a donkey's dick.' That would be kind of sad, wouldn't it, Jack?"

"What's sad at the moment is that I'm sitting here listening to a mad man. What in the hell are you talking about, Gearheardt? I mean, yes, it is a shame, but weren't we talking about the Mexican mission?"

"Not just Mexico, Jack." He still had that pensive look.

A knock on the door brought Gearheardt to his feet and the Walther PPK to his hand. He went to the door and opened it a crack. I smelled the women before I could see or hear them. A monsoon of perfume was wafting through the small opening. It was the old Gearheardt who smiled.

"Señor, very kind of you. But we won't be needing these women. My friend and I are discussing some very important things." Gearheardt stuck his head almost outside. "Who is this one?" Gearheardt's voice softened. "Buenos noches, señorita. Usted poseer anchuroso leche bolsillos. Hasta luego." He closed the door.

"Gearheardt, did you just tell some woman that she possessed large milk bags?"

Gearheardt grinned. "Sometimes the Spanish colloquialisms escape me, Jack. That señorita took my breath away. But back to our mission."

It was *our* mission now.

"I need you to stay right in the embassy. Doing whatever it is you're doing. Keep an eye on Crenshaw. Get any information to me that seems like it might be pertinent, and on Cinco de Mayo, shoot the President." He was looking in his jacket pocket, searching for more cigarettes.

"Seems easy enough, Pepe. That 'keeping an eye on Crenshaw' might be difficult at times. But the rest seems reasonable."

Gearheardt sat down on the far end of the bed. He blew smoke at the lamp and watched it curl out of the top of the shade. "I told the Pygmy you were our guy, Jack."

"Headshot you think?" I asked.

"Oh you know, maybe a torso hit with a high powered dum dum. That should do the trick."

"Well, I guess that about wraps up the discussion. Thanks for the evening, Pepe." I got up to leave.

"Did I mention that you're insane? Seriously. You must have taken a crap and your brains fell out at the same time. You put the wrong pile back in your head. That would explain it."

Gearheardt smiled. "Jack, did you hear the one about the Congressman that comes into a bar holding a pile of dog crap in his hands and says to the bartender 'Look what I almost stepped in?'"

He cupped his hands and I saw he was holding the pistol I had given him.

"You already had a pistol when I saw you yesterday, Gearheardt. Why did you want me to bring one to you tonight?" I edged toward the door.

"Now we have a free pistol, Jack. Never can tell when one might come in handy. Did you check it out in your name?"

He knew I had.

Gearheardt came to me and put his hand on my shoulder. "This is the way things get done, Jack. Don't take it personal. The Pygmy wants you in the game. The whole game. After the game ends, you'll defect to Cuba and then we'll get you back. A simple plan."

He was right. This was the way things that were ugly got done.

"I'm not working for the Pygmy, Gearheardt." I opened the door, wondering whether or not my pal would try to stop me. "I'm not even sure he exists."

"Well then you have nothing to worry about, Jack. I'll call you tomorrow."

Jorge was waiting in the embassy car. "Home, Señor Armstrong?"

"I think I'll go back to my office for a while, Jorge."

I felt like I had *already* defected, even by talking to that damn Gearheardt without letting my boss in on the fact. But—and there was always a 'but' with Gearheardt, which was what had kept me in trouble all the time I had known him—I trusted Gearheardt. At the end of the day, his ideas usually made as much or more sense as 'official' policy. I had felt for some time that our policy in Mexico was drifting along as if we were hoping something would happen. Maybe Gearheardt was the something.

CHAPTER FIVE

GEARHEARDT BECOMES SANE; WORLD HOLDS BREATH

hree messages awaited me on my desk. They made me immediately glad that I had decided to stop by before I went home. Two were encrypted but the communications room was always open and it didn't take long to have the readable versions in my hand, and me back in my office. The third message was from my mother who, convinced I was an economic development officer, wanted to know if I had received my subscription to *Latin Farming*. She probably also wanted to know about Gearheardt, but that could wait.

The first message was from Gib Wilson. He had been in the Marine Corps with Gearheardt and me (Although he'd never really liked Gearheardt because he made fun of the Marines. Gib had the sense of humor of a body bag.). He was now a junior officer at CIA Headquarters in Langley. His specialty had something to do with technology and I suspected he was a comm officer.

It read: "Jack, something rumbling in Mexico. Lots of traffic but none routed through you, which is strange. Can't say too much but your pal is mentioned a few times. Also new COS has departed CONUS but no arrival date shown in Mexico City. Strange. Keep your head up. Semper Fi. GW."

Not much hard information but it did 'confirm' that something was up for Mexico. Gearheardt *might* be telling the truth. And Gib also confirmed that others thought Crenshaw as strange as I did.

The second message was a bit more official. "To Acting COS. Need current info on Cuban activity in Mexico City. University of Mexico. Cuernavaca. Top priority. Risk unlimited. ADIA."

ADIA was the acronym for an acronym that meant someone at a level immediately below the DCI (Director of Central Intelligence). To even get the encryption device to accept the acronym took clearance far above mine. So the message was authentic.

'Risk unlimited' was a way of telling me that even if I had to risk my life or the life of someone else, the operation must be followed through. This indicated a pretty high priority while giving some weasel room to HQ.

My intercom buzzed. "Are you to go home this evening, Señor Armstrong?"

"Yes, Jorge. Sorry. I'll be right down."

Stupidly—that is without remembering all of my history with Gearheardt—I felt better. He was obviously not just making up all of the Cuban activity out of whole cloth. And based on the unwritten message in the messages, I wasn't exactly expected to share this info with Crenshaw, even though he was my new boss. The ass on an ass, as Gearheardt described him.

I woke in the middle of the night in a sweat. I had dreamed I shot the president of Mexico and the only safe harbor I could find was in Cuba. Defecting to Cuba was not on the top of my 'to do' list and I wished I knew how to find Gearheardt, to tell him that part of the plan wasn't going to work. Not that I had *agreed* to shoot the president of Mexico.

That part of the plan didn't make sense either. Or if it did make sense, based on knowledge that I obviously didn't possess, it wasn't the kind of thing that even the CIA took lightly. No matter what the public might believe, assassination wasn't a casual 'oh by the way, why don't we shoot the president while we're at it' kind of action. I resolved to get down to a few brass tacks with Gearheardt when he called in the morning.

I decided to get a drink of water before I went back to sleep. The landlord usually shut off the air-conditioning sometime in the night so going back to sleep was a struggle.

I had just stepped into the dark kitchen when the assailant struck me from behind. An arm around my throat shut off my air, a knee into the back of my knees crumpled me, and a hard punch to the kidney stunned me as I fell. I was just able to grab the jacket material of the assassin as I went down, and by putting my dead weight into it, threw the man across my body. He landed on his side next to me with a 'whoomph' that indicated the air was knocked out of him.

"Gearheardt! You stupid bastard! What in God's name are you doing attacking me in my own damn kitchen?!!"

Gearheardt sat up, trying to get his breath. "How did I know it was you sneaking around in the dark, Jack? When I fell asleep, you were snoring away in your own little bed. Then I woke up and saw someone sneaking into the kitchen. What the hell should I have thought?"

"That I was up in my own damn apartment getting a drink of water, you asshole. Geezus, you nearly scared me to death. And what are you doing in here anyway?" I got up and turned on the light. Gearheardt sat on the floor rubbing his neck. Good. I hoped the jackass was hurt. My heart was still racing.

"New plans, Jack. Or at least an update on the old plans." He stood up. "Damn, Jack," he said, "you could have really hurt me with that move."

"Gearheardt, you were *attacking* me!" I took a breath to calm down. "But what are these new plans? And by the way, I still need some authentication for this op. I'm not as dumb as I look."

"Not by a long shot, Jack. Let's step in the living room so I can sit down. I think you fractured my cranulus."

I ignored his whining and didn't think there was such a thing as a cranulus anyway. "Turn on the lamp by that table, Gearheardt. I'll start some coffee. I doubt I'll be going back to sleep." The light snapped on and I did a comic double-take. There was a naked woman sitting on my couch.

"Jack, this is Marta. Marta, this is Jack. I think we would all be more comfortable if you both got dressed."

I actually could have taken a bit longer look at the stunning Marta, but went into my bedroom and threw on clothes. My haste was rewarded when I returned to the living room in time to watch a calm and collected Marta slowly (almost reluctantly, it seemed) don hers. She smiled as she stood to zip up the side zipper on her skirt. "Ola, Jack," she said. My heart tingled.

"Ola, Marta," I replied. Then I realized that Marta had been in my living room with Gearheardt, without clothes. I looked at Gearheardt.

"Marta is our ticket into the Cuban opposition, Jack. And whatever Marta wants, I assure you, Marta gets."

"We have Cuban opposition?" I sank down into the large leather easy chair, a gift from another asset in Mexico who also ran a stolen furniture racket.

This is what happens in the CIA and particularly the part of the CIA where you deal with anyone as mysterious and manipulative as Gearheardt. You actually *ask* if we have Cuban opposition, when of course you know that Cuba is obviously an opponent. But there can be elements of the opposition that are in opposition to their own policy of opposing the U.S. So these would be in opposition to the opposition, making them of course our partners. But since Gearheardt was working in opposition to our own policy (as far as I knew for certain) which was in opposition to the Cubans, then if we had opposition from the Cubans, it must be the Cubans which were opposed to the original opposition that put them in opposition with us in the first place. Which was all to say that 'the enemy of my enemy is my friend.' Only Gearheardt's double talk made it seem confusing.

However, in this case, I was giving Gearheardt the benefit of the doubt because of my trust in him, the cable from Gib Wilson, and my basic distrust of Major Crenshaw, who of course might very well be working on the same mission Gearheardt claimed he was working on. By not sharing my information about Gearheardt with Crenshaw, I was now effectively working both sides. Which was where Gearheardt probably wanted me.

A benefit of this brain numbing run-through of scenarios was that Marta was no longer making my heart or plumbing tingle.

"Marta is a friend, Jack," Gearheardt said. Everybody seemed to be able to read my mind. Not a good thing for a spy.

"I don't know what friends are these days, Gearheardt."

"Friends are the ones who you have to go to the funeral for after you kill them."

Marta had just spread her legs in front of me revealing a gorgeous little Beretta strapped to her inner thigh. She adjusted the holster and then modestly smoothed her dress into place. "I say we have coffee and we talk," she said, looking at me.

"Excellent idea," Gearheardt said. "Let me get the coffee. Marta, you can give Jack your background."

Marta sighed, as if she had done this too often. But she went on. "I am Marta Carlingua. I am Cuban. My mother and father were Cuban importers of rubber products. It is very dangerous to be this in a Catholic country. My mother and father were Jewish. When Castro came to power the CIA contacted my father for him to put hot itching powder in some rubber product and to make sure that Castro and his henchmen got the product. This happened. But later the product was traced to my father. The Castro people shot my father and put hot itching powder on my mother in a not nice way. She became a prostitute. I ran away and I hated the Castro people very much. Now I work with Señor Gearheardt to help the Cuban people." She smiled.

"Thank you, Marta. I'd better help Gearheardt find the spoons." I went into the kitchen where Gearheardt was looking dumbly at the coffee pot as if transfixed.

"Gearheardt, I just heard probably the lamest story I've ever heard from *anyone* claiming they want to come over to our side and help us. Where did you find this Marta?"

Gearheardt was happy to lay down the various pieces of the coffee pot he was holding and deal with something he supposedly knows something about. "What do we care, Jack? Think about it. What if she *is* a Castro plant? As long as we know that, we can handle it. But to tell the truth, I think Marta is the real thing."

"A Cuban defector?"

"The daughter of a rubber distributor. She knows every thing you can imagine about them." He smiled. "Can you imagine dating the daughter of a rubber distributor? Sounds like a TV sitcom. Think about—"

"Damn it, Gearheardt. You're a child sometimes. Forget the rubbers, okay. You've dragged me into the cockamamie idea of assassinating the president of Mexico. You've introduced me to a Cuban—"

"She was naked, Jack. I supposed you're going to hold that against me too."

I closed my eyes, not caring whether Gearheardt thought I was just visualizing Marta naked. I counted to twenty before I opened them and spoke.

"Just fill me in on the plan, Gearheardt. This is not Vietnam where I had to rely totally on your gibberish. I have my own resources."

"And I'm counting on you using them, Jack. Hang with me. As you see the beauty of this scenario, I have no doubt that you'll be right there by my side. Like always."

I shuddered at that thought. On the counter I saw a cereal bowl with what looked like ground coffee and sugar covering the bottom. "You don't know how to make coffee, do you, Gearheardt?"

"I do except for the part where this thing with holes in the bottom has to fit in this pot or somewhere."

"Give me that damn thing and go into the living room. Work with Marta on a better cover story while you're in there. I'll make the coffee."

Marta, it turned out, was no dummy. Over the coffee that I finally produced, Gearheardt had her run through her role in the mission, code named (according to Gearheardt) 'Goodbye.'

"As in 'Goodbye Mexico,'" I said.

"Something like that," Gearheardt answered, smiling at Marta.

I admit it was partially to impress the delicious Marta that I pretended (I thought) to go along with Gearheardt's scheme. There were parts of it that made absolute sense. And there were parts that only a madman could possibly think up. A certain macho attitude—the root of most problems in the world— made me discuss with apparent equanimity the idea of assassinating the President of the country. Somehow I assumed that my subsequent refusal, at the appropriate time, would be taken care of by others far more qualified than I was.

"I don't understand the defecting part, Gearheardt," I said. It was nearly three A.M. and even the still delectable vision of Marta on my couch (and the thought of her soft tan thigh with a Beretta strapped to it), was not keeping me completely awake.

Gearheardt yawned. "All part of the plan, Jack. Don't worry about it now. I can assure you that you will be taken care of. Won't he Marta?"

"You will be taken great care of, Jack. I will personally see to that."

"I'm sure you will do a good job. How exactly do you plan to do it?" I hoped she didn't hear the amused condescension.

"I will come with you."

As inviting at that sounded early in the morning in my apartment in Colonia Polanco, the conversation was getting too close to a commitment on my part, one that I wasn't ready to make. Somehow, I had to find out if Gearheardt was acting on his own, or at least on behalf of a small faction in the Company. Or was this a mission that had administration, and therefore Agency, approval and direction? Neither seemed likely. But neither was impossible.

I was beat. Too tired to think through the possibilities. Even the annoyingly perky Marta looked tired.

"I need to go back to bed, Gearheardt. Do you two want to spend the night here? Officially, this time."

"Marta will stay, Jack. I need to see some people. Thanks, anyway." He rose, stretching. "In fact, Marta needs to move in here. She'll stay out of your way."

I wasn't sure what I was supposed to say. The prospect wasn't totally unattractive. Although my current girlfriend from the Austrian embassy might feel differently about having Marta around full time.

"Marta, if you will excuse Gearheardt and me for just a moment." I pulled him into the kitchen again.

"She can't just move in here. In case it hasn't occurred to you, the Agency frowns on its agents having foreign spies live with them. There's probably even a regulation about it, you idiot." I was getting madder as I talked to him. It was easier when I didn't have the luscious Marta protruding through her blouse in front of me. "And you admitted that you're not even positive that she isn't working for Castro. She could slit my damn throat while I was sleeping or something."

"I think you would wake up before she could actually get your throat slit, Jack."

"That isn't the point, you jackass. You're not ducking this one. What—"

Gearheardt stepped to the door and removed the rubber stop with his foot, allowing the kitchen door to swing shut. As it slowly closed he said, "Be with you in just a moment, Marta. Jack's teaching me to make coffee."

He turned back to me. "I need to take you up a level, Jack. I know you think you're not committed to the Goodbye mission yet. But you will be." He dropped his voice from a conversational level to a notch below that. "We're not supporting Castro taking over Mexico. Even the Pygmy isn't that stupid."

"But I asked you about Castro."

"And I didn't deny it. But I also didn't confirm it. I needed to get you a bit deeper in the morass. Did you know that's not pronounced more-ass? A subtle difference but—"

"Gearheardt—"

"Okay. The thing is that we're going to work with the Cubans in Miami. The good Cubans. They need a country. Mexico needs somebody with some leadership ability and a decent work ethic. Who isn't crooked.

And some other stuff. I forget the whole speech. But you can see where we're headed."

The plan had a ring of legitimacy. I had heard rumors that the agency was still working with the Cuban populations in Florida. After the decade-old Bay of Pigs fiasco, there was a still a great deal of mutual mistrust. Maybe we were taking steps to get something started again. That didn't explain all of Gearheardt's supposed mission. Such as the assassination of the Mexican President. But I knew there were significant gaps in the information that Gearheardt was sharing with me. I made a decision to move slightly ahead with my involvement.

"Crenshaw is down here supposedly to work on a very hush hush mission. Do you have any idea what that might be?" I asked Gearheardt.

"No. And I would give your right nut to find out, Jack. See what you can do. He's going to need you. Play along, but just keep me informed." He smiled. "That's my boy. We're a great team, Jack. That's why we were chosen to stop the Vietnam War."

"Which turned into a fiasco of epic proportions, Gearheardt."

"If you say so, Jack. I like to think positively about things. I think history is on our side."

I didn't respond and Gearheardt held out his hand which I shook warmly. After all, he was my best friend. "Do you have any idea what you're talking about?" I asked.

"Not really," he admitted readily. "I think I read it somewhere. Maybe Churchill or Stalin."

"How do I get in touch with you? What's the next step?"

Gearheardt took a bottle of beer from my refrigerator and opened it. "Don't worry about it. I'll take care of everything, Jack. You can just go about your normal routine. Try to keep in touch with the duty officer at the embassy if you're not in the office for any length of time. But let me handle things."

I looked toward the door. "And Marta? What do you expect me to do with her?"

Gearheardt bit his lip in thought. "Don't screw her. We may have to kill her later, and I don't want you having any attachments."

"Damn it, Gearheardt—"

He laughed. "I was just shitting you, Jack. She has her orders. She's just on loan to me now, but she's going to infiltrate you into the Cuban network here in Mexico City. Be careful."

The door was swinging behind him before I could gather my wits to ask him a number of questions. I heard him say goodbye to Marta. When I went back into the living room, the lamp was off again, and Marta was making herself comfortable on my couch, dressed in her thigh holster.

CHAPTER SIX

IS THIS A BREAST
I SEE BEFORE ME?

I was putting breakfast on the table when Marta entered the kitchen, rubbing her wet hair with my towel.

"Marta, you can't run around without clothes all the time," I said, trying not to stare.

"Why not, Jack?" she said. She hung the towel over the back of a chair and sat down at the table.

"It just isn't done. I mean, it's not right." I was searching for a good answer. "Look, I'm just a regular guy, you know what I mean. It's . . . uncomfortable for me to have you . . . looking like that." This was the best I could do.

Marta put jelly on her toast and munched loudly. "This is burned, Jack. Can you not make toast that is not burned? Do you want me to cook for you?"

She put the toast carefully on the plate, then brushed her hands vigorously, throwing delicate crumbs on her breasts. I wondered how I could make it through this.

"Jack, when I was a young woman in Cuba, my body was already an adult. Men would say things to me that I did not understand. I was feeling ashamed. My mother tried to tell me, 'Why should you feel ashamed? The men should feel ashamed.' So now that I am older I do not feel ashamed. If men want to look, they look. In America, I like the nudist camp. On the street, I am . . . okay. But in the house, I feel uncomfortable in clothing."

"I think you've taken it to the extreme, Marta." I started out of the kitchen, trying in vain to avoid the close-up that came when I passed her chair. "Look, I've got to get to the embassy. If Gearheardt says you're to stay here, you can stay here. When I'm in the apartment, I would like you to wear some clothes. How's that?"

"Whatever you say, Jack. I am sorry that you are ashamed."

"*I'm* not ashamed, Marta. That isn't what—" I sighed, telling myself that I had to just get used to this and that it was a noble sacrifice on my part. "How long have you known Gearheardt?"

"I have known Gearheardt many times," she answered.

I decided to not try to deconstruct that reply. After all, English was not her first language.

"I'm going to the embassy. I suppose I'll see you later."

"Tonight, we go dancing," Marta said.

The look on my face must have been easily readable.

"It is business, Jack." She walked to the sink and deposited the dishes, bending over to reach the trash can. At least she was wearing the Beretta.

In my office it was business as usual as soon as I sat down at my desk. On the top of my message pile was a message from Rodrigo, my Colombian project contact. 'Meet me at ten o'clock. There is something that is urgent to tell you. R.'

I had about an hour before I needed to leave so I called security and asked them to change my safe combination and sweep my office. Just as they left and I was putting my files back in place, Major Crenshaw appeared in the door.

"Jack, didn't you get the message to come to my office?" he asked.

"Yes, sir. I was just getting ready to—"

"Do I need to write 'immediately' on every message I send you, Jack?"

"No, sir. I'll come right down."

"No need. We can talk here." He closed the door. Before he sat down in front of my desk he surveyed the room silently. He frowned and made me wonder what he didn't like. Or maybe he was thinking about taking over my office. It was on the side of the embassy and had a choice view of the embassy garden and the tree-lined street beyond. But he took a chair without comment and sat down. He straightened the crease in his trousers.

"I need to fill you in just a bit, Jack. It goes without saying that you cannot repeat what I am about to tell you."

I was fidgeting with my stack of messages and he stared at my hands until I dropped them and sat back in my chair.

"Every successful mission must have excellent support. You know that. You will support me and your efforts will be excellent. That way, my mission can be successful."

I nodded my head and tried to look as if I had heard something profound.

"As you know, Cinco de Mayo is in a couple of days. Officially, the Agency is not tasked with any significant role in that ceremony."

"You mean the speech of the President, Major?"

"Exactly. Obviously the State Department people," he made them sound like scabrous lepers, "will be involved in the ceremony. The Ambassador specifically asked me to be, let us say, unseen. But I did get his agreement that I could provide one officer as a security representative. That officer will be authorized to be armed, the only one who has that honor. That officer will be you, Jack."

A small generator of conflicting and dangerous thoughts kicked off in my head. Did Gearheardt know that I was to be an armed security representative at the introduction of the Mexican president? How could he, if Crenshaw had just made the selection after his conversation with the Ambassador? And why did Crenshaw want me armed and present anyway? For just a moment, I also wondered what Marta was doing back in my apartment.

"Am I keeping you from your day dreams, Jack? Is this a bad time?" The man had no humor but had sarcasm down perfectly.

"Yes, sir. I mean, no, sir. It's just that I need to meet someone in a few minutes."

"Someone?"

"Rodrigo."

I watched to see if he would give away the fact that he had probably read my Colombian file.

"Sounds like a local." He stood and went to the door. "I don't want any jacking around on this Cinco de Mayo assignment. And that's not a pun. See me when you get back." He opened the door and then turned back. "You do know how to use a pistol, don't you, Jack? As in shooting someone? If you had to?"

"I can shoot people, Major. Sometimes even if I don't have to."

"Hmmm," he said and left. Leaving my door open.

"Pepe is for you, Señor Armstrong," Ms. Sanchez said on my intercom.

I got up and shut my door. I had only a few minutes leeway to get through the traffic to Rodrigo, but I needed to ask Gearheardt a few questions.

"Gearheardt, where are you? We need to talk."

"Watch out for Crenshaw, Jack. He thinks he knows more than he knows."

I let that sink in.

"Gearheardt, you rotten bastard, do you have a bug in my office? What the hell do you know about Crenshaw?" I was genuinely upset. Bugging someone's office was . . . well we did it all the time, but Gearheardt was supposed to be my pal.

"Believe me, Jack. It's for your own good."

"I just had the office swept this morning, Gearheardt. How could you possibly get a bug back in here?"

"Let's talk about important things. Not why Hector and Billy might have missed a bug in your office." Hector and Billy happened to be the embassy security people who had changed the combination on my safe and swept my office. "First, Marta will take you to a Cuban nightclub tonight. Be careful, but trust her. She will introduce you to some people it will be good for you to know. And she's a hell of a dancer. You aren't supposed to know anything, so just let whatever happens happen. They'll try to approach you if they get comfortable."

I was trying to calm down and understand what Gearheardt was telling me. "So these are some of your Cubans?"

"Uh, no. Not exactly. These are the opposition. Mean little bastards too. But just take it easy. You're there dancing with Marta. Don't wear your gun. I gotta go, Jack. I'll talk to you later. And congratulations on the security guard job. You're perfect." He hung up.

Rodrigo was in a sweat by the time I got to our meeting place. He met me at the door of the small cantina, and took my arm. "Let's go, Jack. I have my car here. I will tell you on the way." His car was a red 1969 Chevrolet convertible. Fairly obtrusive for a private detective in Mexico City, but that was none of my business.

On the periferico, the freeway that encircled the city, Rodrigo wove in and out of traffic at speeds up to eighty miles per hour. The first few times I had ridden with him, I assumed that all of the Mexican traffic police knew the car and left him alone. A former police officer himself, he had gotten mixed up or crosswise with the vice boys and ended up a civilian. I didn't know the whole story.

We exited on the road to Puebla before he spoke again. "Thees Colombian guy, he is full of bombs in his car. My friends will stop him until we get to there. He will tell us the students that take the bombs to America." He smiled at me. "He will sing like the bird."

"Rodrigo, I am just interested in finding out who supplies the explosives, the bombs, and where the money comes from. I know that you don't like it that he recruits the Mexican kids, but we're more interested in the source. We think the Russians are behind this." I had explained this to Rodrigo more than once, probably telling him too much.

"Then he will sing a Russian song." He laughed and looked at me, expecting me to laugh too. I tried.

We swung off the blacktop and followed a dusty road for another two or three miles. The town we entered was Calixtua. More than a village but hardly a city. One-story pueblo-style buildings in the 'suburbs' and a mixture of American fast food knockoffs and open-front appliance stores on Main Street. All glued together with small cantinas and cafés. Rodrigo turned down a narrow street and after two blocks pulled tightly against the side of a building and stopped.

"From here we walk," he said, not noticing that I was struggling to open my door against the adobe wall. "My friend's garage is not far. The Colombian is there to get his car fixed." He stopped at the corner and turned. "You are armed, Jack?"

I was, but before I could answer, a blast we both felt and heard captured all of our attention. Rodrigo took off running and I followed, instinctively pulling my pistol from its shoulder holster.

Down two blocks and around another corner we ran and then slowed at the sight that awaited us. A car was burning in front of what had been an auto mechanic's garage. The front of the garage was missing. The windows on the adjacent buildings were shattered and shards were still falling to the ground. Two young Mexican men were sitting on the ground, their hands covering their faces, blood showing between their fingers. Alongside the burning car, another man lay prone and motionless. From the corner of my eye, I saw a man twenty yards away on his hands and knees.

Rodrigo and I ran to the motionless man and began dragging him away from the car. As we deposited him on the concrete floor of the garage and rolled him on to his back, he moaned and opened his eyes. Rodrigo began talking to him in rapid Spanish that I couldn't follow. I did hear "Colombiano" two or three times.

I walked to where the two young men now had their shirts off and sat wiping blood and dirt from their faces. They didn't appear to be seriously injured. I became aware of noise for the first time since we had heard the explosion. Turning, I saw a small crowd of people gathering in front of the shop. Some men were throwing buckets of water on the still smoldering car. A baby was screaming from somewhere in the crowd or one of the adjacent houses.

One of the 'fireman' stopped and looked at me. He pointed down the street. "Colombiano," he said.

The man who had been on his hands and knees was now on his feet, supporting himself with one hand against an adobe wall. As I started toward him he looked back and began moving more swiftly. I broke into a run as he disappeared around the corner. I rounded the same corner moments later and crashed into a small wooden cart that evidently had been pulled into my path by the fleeing Colombian. With one knee hurting like hell, I started back after him. Down a pot-holed alley. Then into a small square. Five or so street carts and a small crowd of Mexicans. An overcrowded bus was departing from the other side of the square and I saw the Colombian clinging to the back door. He saw me and gave me the finger.

Back at the garage, Rodrigo had everything under control. No one had been killed, but the two garage workers had been taken to the hospital. His friend sat in a chair brought from one of the surrounding homes. Dust and smoke still hung in the air. A woman stood in what had been the office of the garage, holding a rag to her mouth and crying. A small girl clung to her legs, her eyes following me as I moved around.

"What happened?" I asked Rodrigo.

"My friend says your Colombiano came to his shop to get his car fixed yesterday. My friend knew that I was looking for a Colombiano with thees car so he tell him to come back today and he call me."

"What's your friend's name?"

"It is no matter, Jack." He was not looking at me. "Then my friend told the Colombiano that it would take maybe one hour. The Colombiano left and walked to the plaza just there," he pointed in the direction I had chased the other man, "and when he return he was angry that the car was not fixed. My friend had the keys to the car so the man could not leave and the Colombiano threw a small bomb into the window and then . . . BOOM. And this is what my friend said happened."

In my less than perfect Spanish, I asked the garage owner if he was okay.

Rodrigo answered for the man. "My friend was once in the Mexican army. When he saw the small bomb, he knew he should not try to run away. He fell to the ground very flat." Rodrigo slapped the man on the shoulder, congratulating him for his quick thinking. The blast had simply blown up and out, sparing, for the most part, the garage owner flat beneath the 'cone' of energy and car parts.

I nodded toward the crying woman and small girl. "His family?"

"Si, Jack. Those boys at the hospital are his two sons."

A wave of emotion came over me that I had not expected. I saw a village in Vietnam that we had entered after a friendly artillery shell fell in its center. Only the small children would look at me as I walked through checking the damages. The image was so vivid for a moment that I wondered if I were having a 'flashback.' I had heard vets talk about them, but never thought I experienced anything other than a few bad dreams and some occasional discomforting memories.

"Jack, the local police are coming. I need to speak to them and then we'll go."

"Tell your friend that we will pay to have his garage repaired, Rodrigo." I didn't trust my flimsy Spanish under the circumstances. "Tell him I am sorry that this happened and we will also pay for the doctor bills."

As Rodrigo finished speaking to his friend, whose expression didn't change, two Mexican Policemen, their brown uniforms sweat stained and unpressed, came up to us.

"Buenos dias, amigos," the older one said. He began a long conversation with Rodrigo.

After a few minutes, Rodrigo took me by the arm and led me through the small crowd of on-lookers, heading back to his car. "We will need some money for the police also, Jack. It will cost them extra for security now that they know we have dangerous operations taking place in Calixtua. Maybe five hundred U.S. dollars."

"What kind of security?" I asked. It sounded naïve.

"They will do nothing different, amigo. But this is their town."

On the way back to Mexico City, those irrational thoughts of 'what if' flooded over me. What if the man and his two sons had been killed? What if the little girl had been in the garage? The mother? The fact that they hadn't didn't seem to chase the 'what if's' away.

I could also imagine Gearheardt's comment. *Jack, the garage owner should have put his shop somewhere besides where the United States and Russia are using their surrogates, like Mexico and Colombia, to blow each other up.* Gearheardt and his witticism, his naked cohorts and his cockeyed schemes seemed far away from the realities of my normal routine.

I knew it was dangerous to have feelings in my job. And the man and his family would recover, with a new and probably better shop. Still . . .

"Jack, amigo, here is your car."

We were pulling in front of the restaurant where I had met Rodrigo only a couple of hours before. I got out as he stopped, but held the door open and leaned back in. "Rodrigo, do you think you can still get a line on the Colombian? I would think he would hightail it back to Bogotá after this."

"Maybe, Jack. But I don't think so. He is probably paid very well. And he didn't deliver the bombs. Sometimes that is not a happy thing to tell the Colombian bosses. I will check around. With my Colombian cousin, and at the school with my son. He is a student there." He started the car. "Did you see him, Jack? Did you get a good look at him?"

"They all look alike to me, Rodrigo." I laughed but there was some unfortunate truth there. "I am sure he was young. Probably a student. He gave me the finger. Not the thing a senior agent would probably do." I started to close the door. "You might ask your son to watch out for a Colombian student who shows up on the campus injured or limping."

"Don't forget the money, Jack. I can pick it up at the cantina tomorrow?"

"It will be there. Do you think $2500 will be enough?"

"More than enough. But I might have some expenses also, no?" He drove off.

I had a beer in the café before I started back to the embassy. I knew I needed to be under control to tell this story to Major Crenshaw. Somehow I didn't think Major Crenshaw would worry about blowing up a Mexican auto shop. The money to repair it—that might be a different matter. I remembered the grand that I took from the egg money and felt better that I would only have to request fifteen hundred from the Agency.

As I cruised through Chapultepec Park on my way back to my office, I glanced at the elegant apartment buildings in Colonia Polanco. I imagined a naked Cuban woman lounging in one of them. I shouldn't have, but I felt better just thinking about that. As Gearheardt would say, "If free money and naked women can't cheer you up, you may be dead."

CHAPTER SEVEN

NO SHIRT, NO PANTS, NO MARTA

Luckily, Crenshaw (Major Crenshaw—I was not supposed to even *think* of his name without 'major' in front of it) was not in when I made it back to the embassy. Juanita wouldn't tell me where he had gone or when he would be back. She didn't like Major Crenshaw, but she was a loyal assistant.

"Will he be back this afternoon, Juanita?" I asked.

"Even if I did know, I would not tell you."

"So you don't know."

"I do know. I am his assistant."

"It's okay not to know, Juanita. Major Crenshaw hardly trusts anyone." I started to my office. I stopped and took a wild guess. "Is he riding his burro into the hills, Juanita?"

I looked at her and she was flustered. "I cannot tell you about his riding burro, Señor Armstrong. Especially about the burro." She paused. "He is not riding burro today."

The jackass was probably meeting his Cuban contacts in the hills north of Teotihuacan. That was burro country. Did we have burro parking in the embassy? Did he take an embassy car to where he parked his burro? The guys he was meeting probably had to leave luxury condos in the Zona Rosa and have drivers take them to the hills so that they could meet with the bozo from America who rode around on a donkey. Were burros donkeys?

I closed my door and flopped onto my tattered embassy-issue couch by the window. Thoughts of Marta gamboling around my office in the buff began to overcome the sadness of blowing up a poor Mexican's livelihood. I was Americanized again.

I wrote up the action report for my Colombian file, filled out a request for funds for the auto shop and extra security, and spent an hour with another agent who was also involved in the military intelligence project. His assessment was that the risk of the operation wasn't worth the potential information that we might find.

"This looks like 'make work' to me, Jack. So what if the Mexicans are holding back information from us? I've never seen them generate any intelligence worth buying. And buying is the only way to get intelligence at this level. So why bother to infiltrate?"

"You were enthusiastic last week, Eric. Why the change?"

"Crenshaw has me on a special assignment that's eating up all my time."

"That's *Major* Crenshaw. Under the honor code I'm afraid I'll have to report that you didn't use Major when you referred to him. Your career's over."

"My career is over if anyone finds out what I'm *doing* for *Major* Crenshaw. If I tell you what it is, will you promise on the life of the many brothel children you no doubt have never to reveal to anyone what I'm about to tell you?"

"I have no brothel children, and I'm not really sure I want to know what Major Crenshaw has his top agent doing." I got up to leave.

"I really would like to tell you, Jack," Eric said, rising also and grabbing my arm. "He has me trying to find out how many committed Christians are in the Cuban spy network in Mexico City."

"How do you—"

He shrugged and held his hands out palms up. "Beats me."

I shook my head in sympathy. "Have you thought of checking Sunday mornings in the churches?" It was hard for me to register this information as *not* somehow humorous.

Eric stroked his chin. "Actually I *hadn't* thought of that, Jack. You mean just take our list of suspected Cuban activists and see if I can find them in church?"

It was frightening to me that I might have given Eric the best advice he had so far received. So I left without answering.

Back in my office I looked through the files that had to do with the Mexican intelligence services and decided that Eric might have been right. The danger of the Mexicans finding out that the CIA was targeting them probably outweighed the intelligence we might discover. And there were other ways to find out what they were up to. I wrote 'suspended' on the outside of the file, a short memo to Crenshaw outlining my conclusions, and marked the file for the archives.

The Colombian connection was another matter. I was convinced that money was flowing into student radical groups at the University of Mexico. And I was also certain that American students were getting terrorist training somewhere. Probably through Cuba. There was a connection there and I was determined to find what it was, Gearheardt plan or no Gearheardt plan. The real world of my business shoved wild ideas off of my priority list. Still, there was definitely something going on. Crenshaw had some bug up his butt. Gearheardt knew more than he was letting on. Why I, a lowly junior Agency officer, was in the middle of things, was beyond current speculation.

When I opened the door to my apartment, I saw figures scurrying out of the living room toward the bathroom and my bedroom. "What the hell is going on?" I yelled. I was pretty sure I knew. After a moment, Gearheardt strolled into the living room as I was hanging up my shoulder holster.

"Hey, Jack," he said. "You're home early." He was dressed in Levis and a polo shirt. "I just stopped by to give you a message. I'm heading out to meet someone now."

"Barefooted?"

He looked down at his feet. "What happened to my shoes?"

"Gearheardt, I don't care what you and Marta are up to. I just don't like this arrangement. I used to have a social life of my own before you showed up."

"If you're talking about Greta, from the Austrian Embassy, you might want to check in with her, Jack. She stopped by this afternoon."

"Let me guess. Marta was here nude."

"I prefer to call it 'au natural.' Doesn't rhyme with lewd that way."

"I'll keep that in mind, Gearheardt. So what did she say? What did you tell her?"

"I didn't tell her anything. Marta handled it herself. Convinced her we were just making some blue movies in the bedroom. I was in there yelling 'action' and 'cut' and I think she bought it."

I wished I could even consider that he was kidding. "Great. Good thinking." I ripped my tie off and threw it on the easy chair. "I suppose you led her to believe that I was in the bedroom with you."

"Why would we be using your apartment if you weren't home, Jack? She might have called the police."

He retrieved his shoes from under the couch and was slipping them on. "We could have told her we were a couple of spies just waiting for you to come home so that we could practice some espionage. That sound better, Jack? Imagine that story getting back to the Austrian Embassy."

I plopped onto the couch as Marta, wearing my robe, walked into the living room. Before I could decide my attitude toward her, she said, "May I get a drink for you, Jack? You look very tired. You need to be ready for a good time and good business tonight."

"Ola, Marta. Yes, I'll have some Scotch. And no, I am not going out tonight. I am exhausted. I've had a long day. And I still don't know what I'm supposed to be doing for you," I turned to face my pal, "Gearheardt."

Gearheardt just laughed. He picked up my tie and wrapped it around his neck. "Jack, don't you think Washington was tired when he had to row across the Delaware? Don't you think MacArthur would have preferred staying home rather than marching to Bataan? We're not in a game that allows for 'tired' or 'too busy.' When there are people trying to assassinate our leaders, bomb our institutions, spy on our citizens, do you think we should fight them only from eight to five? When it's convenient and there's nothing good on TV?" He stood and slipped on a sport coat that looked suspiciously like one that I owned. "You know better, Jack. That's why I know I can count on you." He smiled at me. Charming and annoying. "And Marta."

Marta had in fact returned with my Scotch. She smiled and I deliberately did not envision taking her out to a club in her short, tight skirt. "Gracias, Marta," I said. She waited, prescient, while I drank the liquor in one long swallow and sat the glass back on the tray. She headed back to the kitchen. "Gearheardt, even after all the years I've known you, I don't know if you are really as uninformed as you seem to be, or if you just do it to infuriate me. Somehow your inane speeches actually make me feel guilty about not carrying out your idiot plans."

"That's the ticket, Jack." As if I had agreed to something. "Let me tell you about this evening." He looked at his watch and then sat down across from me. "I told you before that I need a certain structure in place to make every thing happen. Right? Tonight you can do me the favor of putting another piece in place. The Cubans that Marta will introduce you to are not on my team."

"So I'm on a Cuban recruiting mission? What makes you think any of these guys will have any interest in being on your *team*?"

"I don't want them on my team, Jack. That's the thing. I want them on Crenshaw's team. And you work for Crenshaw."

"Gearheardt, wouldn't it just be easier for you to tell me what's going on? Recruiting Cubans for Crenshaw? That doesn't make sense at all."

Gearheardt rubbed his chin and looked at the floor. Evidently taking what I was saying under consideration. I knew he trusted me. Finally he said, "Jack, did you wonder why you, a junior Agency officer, were asked to be Acting Chief of Station in Mexico City? You have a number of very qualified agents in the embassy. Ever cross your mind that they were overlooked?"

It had. Frequently. The explanation that the Mexico desk in Langley gave was that since the position was for only a short period, it wouldn't make sense to interrupt the other agent's routines and on-going operations. I really hadn't bought that, but I didn't know of a better explanation. "I suppose so, Gearheardt. I guess you're going to tell me it was your doing."

He laughed. "I wish I had that much pull, Jack. But I'm just a contract officer. They hardly know I exist except when I cause them a bit of rouble."

"In other words, everyone at Langley probably knows you."

"Well, yes. But that doesn't give me much leverage in things like picking the COS."

"So what's your point?" I knew I should shut up, throw him and Marta out of my apartment, and get on with my life. "If you weren't involved, so what? Langley might not have had *any* reason particularly. Maybe it was a typo"

"No typo, Jack. It was the Pygmy." He held his palm toward me. "No, I mean it. The Pygmy is running this show. He thought that if we could get the operation going while you had no boss in Mexico City, we could move things along quickly. Unfortunately, Langley decided to rush a new Chief of Station down here. I knew Crenshaw when he was running around Africa carrying a spear. So I suggested that the Pygmy get him sent down here."

"He rode a burro into town." Not that I was buying Gearheardt's whole story.

"It was good enough for Jesus."

Which could have meant that Gearheardt was a born-again Christian. That he was spoofing Crenshaw. That he simply thought it was a time-honored mode of transportation. In any event, I should have stuck with my earlier notion of throwing him out of my apartment. But it was Gearheardt. And he was under contract to the CIA. And so was I.

"So what do you want me to do?"

"Just follow Marta's lead, Jack. Perfect tits don't mean you're dumb." He smiled at Marta who smiled back. "Maybe it's 'doesn't.' Would it be 'perfect tits doesn't mean you're dumb?' The 'having' is understood. So—"

"Gearheardt, for Pete's sake, just leave it alone. If you don't want me to ask more questions, just say so."

He shrugged and looked at his watch again. He looked very collegiate. A blazer over a polo shirt, worn with jeans and loafers with no socks. I wondered if he were really going to meet someone in the scheme, or out to the campus to cruise for American college girls down for graduate school. He stood. "Jack, I will never not let you know as much as you shouldn't know to keep yourself out of trouble as far as knowing goes."

I think he was serious. "Thanks."

At the door he smiled big teeth at Marta. "Take care of my boy, Marta. And keep your clothes on."

"Gearheardt, you do understand that I have gone far beyond where I should have gone with all this. Just by not discussing it with my case officer, I'm breaking the rules. To say nothing of common sense."

"And I won't let you down, Jack. You will get the authorization you need when you need it." He left.

The club that Marta took me to was unexpectedly not a dive. A watering hole for kings and potentates—probably not. But it was white tablecloths and waiters that actually came to your table. I shouldn't have been surprised that Gearheardt ran with a higher class crowd than my gang of runners and informants.

It was the Club Tristiza, a word only vaguely familiar but sounding festive enough. It was in a part of town that I hadn't visited frequently, near the floating market. Leaving my little BMW 1600 with the white-shirted valet parking crew was the toughest part. I assumed that while I was dining and dancing with the very luscious Marta, my car would be a part of various robberies, kidnappings and sundry criminal transactions; this deduced from the conversation I heard patches of when I handed the youth the keys. Then I felt bad that I was making such bigoted assumptions and followed Marta into the club.

The greeter seemed to recognize Marta, or maybe he asked everyone to please keep their clothes on.

The patrons, I noticed as we were shown to a table near the dance floor, were somber. The music being played by a five-piece band in tuxes and lacy shirts was a Latin American dirge, what the Mexicans called an *endecha*. They sat on the small stage under faint red lights. Two couples moved slowly around the dance floor, neither laughing nor talking. When the music stopped, no one clapped. The couples shuffled wordlessly back to their tables. The ones I observed grabbed wine glasses and drained them as soon as they sat down.

Marta and I ordered our drinks, both red wine, and I smiled the smile of any guy on a first date not sure what to talk about. Marta was scanning the room, looking, I assumed, for anyone that she might know. I saw no signs of recognition cross her face before she looked back at me and smiled.

"Marta," I said.

Before I could think of what followed that, a man whose description might define *swarthy* took the stage in front of the band and tapped the microphone. He began to speak in a slow Spanish, emotional and slurred, very difficult to understand. I heard Cuba and Castro a number of times before the man burst into tears and was led from the stage. The room was silent except for the clink of wine glasses and a few sniffles.

"For God's sake, Marta, what is this place? This has to be the most depressing nightclub in the world."

Marta's eyes were teary when she spoke. "In my country, in all of Latin America, we do not hide our emotions, Jack. We celebrate them. Club Tristiza is a place where we can come and be sad. If we are lonely or missing a loved one. If we are in a strange land and missing our country and our family, we need to share those emotions."

"You took off your clothes in *here?*" It just slipped out.

Marta ignored me, finishing her wine and signaling the weeping waiter for another round. As he slipped into the kitchen through a swinging door I glimpsed bright lights and heard normal sounds of people talking and enjoying being alive.

"I thought maybe Castro died or something," I ventured.

Even the clinking and sniffling stopped. All heads near our table swung toward me. I raised my glass. "Viva Castro," I said. No one joined my toast but they stopped staring.

The band began playing, this time with a young woman singer who was not bad looking except for her streaked mascara. The song she sang evidently had something to do with 'love' falling in a river and something about a horse that was magic and somehow saved 'love' except that someone's lover or carpet cleaner had a knife and someone got stabbed. I wished my Spanish language course had lasted a bit longer before I was posted to Mexico City. For the first time, I felt 'set up.' I was in a strange land, working for strange people, without a language, with few friends (except Gearheardt), and a vague sense of mission. Just before I started to cry, a man approached the table and greeted Marta.

"Ola, Marta. Como esta?" He was slick. I knew that I should not make snap judgments based on first impressions. But my first impression was that this guy had a tee shirt under his suit that said *I'd rather be molesting schoolchildren.*

"Esta es mi amigo Jack," Marta said to the man, pointing to me.

I rose and extended my hand. "Mucho gusto," not meaning it.

The man ignored my hand. In fact ignored me and spoke to Marta.

As I sat down I said, "Why don't you go screw yourself."

His look and raised eyebrows told me he spoke passable English. Marta kicked me under the table. I wasn't sure I understood all he said next, but I was pretty sure that even if he cut my heart out, it wouldn't fit up my ass. We weren't getting along so far and I hoped this wasn't one of the contacts that Gearheardt and Marta wanted me to make. This guy was Cocky, Clever, and Cuban. Long ago Gearheardt and I decided to kill anyone that passed that test with a sixty-six or better, as long as they got the last one right.

Marta seemed all business as she invited the Cuban to join us. His reluctance lasted about five seconds. I said nothing as Marta's spiked heel onto my instep kept my mind busy. They began a conversation that was difficult to interpret as well as to hear with Marta (the shameless hussy) leaning close to the man's ear. I did think I heard Crenshaw's name mentioned, a burro, and me.

My mind wandered, thinking about the Cubans I met in North Vietnam and the stories of their torture techniques. When I checked back in, Marta and the lizard were looking at me.

"Marta says to me that you work in the American embassy," the lizard said. It seemed to pain him to speak to me.

"I am an economic development officer in the embassy."

The lizard looked at Marta and shrugged.

There was a loud thump as Marta's kick missed my leg and hit the booth. "Jack," she said, "there is no reason to be secret. I have known Victor for a long time."

"You have known Victor many times?" The joke was lost on Marta.

"Yes, he is a man that was kind to me after he killed my father." (Maybe I misunderstood her). She went on. "Victor is an important man. I told him that you are an important man also." Why didn't she just paint a bulls-eye on my suit coat? And why did I envision Gearheardt somewhere cavorting with naked women and tequila while I chatted with the *lagarto*?

Marta was still talking. "I believe that Victor would be a good man for you to know, Jack." She turned to Victor, who was the only other person in the club not breaking into tears. "Jack might be able to help with your mission, Victor."

Victor began a lengthy tirade, directed to Marta and suitably subdued in the funereal surroundings. I caught enough of it to understand the basic theme; 'what in the hell have you been telling this slimeball about me?' When he finished he stood and looked down at me. I braced myself for an assault, either physical or verbal. But he turned on his heels and left.

"I think that went awfully well," I said.

Marta understandably ignored my feeble sarcasm. She was writing on a section of the wine list. She tore it off and held it up to my face. "This is the number you will call."

I took the paper, looked at it closely, and held it to the candle. It flared quickly and was gone. "Screw the lagarto," I said. "You want another drink? Or would you like to cry or something?"

Marta might be on loan to Gearheardt (whatever the hell that meant) but she needed to have a bit stronger sense of who was running this particular side of the operation. Assuming there was one. I wasn't about to suck up to a rabid Ricky Ricardo. If the Cubans were interested in me, they could get in touch with me. This wasn't just machismo (although Marta admittedly brought out a bit of that) but good sense. Never go into another man's game with your dick in your hand. (This was advice that Gearheardt had give me. I wasn't exactly sure what it meant, and I knew it was not elegantly put. But I had a vague sense that he was right).

Marta was worried that she had done something wrong. "Gearheardt will not be happy with this, Jack. This is part of his plan. Victor and his friends will be waiting for you to call. And Victor is not a lizard."

I patted her hand. "Don't worry about Gearheardt," I said. "Remember I know something about this game too. If Victor takes the bait," I looked around to see if I had spoken too loudly, "he'll get in touch. You can't force yourself on a man with a mission, Marta." The band broke into an agonizing rendition of *Volga Boatmen* which prompted a brooding Russian type to begin boo-hooing and I decided I had had it with the Club Tristiza. "Let's go. This place is giving me the creeps." I patted her hand again when she didn't respond. "Unless you want to take off your clothes or something."

She smiled and I liked her even better. In the car I tried to find out exactly who Victor was and how much she had told him about me. I found out very little. She was good, or dumb. Or both. Victor had been a childhood friend in Havana. When he went into the Cuban army, he changed. Back in civilian clothes, he was cold and secretive. But Marta, she claimed, had charmed him and became what I took to be his mistress for a short while. I had heard her right; she did suspect that he had been responsible for her father's death. I had begun to make sense of her wanting to help Gearheardt use the bad Cubans for his purpose when she followed up with, "My father was an evil man, Jack. I do not want to tell you."

A girl with an evil father and a mother who encouraged her to run around bare-ass naked becomes the mistress of a man who is responsible for having her father killed and turning her mother into a prostitute. I ould see why Gearheardt trusted her with the Agency's secrets, to say nothing of putting my life in her hands. A nice stable girl. Damn Gearheardt.

But I didn't try to call Greta that night, and wasn't sure that I would try the next day.

I went straight to bed, not thinking for a moment about the lovely Marta prancing around my apartment dressed in her thigh holster. And I left the next morning while she was still sleeping on the couch, my souvenir serape pulled up over he bare shoulders.

WHOSE HAND IS THIS I'M BITING?

"I suppose it would be too much trouble for you to arrange to have lunch with me, Mr. Armstong?"

Crenshaw, Major Crenshaw, had snuck down the hall and opened my office door without alerting me. He scared the heck out of me when he spoke.

"No, sir. I would be thrilled (thrilled?) to have lunch with you, sir. May I arrange it? Or are we in the embassy cafeteria?" Why did I sound like an obsequious suck-toad when I talked to Crenshaw?

"I've had Juanita arrange a table at a small cantina I know near the embassy. I think you'll find the food quite good." He left my door open as usual, and I heard him at Juanita's desk. "Did you check on the carpenters, Juanita? I'm really quite anxious for them to complete the new door."

After I closed my own door, I spoke to Gearheardt. "Gearheardt, you rotten bastard, if you're listening, give me a call. You and I need to talk." I had assumed he would be contacting me if Marta had reported my 'lack of cooperation' with her Cuban contacts. I knew that Gear-heardt would understand that I didn't want to seem too interested in them. Marta did not know the subtleties of the game.

Juanita knocked discreetly and brought the morning's dispatches and messages.

Rodrigo had called. A new lead and a sighting of the Colombian by one of Rodrigo's many 'men.'

The Agency in Bogotá had responded with a cryptic note:

> Your subject son of prominent businessman. No known con-nections with communist organizations or other enemies of U.S. Suggest you use caution if implicated in terrorist activi-ties. Need leather type and color.

It only took a moment to figure out the reference to leather (the jacket I had ordered) but deciphering the "use caution if . . . activities" was as clear as the Mexico City air. Were they suggesting danger to the target? Or fear of diplomatic problems because the kid was the son of someone important? Or maybe they thought he himself was involved in terrorist activities. What were the terrorist activities they referred to? I looked back through my message chart and found I had not mentioned terrorist activities to the Bogotá office. I wasn't sure it meant anything, but as Gearheardt said 'We're paid to be paranoid, and I, for one, like it."

Juanita was in the doorway after another tentative knock. Her blouse was a soft, demure cotton fabric that was impossible to see through. She had it unbuttoned down the front to just above her waist.

"Señor Major Crenshaw says for me to tell you that he will meet you at the cantina, Señor Jack. He had one errand to do before he meet with you."

"Which cantina am I to meet him at, Juanita? I like your blouse, by the way."

"Your cantina, Señor Jack. You do not think it is too, como se dice, revealing?"

"Not by any measure, Juanita. I don't want to embarrass you, Juanita, but are you not wearing a brassiere?"

"It would show unless I buttoned up my blouse, Señor Jack. Señor Major Crenshaw said to me that he did not want to see my brassiere ever again."

"Has he seen this blouse?" I was on my feet, putting on my jacket.

"He will not look at me. He is red in the face when he passes my desk."

I patted her arm as I went past her. Her perfume was exquisite. "I think you've won an important victory, Juanita. You should be proud."

At the door to the hallway, I stopped. "Juanita, if Señor Pepe calls, tell him that I must hear from him tonight. Señor Pepe. If Rodrigo calls, tell him that I also need to talk to him before he talks to his friend. Have you got that?"

"Si."

She seated herself behind her desk, leaning forward as she scooted in her chair. I became red in the face and left for my lunch with Crenshaw.

I stood just outside the door to El Caballo, the cantina owned by my friend, Mr. Chavez, until I spotted Crenshaw inside. Entering, I caught the eye of Mr. Chavez and quickly signaled that he did not know me.

"Well, hello, Major Crenshaw," I boomed at his tableside as if I had run into him by chance, "do you mind if I join you?"

Crenshaw frowned up at me as if I were a child. "Of course, Jack. I invited you to lunch. Remember?" The guy had no sense of humor at all. We were near the back of the cantina, against the wall, with a full view of the small place. Only a few Mexican patrons were resident. Mr. Chavez lounged with his elbows on the bar, chewing a toothpick and studying a prospectus for condos in South Texas.

"You see the bartender, Jack? No, don't look around. Just to put you at ease, you should know that he works for me. Very trustworthy and full of information that you would be surprised to find that he knows." Crenshaw grunted smugly. "It doesn't take me long to start setting up a network, Jack."

Particularly when I pay Mr. Chavez to approach you the first time you are in the cantina, Major Crenshaw. So Mr. Chavez was 'double dipping.' As long as he kept me posted on what Crenshaw was up to, I had no problem. I just wanted to know who Crenshaw was meeting. And I wanted to make sure that Crenshaw was not aware that I had met Gearheardt here on two occasions. Mr. Chavez assured me my association with Mr. Gearheardt was a secret. Or, for only two thousand more pesos, double secret. It seemed reasonable and I paid.

We ordered, with Crenshaw making an elaborate showing of his appreciation of 'real' Mexican food, not the tourista fare. This resulted in him getting something that appeared to be pig entrails stuffed with pig extrails. It looked and smelled ghastly and Mr. Chavez wouldn't catch my eye when I looked suspiciously at him behind the bar, snorting into his fist.

Crenshaw gamely choked down the entire mess, using most of the hot sauce from our table and the surrounding tables to deaden his palate. I actually felt sorry for him and admired his dedication to maintaining his dignity. His patrician face, and bearing, was rather admirable altogether and I made a mental note to try to give the guy a chance at his new job. He could no doubt use my support whether I liked his mannerisms or not.

"Jack," he said as he wiped excess hot sauce from his lips, "I want you to fire Juanita."

What a jerk the guy was. I finished off my tacos without looking up at him.

"She is a distraction in the office (a welcome one I thought to myself but didn't say) and I am not at all convinced of her loyalty to the U.S. mission. I am not sure how a local became secretary to the COS anyway."

I could have told him that the previous secretary provided by Langley looked like Lon Chaney in drag and had less personality. The former COS had vetted Juanita himself and felt comfortable with her loyalty. He also kept her under surveillance almost twenty-four hours a day, she being his mistress.

"I would think that would be your department, sir. She is *your* secretary and, by the way, I believe she's a loyal employee."

"Don't be cute with me, Armstrong. You know what I'm talking about, the distraction in the office. No one who dresses like that can be trusted anyway. And since you seem to have such *affection* for her, I thought you might like to break the word to her. That's enough on Ms. Sanchez. Let me get on to why I asked you to lunch."

"Sir, would it be possible for Ms. Sanchez to just work directly for me? You can get a new assistant and I wouldn't have to break in a new assistant that knows nothing about my projects."

To my surprise, Crenshaw agreed with no objection. "Very well, Armstrong. You owe me one. May we get on with business now?" He shoved the empty plates to the edge of the table, searching in vain for a waitress to remove them. Finally he stacked all of them and set them on the next table, scowling at the apathetic proprietor still lounging at the bar.

"Let me first remind you that you are to discuss this with no one. And I mean no one. Is that clear?"

"No one, right sir?"

Crenshaw hesitated and then said, "Yes, no one."

"Got it."

Crenshaw wrinkled his brow and hesitated again. "Armstrong, I'm not sure why you seem to tip toe around insubordination with such frequency. But I'm putting it down to that damn Marine Corps attitude that everyone who isn't or wasn't a Marine is just not up to snuff in your book. I've seen it before in former Marines."

"Yes, sir." Actually I was as uncomfortable with my attitude as Major Crenshaw was. My responses just seemed to slip out. In truth, the Major was rather intimidating. I wasn't sure whether it was my years with that damn Gearheardt or my nervousness at withholding information about my dealings with Gearheardt that made me appear insubordinate around the Major. "I understand, sir. And I'm sorry that you weren't a Marine." Damn. It slipped out again. "I mean I'm sure you would have made a great Marine."

"I didn't *want* to be a Marine, Armstrong! But let's get on with it. I have places to go this afternoon. We don't have much time. Let me explain." He leaned closer to me across the table in a manner that invited me to lean across the table also.

"The Agency is certain that there will be an attempt on the life of the President of Mexico. It will happen, we believe, at the Cinco de Mayo celebration when the President begins his speech. Are you with me so far? Good. As you also know, you will be at the ceremony, armed. Can you guess why you will be armed, Jack?"

"To protect the President, sir? I assumed that much."

I ordered a beer. As it was set in front of me, Crenshaw looked at his watch and then my beer, but said nothing.

I continued. "Since you mentioned to me the other day that I would be armed at the ceremony I've been wondering, won't the President be guarded by his own men? He surely will have a bodyguard and there will be troops all around. So I'm not exactly sure . . ."

"But none of them will recognize the potential assassin, Jack. You will." Crenshaw smiled and leaned back as if he had trapped me in an important point.

I sipped my beer, needing to think before I responded. I hoped I looked calmer than I felt. This was the time to tell Crenshaw about Gearheardt. If I didn't do it now, I was going to be out on my own.

"And how could that be, Major Crenshaw?"

I'm not sure why, but I had made my choice. My ego led me to believe I could still play this game from the middle. And Gearheardt *was* my best friend. And no one loved America more than Gearheardt. And maybe Crenshaw and Gearheardt were playing on the same team. A lot of 'ifs.'

"Jack, we have reason to believe that the assassin, I am sad to say, is one of our own."

"An American?"

"An American agent."

I blew out my breath. "That's hard to believe." I wanted to get away from Crenshaw before I blurted out something incriminating, but I also needed more information. "Do you know who, sir?"

"Do *you*, Jack?"

I tried to remember a James Bond movie where the hero pissed his pants.

Before I could fumble a reply, Crenshaw laughed. "We're not sure quite yet. But I'm working on it. I haven't been just sitting on my ass down here."

Under different circumstances, I would have had to snicker at that. Gearheardt would have rolled on the floor.

Crenshaw went on. "The Cubans are involved. We know that. In fact I'm working with a Cuban group, the good Cubans, who tell me that the Russians are backing this whole thing. We're not sure why as yet. But we'll find out. This agent has worked with the Cubans, maybe for too long, if you get my drift." Crenshaw paused and bit his lower lip. He appeared to be trying to make a decision. "Jack, I need you to do something for me. It won't be easy. It could be risky. But I'm afraid we don't have much time."

"Yes, sir. I understand. Whatever I can do."

"There is a group of devils here, Cuban devils that are tough as nails. Just absolute killers. We're not sure if they are part of this plot. But it's hard for us to believe that anything involving the Cubans could be going on without them being a part of it."

"I'm still not sure why the Cubans would want the President of Mexico assassinated, sir." And I genuinely wasn't.

"We're not sure either. That's part of what I need you to do. We have a contact that we want you to use to get close, or at least as close as a few days will let you, to a guy named Victor Ramirez. They call him Lagarto, the Lizard."

I gave myself one small point for coming up with that name on my own.

"I think I follow, Major, but walk me through it. Seems unlikely that Lagarto will just blurt out the name of a Cuban who is going to kill the

President. Am I supposed to, like, torture him or . . ." "You're supposed to hire him to kill the President."

Mind racing. Pulse pounding. I think I feel chest pains. Calm down. Calm down.

"You see, we figure that if Lagarto knows anything, he'll have to wonder what the hell is going on. He has one agent from the CIA already scheduled for the job, and now he's asked by another agent to do the same job himself. He'll start to doubt, to think maybe he's being double crossed, and then we watch him react."

"And then . . ." I paused, tilting my head forward to receive the answer.

"If everything goes to hell, and Victor shows up at the ceremony, you shoot him."

"So we hire a guy to kill the President, but if he shows up, we shoot him." I hoped that my insubordination *was* showing this time.

"What we hope happens, however, is that Victor flushes the other agent out into the open. Somehow, with the confusion of two CIA agents wanting the President shot, we find our man."

"How?"

"We're still working on that." Crenshaw withdrew his wallet and signaled for the check. "One last thing, Jack. We have another agent coming into town tonight. He's fully briefed and will be looking for our turncoat assassin full time. If we can take him out quietly, the game is off. I'll let you know." He stood to go. "We'll leave separately. I have a ride to my next meeting waiting. Take care of Juanita, and I'll see you tomorrow. There will be a packet on your desk with information about Victor Ramirez. You'll take it from there. Good luck."

"Wait a minute, Major Crenshaw," I said, rising, "so there is another agent looking for the assassin agent to kill him? Will I meet this agent and compare notes?"

"I don't think that's wise, Jack. He likes to operate anonymously, do his job and get out of town. You understand."

"So he will find this renegade agent and take him out? I just want to make sure I know what's going on."

"The renegade has hired someone local, a gringo we believe. That's the guy our man will hit."

Me, I assumed.

Back in the office, Juanita was busily finishing her nails. What does it say about a man who has just found out an assassin may be trailing him who immediately thereafter stands numbly watching a voluptuous Mexican woman rapidly move her upper body with a buffing motion that pulls one side and then the other of her blouse precariously close to nipple territory and forgets the assassin problem.

"Jack, the thing about breasts is a mystery. Women dress to almost expose them, but are insulted if you stare. On the other hand, they can expose up to a millionth of an inch close to the nipple, but if one billionth of a nipple pops up, hell breaks loose."

"Gearheardt, you tried to lick that woman's breast."

"Only the non-nipple part, Jack. I'm no pervert."

Juanita broke the spell by smiling up at me.

"So, Señor Jack, you are now my boss," she said as the pull of gravity slowed and stopped the jiggling.

"Exactly how did you know, Juanita?"

"Señor Chavez, he telephone me with the news. You will be happy, Señor. Now I wear see-through, si?"

"No, Juanita, let's not antagonize Major Crenshaw just yet." I was mulling over the fact that a secretary in the embassy, in the CIA to be exact, knew of personnel changes from the bartender at the El Caballo. I needed to watch myself in the cantina, and also have a chat with Mr. Chavez.

I started into my office. "Did Pepe call, Juanita? Or Señor Rodrigo?"

"Only one call while you are gone, Señor." She searched her desk covered with makeup and toiletries. Finding a pink message slip, she held it up and read. "Señorita Greta, she called. She says only," she checked the slip again and moved her lips as she spelled it out to herself, "Señor

Armstrong—that is you—es arschloch. That's all she says, but she spell it for me." Her bright face was eager to help her new boss. "I can get translate for you, si?"

"That won't be necessary, Juanita. It means," I was momentarily embarrassed, "something like a bad person. She is mad at me."

Juanita began putting away her beauty equipment. "Eet mean ass-hole, Señor Jack." So she *could* translate it.

"Thank you, Juanita. If I have no other messages, I need to work in my office. You can begin to transfer my files to your cabinet. I think you're already familiar with them."

I went in my office and shut the door. Without removing my jacket, I fell on the couch. Moving to Pago Pago was now near the top of my list of things to do. After living only twenty-nine years and doing nothing particularly significant, I had an assassin coming down to kill me. The depressing thing was that I had had so many opportunities to strangle Gearheardt and took none of them. I sighed and walked to my desk.

As promised, the sealed envelope regarding Victor Ramirez was lying in the center of my desk. I threw my coat back to the couch, sat down, and opened the thick package.

Normal identity stuff. Old crappy photo. Former addresses. Girl-friends (no Marta). Associations known (no surprises, mostly Cuban organizations and people). Military service record and postings (Where did we get this stuff?). Family (wife and two kids in Havana).

Wait a minute. Under military postings it listed Angola. Same time frame as Gearheardt. Was there a connection? I scrutinized the military information listed and quickly found something I had hoped wasn't there. One of the contacts was noted as G. Norea. The odds were that was our old pal Gon Norea who Gearheardt and I knew in Vietnam and who Gearheardt had run into in Angola. Which then meant that there was a good chance that Gearheardt knew Victor Ramirez.

I tried to remember the conversation with Marta and Gearheardt. Had he said he didn't know the guys that she was introducing me to? Or was that just my assumption? And one way or another, did it mean anything?

Nothing else in the file seemed significant. Ramirez had been kicked out of the Mexico City Rotary for slicing up a waiter who dropped his soup, and he was rumored to prefer Mexican prostitutes who could tap dance. (Where DID we get this stuff?). And, no surprise, the last entry was a possible address contact for Ramirez, the Club Tristiza.

"Gearheardt, you piece of baboon dung, you'd better give me a call," I said to the bug in the office. I didn't want to give anything else away by asking questions through the bug. Someone else was probably monitoring the listening device.

Clearing my desk, I checked one more time with Juanita to see if I had missed any calls. I hadn't. It was time for the Armstrong Yellow Tablet Concentrate. That was the name I gave the process of taking a yellow pad and writing down the events of the past week or so as people, places and facts/fiction. At one time I had only written down facts that I had verified. But I quickly realized that the lies people told were often better clues than facts.

Under places, I wrote Office, 203 Isbsen (my apartment), Club Tristiza, El Caballo, and El Diablo Motel. I considered the places I had been on other business, such as that with Rodrigo, but decided they couldn't be connected.

Under people I wrote Gearheardt, Crenshaw, Marta, Juanita, Victor Ramirez, and Mr. Chavez.

Juanita buzzed me to say she was leaving for the day. "Señorita Greta called again, Señor Jack. I didn't want to disturb you. She wanted to make sure you got the message she left."

"That I'm an arschloch?"

"Si, Señor. An asshole."

"Thanks, Juanita. I'll see you tomorrow. Do I have a burn bag in my office?" I looked around where I usually kept them. "I don't see one."

"You have the burn bag in your desk drawer. Hasta luego, Señor Boss."

I continued my yellow sheet.

Connections, known: Gearheardt—Marta, the Pygmy. Crenshaw—Chavez, Juanita. Marta—Ramirez, Gearheardt.

Possibles: Gearheardt—Crenshaw, Juanita, Chavez, Ramirez.

Nothing jumped out that was significant, yet. I tried then to outline the missions.

Gearheardt—Help the good Cubans gain a stronghold in Mexico by having me attempt to assassinate the President and defecting to Cuba and blaming it on the bad Cubans. How would that work?

Crenshaw—Help the good Cubans by stopping the bad Cubans from assassinating the President. Finding the assassin by pretending to be hiring our own assassin. How would that work?

Although there seemed to be a connection between Gearheardt and Crenshaw (in mission and in knowing Victor Ramirez) there was something missing in their missions, or what I knew of them. Which meant that both of them were holding back information from me. And Gearheardt didn't want Crenshaw to know that I was working with him. And Crenshaw hinting the he knew an agent (Gearheardt?) was behind the whole thing.

I felt a headache coming on. After going over them one more time I dropped the sheets in the burn bag which was where Juanita said it would be. I realized that I had forgotten one of Gearheardt's connections that could be connected to me—the Halcones. My friend at the Mexican Secret Police seemed to know Gearheardt and Gearheardt admitted that he had contacts there. I sealed the bag and dropped it in the secure receptacle so the security guys could dispose of it.

Gearheardt had maneuvered me into working for him. And I had to work for Crenshaw in order to work for Gearheardt. I owed loyalty to Crenshaw who after all was my boss and represented the U.S. Government. With Gearheardt, I just couldn't believe that he would do anything to hurt me, or the country. On the other hand, Gearheardt was crazy. What I had to find out (and I had no clue yet as to how to do it) was if the missions were in conflict with one another, or if they were parts of the same mission. It was not at all unusual for the Agency to compartmentalize a mission so that the loss of one man wouldn't blow the entire operation.

The headache arrived in spades.

It was a nice night and I decided to walk through the park back to my apartment, trying to clear my head before I hopefully met Gearheardt. My driver was skeptical, but I waved him off. "I'll be fine, Jorge. And I'll check in with you when I'm home so that you can sign out for the evening. Gracias."

But Gearheardt wasn't at the apartment. Nor was Marta. There were no signs that either of them had been in the apartment except for a wet towel that Marta must have dropped on the bathroom floor that morning.

I called the duty officer at the embassy and told him to tell Jorge that I was at my apartment and didn't expect to go out again. Just as I hung up the phone, it rang.

"Ola."

"Jack, is that you?"

"Who else would it be, Gearheardt? Didn't you dial my apartment?"

"With the Mexican phone system, it could be Adolph Hitler. Anyway, I'm glad you're home. Is Marta there?"

"I thought she might be with you. Did you talk to her today?"

Gearheardt didn't answer. I heard him talking to someone with his hand over the phone.

"Gearheardt, I just asked if you had talked to her today. I need to meet you. Crenshaw and I talked today. I have a few questions. Where are you?"

"Afraid this isn't a secure enough line to divulge that, Jack. Why don't you—"

"Okay, I'll meet you somewhere. How about—"

"Jack, hold up. We can't be arranging a meeting on this line either."

"You worthless bastard, Gearheardt. So we can't talk on the phone and can't set up a meeting. How in hell do we get together?"

"Go somewhere and I'll meet you after you get there," Gearheardt said.

"Go somewhere and you'll . . . wait a minute, are you having me followed?"

"Not unless you go somewhere, Jack."

I hung up, grabbed my jacket and headed out of my apartment. In five minutes, I was in the park, looking over my shoulder but not spotting a tail. Was he that good, or was I that bad?

A few minutes later, Gearheardt sat down beside me on the bench.

"Hey, Jack, I thought you told the embassy you weren't going out again this evening." He laughed and I wanted to punch him.

"So you've tapped all my lines, bugged my office and now you have a tail on me. What's all this about, Gearheardt? I need the straight scoop or I'm going to Crenshaw." And I meant it.

"So you've told Crenshaw about us working together?"

"No. Not exactly."

"And you've told him about Marta and meeting Ramirez?"

"You know I haven't."

"I'm just saying that will be a pretty interesting conversation with Crenshaw then, Jack. Wouldn't you think so? I've heard the major doesn't like his boys jacking around on missions that he isn't in on. Particularly when they might be, to a certain degree, in conflict with what he's trying to do. Just a thought."

I stared at his silly grin. "You're an asshole, Gearheardt. I suppose you don't realize that you've now put me in a situation where an Agency hitman is probably looking for me."

Gearheardt didn't seem as concerned at the news as I had been. "Tell me what Crenshaw told you."

I told him exactly what had been said at the lunch with Crenshaw. Gearheardt only commented with an occasional 'hmmmm' or sometimes 'ah ha' as if he were finding pieces of the puzzle. When I finished, he smiled even broader.

"Perfect. You've done great, Jack. Couldn't have done better myself."

"I have no idea what you're talking about, Gearheardt. What is perfect and what did I do?"

"For one thing, you didn't tell him about me. That's the best thing. I appreciate it, Jack. I really do."

"What about this so-called hitman?"

"That could be a problem. Let me think about it. Maybe the Pygmy can find out who it is and get to him before he takes you out. I'll try to find him tomorrow."

Gearheardt could be a little maddening sometimes. "If it's not too much trouble."

"Happy to do it, Jack. Happy to do it." He patted my knee. "Let's talk about what Crenshaw wants you to do. First, get this Ramirez guy on the hook. This is even better than using Marta. He may be confused by seeing you without Marta, but when he realizes an honest to goodness Agency man is seeking him for a job, he'll wet his pants to get back to you."

"Do you know Ramirez, Gearheardt?" I asked, hoping he wouldn't lie to me.

"I've run into him a couple of times. We're not pals, if that's what you mean."

"That isn't what I mean. But we can come back to that. What you're saying is that I should just do what Crenshaw asked me to do. Approach Ramirez about shooting the President of Mexico."

"Correcto."

"But that's the job you said I needed to do, right?"

"Correcto again, Jack.

"Would you knock off the high school Spanish, Gearheardt? Just talk normally if that's possible for you." I was in no mood for his crap. I needed some real answers. "So who's supposed to shoot the President, me or Ramirez?"

"You don't need to get all insecure, Jack. You can shoot the President if you want to. We just want Ramirez to *think* we're recruiting him to shoot el Presidente. Sorry, President. And remember, you don't really get to shoot him. Just try to shoot him. We'll take care of the rest."

"I'm not *complaining*, you dope." I paused. "Gearheardt, are you really that obtuse? We've got guys trying to assassinate this poor guy up the ass, and you act like everything's hunky dory. You say the CIA, this pygmy guy, is behind your scheme and that seems okay with you even though Crenshaw says someone in the Agency is going to try to stop the assassin by shooting him and hiring another assassin. Are you completely insane?"

Gearheardt leaned forward and rested his elbows on his knees, cupping his chin. After a moment he straightened back up and looked at me. "Obtuse I guess. I think I'd rather be obtuse than insane."

CIA Agents in Murder-Suicide near Chapultepec Park; Rumored to be Former Friends.

The thought of that headline stilled the hand that reactively moved toward my shoulder holster.

"I can see you're pissed, Jack. Let me get serious. I'm an intelligence agent for the United States government. Not some Crap Island stooge for Casteroil. As such, I have the obligation to take some initiative when I see a situation that needs some . . . some initiative taken."

He had almost had me believing he knew what he was doing until he stumbled on the description of whatever it was that needed to be done. He went on.

"And as far as I know there is only one guy trying to shoot the President of Mexico now, and that's you. If you recruit Ramirez, that's two. Hardly a damn gaggle of guys like you make it sound. One of those schemes, by the way, is being run by your very own boss, Major Crenshaw. I guess you're smarter than all the other people in the Agency so you see that you're right and they're wrong. I'm sorry to hear that, Jack. This is not the Jack Armstrong, Almost Captain United States Marine Corps, who I knew and trusted in Vietnam when the whole world depended on us to stop the carnage."

"Are you finished?" I asked, calmly.

"I assume you have something to say."

"Yes, I do. You have successfully managed to meet with me and sit on a bench in Chapultepec Park for half an hour or so and not tell me a damn thing while making me feel guilty that I would question your sanity or the competence of the Central Intelligence Agency. Was that the purpose for this meeting?"

"That and to tell you to watch your ass. There's a guy trying to find you and kill you before you kill the President of Mexico. But I guess you already knew that."

Gearheardt looked up and smiled. When I looked, I saw Marta approaching. Although a block away still, there was no doubt it was my nudist roommate.

Gearheardt grabbed the sleeve of my jacket. "Jack, you worry too much. We're just talking assassination here, not some all-out war. Did you think that these decisions go all the way to the top? That the president calls the cabinet together to vote?"

Okay, gents, who all's for shooting President Rios? Keep your hands up so I can count. Bob, is your hand up or are you scratching that psoriasis? That's one, two, three, okay seven all together. HUD and Interior, you're saying no, right? No, Dave, Defense does not get two votes. But we have enough yeses to kill him. Tell the CIA, would you, Mary? And none of that poison in the beard crap this time. No poison darts, no midgets in the bathtub, no electric blanket accidents, you tell 'em. The United States of America shoots people. I won't be the laughing stock of the U.N. next time.

"Hang with me for a while, buddy. I'll take care of the guy that might be after you." He slugged my arm. "In a day or two you'll see everything. You and I will be working side by side. With Marta of course." He put his arm around my shoulder. "Jack," he said quietly, watching Marta approach, "try to be a bit nicer to Marta. Women have feelings too."

"Ola, Jack," Marta said. She smiled at me and I realized what I had been looking forward to all day.

"Ola, Marta," I replied. "Como esta."

"Muy bien, Jack," Marta said.

"High school Spanish, Jack. Doesn't impress me." He dropped his arm from my shoulder and pecked Marta's cheek. "I've got to run. Tell

Jack about Palanque, Marta. He was jabbering on about someone trying to kill him and I never got the chance to bring it up." As he left he grinned at me. "Where's that damn cigarette kid?"

Which was another thing I wanted to ask him about, but Marta took my arm and pulled. "Vamanos, Jack. I have to get out of these clothes," she whined.

My rush back to my apartment was because I was anxious to hear about Palanque.

CHAPTER NINE

FOR THE
LOVE OF MARTA

Back at my apartment, I fixed drinks while Marta got undressed. "You're sure you don't want my robe, Marta?" I asked over my shoulder.

"Ees okay, Jack. Your apartment is a bit cold, but I have turned down the cooler. My skin will be the goose bumps, but it will warm soon."

Thinking that goose bump skin would be unattractive, I walked to the couch to hand her the scotch. Oh wow! The cold had caused her . . . I looked away, spilling the scotch on her thigh as I handed it to her.

"So Marta," I began when I dropped to my leather easy chair and tried to relax, "tell me about Palanque."

Palanque was a Mayan ruin, one of the best, in the Yucatan peninsula of Mexico. It was there that Mexican archaeologists discovered the tomb of the Corn God, the first known use of a pyramid for the burial of a ruler (if he were one) on the North American continent. The well-preserved buildings near the pyramid were in a style reminiscent of

Chinese architecture. Hidden well into the jungle and so far, undiscovered by the majority of tourists, it was my favorite Mayan site.

"You know the site, Jack. It is beautiful. And very peaceful."

"I know, but how does it fit into Gearheardt's plan?" I leaned forward and placed my empty glass on the coffee table between us. "Marta, how much do you know about Gearheardt's plan? You and I can trust one another. I need to know more."

"Gearheardt said that you would try to find out from me."

"Find out what? What did he not want you to tell me?"

"I am disappointed that you think me so dumb, Jack. Is because I am naked?"

"No, it's not because you are naked. Although I will say that it's a bit disconcerting. I'm not used to talking to naked women."

She smiled.

"Gearheardt does not like his friends to trust one another, Jack. He would prefer that they remain . . . . suspicious of one another. Comprende?"

"That, I'm afraid, is a rule of the trade. If your friends start to confide in one another, then you have to tell the same story to all of them."

"You mean you can't lie to your friends."

"You can trust me, Marta. I am Gearheardt's best friend. If you trust him, you can trust me."

"Tell me what he has asked you to do, Jack."

I might have. I was starting to feel a little desperate about my situation. I knew I needed to do something bold. Take some initiative rather than passively be manipulated by Crenshaw and Gearheardt. But before I could open my mouth, someone knocked loudly at my door.

I nodded toward the bedroom and Marta took the hint.

It was Eduardo, the Halcone who lived in my building. He pushed past me into the apartment at the same time I was asking him to come in. Although he had been inside many times, he looked around now like he was searching.

"You have a girl friend here, no?" he asked.

I smiled and shrugged my shoulders.

Eduardo smiled back and tilted his head toward my closed bedroom door.

I smiled again.

We stood there smiling.

Eduardo broke first. "Okay, Jack, here is why I have come to see you." He plopped down on the couch, picked up the scotch glass that Marta had left on the coffee table, then sat it down and looked back at me. "You may have some information that I, we, would like to know. My friends wanted to ask you to visit our headquarters. But that can be very, como se dice, intima, intermina, very frightening to some people. Not to you, of course, but still I tell them that we can meet with Jack here. Very friendly. Just talk. Okay?"

"I don't think that an economics officer at the U.S. Embassy would just trot on down to the Mexican Secret Police even if you asked him, Eduardo. That would have to go through the ambassador."

"Maybe we would ask him not so nice." Eduardo, usually jovial and joking with me, was nervous, and slightly threatening, or trying to be.

"Let's say that I were down to see you, what could you possibly want to ask me? Again, you know very well that anything serious would have to come through the proper channels." I wanted to keep the upper hand. He was in *my* apartment.

"We would like very much to know where your friend Mr. Gearheardt can be found. That we would like to know very very much." He wasn't smiling now.

"Mr. Gearheardt is not an easy man to find. I have seen him a couple of times in the last week. But I don't know where he is now." I assumed that the Halcones knew that I had met with Gearheardt and lying would not help. I also had no clue as to Gearheardt's whereabouts. "Can you tell me why you would like to see him, Eduardo? If I see him, I will tell him to contact you."

"Jack, you are aware of what I do, and, although you are not telling me, I know what you do also. Let us not fool each other."

Eduardo was a short, rather dumpy character. His black suit was rumpled and his white shirt wrinkled. His face was soft but studded with shifty eyes. It was difficult for me to think of him as a family man, but I had seen him in the building with a woman and two small children.

"I try to assist the trading missions between our countries, Eduardo." I was programmed to stick to my cover, even if I was caught in a CIA tee-shirt kneeling before a portrait of Wild Bill Donovan. "As a friend, of course I will try to help you find Mr. Gearheardt. But I am not sure when or if I will be seeing him again."

This seemed to satisfy Eduardo and he relaxed just a bit, loosening his black tie, and settling back on the couch. "You sometimes make the blue movies here, Jack?"

That damn Gearheardt. "That was a misunderstanding. I am sorry that the story is known in the building. This is a very nice apartment building and I would not want anyone to get the wrong idea. Just a misunderstanding."

"Perhaps I could view the misunderstanding some time. It is for my curiosity. I have never seen the blue movie."

I rose from my chair, hoping he would take the hint. "It was a joke that got out of hand, Eduardo. Why don't we visit the cantina for a beer this weekend, and I will tell you about it." I moved closer to the door.

Eduardo sighed and lifted himself to his feet. "Your friend is here to cause trouble. He should leave the country. The men he is meeting, the Cubans, are not people he should deal with. They caused the trouble in 1968. We are not happy with them. Your friend should choose his companions more carefully." He moved around the couch and stood close to me. "Victor Ramirez is not someone you should want to be with, Jack. He is listed. That's all I can tell you, but remember that." He held out his hand and I took it. His grip was not dumpy.

I sat back down on my leather chair and thought about what I had heard. When used by the Halcones, 'listed' could mean anything from being watched, to being targeted for elimination. Given the seriousness of the situation, I assumed he meant the latter and was warning me to not spend a lot of time in the company of Victor Ramirez.

My bedroom door was closed. I knocked softly but heard nothing inside. When I went into the darkened room I saw Marta asleep on my bed, the sheet pulled up to her bare shoulders.

It had been a long day of talking about shooting people and getting shot, so I took a very cold shower and went to sleep on the couch.

My head was clear in the morning and as I sat in my kitchen with a cup of coffee I could calmly reflect on my situation and make logical plans. I knew there were no direct flights to Pago Pago from Mexico City. So facing the music would have to be Plan A.

Gearheardt wanted me to make contact with Ramirez. Crenshaw wanted me to make contact with Ramirez. The Mexican Secret Police, the orneriest rascals in the world, warned me to stay away from Ramirez. So far so good. I got another cup of coffee.

Marta strolled into the kitchen at seven thirty. "I take your bed last night, Jack. Muchas gracias." She found a cup in the cupboard and brought her coffee to the table. Sitting across from me, she blew softly across the top of the cup and smiled at me at the same time. "You look worried, Jack. How can I help you?"

"Marta, I have made a decision. You must level with me."

"Level?"

"Yes, be honest. You must trust me and tell me everything you know. Can you do that?"

Her cup had left a small ring of coffee on the table and she played in it with her finger. Then she said, "Yes, that would be possible. And you must trust me also."

I reached across the table to shake her hand to seal the deal and get down to business. When she reached across the table, her right breast followed and rested next to her coffee cup. It was an incredible moment.

I rose, clad in my pajama bottoms, and quickly left the room. I returned with the top to my pajamas and held it out to Marta. "When we talk business, Marta, I would like for you to wear this. Is that okay with you?"

She put it on and looked at me. "Now we are the team. I am the top, and you are the bottom. Unless you want to be on the top?"

I have learned, living in SE Asia and other parts of the world, that broken or incorrect English is not a good indication of intelligence. I saw many people make that mistake. I had also observed that the easiest cover for a highly intelligent woman is the dumb sex queen. I suspected that Marta was highly intelligent. I wasn't quite so sure about the sex queen part. Parading around nude in a stranger's home wasn't on the list of things I had experienced. Unless you included The White Rose bar in Vientiane. Kind of a second home when Gearheardt and I were flying in Laos for Air America. But in that case we paid the girls to parade around nude to aid digestion when we were drinking.

So I let the 'on top' reference go by. I also knew that the easiest way for a woman to keep a man unbalanced is through the use of double entendre remarks. I wasn't going to fall for it.

"You can be the leader, Marta. It makes no difference to me." I began clearing the table so that I wouldn't have to look at her while I was talking to her. "Let's begin by agreeing that you and I are committed to helping Gearheardt complete his mission. Right?"

"That is right. Gearheardt is a great man and a great strat . . ."

"A great strategist? Well, I'm not so sure about that. But my point is that I would need to know what the ultimate mission is before I can be completely committed to it. Wouldn't you agree?"

Marta rose and began helping me clean up. The pajama top was tantalizingly attractive. "You go to get dressed, Jack. It makes me upset to have you in pajama only."

After I was dressed, I called Juanita. "I won't be in this morning, Juanita. Perhaps I can check back with you later today."

"Señor Rodrigo he called. He needs to meet with you very bad. He also would like to know if you have check."

"Damn, I forgot to call him yesterday. Juanita, get in touch with him and tell him to meet me at eleven in front of the University where we met before. He'll know the spot. Then find the paperwork on my desk and

walk it down to accounting. Don't leave until they give you a check made
out to Rodrigo. Can you do that? Then send the check with Jorge to my
apartment. Okay?" I could see her nodding her head, a common response
of hers on the phone and one that she didn't seem to realize was extremely
frustrating for me. "You do have that, Juanita? Now, is Major
Crenshaw in?"

"He is not in the office today. The personnel people have given him
temporary woman and she is looking for him. He is disappear since
yesterday."

That worried me a bit. But at least he wouldn't be coming down to
my empty office and asking how my contact with the Lizard was pro-
gressing. "Okay, Juanita, and listen, if you have any trouble at all, go see
Eric. Tell him that this is part of what he is doing for Major Crenshaw."

"Señor Eric."

"Yes. And thanks, Juanita."

"Señor Jack, the ambassador was here to see you this morning."

"What?" This would be the first time that had happened. It couldn't
mean anything good. "What did he say?"

"I was scared for you not being here. I told him you were always on
time. Maybe you have terrible accident. That is why you are not here."

"Thanks, Juanita. What did he say?"

"He says that you are lucky if you are dead before he finds you."

That didn't sound encouraging.

"You don't look so happy, Jack."

"Things are kind of in a mess at the office, Marta. But I can
straighten that out later. Or be spying in Antarctica before the snow
falls." My apartment, on the fifth floor of a six-story building overlook-
ing the central market in Palanco, had a small balcony off the living
room. Just enough space for two chairs and a small table. Marta and
I sat there now.

"The Agency is alerted to the possibility that someone will try to
assassinate the President of Mexico on Cinco de Mayo, Marta. I tell you
that because I want you to trust me and know that I trust you. In addi-

tion, the Agency is also aware that the assassin and the man who hired him might be CIA operatives or agents. You do know that Gearheardt asked me to be the 'assassin,' don't you?"

"I know that I am to get you to Havana after the event, Jack. I am not sure that you are supposed to kill the Presidente."

"Can you tell me why Gearheardt would not have a Cuban do what he is asking me to do?"

"He does not trust them. He must have someone that he has no doubt about. None at all. Gearheardt says that operations are very fluid—I think fluid was the word—and that only someone you can trust can operate in that enviro . . ." she trailed off.

"Environment. I suppose I can see his point. But now he is willing to go along with Crenshaw and have me contact Victor Ramirez to ask him to be, or find someone to be, the assassin. I don't understand that."

"Jack, the Cubans don't trust the Americans. That you know. They do not believe that the American CIA would back them to try to take over the government of Mexico. So to have you, a CIA man approach them is a very good sign for Gearheardt. The world must blame the Cubans, but the CIA must have control. You see? And when Gearheardt takes over Cuba, then all will be clear."

"Mexico."

"Que?"

"Mexico. You said when Gearheardt takes over Cuba."

"Si."

I took a deep breath. In the street below them, a traveling gypsy had led a bear on a chain onto the grassy area near the fountain. The bear looked mangy and miserable. Later the gypsy would make the bear dance.

"So Gearheardt isn't planning on taking over Mexico?"

Marta laughed and then stopped when she looked at my face. "What would Gearheardt want with Mexico, Jack? There are so many problems and . . . oh, so that is what he told you. I understand."

"I'm not sure I do. But why wouldn't he just tell me. It makes a lot more sense than trying to take over Mexico. Surely he would know that I could see that."

"Gearheardt tells me that he only 98% trusts you, Jack."

"The bastard. After all the times I've saved his ass."

"He says to me 'Jack, has a streak of honesty in him that worry me. I never know when he might be tempted to do the honorable thing just at the wrong time.' That's what he told me."

I didn't feel quite so bad.

The square below us was filling up with vendors, carts and some people with just large baskets they sat on the sidewalk. The meat market opened its heavy metal doors and the bread store was giving off its wonderful scent. None of the people in the plaza below looked as if they were plotting any overthrows, assassinations, or general mayhem. How did I get to this place in life?

"So what else do you have to tell me, Marta? Why don't you start with how you met Gearheardt? I'm not sure I understand the relationship."

"First, I am not the girl friend of Gearheardt. I know you think that Gearheardt is always my amour. It's not true. It is just better to have you think that." She patted my hand for some reason. "I meet with Gearheardt when he was in Cuba."

"Gearheardt was in *Cuba*?" Why did anything Gearheardt did surprise me though?

"Si. He came to Cuba with some troops returning from Angola. He says it was easy. No one suspects anyone to try to get into Cuba. So my half-brother bring him home and we gave him a place to stay while he made his plan."

"He met your half-brother in Angola, right?"

"Si. In the bars and nightclubs, he met many Cuban soldiers. They got along very well. Gon told Gearheardt that the Cuban people would be happy without Castro."

"Did you say Gon? Are you talking about Gon Norea?"

"Si. My `half brother from my father and a Panamanian woman. My father was demonstrating the product and it didn't work so well."

"Your father really did sell prophylactics then."

A discreet knock on my door (I recognized it as Jorge) came as she replied. "Si."

Jorge gave me the check in a sealed brown envelope and had me sign for it. As he started to leave, I called to him. "Jorge, are you driving anyone this morning?"

"No, Señor. You would like me to drive you?"

"I'll meet you downstairs in ten minutes. I will have someone with me also. She is cleared, Jorge. We can talk in front of her. Esta bien?"

"Si, Señor. I will bring the car to the front of the building."

Marta was making herself comfortable on the couch. "Get ready, Marta, you're coming with me. I think you and I should stick together now."

"Si, Jack." She smiled and went into the bedroom. When she came back out, she was dressed and looked dynamite.

In the back of the embassy car I told her my plans. "I need to meet a friend of mine. This has nothing to do with you. Stay with Jorge when I am gone. Then we need to find Gearheardt."

"I am not sure we can find him. He will meet with me later in the afternoon near the park. Then we can find him."

"Okay, that's fine." It didn't make exact sense, but this was Gearheardt we were talking about. "How about Victor? Can we find him?"

"You are still wanting to meet with Victor?"

"Until Gearheardt and I work something out, I think I'll just go along with his plan." I had not told her that Crenshaw also wanted me to meet with Victor. I wasn't ready to tell her everything just yet.

We pulled into the parking lot at Universidad de Mexico. The giant campus was quiet, the students on a holiday of some kind. Leaving Marta and Jorge sitting, I walked to the large mural by Diego Rivera that adorned almost the entire side of one of the university buildings. Rodrigo was there.

"Ola, Jack. I was getting worried for you. Come with me quickly."

Rodrigo led me across the campus, through the building where the foreign students took their classes and up the stairs to the library. We stepped beside the doors where we could not be seen from inside.

"The Colombiano is inside, Jack. He is meeting with students. American students."

The rotten little shits. My contacts at the university had been telling me for months that a number of American students, mostly from wealthy families, were in Mexico to involve themselves with bombs and guns being transported to the U.S. to use in the student unrest. The most promising of these students were recruited by Cuban agents, taken to Havana and then flown to Pyongyang for training in terrorist camps. The students were less active now than at the height of the Vietnam War protests, but the Russians and Cubans were still actively recruiting.

We knew that a main source of explosives was Colombia, or at least through Colombian hands. Now, hopefully, inside the library was proof of the relationship between the Colombians and the most radical of the American students.

"Rodrigo, are there other doors?"

"Si, Jack. But they are temporarily blocked by my sons and cousins." He smiled.

"I know you want to bust these guys, Rodrigo, but it is just as important for us to get photos. You understand?" I clutched a small camera that Jorge always carried in his car for me. "Okay, you go in first. In fact, Rodrigo, you should take the photos. Be sure and get the Americans. When I go in, they might panic and rush the exits. What's wrong?" Rodrigo was looking over my shoulder and his face became tense.

"We have trouble approaching, Señor. The Halcones."

"Get in the library, Rodrigo. Get those pictures. I'll try to stall the Halcones. Go."

Rodrigo went through the door and I turned to see two men in black suits and sunglasses come up the steps.

"Buenos dias, Señors," I said. "You are coming to study in the library."

"Buenos dias, Señor. We like to see the guests in our country learn at our university. Sometimes we come to see what they are learning."

The men stopped and, although they seemed on edge, didn't appear to realize what was going on inside the library. They had probably been tipped to the appearance of the embassy car, and might have been alerted to the Colombian's presence. I knew the Mexican police wanted to talk to him almost as badly as I did.

I heard a shout in the library and tried to get in the door. I was brushed aside by the smaller of the Halcones. The larger of the two stood squarely in front of the door, a pistol in his hand. When I finally got inside, most of the scuffle was over. The Colombian was on his face on the floor with the shoe of the Halcone on his neck. The Mexican students were jabbering at Rodrigo. The two American students that I saw were silent, cowed by the pistol in the hand of the Halcone, although their overall demeanor was defiant. Then the rest of the Halcones came bursting through the door, spreading noise and chaos. The Mexican students ran for the exits and were for the most part allowed to get away. The Colombian student was dragged, literally kicking and screaming, by two Halcones out the door and down the steps. Just as I stepped outside his screaming stopped. The policemen lifted him and dragged him away, his toes scuffing the ground.

The American students were now being handcuffed and shoved roughly down the steps of the library. One of them caught my eye and cried out, "I'm an American," either because he thought I looked American, or hoping that someone, anyone, could help him.

"Vaya con dios, son," I answered him. I felt bad for the boys. Transporting explosives and training terrorists seemed to be a man's game. These two looked like school boys again as the Halcones hustled them to the waiting cars. But I could also see the poor garage owner, his shop destroyed and his sons bleeding. Playing with bombs had consequences.

"Are you okay, Jack?" Marta asked as I got into the car. "We saw many people running."

"I'm fine." I patted her hand that rested on my sleeve. "Jorge, I am going to write up a report here. Would you take it back to the embassy for me? After you drop us off?"

"Si, Señor." He hesitated and I could tell he wanted to say more. Jorge had been my driver and friend since I joined the embassy staff. "I think that I should stay with you, Señor. This morning, there were Halcones in the embassy asking the ambassador about you. And there is a small man in town that also is asking."

He looked at Marta and back at me. I nodded affirmatively. "And there are Cubans that wait outside your apartment sometimes."

And to think I was getting paid all of forty thousand dollars a year for this. Gearheardt shows up and three days later I had become a hunted man. It made me realize how much I had missed him when I thought he was dead.

Señor Rodrigo came by the car, walking with a group whom I assumed were his relatives. He smiled and gave me a thumbs up. I indicated for him to call me later, forgetting that I probably wouldn't be in my office for some time

"Jorge, I appreciate the offer for help. I need you to stay at the embassy and keep your eyes and ears open. When you need to contact me, leave word with Señor Chavez at the El Caballo. That would be a great help. Gracias."

Jorge turned and started the engine. He clearly would have preferred staying with me, and I appreciated his concern.

"Jorge, you said that a small man is looking for me. What did you mean?" I realized that this was a new revelation.

"They call him The Pygmy. He was talking to the ambassador yesterday. Then he began asking about you. I don't like him, Señor. Very arrogant and smells like the roast goat."

The Pygmy was in town! Did Gearheardt know this? So there really was a guy that roasted goats in the building at Langley.

In a motion that would be sure to throw a potential assailant for a momentary loop, Marta reached up under her skirt and withdrew her Beretta. "I will protect Jack, Jorge," she said. "We will watch him like the hawk."

I felt a lot better.

CHAPTER TEN

BEARDING THE LIZARD

J orge dropped Marta and me at Los Flores, a small restaurant owned by Mr. Chavez and managed by his oldest daughter, Pilar. It was far out on the road to Teotihuacan, where we were not likely to be disturbed.

"Welcome, Señor Armstrong," the lovely Pilar said as we entered. "And welcome also to your friend." Pilar for some reason had taken an interest in my love life. I knew she would sniff around Marta like a bloodhound and later give me her impressions and opinions.

"Ola, Pilar. We would like a table away from the peasants." An old joke between Pilar and me based on my poor attempt at Spanish the first time I had visited her restaurant. Los Flores was a humble place and I had tried to make a joke about not ordering pheasant under glass which of course had no meaning to Pilar whatsoever and in trying to explain, it got weaker and I got stupider by the moment.

"I have the table for lovers which is perfect, Señor." Evidently she had a positive early assessment of Marta. No doubt because Marta was

Latin American, and not northern European like Greta, or Ingrid before her.

"Very nice place, Jack," Marta said after we were seated and Pilar had taken our order for cerveza.

"I'm afraid this is not going to be a social lunch just yet, Marta. You really haven't told me much about Gearheardt's plan. Other than its Cuba he has in mind taking over. Not Mexico."

"I am afraid that you believe I know more than you think I know, Jack."

She must have been spending too much time with Gearheardt. She had picked up his double talk.

"No. I think that you know more than you are telling me. Not more than I think you know."

"That is what I said. I do not know more than you think I know." She poured her beer into a glass and drank. Then she smiled. "It's good, no? Soon you will be so angry with my words that you will forget what you were asking in the first place. Gearheardt is a very good teacher."

Oh great. A female Gearheardt.

"Did Gearheardt also tell you that many people have knocked the crap out of him for doing his double talk?" I smiled also.

"So what is it you want to know?" Marta asked.

"I know that you are a very smart woman, Marta. I cannot ask all the right questions. You can tell me what I *should* know. I think you can do that."

Marta drained her glass, filled it again, and signaled for another round. *Yes, Gearheardt trained.*

"Jack, you know that the Americans are very worried that the Russians are behind much trouble in Mexico. You are aware that they provided mucho money to the radical students who rioted at the University. Sabe? Maybe some are not so aware that the Russians use Cubans quite often to do their business. It is obvious that Cuban people are less easy to detect in Mexico than the Russian people."

I nodded my head. So far nothing was new to me. In fact it was along the lines of my investigations into the Colombian connections. It was at a Cuban anti-American rally on the campus that I had first spotted the Colombians.

"There are people such as Gearheardt who believe that America will not confront the Cubans. After the Bay of Pigs, and the missile incident with the Russians, some would want to leave them alone. There are many people like this."

"I think I know the rest, Marta. I'm surprised I didn't think of it before now. Gearheardt wants to blame the assassination attempt on the Cubans, believing that will trigger an interest in invading Cuba, and with support from the Mexicans and other Latin American countries. Right?"

"Creo que si, Jack. I think so. There are parts of Gearheardt's plan which I am not in total understanding."

"Such as why he wants me to defect to Cuba after my failed assassination attempt." That one still had me puzzled. "What about Victor? Why does Gearheardt want me to try to use him?" I held back a bit of the information about Crenshaw's plan to use Victor to smoke out the Agency assassin. It just seemed the wise thing to do since I was talking to a Cuban, and the ex-girlfriend of Victor the Lizard Ramirez.

"The Cubans must be convinced that the CIA is actually backing the attempt to take over Mexico. Victor can convince them, if we can convince him."

"Do you think we can?" I asked.

"Probably. Victor wants to believe that he is a more important man than he is. Carrying the news that a CIA group wants to support the Cubans in Mexico would give him great importance."

"Marta, does Victor know that Gearheardt asked me to be the assassin?"

"I don't know that he does. I would not think Gearheardt would tell him that." She excused herself to visit the ladies room.

It appeared that I could still serve both masters, Gearheardt and Crenshaw, for a while longer. Both wanted me to contact Ramirez and convince him that he was dealing with the CIA. The mission objectives parted there, with Crenshaw hoping to find out who the Cubans were working with in the assassination attempt, and Gearheardt hoping that the Cuban leadership would be informed of the alliance and let us inside their organization, Castro egotistical enough to believe that he was needed by the CIA. At least that's what I assume Gearheardt wanted me to do when I got to Cuba. Where I was definitely not going. But Gearheardt didn't know that yet.

I needed to talk to Crenshaw and I certainly needed to talk to Gearheardt. Marta had not returned and I decided to use the telephone in Pilar's office to call Juanita.

"Juanita, this is Jack. Has Crenshaw returned?"

"No, Señor Jack. Many people are looking for him. Should I tell them he is on his burro?" She sounded a bit panicky.

"Do you know that he is, Juanita, or is the burro just gone from its parking place?"

"Que?"

"Never mind, Juanita. I was just being an arschloch. So Major Crenshaw is in the hills. Is that right?"

"Si. He went again to meet the people, and I have not heard from him."

"Do you know where these hills are, Juanita?"

She told me the name of a small town north of Mexico City and I wrote it on a slip of paper from Pilar's desk. "Did he tell you any of the names? Of the people he was meeting?"

"Carlos Benetiz, and Pedro Dominguez. That's all he tell to me. Only to tell me that if they were to call, that he was on his way. Major Crenshaw he was very secret."

"Have you talked to anyone else?"

"I mention to Señor Eric about Major Crenshaw. He told me to tell you."

A real go-getter that Eric. Probably still spending all of his time in church.

"Okay, Juanita. Don't worry. I'll look into the whereabouts of Major Crenshaw. If you need me—"

"I call Señor Chavez at El Caballo, okay?"

Yes, calling the local pub owner when a CIA agent is missing is probably a time-honored tradition.

"That would be okay. But also let Jorge know. Sometimes he can find me."

"What is wrong, Señor Jack? Why is nobody located?"

"It's a bit complicated. You keep things running back there. Major Crenshaw and I will be back in the office soon."

"Wait, Señor Jack. There is one thing more important. The small man came and the ambassador let him into your office. He was in there for a long time and then he disappear."

"What do you mean, he disappeared?"

"I did not see him leave your office. I was working at my desk and then I say "Ola, who is roasting the goat?' and when I look back your door is open but no one is inside."

"Thanks, Juanita."

Back at the table, Marta was eating. She had ordered for me and I joined her. "Do you know the Pygmy, Marta?" I asked. "I mean, has Gearheardt talked about him?"

"I don't know the pygmy. He is small man, right? From Africa?"

"Marta, here is our plan for today. I am going to borrow a car from Pilar. We need to go find Victor Ramirez and talk to him. I don't want that part of the plan to get stalled. I can worry about the outcome later. Then we need to find Gearheardt. Can we do that?"

"Victor is no problem. Gearheardt we cannot find until later. There is a place that I am to appear. After a few minutes, Gearheardt will appear. Maybe we can appear there about six o'clock."

It was five after two. That should give us enough time.

Pilar approached our table. "My father is on the phone for you, Jack."

"Señor Armstrong, this is Chavez."

"Yes, Mr. Chavez."

"There is the new man that is looking for you."

"Is it a small man?"

"Si, Señor. A very small man. He is midget man. He has hired me with money to tell him when you are in my cantina (I wondered how many CIA payrolls the ever-watchful Mr. Chavez was currently on) and I told him okay. But I am telling you that it will cost you next to nothing, a few pesos, to notify you when he is asking for you."

"Consider it paid, Mr. Chavez, and thanks for calling." I started to hang up, but I heard Mr. Chavez say something else. "What was that, Mr. Chavez?"

"This small man is a killer, Señor. You should watch the back."

"Thank you, Mr. Chavez." I sat at Pilar's desk for a moment. There was a good chance that the Pygmy was the hit man in town that was gunning for me. The fact that it made no sense—as Gearheardt was the one who engaged me and he supposedly worked for the Pygmy—put me in no less danger.

In Pilar's car Marta directed me to the place of our first date, the Club Tristiza. I wasn't surprised when she informed me that Victor Ramirez was one of the owners. We met him in an office in the back of the club. It was small, smelled of cigar smoke, and completely barren of personality. This was not Victor's normal place of business.

"Mucho gusto," Victor said as we entered. His smile told me he was mocking the last introduction I had to him.

"Sure, Victor. It is a great pleasure to meet you." Marta and I sat down in two wooden chairs in front of his cheap desk.

"Marta tells me that you have a proposition for me, Señor. I am always open to propositions."

"I think you know my friend Gearheardt, Victor. Is that right?"

Victor's face was expressionless. Finally he gave a small Latin nod. "Si, I know Señor Gearheardt. I have met him. He is a friend of yours?"

"A very good friend. I've known him a long time. And you?" I was still searching for a read on Victor.

"As I said, I have met him. Why do you ask me about Señor Gearheardt? He is not here with us."

"He is a friend of Cuba. He believes that Cuba can be a partner of the United States in South America."

"That would not seem to be possible. The Americans are fearful of uba. It is hard to be friends when one is fearful. Perhaps you are mistaken."

"The Americans are fearful that Cuba will make a big mistake, doing business for their friends the Russians."

Victor's face changed just a bit, harder if that was possible. "Cuba has many friends. The Russians do not tell Cuba what business to do."

Marta cleared her throat delicately. I knew that she was anxious that Victor and I did not start sparring again. I didn't look at her.

"In America we like to look at possibilities. In possibilities there is sometimes opportunity, Victor. So let's assume that Gearheardt is a friend of Cuba and I am a friend of Gearheardt. Let's assume that and think of the possibilities." Victor nodded and I went on. "There is a possibility that America is not pleased with the way that the Mexican government is moving. Maybe not all Americans, but some Americans that work within the government. The Mexican government is not honest with its people. The people are poor and getting poorer. The Mexican country is rich in assets, oil and minerals, that the Americans would like to help exploit, to the benefit of both countries. But the Mexican government does not want to share, because that would mean that the people would share. Does what I am saying make sense, Victor?" I was making it up as I went along, but it sounded good to me.

"In Cuba, we share all of our assets with the people. The people own the assets. Not a few rich businessmen."

I wanted very badly to answer that statement differently than I knew I should. But I had a mission.

"You have a great leader also. That is why I am talking about possibilities." I read into Victor's expression that I was beginning to win him over. Appealing to his patriotism and admiration for Castro was a sure starter. "We are not diplomats, Victor. They always beat around the bush without getting to the point. Shouldn't we just say what we have in mind?"

"And who do you speak for, Señor Armstrong? Certainly you are not a diplomat. And you are only, what did you say, an economic development officer. Do economic development officers make the foreign policy now?"

I kept my gaze steady on him until he dropped his eyes and looked down at the ash of his cigar. He tapped it gently on the edge of a ceramic ashtray until the ash fell. With the end of his cigar, he smashed the large ash flat in the ashtray. The actions of a man who was thinking.

"Victor, I work for the Central Intelligence Agency of the United States government." Instinctively I thought that such an outright admission would elicit a response. I was right.

"So I have been told. But why are you telling me this? What is it to me?"

"I have been told that you are an important man. That you work for the intelligence agency of Cuba." I had been told no such thing. He was a well-connected ex-Army officer according to Marta. "We would like for you to cooperate with us, and we will cooperate with you. If you are not the man that I was told about, there shouldn't need to be any more discussion of possibilities."

I had put Victor into a box. I had admitted, even boasted, that I was an intelligence officer. If he played the 'I'm not an important man' role in front of me and Marta, it was a great loss of face. Or an admission that he was not brave enough to reveal his importance to me. I didn't think he would back down.

"If there were an opportunity for *cooperation* I would be able to talk to people who could make it a possibility. That is certain. But I am tired of possibilities and opportunities, what is it that you want to do?"

"The U.S. is taking a great risk if we cooperate with the Cubans. We are asking you to take a great risk also." I paused for drama. "We want you to assassinate the President of Mexico. Together we will blame it on the Russians (I made this part up). In the chaos that follows, the U.S. will turn to Cuba to help us restore order in this country. We will kick out the Russians, and Cuba will be the savior of Mexico. For this, we want

Cuba to kick the Russians out of Cuba and help us rid all South American countries of the Russians."

"You are crazy. I do not believe that the Americans would do this."

"Think about it, Victor. The largest country on our border is near revolution. The most organized and disciplined country near us is an outpost for the Russians. Imagine the world that I have described. Don't you think we would want to see that world?"

Victor rose from his desk. His cigar had gone out and he searched his pockets for a light. Marta picked up the lighter which matched the ashtray on his desk, and handed it to him.

"When would this possibility occur?"

"Cinco de Mayo."

Victor grimaced and then laughed harshly. "Again, you are crazy. That is only in a few days. How could we do such a thing in a few days?"

"The Americans have been planning for months, Victor. A plan like this is something that is difficult to keep a secret, so we told no one. It would be very dangerous to have it known. Even in the U.S. We prefer that only those Cubans actually involved will know. We don't want to face the Cubans' friends."

"The Russians?"

"Would you trust everyone in the Cuban government not to inform the Russians?"

"Some people are very happy with the Russians." He looked at Marta for confirmation. She shrugged.

"Exactly." I hoped he did not pursue the timing much longer. I couldn't think of any more excuses.

Victor paced around his small office. His cigar smoke was almost suffocating. Occasionally he would look at me and wrinkle his brow. I tried to look impassive and convincing.

"There is something that I don't understand, Señor Armstrong." He sat back down behind his desk. "I have heard this plan before."

Keeping cool was getting harder. "I don't think so, Victor."

"There is talk that the CIA is planning to do something on their own. Just talk of course."

"You know who I work for in the embassy, don't you, Victor? His only boss is in Washington. Wouldn't you think that we would know?"

"This Crenshaw, he is new to Mexico. Maybe he is too busy on his burro."

"I don't know what you are talking about. Crenshaw is a very experienced man."

Victor nodded and then stared into space. He was quiet for a moment.

"You would be a hero in Cuba, Victor."

He laughed. "There is room in Cuba for only one hero, Señor Armstrong." He stubbed out his cigar. "And I would be a dead hero in the event I did this thing. To escape after the thing would be difficult, no?"

I used my last card, feeling very uncertain of my ground. "I am in charge of security for the Americans, Victor. The escape has been arranged. You may ask Marta."

Victor didn't speak but looked at Marta and raised his eyebrows. She nodded.

Victor rested his elbows on his desk and looked squarely at me. "It is okay. This possibility is a good opportunity. Of course I must know more about the plans."

"That will be taken care of. Señor Gearheardt will give you the plans personally." That would teach that damn Gearheardt. Let him figure that out. I had no clue. "I would like you to tell me one thing, Victor, and then I need to get back to my people. Perhaps the person who told you the CIA was planning an event told you who was going to assassinate the President. And perhaps you can tell me who that is." That was as clumsy as I could make it.

Victor smiled. "You, Señor Armstrong."

Marta made arrangements for us to meet Victor again the next day. She also offered to drive Pilar's car, sensing that arranging for the President of Mexico to be assassinated by the Cubans had thrown me off balance just a bit. I didn't protest, nor was I particularly embarrassed that she saw my hands shaking when I handed her the keys.

CHAPTER ELEVEN

IN THE HOUSE OF EMPEROR GEARHEARDT

"You were very brilliant, Jack," Marta said. We were screaming along on the Periferico laying a cloud of exhaust only equaled by the trucks which sprayed for mosquitoes in low-lying parts of Florida. Screaming because Pilar's '49 Chevrolet only had first gear.

It was truly a James Bond moment. A beautiful woman peering over the steering wheel, an angst-ridden man holding his forehead, a Chevrolet that needed a ring job ten years ago, and two chickens in the back seat. (Pilar had neglected to tell us they roosted in the car). The engine noise was incredibly irritating and so was the occasional backfire which not only startled us and the chickens, but decelerated the car momentarily, throwing us into the dash, before catching again and wrapping back up to seven or eight thousand rpm. My head was throbbing and thinking about my next move was impossible.

When Marta missed the turnoff to Chapultepec Park, I began to hate her. I shouted new directions to her and had closed my eyes when the chickens in the back seat started fighting, cackling and pecking. Something blew. Grabbing one, then the other (no small feat) I threw the chickens out onto the freeway. Then I stared at Marta, challenging her to say something, but she kept her eyes fixed on the road.

At the next exit, Marta turned off. She took a side street for a block, then pulled to the curb and shut off the engine. For a moment the silence was deafening. I let out a breath I had been holding for the past five miles.

Finally Marta spoke. "Ees why they don't let economic development officers make the foreign policy. Ees too much pressure."

She started laughing. Then I joined in and we let the tension go, to the amusement of the Mexican women in the neighborhood who walked by the car, herding small children and carrying groceries for their families' dinners.

When we calmed down, Marta and I looked at one another for a long moment. I moved toward her and probably would have given the neighborhood women something else to think about except my slacks and thigh took a one inch rip from a spring that was poking through the woven paper seat covers.

"Damn it," I said. Marta began laughing again as I tried to regain dignity while holding my handkerchief tightly against the side of my leg. "We need to find Gearheardt. See if you can get a taxi for us, Marta."

By five o'clock Marta and I were in the coffee shop of the El Camino Real hotel, not far from the Park, and also close to the National Museum of Anthropology, one of the finest in the world. "Sometimes, I will meet Gearheardt at the Museum," Marta was saying, "sometimes in the Park. But I do not go there until near the time. Gearheardt does not want to allow time for people to notice me."

"That makes sense. Where are you to meet him today?"

"In front of the Museum. Just as they close the doors and the people are coming out."

"We have about an hour. What else can you tell me about Gearheardt's plan? What about the escape to Havana? Is that truly arranged, or just part of the story?"

"It is arranged. I think it is arranged. So many things seem to be changed." She sipped her drink. She looked beautiful.

"How can we find out? I'm not sure this plan is going to go forward. But it would be nice to know."

"The Cubans of Miami, the good Cubans you call them, have the arrangements. They do not know the reason, but they know that they must help a CIA man out of Mexico and into Cuba on the fifth of May. This, they say they can do. And they can hide him there to work with other people in Havana."

"How do we reach these Cubans? Are you in contact with them?"

"Only Gearheardt knows them I think. I cannot work with both Cuban groups and he said he needed me to work with Victor."

I excused myself and found a payphone, hoping to catch Juanita before she left for the day.

"Ola, 34883552." We answered our phones by repeating the number.

"Juanita, I'm glad I caught you. This is Jack."

"The Pygmy no kill you, Jack? This is a rumor I heard."

"No, I'm still alive, Juanita. I need you to do something for me, and then tell me if I have any messages."

"Si, Señor Jack."

"Go see Eric. If he's not there, find the duty officer in the embassy. This is very important. Tell them that two American students were arrested today by the Halcones."

"How you spell Halcones, Señor Jack?"

"Maybe I'm pronouncing it wrong. Fal-con-ees. The Mexican Secret Police."

"Ayyeee. Poor students. What should I tell Señor Eric?"

"I just want the embassy alerted that the students have been arrested. Okay? I think their names are Fred Benson and Nick Blowden. Something like that. Now, are there any other messages?"

"Si. Señor Rodrigo called and said he is happy and wants to work with you more. Señor Chavez call and said that the small man was looking again for you. I think the small man is the Pygmy, Señor Jack."

"Where did you hear about the Pygmy, Juanita?"

"Señor Pepe."

"Okay, we'll get back to that later. What else?"

Across the room I could see that Marta as getting impatient. She gave the signal for the check to the waiter and jerked her head at me.

"You have a box from Señor Major Crenshaw. I put this on your desk. There is no more message except the ambassador has said for you to see him if you come back. He personally come to my desk six times today."

"What are you wearing, Juanita?"

"Que?

"Never mind. What about the box from Major Crenshaw? What is that? Juanita, go get the box and open it for me. It could be important."

I held up my finger to Marta. *Why would Crenshaw send me a box?*

"Ay yi yi, Señor Jack. It is the tail of the burro. Ay yi yi." She lapsed into a lilting panicky Spanish.

"Juanita! Juanita! Calm down. What is in the box? What did you say?"

"It is tail of the burro. Why would Señor Major Crenshaw send you the tail of his burro?" She sounded like she was crying.

"I don't think he did, Juanita. I imagine that is a message sent by other people. Perhaps he is in trouble. I take it that you have not heard from him." I wanted to calm her down, so I spoke less upset than I felt.

"No, Señor. Eets okay now. I have closed the box. Eet surprise me, that's all. I do not like him but I am worry about Señor Major Crenshaw. What should we do, Señor Jack?"

"You should go home, Juanita. After you tell the duty officer about the American students. Forget Eric."

"He in church still."

"Yes. But you should go home. Don't tell anyone about the burro tail. I will look into it tonight. And I'll call you tomorrow. Do you remember who you can call to try and find me?"

"Señor Chavez at El Caballo, and Jorge in the driving pool."

"That's exactly right, Juanita. And Juanita, thank you for staying at your post."

"De nada, Señor Jack. I am CIA."

"Well, I wouldn't let that get around outside, but yes we are all on the same team. Goodnight, Juanita."

Marta was beginning to get nervous by the time I sat back down.

"Jack, we must be at the Museum in ten minutes. If we miss Pepe, I will not know how to find him until tomorrow evening."

"Let's go. I just had business that had to be taken care of. I am afraid that Major Crenshaw has gotten himself into a bit of trouble."

"But he is working with the good Cubans, no?"

"That's true. Maybe he just irritated the hell out of them so they cut off the tail of his burro."

We were almost out the door to the taxi stand. "They do what?" Marta asked.

"I'll tell you later. We need to find that damn Pepe."

Who showed up almost as soon as Marta and I sat down on the wall around the fountain. The Museum was closing and scores of people were making their way out of the building. Gearheardt approached through the crowd, grinning broadly. It nearly always made me feel better just being around the optimistic jerk.

"I am in deep shit," he said as he drew near to us, still grinning like a possum.

"What's up, Gearheardt?" I asked. I assumed he was just pulling our chain. He had a knack for making problems seem small by inventing large ones.

"I must have pissed off the Russians," Gearheardt said. He pecked Marta on the cheek and patted my shoulder. He was dressed in the blazer that he stole from me, khaki slacks, topped with a tan trench coat, British military style. His blue pinstriped shirt set off a brilliant red tie. "The Pygmy tells me they've imported a sniper that can pick the condom off a gnat's pecker at five hundred yards."

I tried not to concern myself with his metaphor because I knew that's what he wanted me to do. "I don't get it. What are the Russians upset about? Not that I doubt you could piss them off easily enough."

"I think someone tipped them off to my plan to blame them for helping the Cubans assassinate the Mexican president."

"So they're going to shoot you?"

"I think they're going to shoot *you*, Jack. Why would they want me?"

I still had the feeling that he was making all this up to cover up some *really* bad news. "Speaking of people shooting me, did you talk to the Pygmy about him not shooting me? I think that's the order of the day. I hate it when midgets are trying to kill me." I laughed tentatively. "So did you talk to him? It's just a misunderstanding, right?"

"I talked to him, Jack. And I really think he is considering not killing you. He has to weigh it against his other commitments, completing the mission without casting undue suspicion on himself, things like that. Remember this is *his* overall mission. I think you can assume that he will rate completing the mission more important than taking out a CIA agent who is working for the opposition."

"But I'm *not* working for the opposition, you nincompoop. I'm working for you. You got me into this." Marta rose from where she had been listening. She took my arm, evidently concerned that I was about to strangle Gearheardt.

"You should have nothing to worry about then, Jack," Gearheardt said. "So how did it go with Victor today? Did we recruit him to be our assassin?"

"It went very well, Pepe. Jack was brilliant in his speech. I am sure by now that Victor is telling Havana that the CIA is backing up Cuba. I hope they will be convinced of the truth." She squeezed my arm, smiling at Gearheardt. "What is gnat pecker?"

"Never goddamned mind what a gnats pecker is. Pepe, you got some 'splaining to do. As far as I know I have a pygmy after my ass, and now a Russian assassin is on the 'shoot Jack' team. Let's head someplace and go over all this. I'm not letting you out of my sight until I have all the nswers."

"Fair enough, Jack. And I think technically the Russian is a Ukrainian. Wears glasses now so he may not be worth a damn as a shot anymore. I don't think they thought you were important enough to fly over one of their top men. This guy is retired here." He took Marta's arm and began guiding her through the thinning crowd to where a car was waiting at the curb.

We were at Gearheardt's 'pad' in less than ten minutes. He was living in Chapultepec Castle.

Up the drive from Paseo de la Reforma we could see the fortress with its turrets, the largest in the center of the palatial structure. Massive cypress trees filled the terraced landscape.

We were greeted by servants dressed in costumes from Maximilian's time. Inside the castle, the very best of extravagant European luxury was evident in every detail.

"I got tired of the El Diablo Motel," Gearheardt said. He was leading Marta and me up the magnificent red-carpeted winding staircase. "I figured since no one was living here, a few bucks spread around the right places could give me temporary shelter." He threw open large double doors. "I thought you might like this, Marta. This was Carlotta's bedroom. The Empress of Mexico. Went mad I think. But she had a bathroom you'll like."

We looked inside the room where Gearheardt pointed. A huge marble tub, green chaise lounges on each side. Opulent. Marta stepped back to the bedroom and lay down on the gold bed. A gold chandelier hung high overhead.

"You would have thought they could afford a mirror on that ceiling, but different strokes for different folks," Gearheardt said. He plopped down on a blue velvet chair and I took the matching one. "Jack, don't think I'm taking your problems lightly. You're my brother." He lit a cigarette and after searching around, finally dropped the match into an urn. "First, bring me up to date. We're approaching 'go-no go' time and I need to let some folks know what's up. Remember, you just have to get you and Victor in place. I'll take it from there. Wham Bam, you're in Havana. Marta will take care of you. And your instructions will be crystal clear. So what's with Victor and Crenshaw?"

I filled him in on my meeting with Victor. Gearheardt was ecstatic. Couldn't have gone better, he said. "The Cubans will be expecting the CIA to be behind them all the way. We will be, but not in the way they think we will."

"Gearheardt, I think Crenshaw might be in trouble." I told him about Crenshaw riding off on his burro to meet a group of Cubans. I told him of Juanita receiving the tail of a burro, in a package addressed to me and from Crenshaw.

"Crenshaw isn't the kind of guy to just do that as a joke, is he Jack?" Gearheardt asked.

"Cut off the tail of his burro and send it to me? Get serious, Gearheardt. Someone is holding Crenshaw."

"Did you check at the embassy to see if anyone saw who delivered the package? We know he didn't mail it, unless he mailed it six months ago and bribed every one from the mailman to the postmaster so it would be delivered in less than two years. This Mexican mail system is a damn disgrace, Jack."

"Could we stick with Crenshaw? And no, I haven't done any investigating at the embassy. I haven't been in there for two days. The ambassador is looking for me. Evidently, he's a bit upset over something."

"You think he knows what you're up to?" Gearheardt asked.

It was what *I* was up to now.

"I doubt it. I would imagine that word is out that the CIA is involved in some kind of shenanigans and he's just on a normal rampage. The reason I don't think it's anything specific is that he hasn't actually sent anyone out to put me under house arrest or anything. As far as I know, he just wants to see me."

"He told the Marine guards to shoot you on sight, Jack. Sorry to be the one to let you know."

"You don't suppose the Marines would actually—"

"Aw, I'm just shitting you, Jack. Those boys wouldn't shoot a former Marine hero like yourself. They'd shoot the damn ambassador first." Gearheardt laughed.

"Very funny, Gearheardt. I've got two people trying to shoot me now. So that isn't exactly humorous."

"One and a half, Jack. The pygmy's only about three feet tall."

"Let's get back to Crenshaw. I think we need to look for him. He is my boss after all."

"I'll put out some feelers," Gearheardt offered. "Where was he last seen?"

"Feelers my ass. We're going to look for him. I know the town that he rode out of yesterday. Its just north of here. He was going to meet some people who he thought could help him get to the bottom of the potential assassination of Rios. Your deal, Gearheardt. So the least you could do is find out if he's in some trouble. Tails don't just fall off burro's you know."

"I was going to ask," Gearheardt said. "I was wondering if it was some kind of shedding thing." He flicked his cigarette butt to the fireplace, not noticing the opening was covered with clear plastic. Marta got up and picked up the butt and put it in the urn. The urn was no doubt an invaluable gift from the Chinese.

"I'm taking a bath," Marta announced. She began taking off her clothes.

"Come on, Jack. Let me show you around this place. It's magnificent."

"You and I are going after Crenshaw."

"Jack, if the Chief of Station is missing, don't you think the CIA has some folks on the job?"

"Maybe, but Crenshaw was so damn secretive about what he was doing. I'm not sure that anyone but I and Juanita knew where he was headed. And I only have a vague idea."

Marta was down to her underwear and I decided that given my new feelings about her, I needed to vacate the premises. I headed out of the room and I heard Gearheardt rise and follow me.

"Everything is set for you in Havana, Marta," he said. "Your halfbrother is in place and making arrangements."

I turned around as Marta headed into the bathroom. "Gon is in Havana?"

"So was I yesterday," Gearheardt said. "I'll tell you about it. By the way, I spoke to Mr. Chavez. He said Pilar wants her car back."

"Pilar does not own a car. She owns a nineteen forty-nine Chevrolet chicken coup. It is a piece of shit, even for a chicken coup."

"Jeez, Jack. I was just passing on the message."

We were in the grand library. Beautiful wood and hand bound books by the hundreds.

"Sorry, Gearheardt. She was nice enough to loan it to us. I'll buy her a new one. I'll call her later. Now, let's talk about Crenshaw. I think we need to get out there and see what we can find out. Even if you don't feel like helping the guy, this could affect your plan."

"Righto, Jack. We'll head out after dinner. I've got a staff downstairs that can make lizard taste like filet mignon."

"I don't want any lizard. I want us to get our asses out to Tahuacan and find Crenshaw." I realized I was shouting. The castle was chillingly quiet. "And we're taking Marta."

"Fine. I'll go get her." Gearheardt started out of the room.

I grabbed his jacket and turned him around. "I'll go get her. You get a car for us."

The scene of Marta in Carlotta's marble tub, her black hair tied back in a scarf, one faultless leg raised as she rinsed, was something that would stay with me a lifetime.

"Jack," she said as she looked up, "there is water for two in here." She smiled the smile that I was becoming addicted to.

"I would like to come in with you very much, Marta. But we must go to find the Major. Maybe we could come back here later."

"But you smell like the goat, Jack. You should take a bath now." She rose from the tub in full magnificence. I realized how contextual nudity is. At my breakfast table it is a distracting joy. Rising wet from a bath, it is incredibly—"

"Hey, I got the car, Jackson. Wow, would you look at that body. Marta you are one luscious babe." Gearheardt was beside me in the bathroom door. "Get your clothes on, Marta. Jack here has a bug up his ass about Crenshaw. And he's probably right. We need to find the guy tonight if possible. Cinco de Mayo is soon upon us."

Gearheardt and I sat in one of innumerable parlors while we waited for Marta. He began to tell me of the arrangements that he made in Havana. "It's a simple plan, Jack. The bomb goes off in Mexico City. Attention is drawn there. The U.S. has a perfect excuse to send—"

A livery festooned young man entered the room and gave a small nod of his head to Gearheardt. "Excellency, you have a phone call from Mr. Chavez."

Gearheardt actually blushed. "Don't start with me, Jack. It was only a few dollars more and the people who work here like it. It gives them a sense of history."

"Go see what Chavez wants, your Excellency. You are a real piece of work, Gearheardt."

When he returned, he was serious. "Jack, have you recently pissed off some Colombians? Chavez says that a couple of cranky looking guys came in asking for you this evening. He's been trying to get in touch with you. Says you should watch your ass." He walked over to a gilded chest and pried open the door. Inside were various size crystal bottles. "I don't know about you, but I could use a drink. This looks good."

"I don't think that's a very good idea, Gearheardt. Those bottles have probably . . . forget that. So now I have cranky Colombians looking for me. At least I can't blame that on you. Where's that phone? I need to see if I can get in touch with Rodrigo."

"Have you ever thought of keeping a list of people wanting to kill you, Jack? You know the Mexican Secret Police aren't exactly big fans of yours either."

"Where's the phone? You can tell me about that later."

Rodrigo, being the trooper that he was, took the news as if he had expected it. "My family and I will go to our home village for a few days, Jack. No problem. You should come with us. No outsiders will harm us there. The Colombians will not search for us for long. They will be angry now, but their leaders in Bogotá will not want much attention on the operation in Mexico. They will find new people and start again."

"I suppose you're right, Rodrigo. Stay safe and contact me when you get back to Mexico City. If you need to get in touch with me, just leave word with Juanita."

"Who is thees Gearheardt?"

"That's a long story. But you can trust him if he contacts you. I'll tell you about it later."

Marta was dressed and having three-hundred-year-old brandy with Gearheardt when I finally found the right parlor. "This is a nice place you have here, Excellency," I said.

"Knock off the Excellency crap, Jack. By the way, how long have you been wearing those clothes? That suit looks like you've been wrestling chickens on their own turf. Try some of mine. I've had some laid out for you in the bedroom you'll be using. Pedro here will show you the way. And I might take Marta's suggestion that a bath wouldn't hurt."

"Gearheardt, we are on our way to help a guy that might be in real trouble. We don't need to smell pretty and we are wasting time."

"Emperors can't be rushed, Jack. That's one of the first rules of Emperoring. Take a damn bath. I need to bring Marta up to date anyway."

CHAPTER TWELVE

ON THE TRAIL OF THE TAIL-LESS BURRO

Spit-polished and fragrant, we finally made it into Gearheardt's borrowed (I didn't even ask) Mercedes and on our way to Teotihuacan. Or actually a small town near those famous ruins.

Gearheardt's driving matched his other skills, more or less car-veat emptor. That is, other drivers needed to anticipate where Gearheardt was heading and make allowances. No lane, speed, turn, traffic restriction nor civilized responsibility impeded his driving. I had forewarned Marta and she had emptied her bladder prior to climbing into the back seat.

"Gearheardt," I said, acting as if I weren't aware of our imminent death, "Marta never did explain Palanque to me. What's all that about?"

"Good question, Jack. Actually has nothing to do with Palanque (of course) but I liked the name. Palanque is the nearest Mayan ruin to the little village on the Gulf that is, as we speak, being invaded by Cubans. Mostly by sea, but some are driving and some have flown into Merida. These are 'good' Cubans of course. Guys I can count on, and the nucleus of the Cuban government after we kick Castro out."

"By 'we' I assume you mean the United States."

"God Bless America, Jack. That's exactly who I mean."

"And I also assume that you believe the U.S. will kick Castro out because you have egged them into trying to take over Mexico."

"By Jove, I think you have it, Jack. You didn't think I really meant to take over Mexico, did you? Lovely country. Friendly people and some of the best tortillas this side of . . . wherever else they make tortillas."

"And what if they don't? Attack Cuba, I mean. It didn't work at the Bay of Pigs. And there was no popular uprising against Castro either. Have you thought through all the possibilities?"

Marta spoke up from the back seat. "Pepe has much help in Cuba, Jack. He is the leader but he is not alone."

"You're the leader? I thought this was the Pygmy's operation."

"The Pygmy *was* the leader. He put things in place at Langley. But he's gone off the deep end. Kind of taken this assassination thing to heart. I've had to change some plans." Gearheardt was lighting a cigarette while balancing an exquisite snifter of fine brandy. Marta and I held our breath as he wove through the evening traffic.

He went on. "Blood lust can do that to a man. Once he got the word from HQ that he was to take out the would-be assassin traitor, he's lost interest in everything else. We get so few killing assignments these days, what with Congress on our ass all the time, you can hardly blame him." Gearheardt took his eyes off the road for a few terrifying seconds while he looked over at me. "I'll stop him, Jack. Don't worry. And I know you're no traitor. Since I was the one who told Langley you were."

"Pepe can do amazing things, Jack," Marta chimed in. "He is the—"

"Marta, could you hold off for a minute on the Gearheardt skill and acumen? I need to make sure that I know exactly what is taking place. Then when I kill Gearheardt, I'll know how to run this show." Although Marta was clearly beginning to look at me the way I was now looking at her, she was in love with the Emperor Gearheardt concept. Hero worship was a dangerous thing for an American in a foreign land. Particularly worshiping someone like Gearheardt.

"And I wouldn't blame you if I let the Pygmy kill you, Jack. For killing me, I mean. But it ain't gonna happen, qien sabe?" He slammed on the brakes throwing us painfully forward against our seatbelts.

"We missed the turnoff to Teotihuacan while we were jabbering. Driving in this traffic takes concentration." He made a u-turn in front of the on-coming traffic and then cut across three lanes to the Teotihuacan road.

"Now where were we? Okay, Jack, get the idea out of your head that the Pygmy is going to shoot you. I'll take care of it. I'm working on the blind Ukrainian sniper situation, and you need to get your back covered with those Colombian assholes. We'll talk to your pal Eduardo with the Halcones tomorrow and see if we can't get that called off too. So now, what's the problem?"

"I feel a lot better, Gearheardt. As Marta says, you are a genius."

"Thanks, Jack." (Sarcasm was lost on the jackass). "How much further, guys?"

"About five more minutes on this road, Pepe. Then we will turn north at the Pemex station. We need to stop at Pemex and let me ask about this village. I am not sure."

"You didn't finish about Palanque, Gearheardt. So you have this army of good Cubans congregating on the coast, which, by the way, is a hell of a long way from Cuba, and then what happens?"

"The boys will not be going directly to Cuba, Jack. First they come up here and help us stabilize the situation. We can't rely on the dopes at the State Department to react very quickly, and the Mexican army is on a five-year taco break, and we don't want to unleash the Halcones." He opened his window to toss his cigarette butt and the brandy snifter went with it. "Shit," he said, "I hope those can be replaced."

"So the guys are coming up here when, and how?" Long ago I found out that seeming to go along with Gearheardt's schemes was the best, maybe the only, way to get any real information.

"I've had a little trouble arranging transportation. Moving guerilla armies around is not as easy as it sounds."

"I don't think it sounds easy to anyone. So what did you do?"

"Taxi."

"You're having the army take taxi's from Calixtua to Mexico City?"

"Don't make it sound like such a big deal. There's only fifty guys."

"Well, that will be a sight I don't want to miss, Gearheardt. Ten or fifteen Mexican cabs, bristling with guns and Cubans, heading into Mexico City."

"My boys can round up the bad Cubans and then be ready to head to Havana when you give the signal. They'll be in place tomorrow night."

"See, Jack, ees all worked out." Marta leaned over the seat and pecked my cheek. "Here's the Pemex station."

Gearheardt squealed into the well-lit gas station and screeched to a halt at a pump. He and Marta got out, leaving me to contemplate the idea of being in Havana within a couple of days, directing an operation that I neither knew anything about, nor particularly believed had any chance of success. I decided not to challenge Gearheardt. We needed to find Crenshaw. I wanted to keep him focused on that.

Gearheardt had the tank filled by a young Mexican lad whose head was snapping between the lovely Marta and the equally lovely Mercedes. Gearheardt gave him a tip. "Never wear brown shoes with a blue suit."

"I don't think he saw the humor," I said as we drove away.

"The best thing we Americans can give to poor people is our sense of humor, Jack. A few pesos would be gone tomorrow. A sense of humor, a good joke, those last a lifetime."

"The kid is standing in the middle of Mexico with the pump in his hand, Gearheardt. And he couldn't possibly understand a damn thing you said. He just thinks you're an asshole American."

"The kid charged me $50 for ten gallons of gas, Jack. He can work his tip out with the manager."

We reached the end of the pavement. At the beginning of the dirt road, a small cantina was lit and loud. "We are to ask in here about the village," Marta said. "I will go in and see where we can find it."

"I'll go with you, Marta," I said.

"No. Too many strangers will cause talk."

"She can handle it, Jack. You're about as subtle as a canker sore in dealing with the Mexicans sometimes."

This from a man who thought sharing fart jokes with people who were bloated from hunger would be admirable aid policy.

As she went into the club, I said to Gearheardt, "I need to talk to you about Havana."

Gearheardt sighed. "Can't you just have faith, Jack?" He took his pistol from his shoulder holster and checked the clip. "You worry too much about the plans. The big picture. I'm not a big picture guy. If the government of the United States puts a gun in my hands and points me at communists, I don't worry about what to wear. I don't worry about *offending* some jackass at the UN. The *mission* is the thing, Jack. We need Castro out of Cuba. My job is to see that happen. Your job is to help me see that happen. Like Teddy Roosevelt, my favorite president by the way, once said, 'Seeing things happen is what it's all about.'"

It was my turn to sigh. "Yes, that's one of my favorite Teddy Roosevelt quotes too, Gearheardt."

A flash of light from the door turned us both toward the cantina. Marta was coming out, a Mexican man following.

"So you're not going to fill me in?" I asked finally.

Gearheardt smiled. "I have my pals in Havana setting things up, Jack. You'll know their names when you need to. I don't want you giving away the details just to save your gonads. And you'll have Marta with you." He looked at me. "And the full faith and support of His Excellency Gearheardt."

"This man will take us to Calixtua," Marta said through the window to Gearheardt. "But we cannot drive this car. The road is too much rock and sand. He will take us in his taxi."

"Si, Señors," the Mexican said. "It is my pleasure. And I am driven by the pursuit of the Yankee dollars."

"A man after my own heart. Good fellow," Gearheardt said as he got out of the Mercedes.

We left our jackets and ties in the car, locked it after assurances from the man that it would be safe, and followed him around to the back of the cantina. His taxi was in the form of a 'dune buggy' affair that had been crafted from a Mustang. After the Mustang had died and decomposed. Large tires, bucket seats, and a roll bar welded to a frame sporting a V-8. I knew it was a Mustang only by the name on the chrome valve cover.

Gearheardt and the old man began talking about the engine in broken English track talk. He had a way to instant rapport with almost anyone as crazy as he was.

"What did you find out?" I asked Marta as she and I climbed into the back seat.

"Crenshaw came through this place," she said. "I am not sure if it was yesterday or the day before. But many of the people remembered the burro and the gringo. They have not seen him return."

"Buckle up, kids," Gearheardt yelled from the front seat over the noise of the engine that didn't have a muffler. "This greaser is going to show us what this baby can do."

"Greaser is not—"

"I said *Geezer,* Jack!"

The engine died. Gearheardt slapped the Mexican on the back.

"My friend has half the United Nations trying to kill him and he's worried that he might *offend* somebody."

The Mexican and Gearheardt laughed.

"Maybe I can try to keel him also. There is money to be made for this?"

"Drive, Pedro," Gearheardt said, slapping the man's shoulder again.

The engine exploded into life and we flew forward, spinning dirt and gravel high behind us.

A 'driving surface' to the 'road' that we followed was as the 'Mona Lisa' is to 'baboon butt.' The lights of the buggy, on the front bumper and from the roll bar, gave us a preview of coming attractions, just like shining a flashlight around the walls of a torture chamber. There were deep gullies, cactus shrubs, large rocks, and an occasional slithering reptile. Gearheardt of course kept up a challenging antagonistic patter: "Hey, is there a speed limit, Grandpa? Don't worry, old man, they'll hold the funeral for us. What time is your beating scheduled for, Gramps? Should I get out and push, Methuselah? Is the parking brake on, Pedro?"

Holding on for dear life, my hands cramping from holding onto the seat and roll bar, I began to lose my anger at Gearheardt. His manic laughter and egging on of the Mexican reminded me of what I liked best about him—his unfettered enjoyment of life and thrills, people and action, women and liquor. I often had suspected that the reason he hated the communists, and his willingness to 'shoot the bastards on sight,' was somehow due to his view of them as lifeless, joyless bureaucrats who hated God and the poor.

"The Communist PARTY? Why those bastards wouldn't know a party was going on if Fatback Annie herself was doing the naked dirty dance on the coffee table with vodka spurting from all orifices. The only way they knew Lenin was dead was that he wasn't fogging up the glass on his see-through casket. Party, my ass."

We began to slow as we left the desert and entered the hills, at first sparsely treed, and then forest. Our lights now shown on trunks and branches. 'Death-defying' no longer described our progress.

"Could we stop a minute, Gearheardt?" I yelled.

"Sure, Jack. You need to pull the Naughahyde out of your butt?" He laughed and winked at Marta, the roll bar lamps lighting his face devilishly.

"No, I would just like to talk briefly about what we might be getting into and how we're going to handle it. And would you ask your pal to kill the engine so I don't have to yell?"

Gearheardt tapped the Mexican on his arm and then indicated my request by drawing his thumb across his throat.

The Mexican shut off the engine (the silence was joyous) and grinned at Gearheardt. "Now we keel him, no?"

"We have a comedian for a driver, Jack. But your idea is a good one. Besides I need to take a leak." He glanced at Marta. "Excuse me, Marta."

"Take a leak, bring a leak. I am hating this car. Jack is right. We should talk after we visit the trees."

We split up in the dark then rejoined a few yards away from the Mexican driver.

"Your show, Jack," Gearheardt said.

"All we know is that Crenshaw rode his donkey—"

"Burro."

"Thanks, wiseass. He rode his *burro* to this village day before yesterday. We also know that he was to meet people, Cubans I believe, to talk about the Cinco de Mayo event. We know he hasn't been seen since. And we got his burro's tail in the mail. That's about it."

"And you're sure the tail is from Crenshaw's burro?" Gearheardt asked. "They all look pretty much alike to me."

"I would think a jackass like yourself would know burro tails, Gearheardt," I said. He had his arm around Marta and that smirking grin on his face.

"So we're looking for a burro with two assholes, right Jack?"

"I know you didn't want to come, Gearheardt, but Crenshaw—"

"Hombres," Marta pleaded, "we need to get started to the village."

Gearheardt had removed his shoulder holster, sticking his weapon into his pocket, and suggested I do the same. "Let's don't advertise the Marines have landed, Jack. Pedro there will keep your leather in the hotrod for now."

"Just let me do the talking. We don't know that Crenshaw is in trouble. We just know he hasn't checked in with the embassy. Remember, we're not at war with these villagers, just possibly the Cubans that met Crenshaw out here. Most of these little towns have mayors. We want to meet with him and ask about Crenshaw. After we look around a bit."

"It's getting late, Jack. What say we saddle up and head on in to Dodge."

"I'm warning you, Gearheardt, this is my show out here. Just keep a lid on your shenanigans. In other words, don't mouth off to the people and don't try to bully them."

We headed for the dune buggy Mustang.

"I like your plan, Jack. Plain and direct. I'm not absolutely clear what it is, of course, but then I'm just a simple troublemaker." He climbed in beside the Mexican driver. "Let's fire it up, Paco. The bars close at midnight."

We had gone less than a hundred ear-splitting yards when the road topped the hill and we began to descend into a dark valley. The road switch-backed its way down the hill and we caught glimpses of lights from the village in the valley. I guessed it to be a town of maybe five thousand people, based solely on how wide the lights were spread. The town square was obvious.

Our driver had assured Gearheardt he made this trip often, so the noise of our arrival would not be a cause of alarm for the people in the town. "Your arrival *anyplace* is a cause for alarm, Gearheardt," I had said when he told me. "Thanks, Jack," he had replied.

There were strollers and sitters around the moderately lit town square. The driver collected half of his fee and was told to stand by until we needed to leave. I didn't like the fact that he smiled and rubbed his thumb and fingers together rapidly when he looked at me. Gearheardt made a pistol with his hand, pointed it at me, and shook his head affirmatively.

"Very funny, Gearheardt," I said. "Why don't you and Marta wait in this cantina and have a beer. I'll scout around and try to find the mayor."

"Sure thing, Jackson." He put his arm around a strangely quiet and compliant Marta and headed into the café. "Why don't you show me that fast draw technique again, Marta? The local boys will get a kick out of that." He stopped and came back to me. "And by the way, Jackson, remember that while we're dicking around out here, we have a major assassination scheme plowing ahead in Mexico City. Just keep that in mind."

"I think that Crenshaw's disappearance may have something to do with that, Gearheardt. And we're not 'dicking' around."

"Poor choice of words. Let's find your boy and get back to the world of international intrigue. That's all I'm saying." He went back to Marta and up the steps to the café.

I turned back to our driver. "Pedro, or Paco, do you know where I can find the Mayor? Or is there a sheriff here, a policeman?"

"There is a mayor. There is a policeman. My name is Juan. I don't know this Pedro-Paco."

I could never understand how I could give a guy ten dollars and he would spit on my shoes because it wasn't twenty dollars. Gearheardt could give a guy a nickel and the guy would *shine* Gearheardt's shoes. I wondered if Gearheardt gave off an aura that told everybody what I knew about him, his love of life and people.

"Bueno, Juan. Let's find the mayor or the policeman."

We started across the square, tree covered with many statues, and the few local people being only mildly interested in a gringo passing by. Crossing the opposite street, I saw the sign above an open door that read *Policia y Oficina de Alcalde*. Police and Office of the Mayor. Juan pointed and smirked.

"Dentro," he said. Inside.

Inside were two genial men playing chess and drinking coffee. They rose politely when I entered and extended their hands.

"Welcome, Señor," the mayor (without the uniform) said. "You are here for tomorrow's burro roast, no doubt."

CHAPTER THIRTEEN

BROTHER, CAN YOU SPARE A CRENSHAW

"I am not aware of the burro roast," I said as I took the offered chair. The policeman poured a cup of coffee for me. "Gracias," I said.

"We are not normally the roasters of burros," the Mayor said. "This is most unusual. A burro arrived in our town yesterday, cleaned and on . . . como se dice . . . a spit."

This precipitated a rapid discussion in Spanish. The policeman, a short muscular man, made a spitting sound, and shook his head. The mayor pantomimed a rod being poked up—

"Señors," I interrupted. "Yes, spit is the proper term. That isn't important."

My two cents didn't settle the argument. The policeman, Capitan Malo, wasn't buying the 'rod up the butt and out the mouth' theory evidently and made his case for expectoration with examples landing precariously near my shoes.

The mayor, Señor Verdago, jumped into the debate vigorously. He cleared the chess table and produced paper and pen, quickly drawing a stick burro and illustrating a rod through its length.

I was biting my lip, hoping that the conference on English Descriptive Colloquialism would adjourn before I had to intervene.

Finally Capitan Malo seemed to agree to argue no more. He nodded his head affirmatively, picked up the drawing and spit on it, wadded it up and threw it toward the waste basket. The mayor smiled. Then the policeman smiled, and it occurred to me that these two gents lived for the chance to find something unique to argue about. Gringos and roast burros must be giving them a field day.

"Pardon, Señor," the Mayor said. "My friend is learning the English late. He went only to a poor technical school that taught police work. I, on the other hand, attended the Universidad de Mexico, the finest university in the world. And with our great educations behind us, we sit next to the square and grow older. But excuse me, you are here with a question, not the burro roast. How can we help you?"

"Believe me, I would love to stay for the burro roast. I have a friend with me that would rather eat burro than make love."

The two gentlemen laughed politely at my poor joke.

"But I am looking for a colleague who came through your town yesterday or the day before. I'm afraid he is now missing. Or at least he has not been in his office for the past two days. I am concerned about him."

"And this office he is not in would be . . . ?" There was a wariness in his voice, and in the eyes of the policeman, that had not been there efore.

"He is from the U.S. embassy."

"And you also, Señor?"

"Yes, I work for the gentleman."

Captain Malo rose from the table without comment and went into the adjacent room. The mayor began putting away the chess pieces, not looking at me.

"There are very few officials who come through Calixtua Señor. I don't believe that I am aware of your colleague."

I decided to up the ante a bit. "Señor Mayor, I work with the security group in the embassy. It would be best if—"

The mayor smiled and called out to the other room. A similarly smiling policeman returned and took his place at the table.

"So you are CIA," he said. "Bueno. We were thinking that you were perhaps an economic development officer. They come to our town often and ask us about crops and the population and how many people are working. They are very tiresome and irritating."

"I didn't say I was CIA," I said.

"And I didn't say I was Mexican," the mayor laughed. The policeman joined in.

I looked at them for a moment and then grinned.

"Okay, let us suppose for the moment that I am CIA. I am still trying to find Señor Crenshaw. Can you help me?"

"If you are certain that you are not trying to change the way we have farmed since Cortez, we can help you perhaps." He looked at his policeman pal. "No?"

"Si, Señor. I will tell you. Your friend arrived the evening before yesterday. He was covered with the dust of the road, and sat on the burro. Many people were at the church for evening mass. He disturbed them and I was forced to arrest him for trying to be the Jesus."

"You arrested Señor Crenshaw for impersonating Jesus?"

"Ees not so simple (as if I thought it was), Señor. There are people in the town who believe our Blessed Guadalupe will visit us. Our brothers from Cuba were at the mass. It was they who began saying that your friend claimed to be the Jesus. I am not sure that was the thing, but people were angry and your friend also began to sing the hymn. For this matter, I brought him to the jail."

Cubans? I needed to know what that was all about. But I asked, "And you turned him loose? Or is he still in your jail?"

"No, he is loose now. The very same Cuban people who complained came to the jail and asked for him. They were very sorry that they caused the trouble. After he was cleaned and fed, they took him in their truck and went away. The burro was in the back of the truck. Then yesterday, the truck came and gave us the burro for a feast. To make sure that the town was not angry."

I wasn't sure what to say. "Didn't that seem a bit strange? The Cubans taking him away?"

The mayor wasn't smiling now. "No, Señor, we did not think it strange. Every summer the touristas come to our town. They take pictures of our houses. They take pictures of our church. They ask for ketchup for their tacos. Some ask to find the Mexican women who make love. They buy rocks which we find in our fields every day. If we tie two sticks together as a cross, they will buy it. No, Señor, we did not think it was strange." The policeman shrugged in agreement. The mayor went on. "The Cubans and the gringo you look for went northwest, toward the ruins of Tula. There is nothing else in the area."

"I understand. But do you often have Cubans in town? Who were these men?"

"They were Cubans, Señor," the mayor said. It sounded like his final word.

While I was thinking of my next question the sound of a man running came behind me. A young, excited Mexican man stuck his head into the doorway. 'Gringo,' 'combate,' and 'cantina' told me how fast I needed to find Gearheardt.

The policeman and I were head and head across the square with the mayor huffing and puffing close behind. Inside the cantina where Gearheardt and Marta had gone to wait for me, the scene was not the chaotic mess I had expected. About ten locals were seated or standing around the room, three were lying on the floor. Gearheardt was at the bar, leaning on his elbows, facing the room. Marta was beside him on a barstool.

"Jack, don't believe a word of what they tell you," Gearheardt said. "I went to take a leak and when I came back, that one (he pointed to a man near his feet) had his hand on Marta's butt. That one (prone beneath a table) was trying to kiss her neck. And that one (sitting on the floor and shaking his head groggily) was . . . I'm not sure what he was doing, but he ran into one of my fists. I probably owe him an apology." He nodded to the man who weakly raised his hand in acknowledgement.

"Are you okay, Marta?" I asked.

She nodded.

The policeman began talking to the bartender and the Mayor introduced himself to Marta. I began to lecture Gearheardt on his seeming inability to be by himself for five minutes without creating an incident. It was more for the benefit of the local crew as I knew it was lost on Gearheardt.

The policeman turned to Gearheardt. "It is as you said, amigo. These two were what you say 'out of line.' We do not treat women so badly as this. You will accept my apologies?"

"No problemo, Capitan. I needed the exercise."

"Don't overdo it, Gearheardt. Just accept the apology and let's get out of here. I'll fill you in."

Marta, however, was heading out of the door on the arm of the mayor. He turned his head. "The Señorita requests to use the ladies room. My office has the best in the town. You may follow me there, Señors."

Marta looked back and smiled. Then they left the cantina.

The policeman was helping the men off the floor into chairs. Chastising them, but not aggressively.

"Jack," Gearheardt said, "have you noticed anything strange about Marta?"

"Such as?"

"What are the chances the Marta we know and love would let some hombre man-handle her at the bar? I'll answer for you. None. And she seems very quiet."

"Women have feelings too, Gearheardt," I said. He missed the sarcasm.

"Yeah, I guess so." He shook the outstretched hand of the bartender, then the policeman, and finally the stranger who had gotten in the way of his fist. Then we left to follow the mayor and Marta.

"Pretty impressive, Gearheardt. What did you hit them with? Or was it just your CIA hand to hand training?"

"It was my orphanage training, Jack. When you grow up in a state orphanage like I did, you get good with your fists. Or you become a girl. I didn't like dresses."

Gearheardt had once explained to me why he grew up in an orphanage and yet had parents. Something to do with them being paranoid about leaving him if they both died. If anyone but Gearheardt had told me that story, I would have doubted it.

We were in the square. Darker now and almost deserted. I was about two inches taller than Gearheardt, fifteen pounds heavier, and in pretty good shape. I couldn't imagine knocking out three men in one evening.

"So what did you find out?" Gearheardt asked.

"Crenshaw was here. Day before yesterday. He started some kind of a disturbance at the church, was arrested, and then the Cubans who turned him in bailed him out. He left town with them and then his burro came back the next day, ready for roasting. That's all I could find out."

"Have you ever thought about a career in plumbing, Jack? I mean, really, you spend time with the mayor and the police and come back with that story. Wouldn't you say there are a couple of things in there that might use a bit more explanation?"

"I was getting to the explanation when some gringo started a slug-fest in the cantina, Gearheardt."

"Jack, you would-of loved it. I came up behind the one guy and actually tapped him on the shoulder, like you see in the movies. He looked around and I just smashed his damn face. The other guy—"

"Spare me, Gearheardt. Look, the policeman told us that the Cubans and Crenshaw left up that road." I pointed north. "And the burro came back the next day. They couldn't have been too far away. Let's get Marta and we'll have Juan fire up the beast."

"Fine with me. But we've got to get back to Mexico City pretty soon." He stopped. "Why don't you get Marta and I'll round up Pedro. And by the way, you say Crenshaw was arrested? What the hell did he do?"

It was too complicated and Gearheardt would forget about it in ten minutes anyway. "He was charged with impersonating Jesus."

"That's against the law?"

"Go get the dune buggy, Gearheardt. We'll meet you back there. Stay out of fights."

The mayor was standing in front of his office, smoking a cheroot. He offered one to me and I declined. "Donde es—"

"Telefono," he responded. He made the sign of the telephone against his head to make sure I understood.

Marta came out of the building shortly thereafter.

"Okay?" I asked.

"Si, Jack. The mayor has a very nice ladies room. The best in the own."

She didn't mention the telefono.

"Paco says there's no way they could have gone to Tula. It's fifty or a hundred miles from here," Gearheardt said. "He's not too precise on distance issues."

We had joined Gearheardt and the driver at the dune buggy. It was getting cold, and the thought of bouncing over the ruts in the buggy was not attractive. The trail leading to Crenshaw was getting cold also.

"I don't like the sounds of all this, Gearheardt. Major Crenshaw is eccentric, but he's no dope. He came up here on a mission and now he's disappeared. Maybe we should try to get some help."

"From who, Jack? Crenshaw has evidently struck out on his own. No one at the embassy seems to know what he was doing. We don't know for sure what he was doing. And the local police don't seem excited about trying to find him. The only guys I know who will look for an errant CIA agent are probably Halcones. Do you want to call them?"

"Then we'll have to push on. I'm not going to just ignore the fact that he was meeting someone here and now is gone. And we're pretty sure it has to do with your damn Cuban mission."

Gearheardt hesitated. He looked at his watch and seemed to be doing a calculation. "Okay, he's one of us, after all. We'll try to see if we can find out something up the road. Seems a wild goat chase, but he's your boss."

"We need to take a leak before we get back in that monster," I said.

"I gave at the office, Jack." He began climbing into the dune buggy.

"I said we need to take a leak." I grabbed his arm.

Behind the buildings Gearheardt lit a cigarette. "So what's the message that you didn't want Paco to hear? Or is it Marta?"

"Marta made a phone call from the mayor's office."

"Probably called her mother. That's what you do at the drop of a hat, Jack."

"Oh, bullshit. Who would she be calling this time of night? She just seems to be acting strange. I can't quite put my finger on it, but—"

"I think she's in love." Gearheardt smiled. "With you."

"That wouldn't explain the phone call."

"Love makes you do things that can't be explained. I was once so in love I bought a trombone."

"You're hopeless, Gearheardt. Don't even try to explain that to me. I'm saying that we need to watch her. And I hate to say it, because if the truth be known I'm more than a little attracted to her. But we have a mission." I started back to the dune buggy. "Let's see if we can find Crenshaw. If the trail is a dead end, we'll go back to Mexico City."

We started back up the switchback, Gearheardt and his new pal, the driver, laughing and chatting as if we were headed to dinner and a movie. Near the top, the driver turned sharply right onto a track that could only be found by someone very familiar with it. It was dark in the trees, the dune buggy's lights illuminating the dense undergrowth and tall pines. The track, two ruts with worn down shrubs between them, looked well traveled. But leading . . .

"Gearheardt, does he have any idea where he's going," I shouted.

"He took some Cuban's in here a couple of days ago. Those were their Mercedes behind the cantina where he picked us up."

"I didn't see any Mercedes."

"They were up on blocks over by the garage, Jack. Paco's pals borrow parts off them while their owners are out here in the boonies."

"Wait a minute. You mean Paco, or Juan, knows where the Cubans are? Thanks for telling me. What were we doing in the town all that time? We could have just asked Juan to take us here."

"And miss the story of Crenshaw impersonating Jesus? That's the kind of valuable information that we couldn't do without."

"Gearheardt—"

Gearheardt turned around to me and leaned closer. "Jack, this guy may look like an old herdsman, but he knows more than he lets on. I had to get closer to him, you know. He's opening up now. He probably wanted to make sure we weren't going to shoot him when we get back to the cantina and find out the engine is gone out of our Mercedes."

"Does he know anything about Crenshaw?"

Gearheardt looked at the driver, who was staring intently at the track, and lowered his voice to just above the engine noise. "We're not that good of friends yet. He's probably angling for some dinero."

"Hell, offer him a hundred bucks."

"I offered him five hundred bucks. Your money of course. He says he's trying to remember." He laughed. "He said he'd shoot you for free. Thinks you're a typical American. But don't worry, he doesn't have a pistol. Asked to borrow mine."

I never knew when Gearheardt was serious.

Marta spoke up, touching my arm. "He is kidding you, Jack. The driver says no such thing."

Paco, Pedro, Juan brought the dune buggy to an abrupt halt that threw everyone forward. He shut off the engine and the lights.

"There," he said, pointing to the darkness.

"There?" Gearheardt and I said at the same time.

"In the trees there is a light. That is the camp of the Cubans. And there is a house not far away."

Squinting ahead, I *could* make out a faint light. I began climbing out of the vehicle. "Marta, you can wait with Juan. Gearheardt and I need to see what's up."

"She isn't Harriet Housewife Jack," Gearheardt said. "She's a professional, and we may need her." He was checking the clip in his pistol.

For some reason, I was hesitant to take Marta and I wasn't sure whether it was concern for her safety or a small nagging lack of trust.

"I will stay in the car," she said, making the decision for me. It only deepened my confusion over what was bothering her. This was not the naked lady in my apartment.

"Let's go, Brother Jack," Gearheardt said. He started off into the trees and I hurried after him before he was lost to me.

"We'll be back soon, Marta. If anything happens, you and Juan head back to town."

"Si, Jack."

On impulse, I leaned back into the dune buggy to kiss her. Spy or not, she was a desirable woman. Supporting my awkward position as I kissed her, my hand rested on her thigh and I felt the pistol she carried strapped to her leg. "Be careful, Jack," she said.

Gearheardt was waiting for me. "Should I go back and kiss Juan, Jack?" he asked. "He probably feels bad."

"Let's go, Gearheardt. I don't know what to think about Marta. But she is getting inside my head, I'll admit it."

He took off through the brush. "I hope she doesn't meet that woman kick boxer you dated in Thailand in there. That would scare the hell out of her."

"*You* dated her, Gearheardt. Not me." I struggled to keep moving forward; branches, shrubs, fallen logs and imagined fauna holding me back.

"You know, Jack," Gearheardt said, his voice low, "I'm not sure I ever told you, but there is something incredibly sexy about making love to a woman who could beat the crap out of you if you did something she didn't like. Kept me on my toes, I'll tell you."

"Could we just get focused on what we're doing? Let's get close enough to see the area and then lie low for a while to check things out."

We were slowly making headway as the light from what was now seen as a campfire grew brighter. Finally we stopped and dropped down, coming to within a few yards of the blazing campfire.

Three men sat on improvised seats, logs and stumps, around the fire. They were talking and laughing. Relaxed. Cubans from their appearance. Behind them another fifteen or twenty yards a cabin sat with its door open and lights on inside. I could tell there were men inside, but couldn't see them. Occasionally one of the men at the fire would yell and be answered from the cabin. My knees began to ache from the crouching position I was in.

Just as I was about to shift positions so that I could whisper to Gearheardt, the sound of singing came from the cabin. A familiar tune, but in Spanish. The men at the fire looked at one another and rolled their eyes.

I gave my pistol to Gearheardt. I didn't want to look threatening when I approached the Cubans. In theory, from what little Crenshaw had told me, these were 'good' Cubans. I didn't know how the scene in Calixtua fit into that, but then there were a lot of things I didn't know. And I wasn't finding out squatting in the bushes. I motioned for Gearheardt to stay put.

"Buenos noches, Señores," I said as I walked toward the fire.

"Buenos noches, Señor." None of the men rose. In fact none of them seemed very surprised that a gringo had appeared out of the darkness, miles from the nearest town.

The man who had said hello turned and yelled to the cabin. "Señor Armstrong es aqui." The singing stopped.

From the open door of the cabin, Major Crenshaw, a book in his hand, stepped out. He walked toward me and smiled weakly.

"Hello, Jack. I've been expecting you."

I'm sure I showed my surprise. "You mean you knew I would follow you? You sure didn't leave many clues."

Crenshaw frowned. "Follow me? No, the Cubans told me earlier this evening that you were coming." He looked back at the cabin.

Another man stood in the door. With the light behind him, his face was dark. A gold tooth caught the flash of the campfire when he smiled.

"Ola, Señor Armstrong. And where is your friend, Señor Gearheardt?"

"He couldn't make it. Trouble in Calixtua made it impossible for him to get away this evening." He hadn't mentioned Marta.

"Ess too bad. But under the circumstances it makes no difference. You will not be here for long." He went down the two steps in front of the cabin and came beside Major Crenshaw. "Our guest is glad to see you, but only for you to take a message."

"What *is* the story here, Major? Who are these guys? The good Cubans you were going to meet?"

"Well, I'm afraid not, Jack. They are Cubans, yes. But unfortunately—"

"You come in the cabin, Señor. There is something—"

Major Crenshaw turned rapidly. "I was *talking* to my associate. Please don't interrupt me again. We will return to the cabin in a moment." Obviously Crenshaw was not broken. "Where were we, Jack? Oh yes, these are not the Cubans that I set out to meet. I have no idea who they are."

"If you are finished, Major, you will come to the cabin. And you also Señor Armstrong."

"We will be there shortly, Señor." He put his arm around my shoulder and led me a few feet away. "Jack," he said, "bit of a mess here. These guys are not who I was supposed to meet. They convinced the sheriff—"

"Police Captain Malo."

"Yes, but how did you . . . never mind. Anyway he released me into the hands of this gang."

"You're sure these are not the—"

"When we arrived at the cabin, there were four bodies piled in front of the door. Shot through the head. They were Cuban."

"Nice guys. So why don't we get the hell out of here? I have a *friend* looking out for us." I looked at him and rolled my eyes toward the spot

I assumed Gearheardt was hiding. "To tell the truth, these guys don't look all that sharp. And what was the singing all about?"

"I was conducting a church service. These men may be killers, but they're Catholic."

I was not sufficiently theologically gifted to respond to that. "So they won't let us leave?"

The gold tooth answered that. "Asshole, (I assumed he meant me) you and the major get inside. We will talk there." He was carrying a Swedish K, a very mean machine gun pistol. Highly lethal if he knew how to use it.

"That's Julio," Crenshaw said. "He's very neurotic."

I stepped through the door and saw half a dozen men sitting in folding chairs in a circle. A fireplace warmed the room. I walked to it and turned to warm my backside. I assumed that Gearheardt had watched the action and was aware of the serious weaponry the Cubans had.

As Crenshaw passed Julio he was hit on the shoulder by the Swedish K. "The Pope can be wrong. He is infallible but he can still make the mistake."

"That wasn't my point at all, Señor Stupido," Crenshaw retorted, rubbing his shoulder. "You are serving that Godless Castro. That can hardly be a moral basis for your ridiculous position on the Holy Father."

One of the men sitting in a folding chair smiled and nodded affirmatively. Julio looked at him and the man turned away. Julio went outside after barking a grumpy 'stay here' in the direction of Crenshaw and me.

Crenshaw made his way to the fireplace, joining me with his back to the fire. "The man is hopeless," he said. "The Catholic priesthood in Cuba must be run by idiots."

"Major, I would imagine that it's a little tough to get good priests in Havana these days." As soon as I said it I realized that I did not have the slightest idea what I was talking about and that once again I was surrounded by mad men. Crenshaw was evidently the new parish priest of this outlaw Cuban murdering gang. Who, I assumed, also had something to do with the upcoming (unless I stopped it) assassination of the president of Mexico. Father Crenshaw had his work cut out for him.

Although they were all armed, the bible class sitting around the room did not look particularly deadly. If Crenshaw had not told me they had murdered the four Cubans he was originally set to meet, I would have expected to break out the hymnals again and get on with the meeting. I assumed that Crenshaw, now strangely silent and contemplative, knew that Gearheardt was about. Even with the overwhelming odds against him, I had no doubt that Gearheardt would devise a plan to 'rescue' us and we could get on our way back to Mexico City. At least the mission to rescue Crenshaw had been a success.

Sounds of laughter came from outside. No one seemed concerned that I moved away from the fireplace toward the door.

Gearheardt was now sitting with the men at the bonfire. He had evidently just finished a seriously funny story. The men were laughing uproariously. Even Julio was laughing, pointing at Gearheardt.

Gearheardt saw me and stood up. "Jack, there you are. And hello Major Crenshaw."

Crenshaw had come up by my side. "Hello, Mr. Gearheardt," he said.

"A little problem on the rescue issue, Jack. I must have fallen asleep and these gentlemen relieved me of our weapons. Sorry about that." He smiled.

"So you thought you would entertain them with a few jokes?" My voice shook with fear or anger. I wanted to shoot Gearheardt.

"Just the one about the donkey in Tijuana. See, he was gay and the club—"

"Damn it, Gearheardt, you were supposed to watch my back." I trailed off, realizing that arguing with Gearheardt was pointless and unprofessional.

Julio finished wiping his eyes with his bandana. He was still chuckling as he stuffed it back into his pocket. He turned to me.

"Now we will tell you, as you say in your country, the cow will eat the cabbage how."

"In our country we have no idea what that means," Gearheardt, the jerk, said.

After a mumbled conference between Julio and one of his henchmen, he looked back at us. "It means that we will tell you exactly what you will do and there will be no discussion. Comprende?"

Gearheardt, Crenshaw and I looked at one another. No one seemed to have a better plan.

Crenshaw, who was after all senior, finally said, "We will listen to what you have to say. I seriously doubt if we will have no discussion. We're not exactly—"

The Swedish K caught him across the face before he could get his hands up. He fell backward, blood already streaming down his face as he hit the ground.

"This is not a joke, Jesus-man," Julio said.

I knelt and wrapped my handkerchief around Crenshaw's head and helped him set up. He was immediately alert and I didn't think any permanent damage was done.

"Well, you certainly have *my* attention," Gearheardt said. "What is it that we are supposed to listen to and not discuss?"

Julio looked at Gearheardt for a moment. Evidently trying to figure out if he was being made fun of. He adjusted his machine gun and stepped closer to Gearheardt.

"You and Señor Armstrong will leave us. Now."

"You drive a hard bargain, Julio (he pronounced it with a hard J). No discussion, right?" He looked at me with that smirk I wanted to kick. "Damn, Jack. Are you up for leaving or should we just draw the line in the sand? I kind of like it here."

I spoke out of the corner of my mouth. "I'm sure there's more, Gearheardt. Could you please just try not to make the situation worse than it is?"

"I'm trying, Jack, but I would like to shove that gun up his butt before we leave." He reached for Crenshaw's arm.

"He stays with us, Señor Wise-guy." Julio stepped forward and kicked Gearheardt's hand away from Crenshaw.

Gearheardt's head was still down, but I could see him biting his lip. He straightened up slowly. "Señor Julio, don't press your luck." He took a step closer to the Cuban.

The Swedish K blast at Gearheardt's feet was incredibly loud. And unfortunately hit one of the other Cubans in the foot. He jumped up and began dancing around the fire, holding his shoe and yelling. The other Cubans, including those who emptied out of the house and drew weapons, started peering at the surrounding forest, looking for the attackers.

Julio looked chagrined but tried to pull it off. "Let that be a warning to you, Señor Gearheardt. We mean the business."

"I dare you to shoot someone else, Julio. Go on, if you really mean the business." Gearheardt's contemptuous laugh even made *me* mad at him and I was on his side.

After a moment the commotion settled, the wounded man only whimpered, and the Cubans were vying to stay farthest out of the line of fire of Julio, who put the gun to Crenshaw's temple and shoved hard enough to cause the major to wince and pull away.

"You are going to make sure that the assassination takes place, Señor Gearheardt. You will not stop the assassin and make yourself the hero of Mexico. You are thinking that the Mexicans will kick the Cubans out of the country. Yes? But that will not happen. We will take the government. The blame will be on the CIA, and my country will be the hero in South America."

"Oh yes, the old 'kill the president and blame it on the Americans trick.' Oldest one in the book."

"You are not the funny man that you think you are, Señor. If the President is not killed, then the Jesus-man (he shoved his gun at Crenshaw's head again) will be tortured and killed."

"You are assuming I give a shit," Gearheardt said.

Crenshaw looked up and smiled at Gearheardt. Blood ran down his face. "The feeling's mutual."

"Thanks," Gearheardt said.

Julio looked confused. He swung his pistol toward my head. "Then I will kill *him*."

"He's the assassin," Gearheardt said. "That would gum up the works for sure."

Gearheardt laughed as if that would be unfortunate and then went on. "And he is also the only one, thanks to the Major here, that is authorized to be near the President, and also carry a weapon."

"You think I am a fool, Señor Gearheardt?" Julio asked. There was a threat in his voice. His men shuffled uneasily away from the area behind Gearheardt.

"I think everyone is a fool until they prove it," Gearheardt replied.

"Then you are not afraid to die? Is that it, Señor Gearheardt?" Julio seemed to be searching for a level from which to confront Gearheardt.

"Being afraid to die is not rational," Gearheardt said. "I will either have an afterlife or I won't. Assuming my afterlife is not hell, and I can't believe that it *would* be, then its heaven or nothing. So those choices are both pretty acceptable. As to missing the life I would have had had I not died—"

"Which you are about to do," Julio growled.

"Hear me out. You asked if I were afraid to die. So the life that I would be missing after I died could only be compared to heaven. I have never heard anyone describe heaven as 'not quite as good as life.' So I think the answer to your question '*Am I not afraid to die?*' is yes. I am not afraid to die. Your double negative makes it awkward to make my position clear. That's why I took the time to explain the logic behind my answer."

Crenshaw loosened the makeshift bandage around his head and wiped his face with it. "I'm afraid there are a few holes in your logic, Gearheardt. Not the least of which is the assumption that you are *not* going to hell."

Julio tried again. "We will do my first thing." He pointed the weapon at Crenshaw. "He stays here. You and Señor Armstrong will go make the assassination happen."

"I think your Catholic fire and brimstone crap is a bit out of date, Major," Gearheardt said. "You might not know the Internecine Creed, but—"

"The *what?*"

"Exactly. So how do you expect me to take your ramblings on the life hereafter seriously."

"I know the Internecine Creed, Señor." It was one of the Cubans standing by the fire, his hand not holding the Uzi stretched in the air. He seemed to be asking permission to recite it.

"Good man," Gearheardt said. He rolled his eyes and shrugged at me.

Crenshaw straightened up on wobbly knees. "By God, I'll not have you mocking the Catholic—"

"Enough!" Julio unloaded another short burst from his machine gun pistol, scattering the Cubans. This time he had fired in the air. "If you are not worth killing." He pointed at Crenshaw. "And you are the assassin." Me. "Then I will kill you all. We don't need no Norte Americano to do our job for Cuba."

I was almost on his side now after listening to Gearheardt goad Crenshaw with his double talk. But not quite. And I sensed Gearheardt was not serious but just trying again to gain control of the situation.

"Jack, help me get the mackerel snapper into the cabin before we leave." Gearheardt put Crenshaw's arm around his shoulders and I did the same from the other side.

"I haven't heard that one since I was a kid, Mr. Gearheardt. Mackerel snapper. Rather childish, isn't it?" Crenshaw winced as he spoke, his legs were still wobbly.

"I've been called that a few times." Gearheardt said. "Didn't bother me."

We reached the doorway and I fell back to let them through the door. Inside, Gearheardt guided Crenshaw to a couch and dropped him.

"So you're Catholic?"

"Fordham University. 1963," Gearheardt said.

Crenshaw threw back his head and laughed. "A bloody Jesuit. I might have known."

"Gents, before you start speaking Latin and swinging around those little silver softballs with holes in them, might we get back to a discussion of what we do. Julio will be in here in a minute."

"Nothing to plan, Jack," Crenshaw said. He sat forward. "Obviously you're not going to shoot the President. And if the Cuban—what was his name, Victor?—gets close, you shoot him. Don't worry about me. I'll have these boys well in hand."

"I'm sure you will, but you can count on us giving you some help. Somehow," I said.

Gearheardt was thinking, his eyes narrowed at Crenshaw. "I'm curious about a couple of things, Major. First of all—"

There was no 'first of all.' Julio and two of his gang clomped into the cabin. "Get out. Get out before I change my mind and shoot you all," he said. He grabbed me by the elbow and turned me around. He started to grab Gearheardt who looked back at him. Julio dropped his hand back to his weapon. "Go," he said.

A delay in our leaving while Gearheardt insisted and convinced the Cubans to give our weapons back. "The paperwork involved in losing your weapon is life-threatening," he said. "Do you ever have paperwork in Cuba?"

All of the Cubans wanted to share a paperwork story with Gearheardt.

"Yep, yep, heard 'em all. Same thing in the U.S." he said. "Look, keep most of the bullets. We just need a few in case we run into wolves or something on the way back down the mountain."

They actually gave us back a few bullets.

"Gracias. Gracias. You guys stay warm up here. There's a burro roast in Calixtua tomorrow if you get hungry." We were making our way through the small crowd, past the fire, in the general direction we had come from.

"What's this about a burro roast?" Crenshaw shouted from back in the cabin.

Gearheardt smiled at me. "Let these Cubans explain it to him."

We were back in the forest. Gearheardt seemed fairly confident in our path. I was lost. It seemed like hours ago when we had been moving slowly toward the Cuban camp.

"They'll take care of Crenshaw," Gearheardt said. "Some decent guys."

"How is it that you always get along so well with the enemy, Gearheardt? Those guys aren't decent guys. Their murdering Cubans."

"Jack," Gearheardt said, continuing to walk and let branches snap back into my face, "in college I met a lot of smart people. They led with their head. In Asia, I met a lot of horny soldiers. They led with their dicks. You see, in politics, you lead with your asshole. So the troops aren't bad guys. They're just led by an asshole. That's why politics is the ugliest of human activity."

"Elegantly put, Gearheardt. But I do see your point."

"When I meet folks, I usually can type them as head, dick or asshole pretty quickly."

"I'm sure they'll be rewriting the sociology textbooks soon. But my question is, what the hell is our plan now?"

We were almost to the road and a small light was dancing in the dune buggy. Gearheardt held up his hand and we slowed, creeping forward.

It turned out to be our driver, using a small flashlight, trying to see up the dress of the sleeping Marta. He saw us approach and came to us.

"Señorita has a pistola," he complained.

"And she will use it if she catches you looking up her dress, Pablo. Let's get going back down the hill. Try to get your piece of junk past the turtle mark on the speedometer this time."

I jumped in the back, waking Marta and warning her to hang on.

"Where are we going? What's happening?" she asked sleepily while the driver was removing the rocks from behind the wheels.

I looked at Gearheardt and saw him shake his head.

"Don't try to talk, Marta. I would suggest you find something pretty solid to hang on to. If that's an appendage of Jack, that's okay. But I've challenged the old man to get us down this hill pretty damn quick. It might be a wild ride."

CHAPTER FOURTEEN

WHY DOESN'T CONFUSION MEAN 'WITH FUSION' IN MEXICO? SO I GUESS WE WOULD NOW BE UNFUSIONED

I have never put myself in a barrel—along with sharp objects, a scream-ing woman and a laughing hyena—and gone over Niagara Falls. Now I wouldn't have to. I had gone down a hill in the dune buggy. The only respites came when the old man missed a turn and ran off the road, slamming us to a halt. It is impossible to destroy someone by focusing all of your hate onto a single object. The old man still lives, res judicata.

The small village surrounding the cantina where Marta hired the dune buggy was sleeping. Gearheardt surveyed the Mercedes and decided to forego trying to recover the non-essentials. He dispatched the old man to re-obtain the back seat and the steering wheel. The local populace were not thieves. They borrowed items from the cars left in their midst, rather than charge for parking.

While Gearheardt and I watched the Mercedes be reassembled, Marta went in search of a bathroom.

"She's hardly spoken a word, Gearheardt. You know what I think?"

"She called the Cubans to tell them we were coming?"

"Exactly. You figured that out too?"

"I know she is . . . different. I liked the old Marta quite frankly. The naked one."

"Something symbolic there?" I smiled, and Gearheardt smiled back.

"But there's a more puzzling aspect of our situation, Jack. That has to do with Crenshaw."

"We'll figure out a way to save him. I don't think the Cubans are all that anxious to kill him anyway."

"That's not what I meant. Think about it. Crenshaw seemed to know more than *we* do about what's going on with the assassination. How could that be?"

"Maybe the Pygmy or one of the guys—"

"I have to run through the possibilities, Jack. Something's not right." He smiled over my shoulder. "Here comes our little mole."

Given the hour, there were limited cars for Gearheardt to run off the road on the way back into Mexico City, so the trip was calm. The streets were dark until we got into the main part of the city. The only people we saw were street cleaners and Gearheardt made it a point to wave at every one of them. Marta slept and Gearheardt and I talked mostly about old times, Vietnam and Laos. I tried to pump him about the time between when I'd thought he was killed in Laos and when he showed up at my office at the embassy. He didn't offer much information besides accounts of the usual Gearheardt romances.

I sensed there was a story he wasn't telling me. Once he started a lurid tale about a nurse, then quickly retreated, saying "Oh I guess that was when I was still in Air America." But I knew all about his time in

Air America, and that story wasn't in it. And once, the scariest time of our drive back to his palace, Gearheardt didn't talk at all. He looked straight ahead over the steering wheel, his eyes unfocused, both hands gripping the wheel. I felt very strongly that he was someplace else. Finally I heard him let out a low breath.

"You're a good guy, Jack," he said.

"You too, Gearheardt."

"No, I mean it. I can count on you, Jack. How many people can you say that about? It means a lot to me."

"You're not about to propose to me are you, Gearheardt?" I asked.

He grunted. "Just remember that when . . ." He stopped.

"When what?"

"When . . . those fucking cows decide how to eat the cabbage." He slapped the steering wheel and clamped his jaws tight. We drove in silence a few blocks.

Then he was Gearheardt again. As we approached a major glorieta, a large statue in the center, he said, "Hold on, Jack."

He sped up into the circle accelerating until the Mercedes was in a power slide, almost sideways, all the way around the circle.

"Holy shit, Gearheardt. Give me some warning next time." I looked back at Marta. She was still asleep on the back seat.

"It's a lot dicier at noon when there are people and cars all over the place," he said, straightening out the car onto Reforma Boulevard and grinning like a possum. "Damn people running everywhere. And boy, are they pissed."

"I can imagine." I noticed he was not turning to Chapultepec Castle, his new manor. "Where are you heading?"

"Look up on the hill. The palace is lit up like a Bangkok whorehouse. We didn't leave it that way. I'm thinking I need a new H.Q. I'll drop you off at your apartment, Jack. Once you're in, I think you're safe. Then I need to do some checking on my network. See where we are." He stopped in front of my building. No one was in sight.

Before I got out of the car, I nodded back at the sleeping Marta. "What about her? I think maybe we just ask her what the hell she's up to." My voice was just above a whisper.

Gearheardt thought for a moment. "I don't think so, Jack. Let's see what she does. She's supposed to be helping you with the plans to get Victor to kill El Presidente. She may be a lot more valuable to us if she doesn't suspect we suspect her."

"I need to talk to you about all that. The Cubans obviously know something is up."

"Think about it, Jack. I ask you to kill the president. Crenshaw asks you to protect him. The Cubans want him dead for their own purposes. The pygmy comes down from Langley to hit you. But it was his plan in the first place."

"His plan?"

"The idea of setting up the Cubans so that we have an excuse to take out Castro." He glanced back at Marta. "Step outside a minute, Jack."

Outside the car he lit a cigarette and leaned on the front fender. He was biting his lower lip. Thinking.

"So what's the point of your deliberation?" I asked him.

"I just wanted to smoke a cigarette. The guy I borrowed the car from doesn't like people to smoke in it."

I looked at the Mercedes. It had no wheel covers, the hood ornament was missing, the trunk was scratched and bent where someone had tried to pry it open. "He might not notice the smoke smell, Gearheardt. But why the evasion all of a sudden? You were about to speculate as to what the hell is going on."

"Let me noodle a while on it, Jack. I don't want you to worry unnecessarily. Something's rotten in Bismark."

"Denmark."

"Who?"

I was going to get no more information out of Gearheardt at the moment.

"Wake up Marta and get upstairs. At least you don't have to worry about getting her out of her clothes. She is one hell of a date."

I opened the door to the backseat.

"And Jack, let's just keep on the plan for now. You get Victor lined up. I've got my good Cubans coming in. You make sure Victor doesn't shoot anybody."

He sat back down in the driver's seat. "I got to check with the whores."

I raised back up quickly from where I was leaning in to raise Marta. I bumped my head and it hurt like hell. "The *who*?"

Gearheardt started the Mercedes. "Crap," he said. "I didn't mean for you to hear that. I'll tell you all about it tomorrow."

Marta was awake and climbing out onto the street.

"It's just the financing source for the operation, Jack. The International Sisterhood of Hookers is financing this for the Agency."

Inside my apartment, Marta took off her clothes and went into the bathroom. I stepped onto the small balcony and signaled to Gearheardt that we were safely inside. The Mercedes burned away from the curb. As it turned the corner, I noticed for the first time that it had diplomatic license plates.

"Jack," Marta said behind me, "I am going into your bed. I cannot sleep on the sofa tonight. I hope you will not mind." She disappeared into the bedroom.

I got a glass of wine and sat down on the sofa, resting my head against the back. Marta was either drugged, or using fatigue to avoid talking to me. But she was in my bed. A sense of mission told me that it would not be a good idea to join her.

Touching base with the embassy did seem like a good idea. Fortunately the night duty officer was my pal Eric. When he came to the phone, he was out of breath.

"Geez, Jack, the kid had to come down and get me out of the com room. Sorry it took so long. You okay?"

"I'm fine, Eric. I just wanted to find out what's happening around the shop. Any news, rumors, death threats against me?"

"Nothing quite that drastic, but you *are* in deep shit with the Ambassador."

"Do you have any idea what's that all about?" I wondered how much the Ambassador knew about Crenshaw's 'mission,' the Pygmy, and all the related issues.

"I know exactly what it's about. He told your secretary to bring your files to his office. She checked with me, luckily, and just took him the non-classified crap."

"And that pissed him off?"

"No. But just before he left the office tonight, he evidently opened a box that had some kind of animal tail in it. Stunk to high heaven and the flies were swarming in his office. Do you know why she took a donkey tail to the Ambassador?"

"Burro."

"Okay, you do know."

"Heard anything about Crenshaw?"

"I was hoping you knew something. The guys around the shop are not sure whether to be worried or not. He's kind of a loose canon."

"Tell 'em not to worry right now. I talked to him. We may need your help, but at the moment we're trying to straighten out a mission that is kind of screwed up."

"We?"

"Gearheardt."

"Say no more. That SOB comes up in every conversation around here. Did you know he was reportedly living in Chapultepec Palace?"

"Why not? The Marines took it a few years back, you know. Anyway, Eric, do a couple of things for me. First, try to get a couple of guys out to my neighborhood. I want to make sure no one comes into my apartment building unexpectedly, if you get my drift. Second, can you find out if there is such a thing as the International Sisterhood of Prostitutes?"

"The ISP? What do you know about that, Jack?" Eric's voice had changed.

"I can't talk about it right now. Jesus, I can't believe Crenshaw would talk to you about it."

"Why? It may be important, Eric. You know you can trust me."

"Let me just pass on the rumor, okay? The rumor is that the CIA has been recruiting prostitutes for years. Now the organization has gotten bigger than the CIA itself. And, this is just a rumor, Jack, they're starting to influence the Agency policies."

"*Whores are running the CIA?*"

"You said it, Jack. Not me. But don't tell me you didn't know anything about it. It's your pal who started the whole thing."

I certainly didn't have to ask who he meant by 'my pal.'

"Anything else you can tell me?"

"About ISP? Not much. I know they pretty well run Hong Kong and Bangkok. At least that's what I've heard. But I'm telling you more than I really know. I've just heard things."

"Eric, one last thing. Would you tell Juanita to meet me tomorrow? Say, ten o'clock at the Natural History Museum. Have her bring any traffic that I should see."

"Why don't you come in yourself? As far as I know you're not persona non-grata around here. The Ambassador just wants to ask you a few questions."

"And I would not have answers. What about the preparations for Cinco de Mayo? Any word there?"

"Glad you asked. I had almost forgotten. Davis has everybody assigned that day. None of us are anywhere near the reviewing stand. Except you're not on the list."

"And Davis is who?"

"Just came in from Langley. Sits in Crenshaw's office and gives orders. We assume that he's in charge while Crenshaw is wherever he is. Not a bad guy, really. Runs around with a midget, but we all have our quirks. Jack, I gotta go. I'm looking through the traffic and I've left the com room open. Your jacket's ready by the way."

"Thanks, Eric. Any luck with finding the Catholic Cubans?"

The agent laughed. "I haven't been able to get to a church yet. Good luck." He hung up.

I needed to think, but I needed sleep even more. I lay down and pulled the serape over me. The faint smell of Marta's perfume was still on it. I fought the urge to go into my bedroom.

I dreamed that naked women were running in the halls of CIA headquarters and Latin dictators and U.S. congressmen were being whipped and humiliated by Amazon like creatures. It frustrated me that I couldn't find Gearheardt. But I could hear his maniacal laughter. In the DCI's office Marta sat behind the desk in a tailored business suit. She was incredibly sexy.

CHAPTER FIFTEEN

GEARHEARDT THE HUMANITARIAN

A timid knock on my door brought me to a level just above sleeping. Another knock, louder this time, got me awake. I found my pistol, checked to see if it was loaded. It was six o'clock in the morning according to my entry hall clock.

"Que es?" I asked through the door.

"Rodrigo, Señor."

I let him inside, shaking his hand, and looked out into the hall before I closed the door behind him.

"I am sorry to bother you at this hour, Jack. But I have information that you should have."

"Sure, sit down, Rodrigo. I'll make some coffee."

"I'll make it, Jack. Buenos dias, Señor." It was Marta. I caught a glimpse of her as she went through the kitchen door.

Rodrigo was smiling big teeth. "She has no clothes?"

"A long story, Rodrigo. Let's talk about that later." We moved into the living room and sat down. I snapped on a lamp and saw Rodrigo looking at my 'nest' of couch pillow and the serape. "Marta," I yelled out, "remember the pajama top agreement."

She answered as she entered the room with two glasses of orange juice. "Of course I remember, Jack. But we have the guest."

If Rodrigo didn't have a heart attack now, he was missing a good chance. Marta was leaning toward him, her luscious breasts swinging precariously near the brimming glass of juice she was offering.

"Muchas gracias," Rodrigo managed to get out. "I am Rodrigo."

"I am Marta, Jack's friend."

I thought the last was superfluous.

"Marta, Rodrigo and I need to talk for a few minutes. Maybe you would like a shower."

Rodrigo sat immobile. I think he could not bring himself, or perhaps trust himself, to reach a hand toward Marta's breasts to get the orange juice. His molars were still exposed. I grabbed the juice and sat both of the glasses on the coffee table.

"Thank you, Marta. We won't be long."

She smiled and left the room.

"The coffee will be ready soon, Jack." She seemed her old self and I wondered abut that.

Rodrigo was shaken but had not stirred. I prompted him. "So you have some important information, Rodrigo."

"There is nothing like the beautiful woman to stop the mind. Don't you think so, Señor Jack?"

"It starts you thinking with another part of your brain, yes. But you didn't come here to discuss beautiful women, Rodrigo. Are you in danger? Are the Colombians after you?"

"Not to worry, Señor. My friends in Mexico are far greater than the Colombians. Yes, I am careful for my family. But we keep the eye on the Colombians." He finally picked up his juice and drained the glass in one swallow. He might have been hoping for another serving. "And this is what I tell you we have found."

He grew serious and leaned back in the chair. "You and me, amigo, we chase the Colombian bomber. The men, boys more, that smuggle the bombs and turn the Mexican students to terrorists. The American students, also."

"And you have done well, Rodrigo. The American government is very grateful. Certainly I am very grateful and I enjoy working with you."

"The same, Señor. But what I am to tell you is this, the Colombians do not care about the bombs and the terrorist training. I am thinking to myself 'why would the Colombians risk anything to hurt Mexico. Or the United States. They are not communists in Colombia. They do not play with the Russians. So why?'"

"And what did yourself conclude?"

"It is the drugs. The bombs are nothing. The network is being set up to sell the drugs. In Mexico but mainly in the United States. This is my thinking."

I sat forward. Drug trafficking was just becoming an issue in the Agency. Rumors that the CIA had been involved in the drug business in Southeast Asia turned the company upside down for a while. The Church Commission had found no evidence of a program that involved the CIA in drugs, but we were all aware of the growing importance of the traffic. "So the Colombians are getting the students hooked on drugs? To create customers?"

"The Colombians are getting the students hooked on the drug *money*, Señor Jack. There is no cure for this addiction."

"I'm not sure what you mean, Rodrigo. Excuse me, but how do you see this working?"

"The Colombians can supply a few bombs, some training, some weapons, si? And the students, they are happy and feel like the revolutionary. But then how can they pay for the weapons when the Colombians present the bill? As you say 'the Colombians are not in the business for their health.'"

"So they get them to smuggle drugs."

"Exactlemente."

"I'll have to think about this, Rodrigo. Drug running is not really my business. But I'm not sure who should handle this at the moment. Can you tell me your sources? How we would get more information?"

"Unfortunately, I cannot tell you. But it is the good source. My cousin is involved."

"Sorry to hear that. But you know the information is reliable, right?"

"My cousin is a bad man. When I was the policeman, I ran into him many times. I can always find him. And he will tell us more when we talk to him with the battery attached." He smiled.

"Yes, I imagine he would."

It was beginning to get light in the apartment. I needed to get working on a plan to get Crenshaw back. Drug runners might have to wait. I was tempted, but something kept me from asking Rodrigo for help in rescuing Crenshaw. Was it something Gearheardt said?

"Rodrigo, do you need anything from me right now? I will have to get back to you about the Colombians. Can we meet after Cinco de Mayo? Is there anything urgent?"

"Nothing urgent, Señor Jack. I have my friends and my sons working on finding all of the Colombians in Mexico City. I have friends at the police who are also helping. They will tell us the drug people in Mexico City also. I do not trust the list, but it will help."

"Good. Let's find out who is involved as much as possible. In the meantime, I will find out who in the U.S. government should be working with us. I think this is important information, Rodrigo. Thanks for coming to see me."

I rose from the couch, needing to take a shower and change out of the clothes that Gearheardt had loaned me what seemed days ago.

Rodrigo didn't get up. "Señor, you had mentioned about the coffee."

If he hadn't smiled and looked toward the bedroom I might have believed he just really wanted some coffee.

"I'll see if it's ready."

"No, I can wait a while longer. Perhaps I can tell you more about the students we found at the library. The ones who the Halcones took." He looked at the bedroom again.

I sat back down. I had almost forgotten those poor bastards.

"What do you know?"

"They have been taken to the border and made to swim the Rio Grande. They are lucky they were able to swim. Or walk. My friend, Jaime, the Halcone, said they were questioned and knew very little. They wanted to go to Cuba and cut cane with Castro. Their families were wealthy and sent a great deal of money to the Halcones so that their sons could swim the Rio Grande. Little fish, Señor Jack. But the Colombiano, he is still in the cage, singing."

Marta appeared from the well-watched bedroom and signaled she would bring coffee. The unbuttoned pajama top she was wearing nicely covered her back and arms. Rodrigo looked back at me and grinned. "We get coffee now," he said. He leaned toward me and spoke, sotto voce. "Señor Jack, she is wearing pistola here." He pointed to his inner thigh.

I matched his sotto voce. "She is crazy, Rodrigo. When she returns, you must remember to look only at her face. If she sees that you are looking at her . . . her woman parts, she will shoot you."

Rodrigo's grinning mouth snapped shut. He looked toward the kitchen doorway and then back at me. "Perhaps I should go. My son is waiting for me downstairs."

He rose as Marta carried in a tray with coffee. The open pajama top made her look even more naked if possible. Rodrigo raised his chin to a point where he had to look down his nose to see Marta's face. He was practically facing the ceiling. "Gracias, Señorita. I am afraid that I must go."

A noise from the front door caused the three of us to turn. Unmistakable sounds of someone trying to jimmy the lock had us pull three pistols out.

"Hey, coffee," Gearheardt said as he burst open the door. "Hello, Rodrigo. Long time no see. Marta, gorgeous outfit. A good night's sleep always helps. Jack, aren't those my clothes you're wearing?" He hung his coat on the hook.

"Well, looks like pistola inspection. Jack, yours could use some oil. Rodrigo, is that rust I see? Marta, you have . . . well I'm not speculating on what you have on your barrel." He took a cup of coffee from the tray and turned to shake Rodrigo's hand.

"Ola, Rodrigo. How's the detective work?"

"Señor Gearheardt, the last time I saw you I say that I will kill you next time, no?" But he was smiling.

"Just a misunderstanding, amigo. Just a misunderstanding." He stepped past me and plopped down onto the couch. "Pardon me, Jack. I didn't make it to bed last night."

Marta went to the kitchen for more coffee. I noticed that Rodrigo had forgotten the curse of only looking at her face. It made me slightly angry although I had no right to be.

When the four of us were comfortably sipping coffee, I turned to Gearheardt. "So how do you know Rodrigo? I mean other than me talking about him."

"Rodrigo helped me, although he didn't know it at the time, to set up the network in Mexico City before I contacted you, Jack. Over a year ago."

"You mean you were coming down here for a *year* before you called me? Damn it, Gearheardt, that's unforgivable."

"What difference did it make if you thought I was dead a few more months, Jack? I knew where you were. Knew you were safe and gainfully employed. I didn't want you worried about my networking problems."

"The union," Rodrigo said. He didn't sound as if he liked the word.

"Yes, the union. You probably don't know this, Jack, but I worked for a humanitarian organization that was trying to unionize the prostitutes. You know, just give them some bargaining power with the johns and pimps. Rodrigo had some buddies who didn't think that was a very good idea." He tipped his cup toward Rodrigo.

"You mean the IS—" I started to say.

"Yes, the Eyesis organization."

The way he said it told me that Rodrigo didn't need to know about the International Sisterhood of Prostitutes. But then I caught a look between Gearheardt and Marta that I almost wished I hadn't seen.

Marta? Damn, that might explain a lot of things. Not all things, but some. I tried not to stare at her.

Rodrigo was saying ". . . so my friend was telling me that a gringo was in Las Palomas. Upstairs with ten women. And when he finish, he ordered ten more women. He pays for all of them. And they come down with the smile and arranging clothes. But *twenty women*. My friend call me to tell me that he wanted to kill the gringo, but only if it was okay with the policia."

"You know, Rodrigo, that's a system that we could use in the states. You call the police before you shoot someone. Just check out their reaction. Kind of like filing a flight plan." There was an edge to Gearheardt's voice.

Rodrigo shrugged. "It's my job, Señor. I keep the peace. The owner was a business man. You cause the trouble in his business." He paused and looked at Gearheardt. "When we came to keep the peace, the owner he has disappeared. Maybe you know where he goes?"

"He was beating the girls when I found him, Rodrigo. If you want to find him, you should look where they employ eunuchs."

"So you are CIA also?" Rodrigo said, nodding toward me.

Gearheardt shook a cigarette from a rumpled pack. "Lots of men have tried to find that out, amigo. A lot of men tried. A lot of men died." He lit the cigarette and blew the smoke up away from his face. "Sounds like a song doesn't it?"

Rodrigo finished his coffee with a slurp and then rose. "Jack, you will call me after Cinco de Mayo. We will find the drug people." He nodded at Marta, taking a good look as he did, and left.

"He's not a bad guy, Gearheardt," I said. "He's been helping me with the Colombian bombers, who now turn out to be drug runners."

"I'm sure he's a *good guy*, Jack. Just don't miss a payday with him." He paused and looked at the door where Rodrigo had just disappeared. "Before they threw him off the police force, he worked the prostitute market with a pretty firm hand, shall we say. I'm surprised he still needs money."

Marta rose suddenly, gathered the juice glasses and coffee cups and went to the kitchen. We heard her start to wash the dishes.

"I'm using him to find the guys supplying the money and weapons to kill Americans, Gearheardt," I said.

"I'm not saying you shouldn't. Just remember what bastards some of these guys are." He put out his cigarette. "I was recruiting in South America last year. These *business men* took me to a place where we watched a teenage boy attack a teenage girl in a cage. The *winner* got to be free. Sent back to his or her village. She was a virgin. He was hopped up on drugs. The men thought it was hilarious that the girl won."

"So she got to go free?"

Gearheardt's laugh wasn't funny. "Sure, Jack. Some of the men used her and then she was to be sold to a whorehouse somewhere. You knew that didn't you? You just always like to hope for the best for people, Jack. I know better and they say I'm the one who's nuts."

"Where was this?"

"I'd rather not say, Jack. They kind of think I might know something about the three missing businessmen. The ones who took me to the show."

"You—"

"Jack. You know me better than that. I got the boys drunk. Stripped them naked and took them to a whorehouse near the coast. I might have mentioned to the girls who they were and what they had done. That's all. I think the girls took them swimming. Probably had a hell of a time." He smiled at the thought.

"You know why I like whores so well, Jack. Aside from the obvious. They are in the only business in the world that has any honor in it. A whore says, 'I'm going to fuck you and take your money. I will humiliate you and force you to come down to the scum bucket level I live on. In the end you will feel like you've been screwed, you'll be poorer and feel like a dope. So come on in.' How many business propositions start with that kind of honesty?"

My face must have told Gearheardt what I was thinking, that he had lost me.

"Jack, here's the point. Focus on the mission. Remember who you're working for and why you're doing it. But never forget what bastards some of these guys are."

I heard the shower start, reminding me of my house guest.

"Marta?"

"President of the Havana chapter of ISP."

"But you're not sure we can trust her, right?"

"I'm not sure that she is convinced we're going to win this one, Jack. I think she's hedging her bets. Keeping in contact with the bad boys. Hoping we'll pull it off. I can't really blame her. She was just a kid when the Bay of Pigs happened, but all Cubans know the U.S. of A. backed down at the last minute."

"It wasn't quite that simple."

"It never is, Jack. Not when you're trying to explain your sniveling ways to the survivors." He searched for a cigarette, not finding one. "Every country has its Rodrigos and Argo Buzzards, Jack. We throw ours in jail when we discover them. They promote theirs. That's the difference. Rodrigo was kicked off the force because he caused a lot of people to lose money. Not because they didn't approve of what he was doing."

"I'm not as stupid as I look, Gearheardt."

"Not by a long shot, Jack."

"I mean I'm not as naïve as you think I am."

"You couldn't be, Jack."

"You're not going to let me talk, are you?"

"Nope. You'd just say something patriotic and stupid. Just get the job done. That's my motto. That and find women. And strong drink."

I waved away his return to foolishness. "Before Marta gets back out here, Gearheardt, I need to go over this plan with you. Given all we know now, does it still make sense to try to fake the assassination of the president so that we can blame the Cubans and hope the U.S. invades Cuba?"

"We have to make some adjustments. And I need to fill you in on the 'taking over Cuba' aspect. But generally speaking, we need to press on. We've only got today. Take your shower and then you and I will head out. I have another mission for Marta this morning. One that will help us decide if we can count on her. I'm not worried about her in Mexico, but she's critical to my plan in Havana."

I began unbuttoning my shirt as I stood up. "Did you really go to Fordham?"

"Naaa. I just told that to Crenshaw because I knew how he would react to a Jesuit."

"When I first met you in Pensacola, in flight school, you told me you were home schooled through college. I knew that was bullshit, but it wasn't important at the time. So where *did* you go to school?"

"Princeton."

"You went to *Princeton?*"

"Yep. I didn't mention it after you told me you went to some dipshit cow college. You're smarter than I am, Jack. Doesn't matter where we went to college."

"Princeton," I muttered as I headed for my bedroom to get fresh clothes. I met Marta coming out of the bathroom, a towel around her head, only her head. "Did you know that Gearheardt went to Princeton?" I asked her.

"When will he return?" she asked before she looked in the living room. "Que passo?" she asked.

Behind me I heard Marta as she went into the living room. "Gearheardt, you are here. Jack says that you are gone."

After my shower I joined Gearheardt and Marta. We went over the situation with Victor and Marta's role. I watched Marta closely, because she was lovely and because I felt uneasy about her being alone with Victor. I was curious to see if she was apprehensive. She didn't seem to be.

"Gearheardt, what about Crenshaw? We can't just ignore the fact that Cuban's have a CIA agent captured up in the mountains. What are you going to do about it?"

"I'm working on it, Jack. You saw him up there. Did he look in any real danger of being shot? By now he's probably converted the rest of that lot."

"I get the feeling that you would just as soon he stay there for a while."

"Well, it might be—"

"Forget it. I'm not going to have that on my conscience. Either get cracking or I'm taking some Marines from the embassy and going after him myself."

"I'm working on it, Jack. What more can I say? And I don't think even Crenshaw would like to see the embassy involved."

He was right of course. "Just make sure that you get him back. Soon."

"We should have some lunch and then head to our headquarters, Jack."

"Which are where?"

"Jack, did you ever dream of a work environment where you were surrounded by beautiful scantily clad women?" He paused and looked at Marta. "Of course having Marta naked around here for the past few days has been pretty damn good I'll bet. But—"

The phone rang.

CHAPTER SIXTEEN

PYGMY DOWN YONDER

"You've got to help me, Señor Jack," Rodrigo pleaded. "I am go crazy and kill everyone. Those bastardos and their own mothers."

"Slow down, Rodrigo. Tell me what happened and what you want me to do."

"The Colombians have taken my son. He was on the campus, waiting for me. I will kill all of them, every one!"

"Where are you now?"

"I am near the Universidad de Mexico. They are still in this area. These are the people who are angry that we took their courier. You and me should find them."

It made a sort of sense. Although I wasn't sure how I could help more than the Mexican police.

Gearheardt was watching me from across my apartment. He wasn't a fan of Rodrigo, that much I knew. He rolled his eyes and looked at his watch. We were supposed to meet the Pygmy in fifteen minutes. Gearheardt had agreed to talk the Pygmy out of killing me. And to find out what the heck the Pygmy's mission was in Mexico. We were to meet him in Chapultepec Park.

I put my hand over the phone. "Gearheardt, can you get hold of the Pygmy and tell him we'll be late?"

"He's already in the park."

"He's in the park? How do you know?"

"He sells cigarettes there. I thought you saw him."

"*That's* the Pygmy? How in hell would I know? Damn, Gearheardt, you spring these things on me like they were nothing. What if he had decided to go ahead and kill me like he was threatening to do?"

"I'd of run the little bastard out of town on a popsicle stick, Jack. But I knew he was all mouth. He wanted to run Cuba and thought he had a deal with Crenshaw, but the Pygmy also knew that you worked for Crenshaw, so he wasn't sure whether or not he could kill you."

"*Does* he have deal with Crenshaw?"

"Not since Crenshaw found out the little twerp was an animist. You know Crenshaw. That animal worshipping stuff doesn't cut it with him. He also found out that the Pygmy took the burro tail from the ambassador's office and cooked it in the embassy parking lot in some kind of animist ritual."

"Wait a minute. We're talking about that little cigarette kid that you always buy from in Chapultepec Park, right?"

"Holy smoke, Jack, you really should look into a career selling bibles door to door. Didn't you ever notice the kid had a hell of a five o'clock shadow? Not to mention, he smelled like a roasted goat. Yes, the kid in the park selling cigarettes is the Pygmy." "Where in the heck is Marta? We need to get a move on." I could deal with Gearheardt later. But now I needed to help Rodrigo first. I spoke into the receiver.

"Rodrigo, I'll meet you at Chalupa's in an hour. I'm going to bring Gearheardt."

Rodrigo was silent. Then, "If Gearheardt can help me get my son, I will forgive him. My son, Manuelo, is on his way here. It will take him maybe one hour. Only he and you do I trust, Jack."

I hung up and looked at Gearheardt.

"Don't get *me* involved in your operations, Jack. I've got work to do. Remember this meeting with the Pygmy was your idea."

"You're going with me. And maybe we take the Pygmy. If he's so damn set on killing someone, he can shoot the Colombian drug dealers." I tried to get Gearheardt to be serious. "Can we trust him?"

"You mean can we trust a three-foot aboriginal wild man? Sure, why not?" He leaned back in the easy chair and picked up his coffee cup. "But I ain't going."

"Yes, you are. Get your butt up and grab your coat."

"Jack, this is *your* operation. You don't see me begging to have you help *me* out all the time."

I stood over his slouched, coffee slurping, figure. "I won't even dignify that bullshit with an argument. Get up."

Gearheardt grinned as he rose. "Well, I guess now and then I have asked you to lend a hand. Let's go find the Pygmy."

Gearheardt filled me in on the latest about the Pygmy as we left my apartment building. The *Blame-O-Matic*™ policies had once been wildly popular, but senior agency management had recently begun an investigation. The Pygmy had gotten cocky and sometimes didn't bother to read the mission objectives. A failed CIA mission to destabilize the Kobe beef market in Kyoto had the excuse *No One Spoke Italian* scrawled across the OFR (Official Failure Report) with Bernard Ruffkowski's signature underneath. Bernard Ruffkowski was one of the Pygmy's registered and official aliases.

The unwitting new DCI had boasted that he was going to 'cut this Ruffkowski down to size' when he found him. When the three-foot 'Ruffkowski' appeared in front of his desk, the DCI knew he was about to become the laughing stock every agent in the field so he promoted him on the spot from Midget to Extremely Short Person, increasing the Pygmy's pay by one third.

In recent years, the Pygmy's importance was on the decline. The Agency had officially adopted a policy of 'no failures' and although his imprimatur was sometimes sought as insurance (mostly in Democratic administrations) the Pygmy had put in for an in-grade transfer and was accepted as an assassin pro tem. No one was sure what that actually meant.

"So he's not in charge of the Goodbye Mexico operation," I said to Gearheardt.

"I'm pretty sure he's not, Jack. I just told you that to lend some credibility to my proposal." We crossed Reforma, the main thoroughfare running by Chapultepec Park. "But I'm confident I can talk him into shooting Rodrigo. If he doesn't assassinate someone by year's end, he has to reapply."

"You really don't like Rodrigo, do you?" I asked Gearheardt as we walked into the park. "We're surrounded by assholes in this business. Why do you have a hard-on for *him*?"

Gearheardt stopped and purchased flowers from a small girl at the entrance to the park.

"I don't like or dislike Rodrigo, Jack. Liking or disliking is not in my job description. I didn't help old people across the street when I was a Boy Scout either."

"I think there's more to it than that. But I don't care. Where the hell are you going?"

Gearheardt stepped to the side of the broad walkway and approached a young woman holding a baby while keeping an eye on a toddler playing nearby in the grass.

Gearheardt grinned and bowed. "Para usted, Señorita," he said, holding out the bouquet.

The woman smiled and murmured "gracias." The baby grabbed a flower and began eating it.

Gearheardt rejoined me. "Let's find that little shit." He stopped and pointed. "There he is! Damn it, he's bolting. Jack, go that way and head him off. I'll drive him toward the fence."

I caught a glimpse of a small man in a white vendor's coat who quickly disappeared into a crowd of strolling Mexican families. Gum and cigarettes flew from his wooden tray and the children dove for them like they were treasure from a piñata.

"Jack, stay here. I'll drive him back this way. There's no way out of the park the direction he's running. The little jackass." Gearheardt took off.

I watched the sidewalk intently for a few minutes. After a while I began looking around, trying to catch sight of Gearheardt. Finally I sat down on a bench, beginning to feel like a freshman on a snipe hunt. For some reason, I didn't expect Gearheardt to return.

Just as I rose to find a taxi to take me to the University campus where Rodrigo needed my help, Gearheardt returned. He was breathing heavily and his shirt was dripping wet with sweat.

"He got away," he said, dropping on the bench. "I had him for a minute, but he slipped out of this," he held up the white cloth jacket, "and took off like a greased pig."

"Or a greased pygmy." I wasn't sure Gearheardt really wanted me to meet the Pygmy.

"You sound skeptical, Jack. He got away. But I told him that if he tried to shoot you, he would have me to deal with. He got the message."

"Thanks. You going with me to help Rodrigo?"

Gearheardt looked up. "I'm going to help you. But I'm not going with you. Rodrigo is not in my mission statement. I need to find out what's spooking the Pygmy."

"So how will you help?"

"The Halcones can get his kid back. I'll head over there and brief them. If it can be done, they'll do it. And they owe me a favor."

Far down the sidewalk, behind Gearheardt, I saw a young boy who appeared to be crying. A number of street vendors, in white jackets and hats, were consoling him. The boy had a white hat, but no jacket. And it was definitely a young boy, not a pygmy.

"Gearheardt—"

"Gotta run, Jack. I have the address where you're meeting Rodrigo. Some people will show up. Use them."

"Why do the Halcones owe you a favor?"

"Not exactly a favor. I'm blackmailing them." He stood up. "Jack, the thing is that I'm afraid the Pygmy is double-crossing me."

It was pretty difficult to follow Gearheardt's stream of consciousness. As usual.

"We were talking about the Halcones."

"He's in cahoots with them. That's why I'm headed over there. He wants my network and he's willing to—"

"You mean the International Sisterhood of Prostitutes?"

"The only network I have." Gearheardt was glancing around how. Anxious to leave.

"What actual evidence do you have that the Pygmy is in cahoots with the Halcones?"

"None whatsoever. These guys are smarter than you think, Jack." He took my arm. "Let's head for the taxis."

Inside my head little tornados of thoughts were forming. I tried to grab something as it spun by.

"Wasn't this supposed to be the Pygmy's operation?"

"Yes."

"The Halcones are not in favor of attempting to fake the assassination of their president, right?"

"Right."

"So why would the Pygmy be—"

"The Pygmy is probably just trying to make sure I screw this operation up. He knows his insurance scheme is history. The Agency has a five-year program going that will shift all blame outside of the Agency. No need for fall guys if the fucking congress or the administration is going to take all the heat. The Pygmy wants me out of the picture."

"To gain what? What does Cuba have to do with your network?"

"I've promised the boys in Langley that my network is foolproof. If I fail, it's like I can't manage whores. The Agency doesn't like guys that can't handle their women."

"How will the Agency manage to shift all blame to congress?"

"Jesus, Jack. We've created havoc and chaos in damn near every country in the world at one time or another. You don't think we can manage a campaign in our own backyard?" He waved at a taxi. "The program is called 'Change Truth.' I know you're thinking something horrible is happening, Jack. It's really just a budget issue. We simply cannot afford to find actual truth anymore. But if we can *manufacture* data out of rumors and innuendos, the politicians are given the raw materials of truth and they can use it however it suits them or the country, whichever is more important at the moment. We'll need a lot fewer folks, and a few more computers. Computers just give us the best guess at truth without a lot of hand-wringing. Saves tons."

He slapped my shoulder. "So you can imagine the value of the only real surviving intelligence network."

"You never intended to help me save Rodrigo's son."

"Jack, I'm a big picture guy. We have a mission that will affect thousands of lives. We can't save everyone."

"But this kid is where he is because his dad tried to help us, Gearheardt. How do you just walk away from that?"

"In Mexico City, I use taxis." The taxi pulled to the curb. "Remember what LBJ said, 'If I had to worry about ever sonofabitch who got killed in Veetnam, I couldn't get my presidenting chores done 'til midnight.'"

I stood on the curb, watching him get in the taxi, feeling depressed.

"Aren't you supposed to be trying to save a kid's life or something, Jack?"

Probably because I had managed to find the only taxi driver in Mexico who actually feared death, Rodrigo was already arguing with four black-suited, sun-glassed Halcones when I reached the meeting place near the University.

"Jack," Rodrigo said as he saw me exit the taxi, "these men are no help. They will get my son killed."

"They were sent by Gearheardt?"

"Yes. But they—"

"Let me talk to them." I walked to where the four expressionless men were standing. "Habla Inglais?"

No one answered, but one man pointed his chin at me and nodded his head once quickly.

"You know why we are here? We have Colombians holding this man's son hostage."

The same man shrugged. "Tell us where they are and we will kill them. This is not surgery for the brain." One of the other Halcones smiled.

"We don't care what you do with the Colombians. But we want to get Rodrigo's son alive. Sabe?"

"Ohh, Señor. I thought that you did not speak the Spanish. Sabe? You are from Madrid, Si?" All of the Halcones laughed and then the leader grew solemn. "We are not the firemen to rescue the kitten, or the diplomat to bullshit. If you want us to help, we will help. If you want us to go, we will go."

I looked at Rodrigo. His oldest son, Manuel, had joined him. They looked warily at the four secret policemen.

"We'll handle it," I said. I held out my hand and after a moment it was shaken by the Halcone who had spoken and then each of the others.

From a breast pocket the evident leader withdrew a pen and a business card. It was one of Gearheardt's. The pen had a clear plastic top which revealed a naked woman when pointed down. Gearheardt Group was embossed on the side. "You will initial the back, please. We must show Señor Gearheardt that we were here to help you."

I grabbed the card and extended pen and scribbled 'thanks, asshole' on the back.

The Halcone frowned and then smiled at me. "Para su amigo, si?"

After the Halcones left, Rodrigo, Manuel and I ducked into a cantina and sat down at a small table.

"Tell me everything you know, Rodrigo," I said to the clearly worried and impatient man. "It is important that we—"

"I know, Jack. But the Colombianos cannot be allowed to leave. My son is surely dead then." He nodded at Manuel. "They have been dishonored by our success. To gain their face in Colombia, they must hurt us."

"There are three Colombians, Señor," the boy said in nearly perfect English. "They are not large, but they are all armed. When they took

Pablo, my brother, they all had pistols. Now they are in the Colombian house across the street, apartamento two-two at the top of the stairs. In the apartamento are two rooms. One for sleeping and one for the kitchen and eating."

"There's no bathroom?"

"Down the hall, Señor. When you walk in the door you will be in the eating room, the bedroom is to the left."

"You've been in the room, I take it?" Why would Rodrigo's son know the layout of the Colombian's safe house?

Manuel looked at his father before answering. "Si. At one time we were in the apartment. My friend, Carlos, is watching the building now. We have locked the back door to the building. But I don't think that the Colombians will come out of the building before night time." He paused and looked at Rodrigo. "My father said that you will have a plan."

"Jack," Rodrigo started, laying his hand on my arm, "in the past there have been times we must meet the Colombians. Before the drug business and the—"

"We can talk about that later, Rodrigo." I knew we never would. Everybody dealt with everybody else at some time or another in this business.

I leaned back in my chair to think. Three armed men in two rooms, with a hostage. Firing inside the room would be dangerous. If we waited until one of the men left the room to go down the hall, that might give us a chance for something, but if they didn't come out until they were ready to leave the country, then Rodrigo's son would be with them and a lot of shooting would—

"A drink for Conchita, Señor?" It was a woman's voice, close. I hadn't notice any bar girls working when we had entered but the mostly exposed breasts in my face demanding a drink caught my attention. I had a fleeting flash of resentment that a woman was interfering with man's work again. Then felt bad. After all, this was her place of business.

"No, gracias," I said, gently pushing her away.

She ruffled my hair, which I didn't like. "So serious, Señor. Who are you planning to keel?"

Her cohort, who had attacked Rodrigo with the same directness, laughed. "Hey, gringo, who you planning to keel?"

Rodrigo had been less effective in repulsing the attack, and the woman was now on his lap. His son looked uncomfortable.

"Ladies, ladies," I said, "here is plenty of money for drinks, but you need to go back to the bar." I took five hundred pesos from my wallet and, when she wouldn't extend her hand, stuffed it between the breasts of my potential paramour. She pulled herself away and gave me a look of disgust. She was a lovely girl, with a trim waste below a substantial bosom, and surprisingly little makeup. In fact she looked more like Miss Sanchez than a bar girl. She jerked her head at her companion and they walked away and seated themselves at the bar not far from us.

"So what do we do, Señor?" Manuel said.

I was gazing at the two small butts perched atop the bar stools. A course of action and perfect cheeks were wrestling in earnest for attention. It hit me that I needed to use them and it was this hesitation to do so that made me sometimes question my career in the Company. Not my ability, but my halting willingness to follow a basic Agency rule—use *everyone* to accomplish the mission, everyone it takes. When I was going through training, an instructor at the Farm once told me "*You* think of them as bystanders or friends. To me they're just assets. Everyone pays the same price to get in, Jack. Why should some get in free?" I *think* I knew what he meant.

The one thing I did know for sure was that a decision needed to be made. We needed to get on top of the situation quickly.

"I'll be right back," I said. I rose, walked to the bar and sat down next to Conchita. "May I buy you that drink?"

Conchita smiled into the mirror behind the bar. "You must buy a drink for my friend also," she said.

Conchita and her friend both ordered rum and Coca Cola. When I withdrew my wallet, she pushed it away.

"You have paid for the drinks, Señor."

I held up my beer in a toast. "To the beautiful women."

The women took small sips.

"Yes, well, here's the thing, Conchita. My friends," I nodded at the table, "have some . . . business with some men in the building across the street. We believe it would be . . . helpful to perhaps have you and your friend accompany us to visit them."

Conchita turned her upper body toward me and stared into my face. "You want us to accompany you to see your friends?" She looked over my shoulder at Rodrigo and Manuel, then back at me. "And we would do what when we accompany you across the street to see your business friends?"

My mind had wandered while I was looking into Conchita's eyes. I had flashbacks that were both unpredictable and troubling. I was briefing a Vietnamese lieutenant and his four men about the procedure for picking them up from the jungle. We were heli-lifting them into the vicinity of a known North Vietnamese encampment. They were to spend three days gathering information and radioing it back. Then we were to pick them up. The lieutenant did not believe he could last three days in the area. I thought he was right and didn't believe that we would ever pick them up. But we had no Marine recon teams available and we needed the information. It turned out that his team was wiped out within an hour of being dropped off. It wasn't the fear in his eyes that had haunted me later. It was the effort that he was making to keep me from seeing it.

"And we would do what, Señor?"

"It could be dangerous. But we will pay you well. That man," I pointed to Rodrigo, "believes his son is being held in an apartment across the street. I would like for you to get into the room, find out if this is true, and then remember where each of the men are in the room. You come out of the room, maybe to use the bañyo, and that is all you have to do."

Conchita looked at her companion to see if she had heard. The young lady nodded.

"The plan is okay. We will do it."

"Both of you?"

"Sometimes things do not go as we hope. We might need my friend. Her name is Isabella."

I didn't hesitate now. "Very good. Hello Isabella." She extended her hand and I shook it. "Again, you get in the room. Maybe you knock on the door and ask for Pedro or someone. Then I will leave it up to you."

"They will invite me in the room, Señor. I can promise you that."

"Remember. Just find out where Rodrigo's son is. And where the three men are. Then you come out of the room. Comprende?"

She shrugged, seeming terribly calm. But prostitutes must get used to strange requests, I reasoned as I returned to Rodrigo and Manuel to brief them.

"When we know where Pablo is, Manuel, your job will be to make sure he is out of the way if shooting starts. I'll take the guy who opens the door. Rodrigo, you go left and I will go right. If we're lucky, we'll have the drop on them and we just clear them and get out with Pablo. If not, we do what we have to do. Manuel, if shooting starts get Pablo on the floor. Then, as soon as you see your chance, get him out of the room. Don't worry about your father and me. You have that?"

Manuel again looked to his father before turning back to me. "Si, Señor. But what if Pablo is being held in the other room? The sleeping room. Then . . . "

"We will find out when the woman comes out of the room. Maybe she can convince the Colombians that they need to have the bedroom for other things."

Rodrigo was silent, staring at the table top.

"Señor Jack, this seems to be a dangerous plan."

"Rodrigo, you've got about three minutes to come up with a better plan. I'm going to talk to Conchita and her friend and then we had better go. I want them to make a lot of noise coming up the stairs to cover for the three of us. And we need to find a place to stay out of sight when she knocks on the door. If you can think of a better way to get into the room, I'll listen." I paused. "Or we could just wait and see what happens when they leave the room to go to the airport or train station."

Ten minutes later, Rodrigo, Manuel and I crouched out of sight of the door to apartment twenty-two. I had chambered a round in my 9-mm pistol and Rodrigo had repeatedly assured himself that his large revolver held six shots. Manuel was not armed. He had to focus on getting to Pablo and helping him out of the room.

Conchita and Isabella were in the hallway bathroom. As they came out and proceeded by us, Isabella stopped and crouched behind Manuel. I saw him smile briefly at her. Conchita continued around the corner and I heard her knock loudly on the door.

"Pedro!" she shouted as she knocked. "Pedro, abierto!"

After a moment, I heard the door open. A rapid Spanish exchange began. I heard the door close and then Conchita yelling again. She had not gotten in.

"Pedro!" Then a long rant which had the word *bastardo* used more than once. The door opened and I heard a man's voice, at first angry and then jocular. The door closed and the sounds were muffled and then quiet. When I peeked around the corner, Conchita was gone.

As we waited, I wondered briefly about Gearheardt and his scheme. I was angry at him for not being more helpful with Rodrigo's son, but somewhat chagrined that I was here on a private errand of mercy, probably illegal for an agent of the U.S., and having little to do with the mission of the Agency. Was foreign policy a mass effort or the result of our own individual actions? I smelled Isabella's perfume and felt her thigh against mine.

The door opened and closed and I heard a woman's steps coming toward us down the hall.

"Esta bien," Conchita said to Rodrigo. "Your son is fine." She turned to me. "I do not have much time. Yes, there are three men. One is sleeping in bedroom. One is fixing food and one who answers the door is in chair, watching the boy."

"Did you see weapons? Is the bedroom door open?" I asked.

"Yes, they have weapons they are wearing. The bedroom door is open." She smiled. "I must hurry before they come to see me."

"You're through, Conchita. Just knock on the door and make sure they know it is you. Then get out of the way."

As I was talking, Conchita was adjusting the top of her peasant blouse, pulling it far down below her breasts and exposing a brassier. She reached behind and then shrugged the bra off. I heard Manuel gasp.

"When the man opens the door, he will be distracted," she said. "I will get him into the hall and do not worry about him. Isabella and I can handle him."

The distractions would no doubt work—they were almost working at the moment as I tried to think of a response—and for some reason I believed that she and Isabella could handle one of the Colombians.

Rodrigo and Manuel flattened themselves against the wall on the far side of the door, Rodrigo with pistol in hand. Isabella and I did the same on the near side.

Conchita rapped. "Estoy aqui," she sang.

The door opened a crack and then wider as a young man stuck his head out, grinning. It was the man from the car bombing. The one who gave me the finger as he escaped.

Conchita leaned forward, smiling broadly. She slowly brought her hand up toward the man's face, then abruptly grabbed his tie and yanked him into the corridor. Isabella rushed to help Conchita as Rodrigo and I burst into the apartment. I had my pistol in the face of the Colombian next to the stove before he could react. The door to the bedroom slammed shut, nearly hitting Rodrigo in the face as he lunged toward it.

"He is jumping out the window," Rodrigo cried.

"Let him go," I said. "We're after Pablo."

By now, Manuel was leading Pablo from the room. I backed away from my target after taking his weapon. He kept up a steady stream of angry, sneering language, most of which seemed to concern the short yet painful life I was going to experience.

A non-verbal response from Rodrigo—the barrel of his pistol across the man's forehead—silenced him. He hit the floor and was still. Rodrigo aimed his pistol point blank at the man's temple.

"No," I said, not sure why.

Rodrigo hesitated and then kicked the man in the chest. You could hear the wind rush out of his mouth.

In the hallway, the other Colombian was well under control, blind-folded, his hands and feet tied, and mouth gagged.

"Give him to the Halcones," I said. Behind me I heard a noise and turned to see the bedroom door burst open. I raised my pistol and shot the Colombian squarely in the chest, knocking him back onto the bed. Evidently he had not tried to escape when he had the chance. Rodrigo brushed by me, stood over the Colombian on the bed and put three more slugs into his chest.

"You must have missed him, Jack," he said as he rejoined me at the door.

Manuel and Pablo disappeared down the stairs, the disheveled younger boy murmured "gracias, gracias." Conchita was arranging her blouse, moving toward the stairway right behind them. Isabella stepped over to me and took my hand.

"Hasta luego, Jack." She left with Conchita.

"We must leave now, Señor Jack," Rodrigo said. He was clearly relieved and much happier than he had been half an hour before. "Someone will come. This one," he pointed to the bound man, "will tell us what we should know."

We stood for a moment and my heart dropped to a normal pace. We shook hands and I stepped over the trussed Colombian.

"I'll see you later, Rodrigo." Gearheardt was wrong. Rodrigo was a good man, a family man. Like most of the Mexicans I had come to know who were not attached to military or police organizations.

"Thank you, Jack. Thank you very much. Muchas gracias." He didn't turn away quite fast enough to hide the tears in his eyes.

I stopped by the bar, but didn't see the women. At the curb I caught a taxi.

"Colonia Polanco, por favor. Ibsen."

Celebration and emotional release should follow action. But I was always too tired. I leaned my head back against the seat and wondered how Isabella knew my name was Jack.

CHAPTER SEVENTEEN

DAISY SAY SHE GOT THE WHOLE WORLD BY THE BALLS

B ack at the apartment Gearheardt was dispatching Marta to meet with Victor. "See if you can find out if he's buying into the plan," he said. "Jack and I will meet you later. Come to the Camino Real hotel about five and wait in the bar."

"Okay, Pepe," she said. "You and Jack will be careful. Also, I am . . ."

She grabbed Gearheardt by the shoulders and kissed him. Then she turned to me and kissed me without grabbing me. "I will see you later, Jack." She remained close for a moment, and put her hand to the side of my face. She left before I could think of anything to say.

"Seems like her old self, Jack," Gearheardt said. "Maybe she's made her choice."

I blushed, then realized that he was talking about us or the Cubans.

"The story about her father?"

"More or less true. And her step-brother *is* Gon. That's how I found her. I think at one time she believed she was the mistress of Victor, when he was a Cuban army officer. But he started passing her around. She told herself it was for the good of Cuba, a service for her country. One day she realized that she was just a whore."

"She still seems friendly with Victor."

"She knows now that he is a source of information and access. She's pretty smart, you know."

I wanted to ask him if she had been in a bordello when he found her, but didn't feel ready for the possible answer.

"So how did the rescue go, Jack? You seem pretty calm with just a taste of cockiness. You get the boy?"

"We got him. And two of the Colombians. One dead and one delivered to the Halcones." I dropped into a chair.

Gearheardt didn't seem particularly interested. He bent over his paperwork, humming and ignoring me. I rose and went in to take a shower.

Afterwards I returned to the living room dressed in slacks and a shirt. I looked for my blazer for a minute before I remembered Gearheardt had borrowed it. At the cleaners, he said. I put on a dark blue wind-breaker and we left. Gearheardt was dressed in a gray suit, light blue shirt and a maroon regimental tie.

"Where did you change clothes last night? You said you didn't sleep, but you obviously cleaned up."

"As a matter of fact you'll know in a few minutes, Jack. You see, I haven't totally leveled with you about everything going on."

"No shit?" I said.

The Mercedes was at the curb. A mangy yellow dog had his leg lifted against one of the tires. Gearheardt went to the back of the car and deftly removed the license plate.

"Let's find another car, Jack. This damn thing looks like crap."

We walked through the quiet streets of the apartment buildings. Gearheardt spotted a fairly new Impala that was black and recently washed.

"Here we go," he said. He knelt behind the car and switched license plates, giving the Impala instant diplomatic status. I just watched and didn't ask questions. An elderly couple rounded the corner as he was leaning in to hotwire the ignition. "Buenos dias," Gearheardt said. "Como esta?"

The couple grinned and responded. "Muy bien gracias, y usted." Their fritzy poodle sniffed my leg. The man and woman seemed interested in Gearheardt's work under the steering wheel, peering in the side window.

"Esta es su Impala?" Gearheardt said. He rose and pulled a wallet from his jacket pocket and flashed a badge.

"No, no. Aya." They pointed across the street to a brown Ford.

The engine caught after a few turns and Gearheardt got in. "Let's go, Jack," he said. "Adios," Gearheardt called to the couple. We burned rubber to the corner and screeched around it with the back of the car fish-tailing wildly.

"Why do you always drive like a maniac, Gearheardt?"

"For the sheer hell of it, my friend. No worries about insurance and I've got diplomatic immunity. Why not enjoy the thrill?"

"I'm not sure diplomatic immunity applies to stolen cars."

"Damn, then we'd better get the hell out of here." He accelerated through a four way stop.

On Paseo de Reforma, a six lane street, Gearheardt slowed to only twice the speed limit. There was little traffic.

"Okay, Jack. You've been a good and faithful companion. You deserve to know what's taking place in Mexico City." He mercifully slowed to circle a glorieta. "Actually you know more than you know you know. When I fill in the pieces, you'll say 'oh yeah.'" He was steering with his knees while he lit a cigarette with the car's lighter. My feet were pumping the floor in front of me as if I could brake from the passenger's side. I was beginning to hate him again. Finally he blew out the smoke, shook the cigarette lighter and tossed it out his window. "Oh, shit," he said. "Where was I?"

"I know more than I know I know."

We had reached the center of town. Cars and people with fruit and flower-laden pushcarts filled the road and Gearheardt slowed to their speed. We entered the Zona Rosa. The shops were still closed, but a few tourists in their colorful native costumes roamed the streets.

We pulled to a stop in front of a small, three story building that sported a green awning reaching to the street. A restaurant was on the street floor called Los Palomas.

A smiling Mexican boy came out of the building and approached Gearheardt, who began a rapid conversation in Spanish.

Gearheardt turned to me. "I told him to get the plates and then ditch the car."

"Your Spanish is better than you've been letting on, Gearheardt. What's that all about?"

"Good question, Jack. Let me ask you one. Did you ever wonder why the CIA would send you down here when you only know a smattering of Spanish? Doesn't it seem to be a handicap to not know the language of the people you're working with?"

I didn't answer. I had wondered about that almost every day. I assumed that the Agency thought I was sharp enough to do a job and learn the language as I went along. It didn't seem reasonable.

"The Company has dozens of agents in Mexico City, Jack. How many of them do you work with? Any of them?"

"Eric helps me out. I just assumed that everyone operated in his own little world."

"And you're partially right." He opened his door. "I have a better explanation that is becoming more than a hunch. I'll tell you inside." He turned back. "And my Spanish is damn near perfect. The less people that know the better."

I was a bit hungry but Gearheardt passed by the inside entrance to the café and went up the stairs one flight. At the landing, double doors faced us. *Los Palomas (Private)* was painted in flowers above the doors. Although the hallway had been shabby, inside the Las Palomas private club was nice. We were in a large waiting room, leather chairs, a large leather couch, and dark wood tables and trim around the walls. A men's club atmosphere.

Two young women, maybe seventeen or so, sat cross-legged on the floor in front of a gas fireplace. They were eating tacos and rice. As Gearheardt and I approached, one of them placed her hand under a breast and lifted it up, as if offering it to me. She made a kissing sound.

Gearheardt raised his hand as if to slap the girl. The girls looked at each other and began giggling. Gearheardt laughed.

"They're Daisy's daughters," he said. "They mock the girls all the time and flirt with the customers. If you touch one of them, Daisy will have your skin hanging on that wall over there." He pointed to a wall which had mounted game heads. "Come here," he said, and walked to the wall. He pointed to a wooden plaque upon which was nailed a brown shriveled pouch. "The sign says *The Balls of Hector Ortega*. Hector didn't get the message about not touching the teenagers."

I heard the girls giggling behind us. I didn't turn and look at them again. They were very nubile young women and I didn't want to chance offending them.

Gearheardt spoke to one of the girls. "Chiquita, go tell Daisy that I am here. And tell Benito that I would like coffee and rolls brought to the office."

The girl rose quickly, brushing off her blouse and approaching Gearheardt. "Someday I will be working, Señor Gearheardt, and you will be my first customer."

"Not likely, Chiquita. Someday soon you will be a nun and your mother will be at peace at last."

Gearheardt beckoned me to follow him through a door next to the fireplace. Down a dark hallway, and up a metal circular staircase. "It's quiet in a bordello in the morning, isn't it Jack? The customers usually come in starting around lunch."

Gearheardt unlocked a door. When he flipped the light switch I saw a large room with four desks and a great deal of radio equipment. He sat down in front of a teletype machine. "Let's see what the night's traffic brought."

He flipped through a number of light brown pages, pausing occasionally and humming. He extracted half a dozen pages and dropped the remaining in a wire basket on the desk.

"Here's something that should interest you, Jack. A certain military strongman in your favorite Asian country is moving a lot of money to Switzerland. A *lot* of money. And it's a guy that the U.S. is counting on for stability in his country." He threw the page onto the pile.

"How about this? The South African government officials visiting Thailand are making private investments with government money. Let's see. One bought a house. One a villa on the island of Phuket. And another is gambling his money away."

I walked to his side and took the paper. "Where are you getting this?"

Gearheardt leaned around and pointed to the top of the paper in my hand. "Those numbers are the time sent. Those letters are the code for the city. And those letters are the code from the location in the city." He turned back to the desk and spoke over his shoulder. "You might recognize the one you're holding, Jack. Shows it was sent last night from Bangkok. And those letters mean the information came from the Happy Times Massage Parlor. Near Pat Pong to refresh your memory."

"You mean this is your network? You actually have, what do you call them, agents, in these places?

"That's exactly what I mean. Of course those are raw reports. If we see something we have an interest in, then we cable back for verification. We get lots of reports that are just guys mouthing off. But if the information is more or less critical, we cross-check using those forms there." He pointed to a bookshelf with stacks of forms in various languages.

"You have radio and teletype equipment in every bordello and massage parlor?"

"Just the major cities of the world. A few minor cities that are hot spots. And we have stringers in even smaller cities that report to girls in the larger cities."

"Amazing."

"Not really. We're coming out of the dark ages of interrogation, Jack. I just happen to be the technology leader. I use alcohol and sex to get my answers. Saves hauling car batteries around to attach to genitals."

"The girls are able to do this? I mean the gathering part is probably easy, but the reports and the analysis follow-up? Come on."

"Jack, I have yet to visit a brothel that didn't have girls working there who would have been lawyers and doctors had it not been for some bad luck. Usually in the form of some asshole raping them when they were kids. Or their parents exchanging them for cash. No, it's not hard to find good agents. Just takes a lot of work. I spent about two years on it."

"So you weren't in Angola?"

"Not all the time. The Company sent me over there after I got out of the hospital, but there wasn't much I could do. So I hired a guy to write reports for me and took off traveling around the world visiting whore-houses and massage parlors."

I sat down at one of the desks. "This is all a bit much, Gearheardt. You must have a huge network."

"Probably the biggest in the world, Jack. But it's all CIA now, or at least it's on contract to the CIA. I do some work for Mossad and even the French sometimes. But mostly just the boys in Langley. Oh, last year I did some work for the Russians. But those bastards would just get drunk and brag about how they had a new intelligence network. They got tired of paying to see themselves blabbing about hiring me. Intelligence is not a pretty business. You have to—"

The door opened and slammed against the wall. I jumped up and watched Gearheardt to see if I should be reaching for my pistol.

"Gearheardt, you son of a bitch," a massive Mexican woman yelled. "Chiquita told me you promised to be her first customer. I'll have your balls on the wall before—"

"Daisy, this is my best pal, Jack," Gearheardt said calmly." He's going to be working with me here for a while."

Daisy laughed. It was a joyous sound. "You don't scare so easy, Gearheardt. I'll give you that. Chiquita is telling me this every time you come here. She likes you."

"And I like her. Say hello to Jack."

"Ola, Jack. Como esta?" She came toward me like a bulldozer, the chair in front of her swept aside.

"Muchas gracias," I said stupidly. "I mean—"

"Another gringo who speaks third grade Spanish, Gearheardt. Where do you find them?"

Daisy was probably fiftyish. A classic Castilian beauty with layers of makeup to hide aging skin. She only looked massive, now that I had a better look, because her enormous breasts hung the black dress far out from her body. At seven in the morning, her face had already undergone the plastering job for the day. She wore high heels and I crazily imagined a garter belt. This was a 'Madame.'

"Gearheardt has talked to me about you, Señor Jack. You save his life. You screw his girlfriend. Es correcto?"

"That pretty well covers the high points of the relationship, Daisy." I stuck out my hand. "Pleased to meet you." Her grip was powerful and strangely comforting.

Benito, I assumed, brought coffee and rolls and we gathered around one of the desks to fill our cups. The coffee was the best that I'd had since I came to Mexico. This pleased Benito to no end. His enthusiasm for my pleasure made me quite sure he was homosexual. Probably a good thing to be for a man working in a brothel.

"Let's get to work, Daisy. Jack's one of us. He can hear or see anything."

We arranged ourselves around a small conference table near the window. I was nearest the windows. Below me Mexico City started to fill with people and noise.

"First of all," Gearheardt began, "what did we get last night locally? Let's deal with that first."

A redhead had come into the room, closing and locking the door after Benito had exited. She was a knockout, if you liked redheads.

Without makeup she had a wholesome look, discounting the fact that she was 'dressed' in a diaphanous yellow gown. And not much else that I could see.

"Lisa was on duty last night to collect and write the report, Señor Pepe," Daisy said.

"Ola, Lisa. You are lovely this morning. Anything of note?"

Lisa smiled her acknowledgement of the compliment and nodded at me. She consulted notes that she had brought in. "A policia major is bringing in men from Cuernavaca and Taxmil," she said. "They will arrive tonight and be here until after the sixth of May. Maybe twenty men."

"Not surprising, but good information. What else?" Gearheardt asked.

"Another police captain has on his team a sharpshooter who is one of the best in Mexico. He will be on top of the Angel's tower, across from the park." She looked up at Gearheardt. "He is trained by the Russians. This captain I entertained myself. He was very proud to have the honor of providing a sharpshooter from his station. If you want more information, I believe he will be back this evening. I promised him something special." She actually blushed.

"I'll let you know, Lisa. With the president giving a speech in the park, none of this is surprising. Anything unusual at all? From here or from our other offices?"

"I think so, Señor. An office near the palace had visitors from Russia and Cuba last night. The black men from Cuba were angry and the Russians were buying the drinks and paying for the girls. This is unusual for the Russians to pay for anyone."

I spoke up. "Lisa, my name is Jack. I wanted to ask if the Cubans were living here or if they were from out of town. Did the 'office' tell you that?"

"Good question, Jack. I see where you're going. What about it, Lisa?"

"I have no information on that, Señor Pepe. But the girls did say," she checked her notes again, "that none of the men were regular. The other thing is that the girls promised to the men that new young girls, perhaps virgins, were coming to the place on the day after Cinco de Mayo. None of the men had interest." She looked up at me and then Gearheardt. "This is unusual. Perhaps the men would not be in town."

"A good assumption, Lisa. Tell the girls to have extra security men that night. If someone comes expecting a new young girl, they can get very angry to be disappointed," Daisy said.

"Okay, Lisa. If you can get your notes typed up and back to Daisy before you start work today, I would appreciate it. Daisy, if you have nothing further, Jack and I need to pow wow and go over everything." He stood up as Daisy and Lisa rose. "Perhaps we can have lunch brought in. If that could be arranged."

"We did not discuss Nairobi, Pepe," Daisy said. She nodded at Lisa, instructing her to go ahead and leave. I couldn't help but follow Lisa's departure.

"I'm afraid I have nothing new, Daisy. I may have to go there myself." He turned to me. "The girls in our biggest office in Kenya unfortunately were discovered sending a teletype. We are not sure any of them survived the beatings but one or two may be in the Nairobi jail. I'm trying to get more information."

"And Cuba?" Daisy asked.

"I'm working on it, Daisy. It looks pretty good, but there are a lot of 'ifs.'"

After Daisy left, promising to have lunch brought in, Gearheardt moved to a desk.

"You'll have to excuse me for a while, Jack. I've got a briefing paper that has to go out by nine. Part of my deal with the Agency. One for the DCI and one for the President."

"Of the United States?"

"I spice that one up pretty good. Every once in a while we catch a mistress that's pissed or has been dumped. France is good for one about once a month and we've had a couple of scoops from our Italian office in Rome." He buried himself in teletype pages, pecking on a typewriter every few minutes.

"Can I look through some of these files?"

Gearheardt considered for a moment. "Sure. Just remember that the files you're looking through are raw files. The girls are not always reliable. Those that say things like *the police chief is planning to bomb the embassy on Tuesday* are more than likely grudge reports. Guys let things slip and brag a lot, but usually don't give away dates and times."

"So how do you—"

"I don't. I have an office in Paris staffed with ex-spy types from about half a dozen countries. They go over everything for hard data, cross-check with other references and write a report once a week. Or they flash it to me if they think they've found something really hot. We sell a lot of business information too. Those traveling bastards will tell a girl everything but the formula for Coke."

While Gearheardt typed away I learned about a general in Africa who liked to wet the bed, a diplomat from a European country involved in shipping mines to Pakistan, a Saudi who insisted on whores with Jewish names and features who frequented a brothel in Egypt, and dozens of troop movements, assignments, and coming military promotions around the world. At once funny and immeasurably sad, the reports were evidence of a lot of drunken blabbermouth officials, feeding their egos by trying to impress women who hated them. I found I couldn't open the Nairobi file. I didn't want to see what the girls there had been beaten to death for finding out.

"What about Daisy, Gearheardt?" I forgot I was not to interrupt him.

"Daisy? She's pretty unusual, actually. A lot of the madams are threatened by what the girls are doing. You can imagine. They're in cahoots with the police or the brothel owners or both. That's one of the things that make this business so dangerous for the girls. If the mama-san finds out you're ISP, you better have an escape plan. And of course few of the girls do. We buy off the madams where we can. They're usually even worse than the men because they fear the owners both physically and financially. The girls have the physical fear, but most of them don't expect to be driving Ferraris any time soon."

He shrugged. "Give me just a moment more, Jack. There's a financial summit coming up in Lima and I'm outlining the traffic concerning the security."

"Do you tell the girls to target certain people?"

"Hold on." Gearheardt typed steadily.

"Okay." He pulled the last sheet from the typewriter and put the stack into a large manila envelope. "Didn't you say you're meeting your secretary this morning? Save me a courier fee and give this to her. You can trust her can't you?"

"Absolutely."

"Good. I've got the name of who she should give it to." He tossed the envelope to me. "Now you were asking about targets? Never. We don't ever ask the girls to do anything. We never encourage them to take risks, ask questions, or go through a guy's pockets. Their job is dangerous enough as it is. And we don't pay them, in case you were about to ask. If they started having money, the pimps and owners would just take it, and beat them until they found out where they got it."

He unlocked the side drawer of his desk and pulled out a thin file. Tossing it over onto my desk, he stood up and came over to where he could read over my shoulder. The file was marked "Goodbye Mexico."

"That's all we've gotten on our own mission so far, Jack. No one is talking."

I was uncomfortable with him behind me, so I scooted back my chair and went to the coffee pot. I poured a cup and held it out to him. He shook his head no.

"Gearheardt, don't get pissed because I ask you this, but helping these girls, or using these girls, isn't it more or less hypocritical to—"

"Because I chase whores all the time, Jack? Is that what you're asking?"

"I guess so. It just seems strange."

"I didn't say I was Mother Teresa. You can discuss the morality with Crenshaw, Jack. I treat the girls anywhere in the world with respect and always pay them well. And now I run one of the best damn intelligence companies in the world. I don't apologize for that, or for frequenting the women."

"But you use their information and you don't pay them."

"I don't give them cash, Jack. But I give them a weapon to use against the rotten men they have to be with. And I give them hope for the future. ISP wants to prepare a place where they can go." He paused, looking embarrassed. "I'll be king there, Jack."

I couldn't tell if he was serious. His serious smile and his jerking me around smile were too similar.

"I'm going to go meet Juanita. Walking will be good for me. I'll be back about eleven."

Gearheardt slapped my shoulder as I went to pick up the envelope. "That Lisa was a doll wasn't she Jack? Did you notice she was a natural redhead?"

He sat back down and opened the Goodbye Mexico file. "Don't get too introspective on me, Jack. You're probably going to have to shoot that damn Victor day after tomorrow." He paused. "Damn this mission is screwed up."

At the door I turned back to him. "You mentioned something about me being sent here without knowing the language. Of course I know it's strange, but what did you mean?"

"That someone at Langley is way ahead of us, Jack, me boy. The question is are we being made to 'play the fool' as they say." He laughed. "Don't you hate the missions where you have a bunch of people lined up to assassinate someone and then everything gets mixed up and no one knows who's killing who?"

So he was as confused as I was. That was bad.

CHAPTER EIGHTEEN

TO ASS* OR NOT TO ASS, THAT IS THE QUESTION

(*UNOFFICIAL ABBREVIATION FOR ASSASSINATE)

As I walked through the Zona Rosa toward Chapultepec Park, I tried not to think how much better my life had been running when Gearheardt was dead. I had a nice Austrian girlfriend. My Spanish was coming along. And I had a mission that was paying off. My assets and I had broken into a ring running bombs and weapons to American and Mexican would-be terrorists. The fact that we had discovered that the real object was drugs made it all the more important. Sure Rodrigo was not Father Flanagan, but he knew the ropes of the near-underworld trades and he was diligent. The Agency was beginning to get some heat for working closely with the criminal class, but it was laughable to think we could do the job without contacts in the gangs involved in the trafficking.

Now Gearheardt was drawing me into the foreign policy and global manipulation bullshit that I had avoided even thinking about since Vietnam. Namely, taking over countries, assassinating leaders, looking to change hearts and minds (nearly impossible) and being a part of some long term 'strategy' that was sure to leave the splintered flotsam and jetsam of third world societies in its wake.

It wasn't that I disagreed with it, or could think of an alternative course of action for the U.S. I just didn't want to be a part of it. I liked my intervention on a local level. As Gearheardt had said, "Nuclear bombs, smuclear bombs. I want to run over the sonsabitches in my car. Throw it in reverse and run over 'em again. Nuclear warfare just means we've lost the will to get our hands dirty, or bloody." Of course Gearheardt was crazy. And his scheme now was more 'global' than 'local.' And, and . . .

It was just damn confusing.

Turning the corner to reach the park I passed one of many flower vendors and decided to get flowers for Juanita. I was early, and therefore surprised when I saw Juanita sitting on a bench waiting for me. She had a briefcase which I assumed contained my files.

"Ola, Juanita. Thank you for coming to see me."

"De nada, Señor Jack. It is good to see you. Very good." She squealed with delight at the flowers, made to hug me and then awkwardly drew back and shook my hand.

We discussed the gossip around the office while I went through my files. Nothing very exciting. My jacket from Colombia was becoming an issue as the offices traded faxes over the payment of shipping costs. Finally it was sent by diplomatic courier.

Then a page of traffic caught my eye. It was actually addressed to Crenshaw. From the Bogotá office:

> Request scope of Armstrong activity concerning Colombian citizens in Mexico. Top State (the ambassador) questions authority to prosecute without explicit finding.

Which meant that someone in Bogotá had been feeling heat about the missing Colombian student in Mexico City. It was more or less a fishing expedition. Probably a high Colombian official had made an unofficial inquiry on behalf of a friend. The Ambassador said he would look into it. It didn't concern me. Yet.

"Anything else, Juanita? Has anyone heard from Crenshaw?" I wanted to give her the comfort of knowing that he was alive, but for now, she was better off only knowing what was official.

"They have said he is in the mountains. That is all that I know. The new Agency man, Señor Davis, tell me not to worry. He is taking care." She came closer and lowered her voice. "He is look for you, Señor Jack. I don't like him too much."

"Juanita, tell him that you met me. Tell him that he needs to check with the ambassador to find out where I am and what I am doing."

"The Ambassador, he knows?"

"No. But that conversation will buy me a few more days. Neither will trust the other to tell the truth. Since they will both say they don't know where I am or what I am doing, then both will assume the other is lying."

"Que?"

"Each will think that I am doing something that only the other one knows about."

"Is smart, Señor Jack. You are good CIA man."

"I'm not so sure about that. But listen, Juanita, I need another favor. Tell Eric that I need to see any traffic that comes through that mentions Cinco de Mayo or Goodbye Mexico. No matter whether I am copied or not. Can you do that for me? It's only for a couple of days."

"It's no problem."

"If you need to get in touch with me, you have my apartment number. I will give you another place. Don't write it down, just remember it and give it to *no one*. Qien sabe? This number is only in case of emergency." I gave her the number in Gearheardt's office in Las Palomas.

"Oh, so you will be with Señor Gearheardt."

I didn't know whether to laugh or cry. That damn Gearheardt was ahead of me every where. "Yes, you can reach me there if you have information that you think I need to know."

"Señor Gearheardt has good mission, no?"

I wasn't sure which of Gearheardt's many missions she might be referring to so I just said 'yes.'

"Cuba," she said. A broad smile.

I nodded my head as if I had full and complete knowledge of what she meant.

"Vaya con Dios, Jack." Juanita stretched up and put her arms around my neck. I had always suspected she had a crush on me. When I leaned into her, she whispered, "My sister, ISP." She released my neck and smiled shyly, gathering up the papers and shoving them into the briefcase borrowed from the embassy.

"Your sister? I am sorry, Juanita. Can I help?" I assumed that dire straits led her sister to prostitution. "Where is she? Who is she?"

She shrugged at the 'where.' "Her name is Maria Teresa Sanchez."

It was one of the names Gearheardt had given me when I was to pick up two women and take them to the motel the first night I met Gearheardt.

"Juanita," I said, "this package is from Gearheardt. It has to do with the economic summit. Can you drop it to the name on the envelope?"

She took the package, folded it and thrust it into her purse. "Asta luego, Jack."

"Asta luego, Juanita."

I sat back down on the park bench and watched her walk away, disappearing into the crowd on the sidewalk. The sun was warm on my face and the beautiful young girls that strolled by were a distraction. Out of the corner of my eye, I spotted the little 'cigarette boy' that I now knew was the Pygmy. "Hey," I shouted, "over here."

He saw me waving and began walking in the other direction. He looked back as I stood up and then began to run. His cigarette selling technique seemed poor.

I lost him in the crowd and sat back down. The flower vendors and tourists swirled around me. Chapultepec Castle was above me. I had dirty clothes in one of the many bedrooms. Did the tourists get to see those? Why had Gearheardt's plan of using it for his headquarters gone wrong? There were so many things that I wanted to have answers for.

But who to ask? I trusted Gearheardt but he was a genius of evasion and contradictions. Crenshaw? Aside from the fact that he was trapped in the mountains, I had betrayed him by working for Gearheardt without telling him. I doubted if he would have leveled with me. Marta was unreliable. She was obviously conflicted in her mission, whatever it was. And what had Gearheardt meant when he said 'I'll be the king?'

I took a taxi back to Gearheardt's new headquarters at Las Palomas. At the front door I met Marta, also just stepping from a taxi.

"Did you find Victor?" I asked.

"Si, Jack." She looked up the building. "What is this place that I am to meet Gearheardt?"

I took her arm and led her inside, up the stairs and through the double doors which were now open. A number of young Mexican women were sitting in the room this time. Several of them whistled lowly when they saw Marta. Chiquita saw me and got up to let me through the locked door where Gearheardt had taken me.

"Now do you know where we are?" I asked Marta. As soon as I said it, I wondered if Marta took it as an insult. But I was probably being too sensitive.

The office was now busy. Gearheardt sat at the conference table, directing traffic and speaking in Spanish to the half dozen girls in the room. He didn't notice me or Marta right away and we watched him as he ran his global intelligence agency. His staff was voluptuous. Lisa walked by close to me and smiled, her red hair flashing at both ends. Marta didn't seem as intrigued with her yellow outfit as I had been.

"Hey, there you are," Gearheardt said. "And you found Marta. Great." He began closing files on the table, indicating for Marta and me to take a seat.

"Ladies," he said loudly, "Marta is from Cuba. Jack prostitutes himself for America." The ladies, some of whom I doubted spoke English all that well, laughed and said hello to both Marta and me.

"I suggest we take a lunch break. Those of you with customers, be sure and wash your hands before you come back here to work."

The ladies laughed again.

"Jesus, Gearheardt," I said, "how embarrassing." I sat down with Marta by my side.

"These women are prostitutes, Jack. You know it, and I know it. The men screwing them know it. Should I pretend that I don't know?" He smiled at Marta.

"Ola, Marta. How was your morning?"

"Es fine, Pepe. I met with Victor." She looked at the retreating women and then at me.

"And?"

"He is very happy to be working with the," she waited as the door closed, "CIA on this mission."

"By golly, who wouldn't be, right Jack? Finest organization in the world. Maybe that should be finest 'unorganization' in the world." He rolled his eyes at me, and then smiled at Marta.

"So Victor is game for being our assassin? Super. It's nice to know you have psychopathic people eager to work with you."

Marta looked puzzled, and I was taken aback by Gearheardt's manic enthusiasm.

"Marta, I hate to keep running you around, but would you mind finding Daisy and spending a bit of time with her? Ask one of the girls to help you find her. Tell her about your group in Cuba. Jack and I will finish up here and then come find you."

After Marta left, somewhat reluctantly, Gearheardt leaned back in his chair. He stretched his arms and yawned. Then he leaned forward toward me, his forearms on the table.

"Things have gotten complicated, Jack," he said.

I buried my face in my hands. "Oh, Lord. How could this get more complicated?"

"It seems we, that's you and me, pal, have been double-crossed."

I looked up. "By who?"

"It appears by just about everybody."

I straightened my back and sat up in my chair. After all I was a former Marine and a full-fledged employee of the Central Intelligence

Agency. Gearheardt and I had been in tough spots before. Almost all of them as a result of his unbridled enthusiasm for an idea.

"So where are we?" I asked.

"How well do you know Eduardo?" he asked.

"The Halcone? Why do you ask?"

"We need them. So do you trust him? Can we work with him?"

"I have no idea. I've used him a couple of times and I share some information with them from time to time. I don't really know how high up in the organization he is."

"He's pretty high up, I can tell you that. Daisy says that he's one of the top guys."

"Daisy . . . the Madame. You mean Eduardo is a customer here?"

"No. She just has the org chart for the Halcones pretty well memorized. She can't afford to screw around with them." Gearheardt picked up the Goodbye Mexico file. "I've made a few more entries. Take a look and then we'll talk."

"You went with the Halcones that night in the park. What was that all about?"

"They've heard about my network. Wanted to see if they might buy some information. I told them I didn't know what they were talking about. Made them mad since they knew I was lying."

"They didn't blowtorch your nuts?"

Gearheardt laughed. "They wanted to, but I convinced them that I had some files that they didn't want to see in the press. I'm not sure they really gave a damn, but there was some professional courtesy in the chat and they just let me go."

"Professional courtesy?"

"Rat bastards recognize one another."

"Eduardo told me that they were looking for you. They didn't like you talking to Victor Ramirez."

"They know the Cubans are up to something. They think I might have something to do with it. In my capacity as an international trouble-maker."

"So why do we need the Halcones?"

"Do you want to kill Ramirez?"

"Not particularly, but I will. That's my job, right?"

"Let's get the Halcones to do it. Kind of a joint venture."

A key rattled in the door and it opened.

"Knock, knock," Benito sang. He winked at me as he sat a tray on the conference table. "I have something very special for you, hombres. Carne asada de Benito."

"Muchas gracias, Benny. It looks great. I told Jack that you were an excellent cook."

Benito beamed. I glared at Gearheardt but said nothing.

"Call me if you want *dessert*." He swished out of the room, flapping his folded towel over his shoulder.

"Gearheardt, you're going to have half of Mexico City thinking I'm a homo for God's sake. Would you knock it off?"

As soon as we began eating, I tried to get Gearheardt back on track. "You said things have become more complicated. That we have been double-crossed. What's that all about? Level with me, Gearheardt."

Gearheardt was inspecting a string of meat he had found on his plate.

"I've gone back over all of the traffic while you were gone. Some things jumped out that I was too gung ho to see before."

"Too gung ho? I know what gung ho means but—"

"I let my enthusiasm for the mission blind me to the obvious. First, Crenshaw knows everything. He didn't work for the Pygmy, the Pygmy works for him. Second, and this is going to hurt, your secretary, Juanita, is not the innocent twit she sometimes acts like."

"Juanita? She's no twit."

"She and Crenshaw have been fooling you about a lot of things. But she doesn't know that she's been taken for a ride too." He paused and took a drink, then continued.

"But let me finish. Third, the Russians have gotten wind of things and are pissing in their pants. They know that Cuba will ask for help if the U.S. tries anything and they are going to be put on the spot. I suspect that the Cubans have already asked for assurances and the Russians aren't telling them what they want to hear. You remember the report we read this morning."

"Gearheardt, this is all very interesting, but I'm no closer to understanding what the hell is going on than I was before you started." I paused and put down my knife and fork. "And I'm still not convinced that Juanita is a mole."

"Jack, just remember that spying for an ally is still spying. But you'll understand about Juanita later. This is damn good carne asada, isn't it?"

I was thinking about Juanita whispering her sister was ISP. Maybe she was trying to tell me more than I realized. I watched Gearheardt finish his lunch and stack the plates on an adjacent desk. I knew that he would tell me what he wanted me to know in his own good time. He had always had an aversion to answering questions.

"Here's what I think has happened, Jack." He stood and went to the window. His best efforts couldn't open it and he sat back down. "That darn Daisy doesn't allow smoking in Las Palomas. Says it's not good for the girl's health. Anyway, about six months ago I took my plan to the agency—how we could basically get control of Cuba and win the appreciation of South and Central America at the same time."

"Why were you so concerned with getting control of Cuba? You were the one who told me how good the Cuban troops were and how Castro was 'the man.'"

"Well the part about the troops was, is, true. I wanted to make sure that no one thought the invasion would be a piece of cake. As for Castro, I was actually being sarcastic when I presented to the Agency, but they don't understand sarcasm much in Langley. I thought you knew I was kidding."

"Nope, you fooled me too."

"It doesn't make any difference. Cuba will never be worth a shit with Castro running it. The boys in Langley at least know that much. I just wanted to have a plan that wasn't a personal vendetta against the man."

"Okay, okay. I get it so far. The Agency bought your plan, which I still am in the dark about, and you started getting things set up. So what's gone wrong?"

"The Pygmy was my man in Langley. He had a lot of influence; basically from reading Tom Wolfe's book *Radical Chic and Mau Mauing the Flak Catchers*."

"I've read it. *That's* where he got his inspiration?" I could see where a four-foot African wearing animal skins and building cooking fires in the halls of CIA headquarters might be able to develop an intimidation factor. "So what happened next?"

"The Pygmy blabbed around about my whole plan and unfortunately caught the attention of the Vatican's spy in the Agency. You can probably guess—"

"Wait a minute. The Vatican has a spy in the CIA? Come on, Gearheardt. You've finally gone around the bend. This is just bullshit."

"As I started to say, Jack, you can probably guess who that spy is. Our boy Crenshaw."

I slammed the table with my fist and then stood up.

"Damn it, Gearheardt. This is just too much! If I believed any of this crap, and I'm not saying I do, then what was all that bull you gave me the last two days? Why didn't you just tell me your stupid plan and that you suspected Crenshaw or—"

Gearheardt got up and came over to my side of the table. "Jack, listen to me. I feel terrible but I'll tell you the truth. I had to get my plan started before you could talk me out of it."

I started to protest.

"No, listen. Remember, although you didn't know it, you were Crenshaw's pick to come down here. That surprises you doesn't it? But think about it, who better to have in Mexico City when I'm down here setting things up than my best pal? And better yet, a guy who actually has a conscience and a sense of duty. They knew you'd try to do the right thing. I knew that too and that's why I didn't look you up until I had things pretty well squared away."

He stuck his hand out and I debated whether or not I wanted to shake it, but he was only reaching past me to get my unfinished beer. Gearheardt was not overly sentimental.

He sat back down at the end of the table and finished my beer in one long swallow. "Nectar of the gods," he said. "This particular brand is 'piss of the gods,' but still pretty darn good." He tossed the bottle noisily into the trash can. "So are you with me now?"

I dropped into my chair. Still wrestling with the realization that I wasn't the Agency's 'golden boy,' ready to take on assignments with little experience and a woeful lack of language skills, but just a tool in the toolbox. I actually didn't resent that; I wasn't as naïve as Gearheardt didn't think I was. I felt foolish for letting my guard down and not realizing what I was doing. The Agency was right. I would always try to do the right thing. I just needed to know what it was.

"No, I am not with you now. I thought that I had figured out that Crenshaw's mission and your plan were one and the same. To tell the truth I assumed it was just ego that had you two vying for who was in charge. Not that I didn't think you probably had a few 'out-factors' that would give the Agency some heartburn. But now you tell me Crenshaw has double-crossed you. So I guess I am not *with you* quite yet."

Gearheardt went to the door and made sure that it was locked from the inside by turning the deadbolt. He shut the blind on the window.

"So I'm finally going to hear the truth?" I couldn't keep the sarcasm out of my voice. But I was also excited to finally know what was really going on.

"What? Oh sure, but I just decided I really had to have a cigarette. I don't want that damn Daisy busting in here."

Gearheardt lit his cigarette, puffed a couple of times and then dropped the remainder into a beer bottle. "Never as good as you think they're going to be."

"Would you please get on with it, Gearheardt? You're the most frustrating sonofabitch I've ever known."

"Thanks, Jack. Look, the idea of finally getting Castro out of Cuba wasn't a hard sell in the Agency. I think the President had to think it over for a couple of days. But they convinced him I could pull it off and that's what he was really concerned about. But my *whole* plan included putting the right people in office down there. There's where I had to make a deal with the devil. The devil in this case being the DCI. I agreed to give them exclusive rights to the information my network developed. It was too good for them to pass up. But Crenshaw evidently found out about it and brought in some big outside political guns to support his agenda."

"Which was?"

"Jack, he wants *the Vatican* to run Cuba. Mackerel snapper's heaven. They've been looking for a big success in Latin America ever since Montezuma kicked Cortez's ass."

"I'm not sure he did. But believe it or not, that doesn't seem so outlandish. It's hard to believe the Vatican has that much influence with the CIA. But I guess there is some history there." I looked at Gearheardt and felt almost proud of being involved in something as momentous as the Catholic Church taking over and running a country. Crenshaw's questions about the number of committed Catholics among the Cuban gangs made some sense. Maybe the Church could create the counter-revolution that the free Cubans couldn't. But that was only one side.

"So what was *your* plan, Gearheardt? The Marines? They're already on the island."

"I promised it to the girls, Jack. I told the ISP they could have their own country. Damn CIA and the Pope are trying to back down on their assurances. We're not going to let that happen, are we?"

After a moment, Gearheardt went on. "The thing is, I think the Pygmy has double crossed me. He's willing to get rid of me just so he can take over my network."

"The International Sisterhood of Prostitutes?"

"How many networks do you think I have, Jack? Yes, the ISP. So he puts out the word he's trying to kill you, but it's me he's after."

"That's a switch. But why hasn't he killed you?"

Gearheardt thought for a moment. "I think it has something to do with Crenshaw. They have to get my plan in place before they grab for it. Remember the U.S. has to invade Cuba or the Pope is left sitting with his di—"

"You're not really Catholic are you, Gearheardt?"

"Well anyway, the Pope gets squat if we don't bomb the Cubans. That ain't gonna make him happy."

It may be childish but even in my young manhood I had often relied on a basic test of proper behavior: Could I explain it to my mother?

This one would be interesting.

CHAPTER NINETEEN

IF GEARHEARDT WERE POPE, WE'D *ALL* GET TO WEAR FUNNY HATS

"**I**f I had explained it to you before, would you have helped me?" Gearheardt asked.

"It's just crazy, Gearheardt. How could you possibly expect your scheme to work? I'm surprised the DCI let you out of the building without calling the loony bin folks to come get you."

"If the CIA called the loony bin every time someone came up with a cockamamie idea—"

"But giving Cuba to the prostitutes? Evan if it *is* a good idea. I can't think of a more impractical mission to pull off. No politician is crazy enough to publicly back the idea. And that's saying a lot." I still couldn't quite believe he was serious.

"You're thinking of a big ceremony where the key to the country is handed over to a lady dressed in black lace and high heels, Jack. That's not the idea. When the Marines have control of Havana, we just put our team in office. Wham, bam, you've got New Whoreville on the map. Of course they'd come up with a better name."

I was having a hard time coming up with responses. The idea was so ludicrous that normal debate was impossible.

"It's not going to happen, Gearheardt."

"Not if we sit on our asses and let Crenshaw control the process. We need to get moving."

"How can Crenshaw do anything? He's being held in the mountains."

"Not anymore. We have him."

"We? And who would we be?"

"The ISP Guard. Some ladies I've been training for times just like these. Last night after we came down the hill, I met with the team leaders, gave 'em the location, suspected enemy strength, and they had a plan within the hour. I expect to hear from them any time now. Mission accomplished."

"So the ISP has a military wing?" I asked. I would go along with the joke.

"I'd put them up against Special Forces troops any day. Jack, what do you really need to have an effective fighting force? I'll tell you. You need weapons, motivation, and intelligence, I mean the information kind. These ladies have all the motivation in the world, we supply the best intelligence available, and I've been able to find a few weapons here and there."

"I'll bet you have. So you've trained your own guerilla army now. That's just great."

"They know the strengths and weaknesses of their opponents better than any troops in the world. They're motivated because they have zero alternatives. None. And they're fighting to get their own country." Gearheardt sat down beside me.

"Jack, imagine you're seventeen and some greasy bastard is beating you and getting ready to rape you. But you know if you can just get to an ISP unit, you have a chance to get to Cuba and a whole new life. One of the things that keep these women down now is they have no place o go."

"I think it's a bit more complicated than that, Gearheardt. I'm just saying the impracticality is staggering. Forget it. This is silly."

I was now fully aware that Gearheardt was 100% serious. But being serious didn't solve any of the problems with his scheme. I was afraid that he had misled hundreds or thousands of poor women around the world.

Gearheardt slumped back in his chair. After a moment he went to the window and opened the blinds, staring silently down into the street. I felt sorry for him. It was a dream that obviously meant a lot to him. It was just that it was . . . childish. A pot of gold at the end of a rainbow kind of dream.

I decided to humor him just to let him talk it out. Maybe my lucid comments would begin to bring him around.

"What would you say to the Cubans in Cuba now? They might have something to say about a few thousand whores coming in to run the country."

"Screw 'em. That's what I would say. They've let Castro beat them into farm animals anyway. As for the Cuban army, we'd kick the shit out of them while we were taking over. And the Marines are already on the island." He turned back to me. "Gitmo."

"When I was training the girls to be information gatherers, I would ask them why they didn't get out, get away. They all said the same thing; they had nowhere to go." He walked back to the table and sat down. "We bring whores to Cuba and we send doctors and lawyers and business women back to the world. *If* they want to leave the island. Funding this would be a drop in the bucket."

"Ventures almost as screwy as this have been tried before, Gearheardt. Not many, if any, work. The people are just as bad off as they were before."

"Jack, you're talking about places where the leaders were chewing on missionary thigh bone one day and trying to run a parliament the next. This isn't like that."

He squared himself facing me. "Let me take one more shot at you, Jack. Then we have to get back to keeping the Cubans from killing the President of Mexico. That's still a possibility you know." He drew a deep breath. "Jack, do you think we should help the prostitutes, the sex slaves, the whores of the world? Do you think that's a worthy cause?"

"Lots of people are trying, Gearheardt. Well, maybe not lots of people, but there *are* organizations."

"You're right. And do you know what simple task those organizations have as their goal? Their easy way to fight the battle? I'll tell you: changing human nature. They're going to educate and support and preach and diddle around until men don't want to screw whores. How long do you think that will take? What are the odds of changing men's nature?" He paused. "And you think I am a lunatic for just trying to get the girls the hell out of their situation physically."

After a moment he rose and went to the door. As he unlocked the deadbolt he said, "I'm disappointed in you, Jack." He left.

I sat stunned. I had just been lectured on the sad state of affairs for prostitutes by the wildest, booziest, whore-mongering bastard in the free world. I was speechless.

After a moment, Marta came in through the door Gearheardt had left unlocked.

"Ola, Jack. Señor Pepe is mad at you. What is it that causes the argument? Maybe I can help you."

"I don't think so, Marta. It's nice of you to want to patch up things between Gearheardt and me, but don't worry about it. We've had disagreements before." I got up and pulled a chair out for her at the conference table. "Tell me about Victor."

She hesitated and I wondered if it were her facts or her loyalties she was considering. "He says that the Cuban government is very unbelieving but that they have given him resources to move forward. He is wanting to meet with you tonight. There are plans to go over."

Unfortunately the plans I needed were in the head of a friend who was pretty pissed at me. "Set up a meeting for late. Maybe nine o'clock. We'll have the info we need by then."

"And the maps and the papers, no?" Marta seemed skeptical.

"Yes, we'll have whatever is needed. Cinco de Mayo is tomorrow, right? We have the rest of today and tonight to make sure everything is in place."

The teletype clattered and I went to see the traffic spewing out. I was uncomfortable in the room with Marta and it gave me something to do.

POTUS REQUESTS INFO ON SENATOR X4X VISITING RIO BROTHEL. PHOTOS IF POSSIBLE. PLEASE USE PLAIN BROWN ENVELOP TO POTUS PERSONAL PO BOX.

I had the feeling that Gearheardt had created a monster. I didn't bother looking up the code for the Senator's name, just wrote the time and date received and dropped the message in the in-basket.

"Jack," Marta said, "do you think that Pepe's plan can succeed?"

I faced her. "I'm not sure, Marta. I know that there are many people who would like a reason to take out Castro. He is too dangerous to have ninety miles from our coast when he's playing with the Russians."

"Yes, but that is not the plan that I am talking about. Will the U.S. government—"

"I really wouldn't know." My answer sounded cold. I didn't want to hear her question.

"I do not want to go back to being a prostitute, Jack."

Gearheardt entered and saved me from having to respond. "Jack, Crenshaw is heading back to the embassy. I've worked out a compromise with him."

"Crenshaw was here? Why didn't you come get me?"

"He was pretty pissed off, particularly at you. We cleaned him up and let him go." Gearheardt smiled. "I told you the girls were good. Maria, the team leader, said they didn't even have to kill anybody. Marta, you should let someone know there are ten or so Cubans tied up at the cabin. Can't let them starve to death."

Marta looked a bit shocked. "But how would I know who to—"

"Don't worry about it, kiddo. We know you tipped off Victor. Jack might have done the same thing. But you're with us now. I need to know we can trust you. Can we?"

Marta looked at me and I think she was considering my lack of response to her last question. She turned to Gearheardt. "Yes, Pepe. You can trust me."

"Good girl. Find Daisy or Lisa and have them help you get the message out. Don't go to Victor by yourself. Everybody is double-crossing everybody in this lash up and I don't want to lose you." He laughed. "I really never thought I could have as much fun as I did in Vietnam, but this is getting close."

After Marta left, Gearheardt came to me and put his hand on my shoulder. "No hard feelings, Jack. Maybe you're right. It was a crazy idea." He squeezed. "I can always count on you to keep me from doing anything rash, can't I? That's a true friend. Standing up for my best interests even when you have to be a screaming asshole."

I wasn't sure what to say. When Gearheardt sounds rational, the world should be on alert. Finally I said, "So where are we? What's this agreement with Crenshaw?"

"Sit down, Jack. Time to quit screwing around and make some plans. We don't have a hell of a lot of time."

At the table, he grabbed a note pad and pencil. "Okay, here's the deal. Crenshaw believes, like we do, that we should take over Cuba. He also agrees that the attempted assassination of the Mexican President is enough provocation—I told you I went to Princeton, didn't I?—to get the Central Americans and South Americans on our side. Before he found out what a traitorous miscreant—his words—you were, he had already arranged for you to be a part of the President's personal bodyguard for the speech on Cinco de Mayo. He also knows that you're the only one who can recognize Victor. You with me so far?"

"I thought Crenshaw knew Victor."

"He does, but he can't be one of the bodyguards. Too obvious to have the Chief of Station of the CIA tailing along with the President. You're the man."

"So what do I do?"

"Crenshaw will have his guys, so he says, in the crowd and in the area. That will give you a bit of protection. But I want our boys, the guys coming up from Palenque, to be your real protection. They can pick off the Cubans that Victor is sure to have around. And, this is the important part, they have the means to get you and Marta to Havana right after we save the President."

"Tell me why I have to go to Havana again?" I had never been comfortable with that part.

"We have to have someone there who can monitor things for a few days and get the network up and running. It won't be possible for the U.S. to launch an invasion immediately."

"As you have pointed out, Gearheardt, I don't even speak Spanish."

"Marta will be with you all the time. Don't worry about it. I have *got* to have someone there I can trust. Seriously, Jack, don't worry about it." I had the feeling there was something else he wanted to tell me.

"Victor says he needs information and some kind of papers."

"Let me worry about Victor. He needs the schedule, and he needs some identification paperwork so that he can get close to the stage. You can get that from Crenshaw."

"I doubt it."

"No, it's part of the deal I made with him. Head on over there now and I'll see you back here late this afternoon."

"Where are you going?"

"I need to visit the Halcones. We somehow have to get them to stand by and let all this happen. The Mexican police aren't a problem, but the Secret Police boys could step in and give us all a big hole in our head."

"Can you get that done? I thought they were not too happy with you."

"I'll give 'em what they want. No skin off my nose. I've got an appointment with your pal Eduardo. Horniest guy in the world. This should be fairly easy."

"You're probably right. He was pretty interested in your amateur porn movie."

"I'm taking Lisa with me." He got up and idly checked the in-basket. "*Photos if possible*," he read. "Do these dopes think we're some sleazy detective agency?" He wrote a note on the paper and dropped it back in the basket. "I've told the girls to grab some pornography, as graphic as possible, and send it along. What are they going to do? Complain about the quality?"

He turned back to me. "Better get a move on, Jack. Tonight we need to brief the Good Cubans heading up from Palanque. They'll need that same information that Victor wants."

I wanted to say something to him, but I wasn't sure what. He had been so passionate about helping the 'girls.' I was having a hard time believing he was giving up so easily.

"Jack, get the other thing off your mind, you condescending bastard. Remember I'm an American first. Getting rid of Castro is important."

He knew me better than my poor old mom.

Gearheardt grabbed the phone on the first ring.

"Ola . . . Hello, Lisa . . . No . . . I said no, wear something else . . . because I said so . . . be ready in five minutes." He grinned as he hung up. "I love these girls."

Juanita was sheepish when she saw me approaching. I wondered how much she knew about what was going on. Then I remembered that Gearheardt said she was passing information to someone. My mind was so screwed up that I couldn't even remember who she was supposed to be spying for.

"Ola, Jack. I am glad to see you in the office. You no look so good."

"Just tired, Juanita. I've been over at Las Palomas ever since I saw you this morning."

Juanita blushed and looked at her typewriter. "Señor Crenshaw would like to see you. He is in his office. He looks more bad than you." She paused. "What is going on, Jack? Is all America go crazy?"

"It appears so, Juanita. Have I had any calls today?"

"Señor Rodrigo says . . ." she checked her notes . . . "he moving to Alaska. I think he is joking. For you to call him. And Eduardo called. He is meeting Señor Pepe. He says for you to not worry."

"Thanks, Juanita." I started into my office.

"Oh, and Señor Jack. Señor Chavez from El Caballo called also. He says to tell you no one come to kill you all day today."

"Thank you, Juanita. That *is* good news. I'm sure Señor Chavez must be bored silly over there."

My office looked a bit bare. The desk was clear of files. The file cabinet drawers were standing open and empty. Not even a burro tail or two.

With nothing in my office to delay me, I walked down to the break room to cross into Major Crenshaw's office. The candy machine, the one jokesters liked to slide in front of the station chief's door, lay on its side, the little windows broken and candy spilling out. I assumed the Major was not in the mood for jokes today.

"Come in," the Major boomed when I knocked.'

"Yes, sir. Good to see you again, Major Crenshaw. I was quite worried about you when we left the mountains last night."

To my surprise, he was calm, even jovial.

"No reason to be, Jack. You and Gearheardt did what you thought best. Those boys meant no real harm to me."

He had a bloody bandage around his forehead which he must have seen me looking at.

"I should have known better than to goad that Julio fellow. Very conflicted in his allegiances, you know. Makes him insecure and dangerous. I have to say I had one hell of a headache this morning." He gingerly touched his bandage. "But I'm always ready to take a pounding for the Agency. What they pay me for. Those ladies that Gearheardt sent to get me knew their stuff alright. Nice looking girls too. Don't know if you've seen them, but maybe a bit too much makeup and perfume for good soldiers."

"I haven't met them, sir."

"Okay, so I am ready to forgive you, Jack. Gearheardt is not to my liking. Shouldn't have renegades like that in the Agency. But I know he is persuasive and he did come with an imprimatur that probably seemed valid." He smiled and I smiled back.

"So let's get back on track. The plan is simple and I think you know it. The Agency is to foil an attempt by the Cubans to overthrow the government of Mexico. You know your role in that, and I know that I can trust you. Gearheardt seemed to have his own idea of what would happen then, but that's not important now. What *is* important," he walked to the door and checked that it was locked, then turned on a small cassette on his desk that played marching music, "is that I will be going directly to Cuba. I'll be running things there with my own network until our government can come to the 'rescue' so to speak. I don't need to tell you that this is top secret. Very dangerous work, spying in Havana, but I'm up to it."

"Sir, is Gearheardt aware of what the plans are?"

"Only the Mexico City part, Jack. He needs to reign in his grandiose vision of himself. I'm not interested in his view on national strategy. I'll give him that he was the first to come up with the staged assassination idea. But after that, he needs to get on with whatever else he was doing."

"But won't you need his help to get—"

"Jack, I didn't have in mind discussing my plans with you. As I have told you before, I haven't been sitting on my ass since I came to Mexico. I have my own support and believe me, it is of the highest . . . shall we say caliber."

After a moment, I started to rise. "Is there anything else, sir?"

"Juanita will have the package I have prepared for you, Jack. Follow the instructions."

Crenshaw rose also. "Don't hesitate to shoot if you have to, Jack. If something happened to the President and it should come out that we knew about the attempt beforehand . . . it could be quite bad for us."

"I understand, Major Crenshaw."

The Major came around the desk. "If it will make you feel less uneasy, I can tell you that I have talked with the Halcones. Although they don't know the whole story, they are alerted and know what to do. I don't think it will come down to you shooting Victor." He patted my shoulder. "If you're worried about your future, Jack, you shouldn't be. More than anyone else, I know what pressures you have been under. And I value loyalty, even to a renegade like your friend."

I should have felt better. In my office I went over the package that Crenshaw had prepared. The President's movements were detailed down to a piss break just before he went on stage. The entry point for Victor was just as the President came in view of the crowd that would be in front of the platform. Although held twenty-five yards back, they would be able to see the action, and my reaction.

It seemed at this point so utterly reckless. Staging what was in effect a quick draw contest, even though I had the benefit of prior knowledge, with the life of a country's leader at risk.

Gearheardt's plan for me took over where Crenshaw's stopped. After Victor was disarmed, or dead, I was to yell out that I saw another potential assassin and pursue him. Most of the attention would be on the President and Victor. The Good Cubans, after eliminating any Bad Cubans they saw, would then assist me into a waiting car, out to an airstrip and off to Cuba. The plans for landing in Cuba were a little vague, but I had what was probably an unreasonable confidence in Marta once we were in Cuba. I could see that this was something she wanted very badly.

I was going to work to put the Sisterhood of Prostitutes in place as the new rulers of Cuba. Now I knew why Gearheardt wanted me there. Whoever had that first knowledge of the situation in Havana had a great advantage in calling the shots.

I placed a quick call to my mother in Kansas. It seemed like the thing to do.

"Is Gearheardt taking care of you, Jack?" she asked almost immediately.

"Yes, mom. He is certainly taking care of me. You do know he's kind of wild, don't you, mom?" I didn't know what she might hear about Goodbye Mexico if we failed, or if we succeeded, but I needed to start breaking her in on Gearheardt's other side.

"Oh, I'm sure he is. You should get him to settle down. Find a nice girlfriend. Are you still dating that little blonde Austrian girl, Jack? She seemed sharp as a tack."

I hesitated, telling the truth to mom was as hard as lying to her.

"She didn't work out. But I've found someone I do like." Holy shit. Why did I say that?

"Well?"

"Oh there's not a lot to tell. If it works out, I'll bring her up there."

"Does she work at an embassy? You seem to date a lot of those girls."

"She was a Cuban prostitute before she came to Mexico City, Mom." I had lost my mind.

"Oh, Jack," she laughed, "you sound just like that damn Gearheardt." She giggled at her bold language, so I said goodbye and hung up.

CHAPTER TWENTY

I'LL BE DOWN TO GET
YOU IN A TAXI, HONEY

I dropped by my apartment to clean up and change clothes, as well as fill a leather case. I wasn't sure when I would be going, or where for that matter. If things worked out, I could possibly return and stay in my apartment again, but with Gearheardt in charge of planning . . .

The apartment had a slight odor I didn't recognize. Almost like someone had cooked a meal, or roasted a goat. The Pygmy had been in my apartment. Gearheardt was supposed to have called him off. And I meant to ask Crenshaw about him. But I just had too many things on my mind.

Sitting on the sofa sipping one last Scotch and water, I thought about Marta. It seemed ages since she was tripping around the place au natural. I missed it. I knew that one of the reasons I had decided to back Gearheardt's plan (although he didn't know I was backing it yet) was Marta. I didn't want her to have to go back to being a prostitute either. I found a couple of spare clips for my nine millimeter, made my bed (once a mama's boy, always a mama's boy) and left to hook up with Gearheardt.

I found him hard at work on the plan . . . if you call MC'ing a butt-measuring contest on the second floor of Las Palomas working on the plan.

"Jack, just the man I want to see," he said as I walked in. "How thick would you say that two layers of material, say silk, could be? I'm trying to convince these girls that getting measured in their underwear is misleading. Don't you think?"

"I'm not sure, Gearheardt. I wouldn't think that your measuring was all that accurate." I didn't know whose side I was supposed to be on.

The girls, all fifteen of them, squealed. "You lie to us, Gearheardt. Maybe we pull off your pants and measure you," the bleached blonde said. She had on what I think was called a Baby Doll negligee. Folded up twenty times I couldn't imagine the thickness of the material was more than a thousandth of an inch.

"I show my butt by appointment only, Victoria. But we'll just have to declare Teresa the winner. Come here, Teresa, and get your prize."

"I take the prize in appointment only, Señor Gearheardt."

The girls thought this was a great comeback and everyone laughed at Gearheardt's embarrassment. He started to get out of his comfortable leather judging- chair.

"Señor Gearheardt," a lovely, sure bottom measurement winner said loudly, "why are we not living in the Chapultepec Castle? You said that we would move there."

Gearheardt looked at me as if I was supposed to have an answer. I shrugged.

"I'll tell you the truth, ladies. I did promise that, but I'm having the place redecorated. It was way too trashy for your tastes."

The girl spoke so rapidly in Spanish that I could tell even Gearheardt was lost.

"What was that, Laquita?"

"Es sound of toro going bathroom."

Gearheardt held his head high in defeat as we left the room. In the hallway, he stopped me. "All of the girls are not ISP here. I have to be careful what I tell them."

"So how did you do with the Halcones? Did you see Eduardo and get their cooperation for tomorrow?"

"Are you kidding me? Eduardo almost wet his pants when I told him he could look at the traffic from Mexican brothels as well as the overseas brothels that Mexican diplomats might have visited. He's up there right now with Lisa."

"Isn't that a little dangerous, to turn him loose with the files?"

"He's only seeing traffic a year or older. I called ahead and had Daisy move everything current into her room. Jack, the Marines couldn't get into Daisy's room without suffering major casualties. How'd you get along with Friar Crenshaw?"

I looked up and down the hall. It was empty but sounds of music and muffled laughter came through the walls. "Its okay," Gearheardt said. "The only customers right now are foreign businessmen. But I don't want to go upstairs until that damn Eduardo is gone."

"Okay. Well, the Major was pretty nice actually. Said he understood how I got into this. Thinks you're the anti-Christ. Gave me the plans. Said he'd take care of things tomorrow on his end." I paused, sorting our loyalties. "You do know he's personally planning to go to Havana?"

Gearheardt looked around, probably to see if Daisy was about, and then lit a cigarette. "Not a shock to me. Some guys think they can do anything." He smiled. "So it looks like we're just about all set to go. We'll brief the Good Cubans tonight. I meet with Victor at eleven o'clock. Then tomorrow, we change the world."

"Hmmmm," I said. "Gearheardt, about your plan. I know that it means a lot to you and that you seem to have things all worked out. I just—"

A few of the girls came into the hall and excused themselves by us. They smelled terrific. Just as Veronica passed she dropped her magazine and leaned down from the waist to pick it up. Gearheardt bit his knuckle. Then rolled his eyes at me.

"Jack, don't even mention it. I should have told you the truth when we were holed up in the El Diablo that first night. We're on track now. Let's just move ahead." He held out his hand and I took it.

"You do understand that I mean—"

"Jack, let me tell you something. Women who have had babies on average have bigger butts than those that haven't. Seems logical, but I just never thought of it. You have to allow for age and bone structure, but—"

"Oh for God's sakes, Gearheardt. I'm trying to tell you something important."

"*Gearheardt, you are smoking out there?*"

"Shit." He handed the cigarette to me and took off down the hall in the opposite direction from where Daisy's voice had boomed out. This was a man who flew unarmed helicopters into landing zones where people were shooting fifty caliber weapons at him.

Daisy came thundering around the corner. When she reached the spot I seemed to be glued to, she grabbed the cigarette from my fingers. Opening the door nearest her, she stepped in and dropped the cigarette into a glass of water on the bedside table. The couple on the bed, infla-grante delecto, were in stop action. Some ugly Spanish flew over the man's shoulder until Daisy walked to the bed and slapped his bare butt. The man quieted and Daisy came out and shut the door behind her. She glared at me and then tromped back in the direction she had come from. Her high heels clicked and I saw about half a mile of bare leg when her negligee flared as she turned the corner. I blew out my breath.

Gearheardt was no where to be found so I went back into the reception room. Chiquita and her sister were cleaning the place up, picking up magazines, replacing cushions onto the leather couches and rearrang-ing the flower in the vases. Getting ready for the evening rush hour.

"Ola, Señor Jack," Chiquita said. "You are a very handsome man. I am telling my mother that you will be my first." She blew a kiss to me.

"That's very flattering, Chiquita. I don't think that would be a very good idea. I am a homosexual." I never thought I would be saying that to a beautiful girl. In the game room, I sat down without looking at the plaque underneath the Ibex horns, the one that had the small brown shriveled bag mounted on it. I could see Chiquita and her sister through the open double doors, whispering and giggling, looking at me with pity.

After a while, I closed my eyes and began to relax. The die was cast. My fate was in the hands of a lunatic. But it had been there before. My job was to keep Victor Ramirez from shooting the President of Mexico, and then to hole up in Havana, presumably running Gearheardt's network of prostitutes, until the Marines came. The plot was pretty thin, but then I could remember when we unleashed a trillion dollar bombing campaign because some fishing boats took potshots at boats the size of Rockefeller Center in the Gulf of Tonkin.

I was becoming resigned to the fact that history books were filled with borders and politics and grand strategies, heroes and heroines (infrequently), God, family and country. In the Agency, we dealt with whores, drugs, greed, and madmen. Not to mention thugs, gangsters, zealots of all description, double dealers, triple dealers, turncoats, thieves and some good people (more often than one might think). I supposed that somewhat like policemen on the local level, we saw the underside of societies on the global level. And we were a part of it.

"Ola, Jack." I felt a hand on my arm, gently squeezing. It was Marta, perched on the arm of my chair. "So now you are homosexual, si?" She smiled.

"I was just—"

"I know. The girls can be a nuisance. And Daisy, she is fierce, no?"

I slipped my arm around Marta's waist and pulled her onto my lap. She didn't resist.

"Marta, we should talk. Tomorrow, if we're lucky, we may be heading to Havana. I want you to know that part of the reason I am going is because of you. I don't know how you feel, but . . . " I wasn't sure what to say next.

"I am glad that we will be together, Jack. I am glad that you trust me to take care of you. It is a scary thing, to go to Cuba now."

"I'll admit that. But on a personal basis (why did I always sound like a bureaucrat when I tried to discuss emotions with women?) you do understand that I like you very much."

"I am beginning to embarrass to be nude in front of you, Jack. I think this means that I like you very much also."

Well, that was a start. I thought I knew what she meant. I had noticed before that when she became excited or emotional, her English started to fall apart.

When Marta turned her head to look at me, I pulled gently on her neck and brought her lips to mine.

"Hey, knock that shit off. We're in a respectable whorehouse here."

"Gearheardt, you rotten bastard. You scared the hell out of us."

Marta stood up quickly, but she was smiling.

Gearheardt grabbed my hand and pulled me out of the chair.

"Marta, Jack likes you. Jack, Marta thinks you're cute. You can get back to the courtship later. We've got some problems to address." He turned serious. "Jack, brief Marta quickly on the information you got from Crenshaw, then I'll give her a couple of messages also. She needs to meet the Palanque contingent and get them squared away. You and I have bigger fish to fry. First that damn Victor is off the reservation. And if that's not bad enough, the Pygmy is on a rampage. Claims he's being cut out of the deal."

"What do you mean Victor is off the reservation?"

"The asshole sent word that he wants Marta to . . . well in effect he wants her as hostage against a double cross tomorrow. Don't worry Marta. No way in hell we'll let that cutthroat get his hands on you. But Jack and I need to go talk to him. You go get the envelope from Crenshaw off of my desk and bring it down here. We'll go over it with you."

After she left, Gearheardt and I went to a dark corner of the game room and pulled two chairs together.

"Jack, this deal with Victor could throw a monkey wrench into the works. If we don't have a bona fide Cuban brandishing a weapon around El Presidente, then we can't look like heroes."

"What about using one of the Good Cubans you have coming up?"

"You want to try to convince one of them to let us shoot him?"

"Oh, yeah, I guess that wouldn't work."

"Don't feel bad. My mind is spinning right now too. But you and I have to convince Victor we are 100% behind him. No way I'm throwing Marta into his greasy hands."

"I agree. What about the Pygmy? What's that all about?"

The little asshole still thinks he's going to take over the ISP. He's pretending to be confused about who he assassinates, but he's not fooling me. And he thinks if he does get control of my network, he can run Cuba. The little prick."

"Is there anybody that doesn't think they have a right to run Cuba?"

"I don't know anyone in this fucked up mess that hasn't put themselves on the list, except you. But we need to head out. We can find the Pygmy in the park and either talk some sense in him, or just tie him up and leave him in the refrigerator at your place. I'm tired of dicking with him."

Marta unfortunately came through the door into the reception room just as three well-dressed and well-oiled Mexican gentlemen arrived through the front door. Chiquita tried to head them off, but the allure of Marta was too strong. Gearheardt stepped into the room. Marta lifted her skirt and drew her Baretta and the three amigos were almost on their way to amigo dreamland, when Daisy showed up.

"Aw, Señors," she sang. "Buenos noches." After a bit more Spanish, a finger pointed at Gearheardt and a discrete jingling of her necklace, the gentlemen accepted champagne and seats in front of the fireplace to wait for other entertainment, concocting a to-be-told-later of the whore who kept a pistol in her woman parts.

"Gearheardt, it is time for business. You and the smoking man should do your talking elsewhere," Daisy said.

"We need to use the office for five minutes and then we're gone, Daisy."

In the hallway I asked Gearheardt, "What the hell was that Daisy was wearing around her neck. Ugliest damn necklace I've ever seen."

"Its what they use to de-nut sheep."

"Oooooh," I said. I felt my testicles crawling up into my groin. "That's what I thought."

In the office we briefed Marta quickly. She had the information in Crenshaw's papers. And she was the one that had to coordinate the getaway with the Good Cubans. She said she could handle it and took off.

"Where is she taking them after the briefing?" I asked Gearheardt.

He thought for a minute. "I'm not sure. But we agreed to meet back here no later than midnight. She can tell us then." He took out his PPK and checked to see if the clip was full. "You ready to go see Victor?"

"Ready as I'll ever be."

On the way down to the street, Gearheardt put his arm around my shoulders. "You remember going to see old Ho Chi Minh?"

"I remember his sidekick, Giap, getting ready to shoot you with a pistol that must have been a 75 caliber. Biggest damn thing I ever saw."

Gearheardt laughed. "Me too."

"I also remember why he wanted to shoot you. Because you were such an insufferable wise-ass. Remember that?"

"Must have been another trip to Hanoi you're thinking of, Jack. I was on my best behavior."

We were at the street. The young Mexican Gearheardt had left the Impala with was there holding the door open on a gray Mercedes. The plates looked suspiciously like the diplomatic plates on the Brazilian embassy cars.

"Muchas gracias, muchacho," Gearheardt said. "How long will the gentlemen not be needing his car?"

The boy grinned as he accepted a wad of pesos from Gearheardt. "He just went up with the lady. He is quite old and quite drunk. I would say maybe one hour, two hour. His driver is quite content to wait in Las Palomas restaurant." He pointed through the window toward a man in black who was having his inner thigh stroked to a fair thee well by a lady with long red fingernails.

"We'll be back before then. Gracias."

As usual, Gearheardt carefully strapped himself in and then went ape-shit. Burning away from the curb, he rounded the corner at a speed that threw the back end to the side, and settled down to fifty miles an hour on the straightaway, a street full of shoppers, taxis, strolling police-men, vendor carts and other speeding automotive maniacs.

"My mother said to tell you hello, Gearheardt." A part of me prob-ably thought that reminding Gearheardt that I had family depending on me might slow him down.

"Great woman, Jack. Great. Your dad's still dead, right?"

That's how much he was paying attention to me. It took his total concentration to watch for the openings between men driving donkeys ahead of them and liveried drivers in Cadillacs edging in from side streets. Those were openings allowing him to shoot through the closing gaps and literally get tens of feet further than if we had just waited for a place to pass.

"Gearheardt," I said to keep my mind off dying, "would you like me to get a jousting lance and strap it to the side of the car?"

"Sounds good, Jack. Hey, look at that asshole trying to pass us on the sidewalk. What an idiot." Gearheardt went up on the sidewalk to block the idiot's way. Then we turned at the next corner. "I can't stand guys like that."

"We're coming up on the street that leads to the club, Gearheardt. You might want to slow down."

And I might want to save my breath. He was almost past the street when it dawned on him that I had spoken.

"Hold on, Jack."

My hands, feet, and sphincter were grabbing whatever they could get hold of.

At the curb in front of the club I tried to breathe deep.

"Damn, Gearheardt, riding with you just wears me out."

"We were in New York one night and one of my buddies ran out of money. He walked back to Princeton rather than ride with me. Took him three days."

"At last, Gearheardt, one of your stories I can believe." I looked up at the club. "Remember, we're here to convince him to do what we planned. We're not here to give him a lot of crap, or try to antagonize him. You've met him before and you know he's a cocky jerk. Forget that."

"Righto, Jack. Mr. Diplomat. That's me." He opened the car door. "Let's go see this asshole."

I grabbed his arm just as we got to the front door. "Gearheardt, we forgot about the Pygmy."

"I didn't. Daisy is going to send a couple of her boys to pick him up in the park and take him to Las Palamos. I told her to have them break his damn head if he puts up a fight. She's going to lock him in with Benito. The Pygmy hates homos."

We entered the Club Tristiza and found the manager.

"We're here to see Victor Ramirez," I told him.

"Una momento, Señor."

In just under a minute he returned and led us to the same office where Marta and I had met with Victor the day before. He sat behind his desk and didn't get up or say hello as we came in and sat down in front of his desk.

"Where is Marta?" he said.

"She couldn't make it. What seems to be the problem? You got the information you need for tomorrow, right? Gearheardt and I have everything set up for you." I waited for him to say something.

"I want Marta here, or no deal. I say that very clearly to the courier who brought the papers. Maybe he didn't speak the Engleesh."

"He spoke the Engleesh very well. Do you hear the Engleesh very well? No Marta. You show up tomorrow. I let you through the crowd right by the stage. You shoot the President, head for the doorway to the right of the stage and we'll take it from there. We'll have you in Cuba in two hours." I paused. "By the way, the Halcones think it's a good idea for you to visit Cuba also. They'll let you out if you're with me."

Victor opened his coat and took out a pistol which he laid on the desk. "I talk to my friends the Russians. They say that the plan you have is crazy. That the Americans would never let the Cubans run Mexico. They laugh at the idea."

"Well, I'm shocked, Victor." I hoped he understood sarcasm. "I would have bet that the Russians agreed with every word. And by the way, that was real smart to tell the Russians our plan. Did Castro himself suggest that? Just damn brilliant." I nodded at Gearheardt who sat quietly with his arms folded across his chest, staring intently at Victor. "You know Gearheardt, don't you Victor? One of the CIA's top men, you know that also. He didn't come down here to hear about your discussions with the Russians. He was in Havana three days ago. Setting up things. You doubt that? Call your pals in Havana."

Gearheardt moved his hand to his inside pocket, withdrew a pen and wrote a number down on the top of Victor's desk. It was (I learned later), Castro's actual phone number. Marta had gotten it for him.

"Call him. Tell him that you don't trust the Americans. That you talked to the Russians about the plan that *you* sold your bosses less than twenty-four hours ago. We'll wait."

Victor didn't reach for his phone. Instead he picked up his Russian .45, cocked the hammer back and pointed it at my forehead. At less than two feet, he would have to be an awfully poor shot to miss me.

Gearheardt lit a cigarette, looked around for the trash and finally tossed the burnt match on Victor's desk.

I leaned forward until Victor's pistol was only a foot from my face.

"No Marta. No more pussyfooting. You show up tomorrow and shoot that fat son of a bitch," I said as levelly as I could manage. After a moment, I stood up. "Let's go, Gearheardt. Victor, we'll see you in the morning. We'll take care of you."

The pistol was still pointed at me as I reached the door and held it open for Gearheardt.

"You know, Victor, this is about the stupidest fucking idea for a nightclub I've ever heard of," Gearheardt said. He left.

"Very nice, Gearheardt," I said as we exited. "You just couldn't *not* say something, could you?"

"I don't think the president of Mexico is fat, Jack."

Our Mercedes was still at the curb. Getting in, Gearheardt looked over the top of the car. "I have to tell you, Jack, you did a great job. I actually thought the bastard would probably shoot you. Nerves of steel, that's my boy." He slapped the top of the car. "Why are you getting in the back seat?"

The traffic was bad and Gearheardt couldn't immediately get up to ramming speed. "Was that a good idea, putting the Pygmy in with Benito, Gearheardt? He's a good kid and you tell me that the Pygmy is a killer."

"The kid is a whiz with cutlery, Jack. Worry about the Pygmy if you have to worry." He braked suddenly and threw the car into reverse. "Damn traffic," he said.

At the Las Palomas, the Brazilian diplomat stood sulking at the curb while his driver harangued our poor Mexican automobile valet. Gearheardt screeched to a halt and hopped out, leaving the driver's door open. He gestured at the chauffer to get in, pronto. Coming around the car, he opened the back door and let me out.

He grabbed the shocked diplomat by the coat. "Get in you Portuguese-speaking prick." He slammed the door behind the astonished gentleman and pounded the top of the car. "Let's move it," he shouted. The car moved away quickly.

"Muchacho, next time get the gentleman a fat old ugly woman. I wasn't even gone forty-five minutes." He borrowed pesos from me and gave them to the boy.

"You're in a fine mood, Gearheardt," I said.

"Jack, if my driving is so bad, just say so. Don't go hiding in the back seat. I felt like your damn chauffer." He pushed open the door and went inside. We're taking over a country the next day and he's mad because I insulted his driving.

Upstairs things weren't going well. When I followed Gearheardt into the reception parlor of the Las Palamos, Daisy was chasing a tall black man with a machete. He had a pistol drawn and looked like he was looking for an opportunity to use it if he could get distance between them. Marta was crying. Benito was rolling on the floor laughing, dressed only in a bustier and a vendor's white cap. With all that, the din from down the hall was such that the parlor scene looked like it was a silent movie. Nothing could be heard above the music and general rabble rousing. A half dozen inebriated Mexican gentlemen sat in their underwear in the game room, watching in horror and (I found out later) waiting for a chance to dash back down the hall and retrieve their clothes from the girls' rooms.

Gearheardt braved the melee and crossed the room to close the hallway door. The noise was reduced from a battle to a skirmish.

"*Okay, knock this shit off,*" Gearheardt yelled. He picked up the nearest flower vase and threw it against the wall. Everyone gave him their attention except Marta, who continued crying in her chair by the fireplace.

"Daisy, put down the machete. Right now! Benito, go get some pants on and find that damn Pygmy."

Gearheardt walked to Marta and looked down at her. "Let me guess," he said. "You thought you would bring the boys back here rather than the motel I told you to find."

Marta kept her face in her hands but nodded her head affirmatively.

"And the boys, some of whom have been squatting around a campfire in the rain forest for three days, thought they had died and gone to heaven."

"Señor Gearheardt, is that you?" This strained voice came from the tall black man who was held against the wall by Daisy's machete against his throat.

"Welcome to Mexico City, Mario. You are Mario, right?"

"I don't care if he's Alexander the great," Daisy said through her teeth, "one of his boys has Chiquita back there and if she isn't out here, *unmolested,* in about thirty seconds, this black man will be standing in a pool of blood."

Benito spoke up. "I know where the girls are, Señora Daisy. They are safe."

"I thought I told you to get your bare ass out of here, Benito. Oh, shit, don't throw up. What a damn nightmare."

Daisy had lowered the machete. "I hope you're right, Benito."

"Señor, por favor." The soft voice came from behind me, near the door.

A middle aged Mexican man stood quietly, his eyes drinking in the scene, holding his taxi hat in his hands. "The bill, Señor. For the taxis?"

"Crap, I forgot to get the money to pay the taxis. Jack, I don't suppose you have thirty-five hundred dollars in pesos on you?"

"If my girls are safe, I'll pay the bill, Gearheardt," Daisy said. "I've got the ISP money you gave me."

"Ixnay on the ISP talk, Daisy. But thanks." He sat down next to Marta.

Chiquita and her sister skipped into the room. They didn't look molested.

"Mama," Chiquita said, "we were in the office, checking the traffic."

Gearheardt groaned.

"These men, they are all stinking Cubaños."

Mario made a low guttural sound. He seemed to have taken enough abuse.

Daisy made a faint toward his crotch with the sheep de-nutters. He must have recognized them because he backed off.

"The Pygmy is not here, Señor Gearheardt," Benito said, wiping his mouth on the lace doily from the chair he was now standing behind. "He goes to change the course of history."

In ten minutes, the taxi man was paid, Benito had cleaned himself up and made coffee, Marta had stopped bawling, Mario and Daisy went down the halls checking on her girls and hustling the Cubans (there were only twenty-five) out and down the stairs to her van, and Gearheardt had leaned his head back against the chair and closed his eyes. I thought he might be asleep but he said, "Jack, when I open my eyes if you have curly blond hair, a long coat and talk with a rubber-bulbed horn, I'm killing myself."

CHAPTER TWENTY-ONE

THE LULL BEFORE THE P***ING CONTEST

"**G**earheardt, I'm going to make a run back by my apartment," I said. "I'm not sure when I'll get back there again."

Gearheardt looked at his watch. "Sounds good, Jack. I've got a couple of things I need to take care of too. Meet me back here at eleven and we'll brief Mario."

We were in the office. Gearheardt was making a last minute check of the traffic. Other than my leather jacket now being in the CIA offices in Frankfurt, nothing had come through that was ostensibly for us or our mission. It only occurred to me later that the jacket information was on the network of brothel news.

"Jack, watch yourself. The frivolity around this place can make you forget that we're on dangerous ground here. Have our pal out front get a taxi for you. Don't take one off the street."

"Got you, Gearheardt." I stood and watched him making notes and checking street maps. He was an amazing guy. The idea that the next few weeks could bring a free Cuba was his. Without his craziness and insane devotion to his dreams, it might not have been possible.

"If you're waiting for a hug, I'm busy right now," he said without looking up.

"See you in a couple of hours."

The streets near my apartment were mostly deserted but I had the taxi drive slowly around the block twice. On the second circle I saw them. Two men were slumped down in the front seat of a Volvo (a favorite of the Russians) and just to the side of my building I happened to catch the orange dot of a poorly screened cigarette.

"Keep going, driver," I said. He turned at Ibsen and took us out of the neighborhood through the park. "Drive for a while. Keep in this area. I may want to make another stop."

I remembered that I also had some personal gear at my office. The taxi driver found a telephone box and I got out.

"U.S. Embassy. Corporal Waters."

"Waters, this is Jack Armstrong. Do you know me?"

"Uh, yes sir. You were a Marine, is that right sir?"

"Exactly. I need you to do me a favor. Who's the night duty officer?"

"Mr. Goodwin, sir. Would you like me to get him?"

I didn't know Goodwin except by sight.

"No, that's okay. Have you seen Major Crenshaw this evening?"

"Yes, sir. He's still in his office, sir. Would you like me to ring him?"

"Won't be necessary, Waters. I'm trying to see if I can get into my office and not disturb anyone. I can explain later. Do you think that's possible?"

"I definitely don't think so, sir. There are twenty-five or so guests with Major Crenshaw. Sir, is there something I can do for you?" He sounded like he was getting nervous.

"Do you know the guests? I mean are they visitors from the U.S.? (As in Langley, I hoped he would confirm.)"

"No sir. Major Crenshaw signed them all in at once. I believe they are Cuban, sir." He hesitated. "Sir, are you sure there is nothing I can do for you?"

"There's nothing right now. Thanks, Corporal. Semper Fi."

"Yes, sir. Semper Fi. Goodnight, sir."

"Wait a minute, Corporal. Are the guests about to leave? Can you tell?"

"I don't think so, sir. They're still singing hymns."

"Thanks again, Waters. Maybe I'll see you tomorrow."

"Yes, sir. I'll be on duty at the President's speech. Goodnight, sir."

I walked back to the taxi. What in the hell was Crenshaw up to? Cubans singing hymns at ten o'clock at night in the embassy?

Back at the Las Palomas, I stopped in the downstairs coffee shop and had a sandwich and cup of coffee. I had a strong desire for a cigarette. Probably because the death matron upstairs was so dead set against them.

I knocked on the door of Gearheardt's office. I heard noise inside, but no one answered.

"Gearheardt, it's me. Jack. I'm back."

In a moment, Gearheardt opened the door a crack.

"Jack, I'm kind of busy. Can you give me another half hour?" Over his shoulder, although he was obviously trying to block my view, I saw the girl who had led the team to rescue Crenshaw. There were others, but I couldn't get a good look at them.

"Yeah, sure. I'll wait in the coffee shop. Come on down when you're through."

I was sipping my third cup of coffee when Gearheardt finally joined me.

"It's looking good, Jack. Things are falling into place." He ordered a beer and lit a cigarette.

"You already have a cigarette burning in the ashtray, Gearheardt."

"So I do. So I do." He began to smoke them alternately.

"Are you nervous, Gearheardt?" I asked. When he wasn't dragging on a butt, he tapped his spoon against the table. His knee was bouncing. "You're making *me* nervous."

"Jack, we are so close. I'm waiting for a message from Hong Kong. Things are moving ahead there."

"Hong Kong."

"And Rio," he said without looking at me.

"Rio."

"Are you going to keep repeating the cities or do you have a question, Jack?"

I took a cigarette from his pack, lit it and leaned back in my chair. Staring at him.

"What should I ask, Gearheardt? Should I ask how Hong Kong and Rio tie into Cuba and Mexico? Should I ask why the Pygmy who is disguised as a Mexican cigarette boy is trying or not trying to kill me? Maybe I should ask if you are just balls-out insane?"

"All good questions, Jack. Difficult to answer at this juncture."

"And that's your response?" I was trying to decide between faith in friendship and a blinding rage.

The cute little waitress refreshed my coffee, then brought more beer for Gearheardt. As she poured, the bottle tinked nervously against the glass. Gearheardt smiled benevolently up at her and winked. The girl blushed and spoke rapidly in Spanish, then rushed off.

"Gearheardt, my Spanish is weak, but I'm pretty damn sure she called you Excellency. What the hell is that all about? I thought it was just the servants at your former castle."

"Are you up to twenty questions, Jack? What was it? Vegetable, mineral or . . . what was the third category? Grease?"

I added breaking into frustrated sobbing as an alternative to friendship or rage.

"Just tell me what's going on, you bastard. Why do you do this to me?"

Gearheardt looked slowly around the almost empty coffee shop. He stripped the cellophane from his cigarette package and began shaking his hand, trying to get the cellophane to drop into the ashtray. "Tricky stuff," he said. He didn't look at me.

I grabbed his hand and took the cellophane. Now it stuck to my fingers, but I resisted the urge to shake it. I tightened my grip on his wrist.

"Gearheardt," I said though clenched teeth, "I have a gun under my coat. In just a moment I am going to take out that gun and shoot one of us. You ruined my career in the Marine Corps. You ruined my career in Air America. You have almost certainly ruined my career in the CIA."

"Moi?"

Rage edged back ahead of frustrated sobbing. "Yes, you. I'm not *blaming* you. Hell, I went along with everything. But you had all these schemes and cock-eyed ideas."

Gearheardt raised his free hand in protest.

"No, let me finish. Here's the goddamned point. You never *leveled* with me. You always had some damn *subplot* or *secret agenda* that you didn't trust me with. I know you always say it's for my own good, but when did it ever turn out good? Can't you understand—"

"Would you mind not holding my hand while you talk, Jack?"

I let go of his wrist and took a deep breath.

"You are the most maddening son-of-a-bitch in the world. No, don't thank me. I'm trying to insult you, you idiot."

"But I've explained everything to you, Jack." He actually looked hurt.

"You have explained nothing. I am hours away from participating in an attempted assassination of the Mexican president, at which time I am supposed to shoot the other assassin, whom I hired, so that the United States can invade Cuba, where I'll be hiding, while you are running the international gang of whores—"

"Prostitutes."

"—which is providing all the information gathering and financing for the CIA now, and Rio and Hong Kong and God knows where else are somehow involved, and Crenshaw is either on our side or not and the good Cubans are upstairs in a whorehouse and the bad Cubans are singing hymns in the embassy and are trying to make sure I kill the president although that would also give the U.S. a reason to invade Cuba unless someone found out we started the whole damn thing and a naked Cuban lives in my apartment and—" I ran out of steam.

Gearheardt closed his eyes for a moment as if considering. "It's not that simple, Jack," he said, looking back at me.

I'm ashamed to say I went over the table for him. And I might have thrashed his ass if the entire shift of waitresses and the large hostess had not been beating on my back and head. The small fists hurt, but it was the beer bottle against my temple that caused me to loosen my grip on his skinny neck.

All the while, that damn Gearheardt was laughing.

'That was a shameful display, Jack," Gearheardt said. We were in his conference room. I sat semi-comatose in a side chair. More numbed than injured.

Around me swirled a dozen or so women in various states of undress. Negligees, silken Chinese robes, and slippers seemed to be the uniform of the day. Gearheardt was at the teletype, pulling off messages and scribbling notes on them. The women took the sheets, consulted clipboards, and filed the messages into boxes arranged on the floor around the room. Telephones had been brought in and half of the women were speaking earnestly into them. A map of the world had been tacked to one wall.

The door opened and Benito entered, pushing a cart laden with rolls and coffee. He smiled when he saw me.

"Ola, Jack. You no come for the dessert." He gave a little swish with his hips.

"I'm not a homosexual, Benito," trying not to sound as if that were an accomplishment on my part.

"I ask Señor Gearheardt and he say 'not yet.'"

"Yes, well Señor Gearheardt is an idiot. He is pulling your chain, Benito."

"Sounds nice," he said with a sad smile. He began handing out coffee cups.

I saw Gearheardt laughing at me. "Be good, Jack. I'll be with you in a minute."

I accepted a cup of coffee from the non-grudge holding Benito. Gearheardt rose and went to the map. With a grease pencil he began making notations on its acetate cover.

Hong Kong—3 military, 4 govt. 11 bus
Bangkok—10 military, 15 govt. ? bus
London—0 military, 0 govt 22 bus
Moscow—15 military, 10 govt 0 bus

Looking closer I notice that fifty or so major cities around the world had similar notations. None were in the U.S.

"Isabella," Gearheardt called out, "get Hong Kong on the phone. Find out *which* military the three are from. They could be from anywhere."

I turned and saw Isabella who smiled at me. It was Conchita's friend. I guess I should have known.

"Si, Señor Gearheardt," she answered.

"And make sure the offices are using the lists we sent them. Full colonels and above for the military. You got that?" He turned around to the desk nearest him. "Clara, check with Bangkok and try to find out the story behind the 'zero' businessmen. The chance that no important businessmen are in massage parlors is non-existent."

Gearheardt closed the notebook he was holding and looked up at me. "Jack, I should probably bring you up to date on the situation."

"That would be nice. How many more people will be trying to kill me when I know the whole plan?"

"No one is trying to kill you, Jack. At least no one that is involved with the ISP/Gearheardt plan."

"What about the Pygmy? That half blind Ukrainian guy? What about them?"

"I was just trying to make sure I had your attention, Jack. Get you focused. Thinking someone is going to put a bullet through your head can get you riled up sometimes. Know what I mean?"

I was too dazed and tired to be mad at him. And I was not totally surprised. Over- estimating danger in order to grab assets and assistance was an Agency thing. The fact that Gearheardt was supposedly my best friend was not a hindrance to that practice when a mission was on.

"It doesn't bother you to scare me half out of my wits in order for you to use me, right?"

"Cake walks don't get resources, Jack." He smiled and turned back to the room. "Would someone tell me why there is a red circle around Delhi?" he asked, his voice suddenly edgy.

Three of the women spoke quietly to each other, their heads together, looking up at the map and back at Gearheardt occasionally. Finally the one he had called Isabella came shyly over.

"Señor Gearheardt, we are trying to talk to the office in Bombay who will talk to the office in Delhi, who will visit the front line (I found out later this was what the girls called the bordellos now) to see what has happened." She hesitated and looked back at the map, avoiding, I thought, looking at Gearheardt.

"But the red circle—let me make sure all of you know—is to indicate that the girls have started action. We went over all of this. So why is there a red circle around Delhi?" Gearheardt was didactic.

Isabella looked back at her friends, who looked away. Then she faced Gearheardt.

"The girls have taken the Lotus House and are holding the customers. There has been some 'reaction' and we are in touch with the girls now."

"DAISY," Gearheardt yelled. The room activity stopped. The girls manning the phones continued to talk but lowered their voices.

I had not noticed, but Daisy was at one of the desks near the door. She was on the phone and held up a finger to Gearheardt. After a moment she hung up, rose slowly, and crossed to stand in front of him.

"Daisy," Gearheardt said calmly, "Isabella tells me that the girls in the Lotus House couldn't wait until we gave them the word. Can't everybody get it through their little prostitute heads that this is not a game?" He looked up at Daisy. "So what's the situation?"

Daisy sat down in one of the side chairs. "The girls have taken the house. There are a number of officials and some policemen that are . . . in . . . that are . . . not being allowed to leave. Sari is in charge. We have talked to her. She's trying to hold on, but she is scared and many girls have run away."

"Oh for God's sake, Daisy, we have to be tough. I know these women have gone through a lot for years and years. But we can't let them just fly off the handle and ruin the big picture for everybody. If I have to be a hard-ass, so be it. Let me talk to this damn Sari and I'll see if I can control the situation."

Daisy nodded to a young woman across the room. She punched keys on her telephone and then the unit on Gearheardt's desk rang. Daisy picked up the receiver and held it toward Gearheardt. "This is Sari, Señor Hard-Ass. She is twelve years old." She dropped the receiver suddenly, causing Gearheardt to reach out and grasp it. He held it away from his chest, his palm over the transmitter.

Gearheardt looked stricken. His eyes moist. I found it hard to look at him, so unusual to see him emotional and at an apparent loss for words. Finally he raised the phone.

"Sari, this is Mr. Gearheardt." His voice was honey.

We could hear her response clearly. "We are not surely knowing what to do, Mr. Gearheardt. Will we be having help soon?"

"Where are the older women, Sari? Are you . . . in charge?"

"I am oldest, Mr. Gearheardt. When we are becoming thirteen in the Lotus House, we are moved to not be with our friends. Will we be having help soon?"

"Sari, I am going to put Mrs. Daisy back on the phone. She and the girls here will help you as best that we can. Thank you, Sari. You are a very good leader for the Lotus House platoon."

"Mr. Gearheardt, I would be asking you one thing."

"What's that, Sari?"

"Even if I am to be not living, may I be taken to Cuba to be resting forever? I do not wish to stay in Delhi. I am asking please, Mr. Gearheardt."

Gearheardt turned to the map, away from the room. I didn't hear his answer but after a moment he held out the phone and Daisy took it from him. She punched the hold button on Gearheardt's phone and returned to her desk.

Gearheardt seemed to recover just a bit. "Daisy," he yelled across the room, "get the nearest Alpha team into Delhi asap."

Now Daisy held her hand over the transmitter. "It may be too late by the time the team can arrive, Señor Gearheardt."

Gearheardt thought for a moment. "Send them anyway. If Sari and the other girls are . . . gone, then have them burn the Lotus House and track down anyone that owned it and . . . they'll know what to do."

I caught Gearheardt's eye. "This sounds like war, Gearheardt."

"You're goddamned right it is, Jack. No turning back now." He looked back at the map which was being updated by two young women in black lace. "I need some sleep. Big day tomorrow."

Daisy found two unoccupied rooms and Gearheardt asked her to wake him in just a few hours. Imagined or not, my head was filled with rhythmic poundings, sad cries of ecstasy, and voices alternatively demanding and cajoling. The pillow over my head helped enough for me to fall asleep. I was glad I hadn't been raised in a whorehouse.

CHAPTER TWENTY-TWO

HIGH LATE MORNING

Gearheardt woke me at dawn.

"Better roll out, Jack," he said, "Today's a big day."

"Anything new from Delhi?" I asked as we headed out to have a morning cigarette.

Gearheardt didn't answer but his face turned red and he clamped his jaws tighter. Something not good must have happened in Delhi.

By the time we reached the street, Gearheardt had built up an impressive rage. He lit a cigarette and looked at the passing Mexican people. "Pick someone for me to beat the crap out of, Jack. I trust your judgment."

"The odds of someone I don't like strolling by right now are probably not good, Gearheardt. Take a deep breath. You look like you're about to have a stroke. Not a good look for you." Telling myself it was no use quitting the day I was probably going to die, I took a cigarette from his pack and lit up. "Do you suppose its time for you to fill me in on the global operation you're running?"

We were standing on the sidewalk in front of the Las Palomas building. Gearheardt suddenly flipped his cigarette butt into the gutter. It
barely missed the feet of an elderly Mexican gentleman pushing an
orange-laden cart.

"Buenos dias," I said.

"Buenos dias," he replied, frowning at Gearheardt and then smiling
at me. His cart squeaked on down the street.

"That old bastard saves his money so he can come in once a month
and harass Filona."

I respected Gearheardt's mood, but expected a bit of rationality none
the less.

"It *is* a whorehouse, Gearheardt."

Gearheardt looked at me like I was crazy. I returned the favor.

Finally I spoke. "I'm not putting the girls down, Gearheardt. It's just
that the routine is that if you pay money, you get to 'harass' the girls. I
didn't make the rules." It was only later that I recognized the ridiculous-
ness of explaining how brothels worked to Gearheardt. Now, I was just
trying to calm him down.

I think Gearheardt noticed about the same time that I did that the
orange vendor had evidently left his cart to be valet parked. He was
walking quick-step away when Gearheardt turned and shoved me against
the building, putting his body between me and the cart. "Oh, shit,"
he said.

The explosion was loud but, from a destruction point of view, not
terribly productive. Other than orange pulp and juice coating the area,
including Gearheardt's back, no harm was done. The vendor was still
within sight and Gearheardt took him down with a single fruit plucked
from the still smoking pile on the cart. I started toward where he sat
picking pulp from his head, but Gearheardt grabbed my arm and
stopped me.

"He's not important, Jack. Someone hired him to scare us. Don't
waste your time on him." He returned his handkerchief to his pocket
after wiping the back of his neck. He gestured to the cart of burnt and
split oranges.

"This is the thing to remember, Jack. This smoking pile of oranges will someday be talked about like the sinking of the Maine, the shots fired on Fort Sumter, the bombing of Pearl Harbor and the sexual habits of the Kennedys. This is history, Jack. The first skirmish of the War of the Whores." He grabbed another orange and threw it at the vendor. A perfect head shot knocked the man to the street again. "I trademarked that name, by the way. The girls have tee shirts being silk-screened."

We shoved our way through the gathering crowd of curiosity seekers. Gearheardt nodded to the young valet, who indicated he would take care of things. Back in the coffee shop the waitresses eyed me warily and I knew any sudden moves I might make toward Gearheardt would result in an ashtray and beer bottle beating. We took a table in the back of the shop, away from anyone and the noise coming from the street.

The action seemed to relax Gearheardt. We no sooner had ordered coffee than Daisy appeared at our table.

"Señor Hard Ass," she said, "you should be upstairs. There are things happening."

"I'll be there shortly, Daisy. I need to brief my pal here before he goes off and does something stupid."

"Señor, there is word that the Halcones are coming to Las Palomas. We should make plans."

"Daisy, the Halcones are not coming here. You have my word. The Mexican police might drop by, but we can handle them. Take care of things upstairs for just a few minutes, and then I'll be up there."

She left without speaking, stepping on my toes as she departed.

"I don't think she likes you, Jack," Gearheardt said. "She usually doesn't like guys who smoke in her brothel."

In the past I might have pointed out to Gearheardt that one, he had been the one smoking, and two, smoking was actually allowed in some of the finest whorehouses around the world.

"What's going on?" I wanted to try to keep Gearheardt focused on filling me in. I was to take part in an assassination attempt in a few hours and thought that knowing the plan might calm me.

"Jack, let me give you some background. When I was traveling around the world while I was supposed to be in Angola, setting up the Gearheardt Information Network, I talked to a lot of prostitutes. And do you know what I found, Jack? A lot of these girls would prefer to be doing something else. They don't like this screwing for money for the most part."

"You're kidding." Knowing the sarcasm would be lost on Gearheardt.

"Couldn't be more serious, Jack. It actually became depressing going brothel to massage parlor, city after city, knowing the women were not as happy in their work as I had always thought."

"Yes, that would be a downer."

"I began spending more time talking to the girls than . . . you know, fooling around with them."

"Let me interrupt, Gearheardt. You seem to actually be serious. Are you trying to tell me that up until then, after what must have been hundreds visits to various houses of pleasure, you thought the women were doing what they did because they just liked sex?"

"Hundreds? Gee, I've never thought about how many—"

"That's not my point, Gearheardt. What's going on?"

The windows of the Las Palomas coffee shop shattered at the moment we heard the gunfire. A short burst from an automatic weapon, the crash, and the thud of bullets in the wall behind us. A car squealed away outside.

"Well, for God's sake," Gearheardt said, "so much for the bullet proof windows in this place. These damn Mexican sonsabitches will steal your eyeteeth if—"

"Gearheardt! Who in the hell was that?" I rose back from where I had ducked under the table.

"Probably some of the damn Cubans, but I didn't get a good look." Gearheardt held his orange juice up to the light. "You suppose any glass would fly back this far, Jack?"

"Which Cubans?"

"Both sides have a stake in this, Jack. So either side could be trying to stop the other side."

"That clears that up. Which side are we, you jackass?"

"We're more or less non-partisan, Jack. Our mission is to secure Cuba. We're the only people wanting us to do that."

Around us the staff was sweeping up the glass. At the curb our parking valet was directing a crew cleaning up the orange residue and pulling the still-smoking cart away. Gearheardt was reading the menu, that I knocked out of his hands. "Damn it, Gearheardt, finish the story. Maybe you have time to fill me in before the next assault or bombing. You are the most dangerous person to have as a friend in the entire fucking universe."

Gearheardt picked up the menu and smiled. "I always thought it was *you*, Jack. We never seem to have things happen to us except when you're around." He indicated the pancakes to the hovering waitress.

I grabbed his menu, pointed to the pancakes, and dismissed the waitress. No doubt Gearheardt's would be served on a silver platter, while she would carry my pancakes out in her butt-crack. And *he* was the one who was going to get everyone killed.

I went on. "I've figured out that you sold the CIA on a plan that will have the U.S. take over Cuba for you. This fake assassination attempt. And I guess I've figured out that your plan was to then take Cuba for your International Group of Hookers—"

"International Sisterhood of Prostitutes."

"Okay, the ISP. But even *you* aren't crazy enough to think that the U.S. or any other country affected is going to just *give* you Cuba."

"I'm not going to *ask* them, Jack. I'm going to *negotiate* with them."

"With who?"

"With whoever doesn't want me to have Cuba. Realistically only the U.S. will give a damn. And they'll be dead set against it since they're the ones that have to spend all the money and fight the Cubans. Can't say as how I blame them."

"Hmmm," I said. "And what pray tell are you using for negotiating leverage?"

"Damn it," Gearheardt said. He rose and lunged for a hand grenade that had been tossed into the room through the broken window. Tossing it back to the street, he fell to the floor and yelled for me to do the same. The blast was loud, but again not particularly destructive from what I could see. "Landed under a taxi cab driving by," Gearheardt said, craning his head through the front window. "That absorbed most of the blast. That valet boy has his hands full this morning."

He walked back toward our table, gesturing at the waitress who reasonably seemed to be in shock. "Vicki, mi amor, would you have those pancakes sent up to us in the club? The action down here is not conducive to proper digestion."

Upstairs, changes were being made. Two heavily armed women, in green fatigue uniforms, guarded the door. Inside, the fancy waiting room of Las Palomas now resembled a war room with terse commands and requests thrown out clipped and fast. Mostly in Spanish but occasionally in French, German and English. About half of the two dozen women were in fatigues, the other half comfortable in bordello combat regalia—negligees and garter belts. I doubted if any other 'military' staff boasted the cleavage exhibited. Maps and charts lined the walls, a large globe sat on its stand near the center of the room. Small flags were pinned into various cities.

A sheaf of paper was shoved into Gearheardt's hands. He quickly reviewed and initialed the lot. We continued through the room, down the hall and into Gearheardt's conference room. Isabella met us at the door with more messages. He gently pushed her hand away.

"Girls, girls, let me get situated here. Jack and I have pancakes. Taking over the world will have to wait." He smiled and put his arm around the lovely shoulders of Isabella and led her back to her desk. Then he joined me at the table where a young waitress was setting out our breakfast.

Gearheardt had three small pancakes arranged to look much like Mickey Mouse. My two round pancakes were separated by one long pancake that looked like nothing, or perhaps testicles and a phallus. It briefly reminded me of the Disney knockoff store in Hong Kong—inexplicably named Donald Dick. I realized I was getting paranoid about the differential treatment Gearheardt seemed to get, but it hardly seemed coincidental that Gearheardt got Mickey Mouse pancakes and I got Peter Prick pancakes.

"Gearheardt," I began, "let's get back to this operation. Am I still on for not assassinating the President of Mexico this afternoon? In fact, preventing his assassination?"

"Righto, Jack. Exactly what you're on for. And then you've got to get your ass to Havana before we lose the momentum. When the Marines take Havana, you and Marta will be there to greet them, backed by an ISP Commando Brigade that will discourage the Marines from taking up permanent residence." He finished his three pancakes and looked hungrily at my untouched plate. "Are you going to eat—whoa, never mind."

"So the prostitutes are going to have to fight the Marines? Come on, Gearheardt, this is a dumber plan than bombing halts in Vietnam."

"You forgot the negotiation part, Jack. Light up a cigarette and I'll tell you the rest."

I shook a cigarette from my pack before I caught on. "Bullshit, Gearheardt, light up your own damn cigarette." Out of the corner of my eye I could see Daisy, on the phone but squinting nastily at the pack of cigarettes I was holding. I toyed with the package for a moment, pushing it around the desk, before returning it to my pocket. I didn't want Daisy to think I was afraid of her.

"Okay again, Jack. Here's the bare bones. The International Sisterhood of Prostitutes and Gearheardt Ventures of the Flesh have a joint operation. We're taking over Cuba. And—"

"Why Cuba?"

"Couldn't think of any other country that the U.S. would help us overthrow." Gearheardt made it sound obvious.

"When I put together the intelligence network, a brilliant idea I'll have to admit, the girls wanted to know who they were spying for. When I explained that they were risking their lives for the Free World, they wanted to know what the fuck the Free World had ever done for them."

"So they decided they wanted their own country."

"Over the months, yes. We had a series of meetings among the biggest whores around the world. One in Malta last January, and another in New York. We have a big chapter there. Anyway, yes, they want their own country. You understand this is just the tip of the iceberg. If they get themselves really organized, I would imagine we're talking continent."

"How can you always make insanity sound so reasonable, Gearheardt?"

"It's easier than you might think, Jack."

"You're probably right. But that's the plan, such as it is. What is the operation? I think I've got it figured out, but *you* tell me."

Gearheardt held his palm toward me as Isabella leaned into his ear, whispering rapid Spanish. When she straightened (thankfully lifting her 90% exposed breasts from my line of sight) Gearheardt looked at his watch and nodded up to her. "Thirty minutes," he said.

"Jack, we need to wrap this up and get you over to the assassination scene. Got your gun?"

"Yes, but I'm not running out of here with a gun and no information. Give it to me."

"So the whores decided to begin training a select few as warriors. Some were enrolled in an economics unit. Others . . . well you get the idea. And over the past six months, we've put the plan in place. The catalyst is the attempt by Cuba to assassinate the President of Mexico. You know that. What you don't know is that Operation Double Bola is now underway across the world." He turned in his chair and tapped the shoulder of the young woman manning the phone behind him. "Navaja, por favor?"

The girl smiled and took a small instrument from her purse that looked strangely frightening. Turned out, it *was* strangely frightening.

"They slip these over the nuts and they're kind of like that Chinese finger trap, the harder you pull, the tighter they get. Look here, Jack," he bent down toward the desk, arranging two pencils in guillotine-type fittings, "these little babies are ingenious. Two step pulls. First pull on this wire, snaps this against your nuts. I've heard it hurts like a bastard but usually only brings on screaming and vomiting. That's to get a guy's attention. But the next pull," he yanked an almost invisible line in his hand and the pencils were snapped in two, "gets the nuts cropped at the base very cleanly. You'll be singing Christmas carols like Alvin the Chipmunk the rest of your natural life. Assuming someone stops the bleeding. Pretty neat, huh?" He held them toward me but I declined to take them.

"We had them made in China. Japan had the first contract but tried to double the price. Claimed their original bid only covered one testicle. Damn, Jack, I don't know how businessmen look themselves in the mirror in the morning."

"How many of these things did you order?"

"Somewhere around two hundred thousand, Jack. To tell the truth, we couldn't keep up with the demand."

"Two hundred thousand?"

"Jack, do you realize how many hookers, prostitutes, whores and whatever you want to call them, there are in the world?"

I heard gunfire in the street outside. Gearheardt went on without seeming to notice.

"Probably in the neighborhood of a million girls and women, Jack. But that's just the surface. Gearheardt Enterprises had a survey run before we actually ordered the de-nutting device. Pretty discouraging for the men. If the results were accurate even to the seventy-five percent level, there are over a billion and a half women in the world who would pay fifty dollars or more to have a de-nutting device like this. Shocking, no?"

"A de-nutter?" I was not processing information very quickly.

"Beat the potato peeler by a three to one margin. But that's not the important thing. We aren't running a manufacturing business. We're just trying to get an idea of potential membership in the ISP. We found out that if we allowed associate memberships—where you actually weren't employed as a hooker but had just been screwed over by a man—the potential membership was close to two billion. These are estimates of course. Just extrapolating from the survey samples. We tried to adjust for the cultural differences. The thing is, the support we anticipate getting for the new Cuba could be pretty darn strong."

"Fifty dollars?" My mind was still coming to grips with the thought of two billion women wanting ball removers.

Gearheardt laughed. "Well, not exactly. Again, we tried to make cultural adjustments for various segments of the survey. For example in parts of Africa, the question allowed them to answer 'everything I own' instead of a dollar amount. We weren't really doing a pricing model. We were just considering the demand and feasibility of the joint venture." Gearheardt the marketing guru.

"Wait a minute, Gearheardt. Surveys, manufacturing, uh, de-nutters. Where did you get the money for all this? Are you making all of this up?"

Gearheardt laughed again, harder. "Jack, you haven't been paying attention. The CIA paid for everything. Plus a bit from some other intelligence agencies." He paused. "I have to tell you that on top of everything else, the good old CIA is the most generous of the spy organizations. Boy, those bastards at Mossad wouldn't cough up a dime. The French were tighter than ticks too."

"I thought you told me that the ISP was financing this Mexican operation."

"They are. But it's with the Agency's own money. I sold them on the idea of the spy network in whorehouses and bordellos. Of course they've actually been running that trap for years, but it was never organized until I came along. But anyway, they gave us so much money that we were able to fund the ISP operations and still loan funds back to them."

The gunfire in the street was now sporadic pops. Gearheardt motioned for me to stay seated while he took a quick look out the window. When he sat back down, he pursed his lips. "Where were we?"

"You were going to have some de-balling equipment made."

"We *did* have some made. Remember? Two hundred thousand sets. And most of those are distributed in the cities where we think they can be used to our best advantage." He sat back and pointed to the wall maps. "Look at the numbers now, Jack. A few hours away from your big contribution to our cause and the girls are performing tremendously."

"How?"

"Thought you'd never ask." He studied the map for a moment. "These aren't accurate totals, Jack, but I would say that at the moment there are almost eight thousand bureaucrats, seventeen thousand military officers, and nearly a hundred thousand business leaders with their balls in the ISP/G Double Ball trap. Not quite what we hoped, but sufficient I would say."

"How did they manage—?"

"The girls came up with their own plans. Some houses offered two girls for the price of one. So while one girl kept the customer busy, the other one attached the gizmo. Some places just had the girls offer to lick the guys balls, something no self respecting male John can pass up, and the girls attached the trap while the guy was in dreamland. Luckily most of the customers are stupid enough to think that a girl is grooving on licking around hairy chicken-skin orbs. They never suspect a thing." Gearheardt gestured back to the lethal instrument resting on his desk. "Once attached, the girl calmly explains the situation, pulls the first string, waits until the yelling and puking stops, and then explains what will happen when the second string is pulled. They usually have the guy's full attention by then."

"And there are these . . . thousands of men around the world sitting in traps as we speak."

"Evidently." He flapped his wrist nonchalantly at the maps.

"And they are waiting for the word to . . . " I wasn't sure I understood the timing of the next part.

Gearheardt grimaced. "Well, that's the problem. You see when Sari in Delhi jumped the gun, some of the other houses followed her lead. We underestimated the desire to de-nut folks, and now we have a hell of a logistics problem on our hands." He turned his chair and looked at the maps, scratching his chin thoughtfully. "I don't think we can keep these guys hanging by the balls until the U.S. has time to kick Castro out of Cuba. So I've got about three hours to come up with another plan."

Gearheardt rose and went to the coffee pot. He chatted easily with a young woman (dressed in red bikini panties and a lace bra, barely covered by a man's shirt) who was refilling the sugar pot. As he sipped his brew, his hand drifted down the woman's back and I saw his fingers creep under her waistband. He whispered to the woman, they both laughed, and he returned to where I was sitting.

"Gearheardt," I said, "I truly don't know whether you are a genius or an asshole."

"Oh, I probably am, Jack." He grinned.

"Weren't you just feeling that girl's butt while we are in the middle of a siege and trying to get prostitutes to take over the world?"

Gearheardt frowned and looked at his hand as if it had acted on its own. "Yes, I did." He leaned across the desk toward me. "Jack, I swore to help these women. I didn't swear not to fool around with them. There's a difference."

"I'm sure there is. It just seems like—"

"Jack, you know how much I love women. I'm more or less like that fat Saint guy, Augustine. I want to be cured of my lust, but not just yet while I'm having fun. You know, Augustine the Hippo."

"Augustine *of* Hippo, you nitwit. Hippo was a city in North Africa about two thousand years ago."

"Thanks, Jack. Sometimes I think Princeton didn't demand enough of me." His face grew thoughtful for a moment. "I'll bet I'm still the only graduate that got his degree at gunpoint. I think I have some gaps in my education. But I don't blame *them*."

A burst of automatic weapon fire from the street silenced the room. After another long burst, the firing stopped. The room remained quiet for thirty seconds until a PRC-10 radio on one of the tables squawked. Daisy picked it up, spoke into it and a response in Spanish was given. She looked at Gearheardt.

"The street will be clear now, Señor Gearheardt."

"Thank the girls for me, Daisy." He turned to me. "Jack, we need to get you on your way. I've got a squad of ladies that will escort you to the square where the speech is to be given. You can trust them. They'll hook you up with Marta and she'll get you to Cuba."

Gearheardt stuck out his hand. "See you in Havana, Jack."

A red phone hanging on the wall behind Gearheardt's desk rang. The sound broke through the high noise level in the room, louder and shriller. Gearheardt dropped my hand, held up one finger asking me to wait, and lifted the receiver to his ear.

"Gearheardt," he said.

He listened for a moment, then began to move his lips and rock his head, mimicking whoever was on the other end.

"Yes, yes," he finally said, "but I can't understand a word you're saying. Speekee English?"

He held his palm over the transmitter. "Hold on, Jack. I got some crazy Italian screaming about Crenshaw." He listened for another moment.

"Calm down, 'Guido'. I said I can't understand a word you're saying."

Gearheardt listened and then shrugged toward me, holding his index finger up again. Someone spoke.

"Yeah, it's Gearheardt. Who is this?

Paul? Paul Anka? . . .

No, I was just pulling your chain. I recognize your voice, your Greatness. I mean your Holiness. So what's up? . . .

Sure, I know Crenshaw. And I **am** *working with him . . . . . . "*

Gearheardt grimaced at me. He rolled his eyes.

"Look, Paul. I can see where you're heading with this. But that wasn't our agreement and if you made some sort of side deal with Crenshaw, that's not my problem . . . "

But you already have a country . . .

Right, right. No beaches. Right. Yes, I've heard they can be assholes . . . Of course. Not all Italians, I understand . . .

Well, to tell the truth I assumed you talk to Him all the time. But did He say that you should actually do this deal or are you just reading something into His response? I can tell you that a number of the girls say they have also talked to Him and His response was pretty clear . . .

That's not worthy of you, Paul. They've all had a bit of bad luck but some of them are very spiritual women . . .

Paul. Paul. Look, let's cut to the chase. No deal. This country will belong to the women. You may set up shop there, but that's up to the women. Just like any other government . . .

Yeah, well at least I don't wear a white housecoat and beanie around all day . . .

Try it, big boy. There isn't a cloud in the sky here . . .

And lay off the vino before you call next time."

Gearheardt slammed the receiver back into its holder. The room around him was silent. All eyes, Mexican and Catholic, were on him.

"Paul DiMarzio," he said. "An old pal from high school." His grin was weak. But then I knew his real grin. The women went back to work.

"Let's grab another room, Jack. I think we need to talk some more before you go running off to your assassination."

We went down the hallway and found an open room. The window faced the alley and there was very little street noise. On one table beside the red velvet covered bed was a bowl of condoms. The table on the far side of the bed displayed a crucifix and a statue of the Virgin Mary.

"Kind of an incongruous scene isn't it, Jack?"

"You mean the statue of the Virgin Mary? Does seem rather—"

"The statue? All the girls have the statue. I mean the rubbers. The guys won't use condoms and of course they're against the rules in the church. A man thing I guess. But we have more pressing matters, Jack. I need your help." He lay down on the bed and propped his head against the headboard. "Jack, how about opening that window. I am dying for a cigarette."

The most amazing thing about Gearheardt, the trait I probably admired most, was his grace under pressure. If I understood all that he had told me, he had thousands of girls around the world holding twice that many testicles in miniature guillotines. He was masterminding a to-be-thwarted assassination of the President of Mexico, his bordello headquarters was under attack by any one of a number of groups he was trying to double cross and he had just told the Pope to go shinny up a rope. And there he was lighting a cigarette off of a votive candle and relaxing on a whore's bed.

"Let me gather my wits here, Jack. Damn, this cigarette tastes good." Gearheardt closed his eyes and blew smoke at the ceiling.

"For God's Sakes, Gearheardt!" My grace under pressure still needed some work. I grabbed his arm and pulled him to a sitting position. "We need to get our asses in gear! Victor and the bad Cubans are going to be trying to shoot the President of Mexico in less than two hours. I may be the only hope of stopping them."

The door burst open and a camouflaged Major Crenshaw injected himself into the conversation by aiming a Thompson sub-machine gun in the general direction of Gearheardt's head. "Greetings, gentlemen," he said. "First things, first. Jack, you are no longer an employee of the Central Intelligence Agency. Obviously your pal here, Mr. Gearheardt, is off the list." He kicked the door shut behind him.

"You fought your way into Las Palomas to fire Jack? You must be the leading candidate for Asshole Boss of the Year, Crenshaw. A memo wouldn't have worked?" Gearheardt sneered.

"Listen, wiseass, the reason—"

"Typical Agency bullshit. We have a world crisis brewing and the paper-shufflers start gumming up the works." Gearheardt was on his feet, facing Crenshaw now.

"I didn't say I came here just to fire Jack, you nitwit. I just wanted to set things straight so that Jack wouldn't think he could waltz over to stop the assassination with Agency support." He turned to me. "We'll handle things, Jack." He stepped closer to me and lowered his voice. Holding his machine gun to his side with an elbow, he reached into his camouflaged shirt and extracted a small package of documents. "If I could just get you to sign these, Jack."

Gearheardt snorted. "Bureaucratic dildos. You're as bad as the IRS."

"Which is looking for you, Gearheardt." Crenshaw smiled. He raised the machine gun back in the direction of Gearheardt. "On the floor."

He took a length of clothesline from his small backpack and threw it to me. "Tie up our pal, Jack."

For a moment I thought he was inviting me back on his team.

"I could shoot you both right now. You tried to double cross the Company, Jack. Not good. Not good at all. I'm disappointed in you." Noticing I hadn't moved, Crenshaw waved his weapon at me. "I said tie him up. I mean it. Believe me, I would prefer to shoot this sacrilegious traitor."

"Crenshaw, throwing around 'double cross' and 'traitor' doesn't work for someone who has been spying for the Vatican the last ten years. Don't think I don't know who tipped off the Pope to the potential availability of Cuba."

"Don't mention the Holy See, you—"

"Yeah, well the Holy See holy saw a chance to grab a decent country and he thinks he's going to take it. I told him this morning—"

"*You talked to the Pope!*" I didn't like the look on Crenshaw's face. "Gearheardt, you may not take your obligations as a U.S. citizen seriously. You can make fun of the CIA and run roughshod over its policies. But I forbid you to commit this heresy! The Holy Father will not be denied by the likes of you. I'm going to Cuba. And I will deliver it to the Vatican. Your insane idea of some sort of idyllic . . . pleasure palace for fallen women is beyond—"

"Major, could I interest you in a blowjob before you go off to fight the holy wars?"

The major was not amused. Apoplectic might have been a better description.

"You—you disgust me, Gearheardt," he sputtered.

"I wasn't offering to give you one, Major. I just thought you might let me fix you up with—"

The Major cycled a round into the chamber of his machine gun. "That's enough, Gearheardt. Jack, get this man tied up. Now!"

I started toward Gearheardt who didn't look as if he were contemplating lying down or letting me tie him up. I wasn't sure what I was going to do, but the door slamming open again relieved me of the choice.

"Please lay the gun on the bed," Marta said. Her pistol against the back of the major's head added gravitas to her request.

Gearheardt sat back down on the bed. "Jack, would you check the hall to see if there is someone on Crenshaw's side waiting to come in and put a gun to Marta's head?"

I actually started toward the door before I caught his sarcasm. Crenshaw reluctantly put his sub-machine gun next to Gearheardt on the bed. I assumed he had more weapons concealed in his war gear, but didn't think he would use them. As usual, I was wrong. When Crenshaw turned back to us, he was holding a .45, the weapon of choice for those wanting big holes blown in things. He was pointing the monster at my head.

"I think we will call this a stand off," he said to Marta. "You are not going to shoot an agent of the U.S. government, and you don't want me to shoot your boyfriend here, I'm sure." He was motioning the barrel at me.

Gearheardt was his usual helpful self. "Sorry, Crenshaw, but Marta is a Cuban spy, so to speak, and she has no qualms about shooting U.S. agents. And as far as our pal Jack goes, Marta is a lesbian, so I'm not too sure about the boyfriend business. I wouldn't stake *my* life on it."

The great thing about the male mind is its ability to prioritize issues and make reasonable decisions. Marta the lesbian was moved ahead of the possibility that Crenshaw would spray-paint the wall with blood and gore from my head.

"Wait a minute," I said brilliantly, "what are you talking about? Marta, I thought that we were—and what about Gearheardt? You and he were—weren't you?"

"I think that's personal, Jack. Marta has gone through an experimental stage. I know that your ego is—"

"You people are disgusting," Crenshaw blurted. "I'm not interested in your sordid personal lives. What I *am* interested in is you giving me that pistol, young lady."

Marta lowered the weapon. I wondered if I would ever see her naked again.

"Don't give it to him, Marta. Major Crenshaw is *also* not going to shoot an agent of the Central Intelligence Agency. And Jack can be *my* boyfriend if you don't want him." Gearheardt smiled at me. "Personally I think he's cute as hell."

Crenshaw picked up his sub-machine gun and began backing out of the room. "It pains me that the Agency has to deal with such . . . people. Gearheardt, in about two hours I am taking my team to Cuba. There we will await the Marines and then the Vatican team. Enough of your nonsense about prostitutes. The United States is not in the business of taking over countries to let them be run by whores."

Gearheardt showed remarkable constraint by remaining silent. I sensed he wanted to get back to the situation with the thousands of men in de-nutters around the world. He did allow himself a wide grin.

"Necisito pantalones." A small, mustachioed gentleman stood shirted and tied but pantless in the doorway.

"I think he needs his pants," Gearheardt said. "Must be a customer who was rousted out when Marta brought the good Cubans in last night."

I have often thought that a good intelligence officer has the ability to put himself in the shoes of his enemy. And also to see his actions as they would appear to those in his environment. The thought struck me that this poor man had visited a bordello last night, been thrown out of the saddle by wild Cubans, and now was searching for his pants in a room where a camouflaged American stood with guns in both hands, another gringo (me) was gaping at a beautiful fully-dressed woman with her own pistol, and a third grinning gringo lay with his hands behind his head on a red velvet bed. Did he even wonder what all of that was about?

In a reaction which I quickly recognized as having the potential to lose future wars, Crenshaw started looking around for the guy's pants.

Marta found them draped over a chair. Instead of being grateful and scurrying out, he began a heated dialogue, with first Marta then Gearheardt, which sounded like he was demanding a 'rain check.' Finally, he drew himself up to as much dignity as you can have in baggy BVDs and cowboy boots and left the room.

Crenshaw was right behind him. "You two aren't competent to find your ass with both hands, much less find Cuba and take over." He shouldered his Thompson. "Stay away from Cuba, Gearheardt." He turned to me. "Jack, find a new career. This thing will be a stain on your record until the Second Coming, even if the Company did allow you to stay in. Good luck." He left.

Gearheardt bounced off the bed. "I've got prostitutes to lead. Jack, you and Marta can work out the itinerary for getting you to Cuba."

"We're still going?"

"Who's to stop us? Crenshaw? You just follow the plan that we already agreed on, Jack. I'll take care of the rest. Lying there on that bed, I realized what we need to do about those men with their balls in a trap." He patted Marta on the butt as he went out the door.

"You are sad to see me, Jack?" Marta sat down on the side of the bed and replaced her pistol into its thigh holster.

"I am happy to see you, Marta. I am just . . ."

"You are surprise I am a lesbian, no?"

I sat down beside her. "It's not just that. When you were first in my apartment, running around naked and all that, you seemed very strong. Very sure of yourself. But the last couple of times I've seen you . . ." I seemed unable to complete sentences.

"You want me to be naked again, Jack?" She smiled and reached toward the top button of her blouse. But I could tell she was just kidding.

"Marta, maybe we will have time in Havana for you to explain all this. But for now, do you really have a plan to get me from Mexico City to Cuba?"

Marta put her hand on my shoulder in a sisterly way.

"Perhaps." She stood and pulled me to my feet. "We should go to the square."

The mystery of Marta—victim? Prostitute? Spy? Movement leader? Traitor?—would have to wait. She stood and straightened her dress.

"Maybe not so lesbian sometimes, Jack."

I wasn't sure what that meant, but it sounded promising.

"I need to check with Gearheardt before we leave," I said. Probably grinning like a fool. With Gearheardt running my life again, it took so little to make me happy.

CHAPTER TWENTY-THREE

A DESIGN FLAW
IN THE DE-NUTTERS

Gearheardt was a busy man. Pacing the room with a cigarette in one hand and a phone in the other. He had evidently made tobacco peace with Daisy as she sat unconcerned near him. He looked up as Marta and I approached.

"You all set, Jack?"

"Got my gun. Got my map of the speaker's area. I got Marta who is sometimes not a lesbian. What more do I need?"

"You need to get past Crenshaw's little band of Pope People. And past Victor's little band of Cuban assholes, and past the official U.S. government detachment of sharpshooters and trouble makers."

"What are they doing here? I thought the American presence at this speech was going to be limited."

"Jack, if there's a swinging dick in Washington DC that doesn't know we have a faked assassination of the Mexican President scheduled, he must be locked in the pisser at Pizza Hut. There are Congressional delegations, military fact-finding missions, lobbyists, cabals, bureaucrats and God knows who else arriving like they're lining up for the Oklahoma land rush."

"Why?" I personally wished I were thousands of miles away.

"Who gets a chance to say they were at an assassination attempt? Damn few. And the word is out that we may take Cuba." Gearheardt shook his head. "This is a fine damn way to run a democracy."

"What do you mean?" I asked.

Gearheardt looked at me for a moment. "Damned if I know. Guess I just mean that if *I* were in congress *I'd* be heading down here and if people like me are running the country . . . "

"You certainly have a point there."

"Our job is simple. The word goes out that the Cubans tried to knock off the President. The world is outraged. Congress, those who are sober, are outraged. And we avenge the Bay of Pigs fiasco. But this time, the ladies are left in charge."

"By whose order?"

Gearheardt studied the map for a moment. "By the beseeching and distraught loved ones, assorted flunkies and compadres of roughly one hundred fifty thousand world movers and shakers about to lose their nuts." He turned to the room and shouted. "Navaja!"

The women stopped whatever they were doing and withdrew the metal instruments of pain from purses and brassieres. They held them toward Gearheardt.

The women shouted (too darn gleefully I thought), "Navaja!"

"Okay, now get your pretty asses back to work!" He repeated it in Spanish and the women laughed. "You still here, Jack? That means you too. By the way, you're actually a bit too skinny for me. I was just trying to distract Crenshaw when I told him I thought you were cute. Sorry to disappoint you."

"So I'm too skinny for you and too male for Marta. My love life is—"

"Jack, could you just get on over to the square? We can joke about this later."

I had never seen Gearheardt put business ahead of a good laugh, so I assumed this was serious. "And I'll stop anyone from shooting the President, right? Even though I am semi-officially not a Company man anymore."

"Don't worry about that. We'll make you chief token male in the security department of New Cuba. Get going." He looked up from his paperwork. "And yes, keep the President un-shot."

Marta was on the radio, talking to some of Gearheardt's troops in the streets about a clear path to the square. She put the radio down and gave me a thumb's up. "We can go, Jack. We will hook up with the good Cubans before the speech. You will have to make it to the stage facilities on your own. But we will watch you."

"Jack, take that Walkie-Talkie that Marta was using. It's bulky, but you and I need to stay in touch. You look more official with it anyway."

"Gearheardt," I said quietly, "I understand your plan to negotiate with *someone* to give you Cuba, using your hostages as leverage. I get that. But what about those countries which have leaders that don't screw off and aren't susceptible to your scheme? It would seem that—"

Gearheardt stood up suddenly. His Spanish was too rapid for me, but I could tell he was relaying my concerns to his 'troops' that their 'coverage' might not carry the day.

The room erupted in laughter. Isabella went to the main map and after squinting at it for a moment, placed her finger on a small town in Iceland. The women laughed again.

I grinned sheepishly and nodded my head as if I understood. Gearheardt shook his head as if suffering fools was tiresome but necessary. The women went back to work.

I fixed my tie and brushed off the jacket of my well lived-in suit. I needed to look presentable enough to get to my post next to the President.

"Has anyone heard from Victor? I guess we're all assuming that we will actually have someone there trying to shoot the President."

Gearheardt wasn't listening. His head was tilted into a conversation with Isabella and Daisy.

"Victor is on his way, Jack," Marta answered. "I spoke with him this morning. And he has many 'bad' Cubans with him. We will have to be careful."

I waved at Gearheardt who waved absently back.

As Marta and I passed through the main Las Palomas lounge the din was overwhelming. A row of teletypes spewed out messages. Two dozen or more women manned banks of phones. Baby-doll negligee clad women drew grease marks on clear plastic sheeting depicting bordellos around the world. Evidently the revolution had kicked off in full force. Marta nodded to three women who looked combat ready—trim, muscular, and armed—who rose and followed us out of the room and down the stairs. Marta motioned me to follow her outside and then wait by the door.

On the street, aside from a disabled taxi, bullet holes in the restaurant window and a blackened orange cart abandoned at the curb, life looked normal. I had a fleeting urge to grab a passerby and scream "whores are taking over the world" but decided against it. And, of course, I was in favor of the operation in any event. I wasn't sure it would, in fact I was fairly certain it *wouldn't* work, but the revenge upon Cuba for the Bay of Pigs fiasco was worth the effort. If the U.S. or the Catholic Church ended up with Cuba, it was no skin off my nose. I tried not to think about the thousands of men around the world with their nuts in a chopper. Not that I felt sorry for them, it was just uncomfortable to think about men's testicles, or being without mine.

"Jack, you read me? Over." It was Gearheardt on the radio.

"I read you, Gearheardt. I can probably hear you without the damn radio. I'm still at the front of Las Palomas while General Marta is scouting the route I guess. Over."

"Good. Listen, Jack, we have some problems popping up. You stay on this radio in case we need to change plans. You copy that?"

"What kind of problems?"

"The women in Tijuana just pulled the cord on about five hundred de-nutters. We couldn't talk them into waiting. Now we've got a few Mexican guys pretty upset. Over."

"If I lost my balls, I'd be upset too."

"Naaa. I mean cops and army guys. As well as a few government officials."

I wanted to learn more, but it was cumbersome on the Walkie-Talkies, having to make sure the other person was through and had released the 'send' button before you tried to talk. You spent half your time interrupting each other.

"I'll see you later, Gearheardt. Over and out."

"No need to be so formal on the radio, Jack," Gearheardt said behind me, causing me to jump.

"I thought you were upstairs."

"I needed to give you this," Gearheardt said. He pulled a pistol from his inside pocket and held it out to me.

"That's the one I got for you from the embassy armory, isn't it?"

"The very one." Gearheardt looked squarely at me. "You thought I got it so that I could frame you or blackmail you with it didn't you, Jack?"

"Never crossed my mind," I lied.

"Jack, there is a very good chance that you will have to shoot Victor today. He's more or less off the reservation as they say. After you shoot, drop the gun. We'll make sure we get it and the forensics will prove that a pistol from the U.S. Embassy was the one who shot the assassin. Which of course he won't technically be if you shoot him before he shoots the president. Got it?"

"I think so. I'm not sure I see why it's necessary. But I'm okay with using it."

"Where's Marta? Hadn't you guys better be getting to the square?"

"She took off with those Amazon types and told me to wait here. Listen, Gearheardt, since I am finally about to do the mission I have been about to do for the past seventy-two hours, answer me truthfully, did you at first intend for me to kill the President of Mexico?"

"I would never ask you to shoot someone I wouldn't be willing to shoot myself."

"I appreciate that. And it's not an answer. Was the first plan to shoot the President?"

"Jack, the plan has always been to kick the Cubans out of Cuba and start the New Cuba. A good agent makes the rest up as he goes along. You see, he's dealing with the most dangerous and unpredictable of obstacles, the human reaction. In this case, the sex drive of the—"

"Oh, for God's sakes, Gearheardt, spare me. You're just making this up as you go along."

Gearheardt's grin was maddeningly bright. "Except in this case, Jack, I was counting on the inability of man to think straight when confronted by naked women."

He grabbed my shoulder. "Once again, Jack. Do your duty. We'll be in Pussy Galore by the end of the month."

"We'll be *where?*"

"Pussy Galore is the new name for Cuba. The vote was just tallied. The majority of the women who voted want to name the country after that lady in *Goldfinger*, the Bond flick. Some of the women think it's a good marketing attraction. I'm not sure they totally get the concept of having their own country. Too much influence by the pimps and other assholes in their lives." He sighed. "Running this show is not as easy as you might think." He gave my arm a pat and turned to go into the building.

Marta had not returned so I decided to set out for the square, only a few blocks away, on my own. The streets were crowded with shoppers, tourists, and the hordes of people that seem to always fill the sidewalks of major cities. Except most of these were Mexican and there was a noticeable flow toward the Square of the Heroes, where the President was to give his speech. I decided to go past the square and approach from the other side, taking a look for Victor and hoping to spot anyone that might be tailing me from Las Palomas.

I came into the edge of the square near a statue of a Mexican hero who looked more like a character from a Dickens novel. The four-story buildings, at once ornate and solemn, surrounded the huge park-like plaza, creating a rectangular valley cut by deep canyons of side streets. Near the southwest edge of the plaza, not far from where I stood observing the activity, the oldest church in Mexico City was sinking steadily into the lake upon which modern Mexico City was built.

There were three or four thousand people in the plaza, one of whom was Gearheardt, sitting at a sidewalk café, sipping wine and enjoying a cigarette. He spotted me and waved me over.

"I took a taxi, Jack. Want a glass of wine?"

I sat down across from him at the small table. "How did you know how to find me?"

Gearheardt snorted his annoying laugh. "Who taught you everything you know about spying, Jack?"

"Not you. You were supposed to be dead or in Angola."

"Same thing. And beside the point." He leaned toward me. "Things have kind of turned to shit, Jack. You and I have to get this operation back on track."

"I can't tell you how frightening those words are, coming from you, Gearheardt. No more Gearheardt games. Okay?" I was feeling a sense of heightened anxiety. No matter what was happening, Gearheardt could always make it worse.

"Drink up, Jack (I of course had not had a chance to order), we need to get to business. I'll fill you in as we walk." He opened his suit coat to expose a chrome .45 caliber pistol looking suspiciously like the one Crenshaw had been carrying. "Dumb shit stopped to take a piss on the way out of Las Palomas and the pisser attendant stole it for me." He motioned for me to leave some pesos on the table as he got up. "We'd better hurry, or the President of Mexico will look like a sieve. There have to be half a dozen groups trying to shoot him."

We crossed the street into the main area of the plaza, heading toward the northern end where a sizable stage had been erected. Scores of Mexican army uniformed men were milling around the stage, which was properly festooned with the Mexican flag in various shapes and formats. Behind the stage the VIP gathering area was in a large tent. It was there that I was originally supposed to meet up with the guard unit protecting the president.

I stopped Gearheardt. "Wait, Gearheardt. Let's just get the lay of the land. And tell me what you meant by the operation turning to shit. This was not The Manhattan Project to begin with, you know."

"First off, nuts are dropping world-wide. We passed out the de-nutters to the girls way too soon. I'm not mad at them, but, like I told you, we have massive logistical support problems. Already a few of the shops have been stormed by the local police and we've lost a few girls. That's to be expected. A shame, but you have to break some eggs to . . . have eggs for breakfast or however it goes. I keep trying to explain to the girls that if you chop off a hostage's balls, you have no leverage. We needed to keep some leverage until the Marines kick Castro into the Caribbean."

"It's a simple concept but probably new to a lot of the girls."

"Is that more of that sarcastic shit, Jack? That got you into a lot of trouble in the Marine Corps."

I ignored him. "Needed? Past tense?" I was craning my neck around the plaza, looking for Victor, his Cuban hoods or Crenshaw and his Christian Cuban band. I looked back at Gearheardt. "You did say needed?"

"I think I've got a deal, Jack. Daisy is going to telephone me if or when she gets word from the UN."

"So Kurt's going to call you?"

Gearheardt pulled his head back, impressed. "You know Kurt? You never fail to amaze me, Jack. Yeah, I had the Pope call Waldheim to see if he couldn't get a deal cut right now."

"Gearheardt—"

"Hey, Señor! Yeah you, por favor. Come here." Gearheardt was hailing a Mexican photographer. Either on his way to film the President or just to take photos for the folks for souvenirs.

"Let's have our picture made, Jack." He withdrew the shiny .45 pistol. "Get your gun out." Gearheardt put his arm around my shoulders and held his pistol across his chest like a Mexican bandit. "Come on. Get your gun out."

I thought it would be less hassle to just go along, so I stood Mexican bandit style in the afternoon Mexican sun, posing with Gearheardt. He who had been shortly before wheeling and dealing with the Pope and the Secretary General of the United Nations.

Gearheardt spoke to me through smiling teeth as we posed exceptionally long while the photographer consulted the instruction manual for his new camera. "Jack, we got some of the Pope's boys in a massage parlor in Bali. He'll make the deal, believe me."

"What makes you think that the Secretary General will go along with whatever this deal is the Pope proposes?" My jaws were starting to ache from holding the smile.

"Ha. Surely you're kidding. Guess where about half the UN payroll is at this moment?"

Gearheardt thanked the grinning photographer and let me pay him. He asked that the photos be delivered to Las Palomas and was assured they would be.

"Let's go, Jack." Gearheardt holstered his pistol.

We started into the ever-growing crowd of Mexican people. Festivities were breaking out as offices emptied by government order so that the people could hear the speech of the President. Angling toward the stage, we began to notice stern faced, dangerous looking men in small groups. Gearheardt nudged me and nodded toward the men as we passed. None seemed to take note of us.

"Cuban, you think?" I asked Gearheardt.

"Probably. They are darker and they aren't happy to be here."

"Good enough for me, let's shoot them."

"Not a good idea, Jack," Gearheardt said, forgetting he was my comedic mentor.

We reached a sizable fountain surrounded by a low wall. Gearheardt jumped to the top of the wall and I followed him. We continued to survey the crowd, looking for . . .

"Who all are we looking for, Gearheardt? Did you ever tell me why the operation was going to shit?"

Gearheardt spoke while continuing to look out across the crowd. "First, you need to find Victor. We *know* that bastard will try to kill the President."

"Which we asked him to do, by the way."

Gearheardt looked at me. "Are you going to keep up a running commentary or do you want me to tell you about the operation?"

"Forgive me, your Excellency."

"Knock it off, Jack. But anyway, we need to find Crenshaw and his band of Christians. He must have converted and recruited half of Victor's bad Cuban gang. We need to find your friend, Eduardo, with his Halcones. And of course there's always the Pygmy and the blind Ukrainian. You can never tell what those guys might do."

"Eduardo? I thought you said you had the cooperation of the Halcones."

"That was when they thought my bordello operation was only about intelligence. After the Tijuana episode last night, I think they've thrown in with the Russians."

"Señor Armstrong. Señor Armstrong." My walkie-talkie startled me. I dropped down from my conspicuous position atop the wall and pressed the talk button.

"This is Señor Armstrong. Over."

A pause. "Señor Armstrong is over?"

"No. This is Señor Armstrong." I resisted my training in radio procedure.

"Señor Gearheardt is with you, no?"

"Yes. Señor Gearheardt is with me. Let me give the radio to him."

I held the walkie-talkie to Gearheardt. "It's for you."

Gearheardt joined me below the wall.

"This is Gearheardt. Who's this?"

Rapid Spanish followed from both ends of the walkie-talkie. Finally Gearheardt handed the radio back to me. He smiled. "Good news, Jack. I have a message from Waldheim and I think it's positive."

"Exactly what does it say?"

"They didn't want to read it over the air. Isabella is going to meet us here by the fountain in a few minutes. How long do we have before the President is shot?"

"Very funny, Gearheardt." I looked at my watch. "He is due on stage in about half an hour. I'll need to get up there pretty soon. If we can't intercept Victor, I need to at least be there to recognize him if he approaches the President."

"A half hour is plenty, Jack." He sat down on the wall. "Look, let me tell you where we're at. You usually have things pretty well figured out when we work together, but this operation is a bit confusing." He smiled as I sat down next to him, a bit pissed off.

"The bottom line is this. I've worked out a deal with the Pope to let the Catholic Church off the hook, give them a permanent beach resort on the island, and first crack at setting up the religion of Pussy Galoreland. Not a bad deal for him."

"Pretty common arrangement in deals like this," I said.

"Really, Jack, you're getting to be awfully sarcastic. You keep hounding me to learn the real deal and I'm trying to accommodate you."

"Please go ahead."

"So Paul, the Pope, has made a deal with Kurt Waldheim up at the UN to pressure Castro out of Cuba without a fight. We just walk in and take over."

"You're shitting me. Castro agreed to that? We don't even have to fight or send in the Marines?"

"Castro gets some pissant African country, nothing the girls would want, that has oil and other stuff that Castro needs to become a real player. Plus, let's face it, he's pretty much worked himself into a hole in Cuba. After a while the peasants are going to be getting restless and what can he give them? More sugarcane?"

I looked at my pal for a moment. Could he have really pulled this off? Some things, however, didn't add up.

"Why did the Secretary General . . . oh, I forgot, the scores of thousands of guys around the world sitting with their balls on the line, so to speak."

"The UN switchboard was swamped. Faxes, cables, personal emissaries, telephone calls. One guy even had his people send a carrier pigeon. Seems the world's leaders leave no stone unturned when it's *their* balls on the line."

"I hate to ask, but what's the 'operation turning to shit' issue?"

Gearheardt looked down at the cobblestones between his feet and blew out his breath. "Everything is off if someone kills the President of Mexico."

I tried to think through that. "Because . . . ?"

"The U.S. has its fingerprints all over the assassination attempt. We can hardly try to explain that it was just a CIA ploy to justify going into Cuba."

"And the UN needs the U.S. because . . . ?"

"Waldheim got assurances from the U.S. that we would nuke Cuba if Castro didn't give up. They even got the Pope to wire Castro saying the church agreed with the UN's position."

"So much for the diplomacy. It was get out or get nuked for Castro."

"Pretty much. The Agency did a quick study of the danger to Miami and southern Florida if Cuba was nuked. At least they thought that far ahead." Gearheardt stood up and searched the crowd again, then sat back down.

"So they felt they could safely nuke Cuba?" I asked.

"They found out that Miami was mostly Cuban anyway, and that 'deviates' lived in Key West. It was decided to be an acceptable risk. This was for the good of the Cuban exiles after all." Gearheardt didn't blush when he said it, nor did he look at me. "And the trade winds could start blowing in the other direction. There's always that chance."

Around us the crowd had become joyously boisterous. Mariachi music and the warm smell of street food took the air and made the atmosphere friendly, comforting.

"So we just need to make sure the President isn't shot? Right?" I wasn't quite sure what Gearheardt was seemingly worried about.

"Yep, we need to do that. And we need to keep that damn Crenshaw from getting to Cuba before our girls and setting up shop. And we need to find Marta and shoot her."

"You're kidding."

"Marta has gone off the reservation, Jack. I talked to her on the phone just after you took off. At least she had the decency to call me and say she was sorry. And to try to get the name of the de-nutter manufacturer in China. But she was sincere I think." He turned to me. "She really liked you, Jack. Said for me to tell you that. She was ready to try the old man-woman routine with you. You should be proud."

I wasn't. "So why didn't she?"

"She thought you were homosexual. She ran around naked half the time she was in your apartment and you were just trying to get clothes *on* her most of the time."

"I was just trying to be a decent guy, for God's sake. It's not like—"

"It's not a concept she understands, Jack."

Now *I* was depressed. I had thought I was falling in love with Marta.

"Remember what I told you right after I left her in your apartment the first time, Jack. 'Don't fall in love with her; we might have to shoot her.' Remember me saying that?"

"You said, asshole, 'don't screw her.'"

"The distinction escapes me, Jack. But anyway right now she is a danger to the whole plan." He stood on the wall again. "Where the hell is that darn Isabella?"

Behind us the fountain was filling with mothers and small children, wading in the water and squealing delightedly—ignorant of their proximity to scheming spies. Gearheardt took coins from his pocket and flipped them high into the air so the kids could try to catch them or search for them under the water when they dropped. The mothers smiled, a bit nervously, and Gearheardt bowed to them, smiling broadly. Then he dropped back down by my side.

"Do you see that Señorita with the two little girls, Jack? That's one of the best looking Mexican women I've ever seen." He reached for my radio. "I'm going to call back and see what's happened to Isabella."

"No need, Gearheardt. That's her coming there."

Isabella was dressed in a white peasant blouse and billowing skirt, revealing to me how much I had anticipated her sashaying through this crowd in her yellow peignoir. She barely nodded to me and handed Gearheardt a manila envelope.

"Thanks, Isabella," he said. "Jack, keep looking for Eduardo, Crenshaw, Marta, or those other guys while I make sure I have what was promised." He sat down and tore open the envelope. He ran his finger down the page of the teletype. "Yes. Yes. Yes. The bastards. Yes. Okay. Yes."

"Let's start with 'the bastards.' What does the letter say?" I grabbed for it, but Gearheardt jerked it away.

"Oh just the shitheads at the UN aren't going to give recognition to any diplomats from Pussy Galoreland for the first five years unless Fidel Castro is Dictator Emeritus. They all remember how Hitler and Stalin's reputations suffered after they lost their countries." He started to fold the paper. "But everything else is pretty much what we wanted." He stood and put the paper in his coat pocket. "And of course, Kurt expects a free pass to Havana. Seems like every country he contacted for approval for the girls getting Cuba wants to present their diplomatic credentials as soon as possible. I don't think the PG concept is being clearly understood."

"We've got about fifteen minutes, Gearheardt. What do we have to do?" I found myself greatly wanting the women to get their country. It might be a stupid idea, started by a madman as a money-making scheme or a CIA operation gone horribly wrong, but the women deserved something—something life-changing, something hopeful.

"We can all but forget about Crenshaw. If his crew of jolly Christians helps stop the assassination, fine. If they get to Cuba before we do, fine. The UN and the Pope can deal with that."

"The Halcones?"

"Still a problem. If they are truly in with the Russians, they'll try to shoot the President just to make the U.S. look bad. And Paul and Kurt were adamant, the U.S. has to come out clean in this thing or they won't have the credibility to back taking Castro's country away from him."

I felt 'commissioned' to shoot Eduardo and anyone with him. I became conscious of the weight of the pistol in my shoulder holster and felt a boost of adrenaline.

"Good Cubans? Bad Cubans?"

"Immaterial now, Jack. I'll probably never get that thirty-five-hundred-dollar taxi bill reimbursed, but we can't worry about that now." He took a calming deep breath. "Why does it always come down to stopping the fucking Russians? Can't they just leave well enough alone? Always dicking around where they can cause us trouble. Always—"

"Can it, Gearheardt. If our job is to stop the Russians, let's get to it. I think the best place to be is up near the stage, with the President. We don't have time to search the crowd now."

Isabella drew another document from her peasant blouse. "Señor Gearheardt, this is for you also."

Gearheardt opened the envelope and scanned the contents. "Crap!" he said. "Look at this, Jack."

'This' was a teletype from the Chinese manufacturer of the de-nutters. It stated that the design flaw was being researched but that for the present time there was no way to de-activate the mechanism. Once the device was 'installed' the men whom it was installed on would lose their uts.

"We must have ordered the doomsday de-nutter, Jack. Do you realize that the governments, military and businessmen of dozens of mostly third world countries are going to be neutered?"

I didn't want to realize it or think about it.

"Isabella, get back to the Las Palomas. Tell Daisy everything is going according to the plan," Gearheardt looked at me, "more or less."

She started to leave and Gearheardt continued. "And tell her to get as many names as possible. Those guys will be prime candidates for immigration to Galoreland. Exactly the kind of guys the girls can trust once they get over being cranky about losing their balls."

Gearheardt and I began making our way through the crowd, heading toward the stage at the north end of the plaza. I fell ten or so paces behind him, the Marine Corps mantra "don't bunch up" automatically kicking in when in potentially dangerous territory.

And it *was* dangerous and tough going. Twenty feet later my arms were coated in snow cone syrup, I had tacos on my shirt front, and had emptied my pocket of pesos after stepping on a roast goat head from a plaza vendor unseen until my foot was descending into his spread-out wares. But I still had Gearheardt in sight.

I began to notice Gearheardt making eye contact with various good looking Mexican women. I was thinking at first the bastard could manage to flirt under any conditions known to man, but then realizing that these were 'his girls' spotting for him in the crowd. A Mexican band, now assembled on the stage, began blaring out songs obviously written by tuba manufacturers and the people who make the coverings for bass drums. The oompahing and pounding opened the ears so that the staccato shrieks of the trumpets could quickly penetrate to the brain's nerve centers. My pistol was impotent against the musical assault that was made all the more annoying by the urge to hum along with the music.

I saw Gearheardt stop, glance back at me, and then nod to his left front. There, standing just behind the first uneven rows of Mexican Army uniforms, stood a dozen Cuban hoodlums. They were distinguished by smirks, frowns, and tee-shirts that bore pictures of Castro and Che Guevara. Their desire not to be mistaken for the peasant Mexicans apparently overrode their need for anonyminity.

Gearheardt indicated through nods and subtle hand gestures that I should proceed around the group. I unbuttoned my jacket, making my pistol as accessible as possible, and began moving. It entered my mind that I had no idea what we were going to do, but it was too late to start disbelieving in the powers of Gearheardt. I just moved to my right, keeping Gearheardt and the bad Cubans in sight.

I was kept from finding out if Gearheardt actually had a plan when fifteen or twenty Cubans appeared from the closest 'canyon' feeder into the plaza and waded into the bad Cubans with a holy vigor. The initial assault was made with wooden and cardboard signs proclaiming the Catholic Church's legitimate claim to Cuba. The damage from that assault was minimal but led to disorganization of the bad Cubans and their assuming a defensive, retreating posture.

The Mexican soldiers turned their heads to watch the melee. They didn't move toward it or bother to extinguish their cigarettes. Crenshaw appeared and was confronted by a Mexican officer whose shoulders and chest appeared to be gold-plated. Crenshaw's mouth moved, his cheeks got red and he finally jerked off his beret and threw it to the ground. By this time my friend and fellow agent, Eric, was tugging at his arm, attempting to extricate Crenshaw from a no-win situation. With the band striking up the lovely *Aria for Trombone and Bass Drum with Machine Gun and Artillery Obbligato* it was impossible to hear the verbal exchange, but I was fairly certain that when Crenshaw finally punched the Mexican officer in the nose, the argument was over. Eric let go of the Major's arm so that the Mexican soldiers could drag Crenshaw away to be bargained out of jail by the State Department at a later date.

Meanwhile the Cuban Christians and Commies had started round two. The soldiers moved on the fighting Cubans by forming a skirmish line and pushing the knock-down drag-out brawl through the crowd as the body would expel a dangerous infection. Hair-pulling, shin-kicking, and slugging each other took precedence over any pre-conceived mission for the Cubans and I lost sight of them. I hadn't realized that he had spotted me, but when I looked back Eric held out his hands palms up and shrugged. A Mexican officer evidently saw the gesture and began berating Eric who popped him in the nose. Soon thereafter he joined the short procession of CIA agents being frog-marched toward the gloomiest of the plaza valley walls, the headquarters of the Halcones. He had always been extremely loyal to Crenshaw and the Agency.

Gearheardt joined me. "We've only got about ten minutes, Jack. We have to assume the Cubans have been taken care of. Did you see that shameless mess, by the way? I don't know if you could hear Crenshaw, but he was demanding the Army arrest the bad Cubans. The Army officer was insisting that although he was a sympathetic Catholic, it was obvious that the Christian coalition of attackers were beating the be-Jesus out of Castro's guys and didn't need his help."

"So we really have to focus our efforts on stopping any Russian activity against the President. Right? Aside from the Pygmy and that other guy, the almost blind guy."

Gearheardt signaled to a gorgeous young woman hovering nearby. "I need to talk to Rosarita a moment, Jack. But basically, yes, you're right. I saw the Pygmy by the way. He's in his cigarette vendor outfit. I've asked one of the girls to keep an eye on him. The little shithead." Rosarita came near. "Rosie, como esta? You know Jack, right? We need to find the Russians. Ruso, quien sabe? You said you saw them earlier." He then broke into his own rapid Spanish. I knew that Gearheardt, being my best friend and a decent fellow to the extreme, often used broken Spanish/English in front of me just so I wouldn't feel so dumb.

Rosie was quite animated as well as being cute. She began speaking rapidly, first walking a circle in what would best be described as 'basic Frankenstein monster,' then in a more mysterious gait that had her legs so wide apart that walking was difficult, her face pained.

"The Russians are down by the fountain, headed this way. Evidently Eduardo is with them."

"And the other Halcones?"

"I'm not sure. None have been reported and they usually stand out. They're so damn mean that they don't care whether or not people recognize them." Gearheardt grabbed my arm and looked at my watch.

"Omega? I used to have one something like that." He started back toward the fountain, away from the stage. "Jack, let's take a chance on intercepting them. I don't like our odds up here with the Mexican military."

As we pushed through the crowd, Rosie disappeared, but ten paces further on reappeared with three other girls, obviously from the Las Palomas contingent. They drew alongside Gearheardt and he began what appeared to be a briefing, the girls solemn and occasionally nodding their lovely heads in agreement or understanding.

The crowd was now more or less stationary, the area of the Plaza at maximum holding capacity. It made the going easier, not having to fight against a crowd still moving toward the stage. Around the fountain the crowd was thinner, probably because it was harder to see the stage and the young mothers and children still frolicked. I watched for a moment but could see no signs of Russians, or of Eduardo, my former friend.

Then he came into view and it was apparent Eduardo was the person that Rosarita was mimicking when she described the Russians. Eduardo was walking in severe pain, or at least caution, his legs skewed wide with each step, a cane in each hand supported him, and his pants were ballooned around his butt like he was wearing a hoop skirt that encircled him.

It dawned on me that although I didn't know the nomenclature of the hoop skirt or its foundation, it was obvious that Eduardo was wearing the Model 156 Doomsday De-Nutter, first phase activated, second phase armed. I felt sorry for him. He saw me and said something bitter and short over his shoulder. The Frankenstein monsters, Russians, appeared and moved quickly by him, converging on me and Gearheardt. They looked as if they had piled ten suits of clothes in the middle of a dark room and given prizes for the first ones dressed. But they also looked deadly. I reached inside my coat and put my fingers around the butt of my pistol, noticing Gearheardt doing the same.

One of the Las Palomas girls, Victoria, came quickly from the crowd and bumped into one of the broad-shouldered bozos in dark suits. She fell immediately to the ground at his feet causing him to stumble.

"Ayuda! Ayuda! Violar! Violar!" she screamed, very convincingly I thought. Help. Rape.

The crowd in the immediate vicinity turned as one and several men began moving angrily toward the Russians, who became trapped in the mass.

"Ayuda! Rusos hurtar las ninas! Ayuda por favor!" Help me please, the Russians are stealing my little girl. This came from the edge of the fountain where Rosarita appeared suitably distraught. She became hysterical and began grabbing at the ill-fitting suits of the scrambling Russians.

Victoria had managed to get to her knees, clinging to the leg of a panicked Russian. One breast had appeared through a mysteriously torn blouse. The sight seemed to add a level of interest from the Mexican men who were even more belligerent than before.

Eduardo was in a small circle of his own making, swinging his canes wildly to keep anyone from coming close. I could see the panic in his eyes. He was yelling that people should not press against the Model 156 De-nutter, or something to that effect.

A Russian who had managed to get his pistol from beneath his jacket was quickly knocked into the fountain and his head held under water. The Mexican men swarmed over the Russians and a shot was fired. A roar went up. Quiet thumping. Then the sounds of whimpering in Russian were heard before the military band began a new blitzkrieg against the eardrums, the marvelous *Cacophony in G Minor for Cymbals and Howitzer.*

CHAPTER TWENTY-FOUR

THE ROAD TO HEAVEN IS PAVED WITH GEARHEARDT

Gearheardt and I were trying to make our way back to the stage area. At first, still near the fountain, we were accosted and accused of being Russian. We were able to dissuade the accosters by pointing out our finely tailored apparel and grinning like possums, something no self-respecting Russian would do just to free himself from Mexican peasant attacks.

After a few yards, with Mexican men still racing past us, Gearheardt stopped, causing me to run into him. "Jack," he said, "doesn't it strike you as crazy that men will knock themselves out to get a look at a strange boob? Did you know that the viewing of naked women is the number one money making business in the world, Jack?"

"I guess I wouldn't be surprised. Even though I know you just made that up." I turned him around and pushed him toward the stage.

We reached the stage, out of breath and with less than five minutes before the President was scheduled to appear and speak to the crowd. I fumbled in my pocket for the embassy pass that was to get me to onto

the honor guard where I would have a clear view of the people immediately around the President. I realized that I was not breathing hard only
due to the rush to the stage. I was adrenaline charged. Victor had pledged
to kill the President. I had pledged (to Victor) to help him and (to Gearheardt) stop him. I had to be quick on the draw and fire straight and true
if there were no other options and I didn't think there would be any. I
pushed myself through the small crowd around the opening to the VIP
tent, Gearheardt right behind me. What would happen to me when I shot
Victor? That was what was on my mind, not whether or not I could
shoot him.

"Jack, let me see your pistol," Gearheardt demanded.

I surreptitiously withdrew it and passed it to him. He took a silencer
from his pocket and screwed it on the barrel.

"There he is right there," I heard him say. He shot over my shoulder
and Victor dropped to the ground. Gearheardt shoved the pistol in my
back pocket and pushed me toward the tent. "I'll catch up later."

No one seemed vitally interested as Victor's body slumped to the
ground. Men who I assumed were his bodyguards, gathered around him
and talked among themselves. One of them nudged Victor with the toe
of his shoe and said something that made the others laugh. *Sic transit
tyrannis* came to mind, although I wasn't sure about the Latin. Evidently
Victor had not been the best of bosses.

Stunned to numbness, my credentials held in front of my face, I was
moved along by the crowd. After almost a week of agonizing about
defending the President, worrying about shooting Victor, and all the rest,
Gearheardt had seen him and shot him. I felt let down and redundant.

Inside the tent, the atmosphere was less frantic. The President chatted amiably with his aides and sycophants, glancing at the sheets of paper
in his hand I took to be the speech. He seemed in no hurry to mount the
stage. No one seemed to notice my presence. I tried to relax, knowing
that the Russians, the good and bad Cubans and Victor Ramirez were
no longer threats. I checked in with the Mexican security chief, flashed
my permit and shook hands with the others on the immediate security

team. When I asked the time remaining before the speech, the security chief shrugged and rolled his eyes toward the President.

I walked to a table laden with drinks and food, helping myself to a ham sandwich and a cola after deciding I would wait until after the speech to hit the beer. There were a number of women in the tent, all young and vivacious, dressed in elegance and money. I wondered how many of them qualified for citizenship in Galoreland. And how many of that number would give up the President's tent for their freedom. Was it freedom? Gearheardt's scheme was complicated when it came to women who were not physically confined to bordellos. To hell with that. I just looked forward to the evening at Las Palomas, the girls celebrating, Gearheardt celebrating (always a spectacle) and warm feelings for the success and new hope.

"Ola, Jack."

I should have sensed her, smelled her, before she pressed against my back. The focus point of her body against mine was just below my ribs where the unmistakable form of a pistol barrel was present.

"Ola, Marta." I set the plate and bottle on the table and tried to move away to turn around to face her. She wouldn't let me.

"Let's move to the back. Behind the serving curtain, Jack. We can talk there."

Once there, screened from the guests, I turned around. I didn't need to ask how she managed to get into the high security area. She was wearing jeans and a man's white shirt. It was open to where two mirrored 'commas' marked the underside of her breasts. Almost seen dark circles surrounded small protruding nipple pods for deliberate effect. She looked reat.

"Come with me, Jack. I have a plane to Havana."

I hesitated. "Marta, believe me, it *is* tempting. I'm not sure whether I've ever felt about a woman like I feel about you. But I'm not sure that—"

"I am insisting that you come, Jack. Perhaps some time in the Havana military prison will help you to remember more about the operation in Mexico and other countries."

Blushing, I assured her that I had no intention of going to Cuba with her.

"Jack, the President will be assassinated. The Americans will be blamed. Cuba will be safe."

"And you will shoot him?" Talking was so much better than getting shot, so I wanted to keep the conversation going.

"At some point. Perhaps from the tent. I am too important to Cuba to make a martyr of myself."

I was liking her less. "You're a whore, Marta."

"But a whore to important men in Cuba." By now I was too confused to know if that was a legitimate distinction. "Gearheardt's scheme was of interest to me at one time. To be free. To not be beaten for not having sex. Those are good things."

"I thank God nightly for them." Keeping the conversation going.

"You are not Gearheardt, Jack. Do not be the wiseass." She smiled, or maybe it was a smirk. "There are other things. There is power. I can have power with sex."

"You could have had power in Pussy Galoreland." Still hard to say with a straight face.

Marta laughed. "There will be no Pussy Galoreland. Gearheardt knows this. It would destroy his intelligence network. Did you not think of this? And why would he have himself appointed Emperor of Mexico if he were moving to Cuba?"

I wasn't going to give her an inch. "Maybe he wanted it on his resume."

"Wake up, Jack. Gearheardt is—"

"Right behind you, sweetheart." It was a crappy Humphrey Bogart. He had the .45 at her temple as he reached around to take her pistol. "Jack, I think we finally have all the assassins wrapped up. Sorry Marta, and you can quit flashing your tits. Won't work at this point."

"What was that, Gearheardt?" I asked, taking one last look.

"Better check your boy, Jack. Just to make sure."

I stepped around the screen just in time to see the President take a deep breath and head for the stage. The microphone squealed outside and I heard the President's name announced and a roar from the crowd. As the President strode by me, I noticed that he wasn't the President. It was obviously a look alike with a great deal of makeup. I glanced quickly around the tent and saw the real President of Mexico relaxing in a lounge chair, sipping golden tequila and flirting with ladies who weren't Mrs. President, if I had to guess.

The crowd quieted and I heard a confident and presidential voice begin, "Damas y Señores." A fusillade of small arms fire ended his brief tenure as President of Mexico. The bullets also tore through the VIP tent, sending most everyone to the ground. The President of Mexico, proving himself a resourceful man as well as crafty politician, rolled under the table with one of the not Mrs. Presidents. Gearheardt came running toward me and dove to the ground.

"*What the hell?*" he yelled over the din. "Who's shooting for God's sake?"

"Who *isn't* might be the better question. Are you sure we took care of everybody? How many people did you ask to assassinate the President anyway?"

The gunfire ended and the band began playing again, the classic *March of the One Hundred Tubas*. The crowd noise was loud but of indeterminate tenor. Two loyal Mexican secret service men crept past where Gearheardt and I lay, opened the tent flap and dragged the body of the former temporary President of Mexico back into the tent.

"That son-of-a-bitch better not die," Gearheardt said.

"He must have fifty holes in him, Gearheardt. I think he's earned the right to die without any more of your crap."

We slowly got to our feet, dusting off our clothes and adjusting our coats and ties. The tent was rocking with speculation about the attempted assassination and elation at not being assassinated. The former temporary President seemed to be forgotten where he lay, but still breathing. (I later found out that the poor fellow lost a lung, a kidney, both ears and had trouble walking and feeding himself. His suggestion that the same injuries be visited upon the real President so they would still be twins proved he had not lost his sense of humor).

Marta walked to the bleeding stand-in and knelt beside him. With a sharp whistle she summoned three of her 'girls' who began to stop the flow of blood and were generally trying to keep the poor man from dying within sight of a fabulous arrangement of snacks and sweets being gobbled up by dignitaries.

Then Marta was gone. We found a large pool of blood where she had been standing when the shooting started, but no other signs of her. "I kind of hope she makes it back to Cuba," Gearheardt said.

"Gearheardt, where are we?" I asked. "The President wasn't actually assassinated. Do you think the UN will live up to its side of the bargain?"

Before he could answer, the American congressional delegation burst into the tent. "Good lord," one of them exclaimed, "the man's bleeding to death. Someone get the President a doctor. And I mean right now. I'm a Congressman." He ignored the three Mexican women who worked on the fallen paid imposter.

"That man is not the President, Señor," one of the Mexican diplomats replied.

"Oh. Well where is he?" He stepped over the temporary President and took a beer from the table. The other Congressmen did the same. The Congressmen's people did the same. And finally the Congressmen's wives also stepped over the bleeding body of the former temporary President. "Oh, these foreign countries," they said.

The real President of Mexico must have known the Congressmen and their people wouldn't leave until all of the food was eaten and the wine and beer drunk (and he had ordered plenty), so he came out from underneath the table. The 'not Mrs. President' came out from the table at the same time. "Buenos tardes," the real President said with a broad smile. He held out his hand to be shaken. "We were taking the cover under the table."

"Pardner, your fly is unzipped," said a Congressman from the south.

The real and still alive President of Mexico grinned and zipped. Evidently not at all embarrassed and opening his shirt to display a bullet proof vest which had probably been meant for the presidential decoy. He introduced the 'temporary acting and permanently shot' President's wife. She must have been also a temporary President's wife as she adjusted and sipped and shook hands only about fifteen feet from where the bleeding stand-in gasped for breath.

Diplomatic exchanges were exchanged all around and cards were also exchanged among the staff and lesser diplomats. The Congressman had cards that said Congressman on them. The President apologized for not having cards and all laughed too hard at the thought of a president's card which said 'President' on them. That would be good.

"Mr. President," the southern Congressman began, "you might want to take note of the fact that about half the crowd out there seemed to be drawing a bead on you, or him." He pointed at the stand-in who was being moved onto a stretcher. "Folks might not be too happy with your presidentin' policies."

Gearheardt and I rolled our eyes. We stood just to the rear of the diplomatic gabfest, contemplating our next move.

"I appreciate very much your concern, Congressman . . ." The president hesitated, obviously clueless as to the Congressman's name. "I am sorry that you had to witness this unfortunate event. But no harm is done," he carefully averted his eyes from the now stretchered stand-in, "and we can talk some business."

"Gents, if I might suggest something."

It was that damn Gearheardt. He stepped to the diplomatic circle and beamed at the Mexican and American government officials.

"I represent an intelligence agency which shall for the moment remain nameless. You know, things like this don't have to happen. These Cuban assassins should not be allowed to run rampant among us democratic countries, shooting and . . . and, and . . . shooting stuff."

Perhaps those who did not know Gearheardt would not realize that the bastard was just improvising until he could figure out a way to get either the Mexican or American officials to help his scheme which seemed to be falling apart. Neither the Congressman or the President would look him in the eye.

After a moment of uncomfortable silence, Gearheardt withdrew.

"Jack, I believe that the professionals have taken over. In this case, I mean those people who make their living by protecting their own ass and manipulating every situation for their own gain. Politicians." He turned back to the officials. "Let's hear what happens and then we'd better make tracks."

I was still too numb to respond. I felt bad for Gearheardt. Although I knew that he would let all this roll off his back, I also knew that he recognized how quickly the field men, so important just moments ago, would be now forgotten. The politicians and policy makers moved in like lava flowing down the side of a volcano.

The President was changing tactics. "The Americans were behind this outrage," he said. "It is fortunate that only an impersonator was killed," an aide whispered to him. "Was badly wounded," he corrected himself. "Why do the Americans cause so much trouble in my country?" He wasn't addressing anyone in particular. It was just a speech he had to get out of the way before reparations and oil treaties could be renegotiated.

The aide whispered to the President again.

"It is the American CIA that is causing the trouble according to my sources," the President said.

"I'm not surprised," said a Congressman who had narrowly escaped the Model 156 the previous evening. "It's time we rein those outlaws in. They cannot be allowed to operate outside the U.S. if they don't know how to—"

One of his aides whispered in his ear. The Congressman craned his head around to look at the aide. "They can't? Nothing domestic?"

The President of Mexico, an expert negotiator, spoke up. "So it is agreed. The American intelligence agencies were responsible for the attempt on my life. I will expel them from my country and demand, say, one hundred million dollars."

"You have to kick the Russian intelligence agency out too," said the first congressman. "And we get to drill closer to the Mexican shoreline in the Gulf." His demands seemed well prepared and I wondered who had briefed him that he might have this opportunity.

"It is done," said the President. He wanted to get rid of the Russians anyway. And "closer to the Mexican shoreline" was vague enough to get approval from his business associates at PEMEX. After much hand shaking and back slapping, the President and the Congressmen left.

"We're screwed, I'll bet," Gearheardt said, shaking his head. "I'm not sure we were ever in the game, let alone scored any points. C'mon, Jack, let's get to Las Palomas to see what's happened. I sure hate to face those girls if the UN backs down."

"What about the Pope's support?" I asked. Surely there was a way to save Pussy Galoreland and the dreams of thousands and thousands of girls.

"I would imagine the Pope thinks I pissed in his pointy hat. He's not going to help us out of this, Jack. We're screwed."

I described my vision of the political lava taking over and sweeping us aside, after we had done the hard and dangerous work.

Gearheardt stopped thoughtfully for a moment. "Yes, Jack. I sometimes feel like one of the virgins tossed into the flaming crater to appease the gods of U.S. foreign policy."

"Well that may be a bit strong—"

"Screw 'em, Jack. Let's go." Gearheardt laughed and slapped my shoulder.

"Ayudame," the former temporary President said as we stepped over him.

The contingent of Russians was passing by as we exited the VIP tent.

"Pedophiles," Gearheardt said to them. Luckily they were too beaten up to respond physically. One of them gave us the finger. "Oh, cute," Gearheardt said. I could tell he was aching for a fight.

I grabbed him and pulled him away from the stage. "We don't *know* for *sure* the game is lost, Gearheardt. Let's get to Las Palomas and see what the messages are."

"Jack, even the American congressmen are falling all over themselves to blame the CIA. The rotten bastards."

We were walking past the now deserted fountain area. "It *was* a CIA operation, Gearheardt. I'm not saying I blame *us*, but . . . who else should be blamed?"

The plaza was almost empty except for the sweepers and the men taking apart the stage and VIP tent. It was eerie in the concrete valley. I wondered if we would ever come to a point in America where the President sends a double to the podium to see if any one shoots him, before he himself will appear in front of a crowd. I shared my thoughts with Gearheardt as we walked along.

"Jack, the actual president of the United States hasn't appeared in public since Woodrow Wilson ventured out one time when he was president. With of course the notable exception of JFK, who was promptly shot."

We stopped at the edge of the plaza, near the sinking church, and Gearheardt looked around. "We almost got a country for people who don't deny they're whores, Jack. That would have been something."

We stood for a while, wistful, as the plaza emptied. It seemed fitting that the earlier hoopla was now just a street-mess of half-eaten tacos and crowd debris.

"You know, Gearheardt," I started, "one disappointment I guess I'll always have is Marta. I really liked her. She seemed to be a very nice girl. Smart and . . . well, attractive in a naked sort of way."

Gearheardt smiled, not looking at me. "Jack, Jack, Jack," he said. "You know women like I know Mongolian weaving patterns. Marta didn't betray us."

"What do you mean?"

"Who went to the side of the shot up fake president? Who called her girls out of the crowd to help? Don't you think that if she'd wanted us dead, we'd be dead?"

"She had a gun on me, Gearheardt. And you pulled a gun on her."

"The tent was full of her compatriots, Jack. When I knew that the plan was falling apart, I wanted to let her write her own ticket. She deserved that. She could either throw in with us—the CIA has a great history of hugging Cuban whores to it's breast—or she could choose to go back to Cuba and make the best of things. She did what she thought she had to do." He turned to me. "And I'm afraid that one of the wild shots hit her. That blood she was standing in wasn't all from the perforated president."

I felt sick. Knowing that I had been right in my intuition about Marta didn't make me feel better. We had either compromised her or worse, maybe gotten her shot.

Gearheardt smiled and clapped me on the back. "Jack, it wasn't your deal, and it wasn't your fault. Don't take the world on your shoulders."

I smiled back weakly.

"Hell, maybe since the real president didn't get shot, and we did stop the Cubans from killing him, we can still pull this off. The pope and the UN will step aside and give us Cuba without a battle." Gearheardt squeezed my shoulder.

"You know, you're right. Do you really think there's a chance?"

The smile left as quickly as it had appeared. "Not a prayer, Jack. The Mexicans already have their story. The CIA is bobbing and weaving out of the picture, and the pope is probably boarding the pope-plane for Havana as we stand here, dicks in hand. I just thought you looked so pathetic I'd try to cheer you up before you committed suicide or something. You need to be able to roll with the punches a bit, Jack."

He squeezed my shoulder again and then dropped his hand.

"Let's head over to Las Palomas. Maybe a miracle will happen."

We began a sad walk through the streets of Mexico City. At the corner across from the Las Palomas a policeman brought two fingers to the bill of his cap and gave a lazy salute.

"You know, Gearheardt, we managed to walk around with guns, move in and out of a tent where the fake president of Mexico was lying in a pool of blood, and then stroll out of the plaza. I know the Mexican police are lax, but you would have thought—"

"Rodrigo."

Jack stopped. "You're kidding. Does he have that kind of pull with the police?"

"Daisy told me this morning when you were grabbing coffee. The girls paid for our protection today. Rodrigo was the go-between. He appreciated your help rescuing his son, Jack. Sometimes the lesser of us are the most appreciative."

That statement reminded me of Gearheardt's discussions with the Assistant God—the squadron chaplain—in Vietnam. But I just said, "Well, I'll be damned."

When we entered the war room at Las Palomas, we weren't welcomed as heroes. But we weren't jeered as failure either. Daisy and Isabella both embraced and kissed Gearheardt and shook hands with me. It did a lot for my ego to have two hookers decline to embrace me, but I knew that bigger issues were at hand.

"Isabella, bring the messages to me, por favor," Gearheardt said. He took off his jacket, removed his shoulder holster and hand-held howitzer, and plopped down at his desk. "Have a seat, Jack. Help me sort out the damages and then we'll plan our next move. I think you may be unemployed." He smiled that warm Gearheardt smile that always made me want to punch his face.

Isabella brought a short stack of messages and put them in front of Gearheardt.

"Señor Gearheardt," she said, "we need to talk about the girls in many cities. I will gather the information and then we can discuss, no?"

"You bet, Isabella. Let me see if there are any action items and then we can address the girl's issues. You look lovely back in your yellow, by the way."

Tragedy did not prevent blushing.

"Okay, what have we got here?" Gearheardt picked up the top sheet. "Oh this is nice." He turned the paper around and held it up for me to read.

It said, "*Nice try, jackass. Come over here and I'll kick your butt. Fidel Castro.*"

"Boy, the word got back to him quick," Gearheardt said. "I wish we could send a few Marines in there just to make him piss his pants."

He read a few pages without comment. Then he grimaced and handed a teletype to me.

Quan Zhoe Manufacing to Gearhat. Model 156 is new moder. Engineer have tow suggestin. Warning-do not have election with Model 156 on body, many lawsute. Two, loose screw (metar item not doing) on side of Model 156 with smar knife. Put stick in loose place and remove screw. Pull stuck items from Model 156 with grease attached. Work sometime. You due us $115000. Quan Zhoe Manufacing.

"Well, that clears that up," I said. "What are you going to do?"

"I'll have the girls clean up the message and post it to the embassies around the world. Maybe it will get down to those who need it, maybe not." He put down the sheet he was reading. "Jack, the girls will spring the trap in most cases. Their lives are just going to get worse, so why not put a few of the enemy out of action permanently. A couple more for you to look at and then I'm burning the whole pile, Jack. Victory has a mother but defeat is a bastard."

"Nicely put. Who are these from?" I said, taking the papers from him.

"The top one is from Waldheim. Arrogant asshole."

Your correspondence unclear. This office not involved in Cuba or Vatican activity. Notice to press would be unwise. Skeletons in your background could prove harmful. Go to hell.

"Offhand, Gearheardt, I would say the UN is out of the deal."

"And this one from the DCI. Our boss. It's nice of him to warn me."

Gearheardt. I was obviously kidding about taking the job as DCI for Galoreland. Please destroy the previous teletypes as you must have misunderstood my position. Thanks for your good service to the company. I should inform you that you will be hunted down and killed like a dog in the street.

"Get this, Jack." He handed the next sheet to me. "The Agency always overreacts to situations. This came in the same time the DCI's message came it. I think it was meant for your embassy office."

Office of DCI. Effectively immediately the Central Intelligence Agency will be known as the Agency of Central Intelligence, the ACI.

*To avoid confusion, destroy all letterhead and monogrammed material including hats and tee-shirts. Do **not** notify foreign nationals or allies. Blame Gearheardt. This will be my last communication as DCI CIA. Vernon Savage, ACI DCI. (Not my real name).*

He took two more pages from the stack and then shoved the remaining stack off his desk into a waste basket. "I like this one," he said.

Gearheardt. It may be easier for a camel to pass through the eye of a needle than for a lightning bolt to bounce off the pavement, penetrate your anus and fry you from the ground up. I am praying, however, that God will find a way. My money's on Him. Love, Pointy Hat.

PS: I can assure you, you sad sack of sacrilegious impurity, or Mr. Excommunicado as we call you around the palace, the Church adopted its attire long before the appearance of the KKK.

"Wow, Gearheardt. There are some unhappy folks out there. What are you going to do?"

"Did you ever think you'd see a message from the Pope about my ass, Jack? I'm saving this one." He folded the paper and stuck it into his jacket hanging over the chair.

"Isabella, come on over and let's see where we are and what we can do."

The woman walked over and pulled a chair up to the desk. Three other women, including a subdued Daisy, joined us also.

"I apologize for what has happened, ladies. It was my responsibility. I don't blame the girls who jumped the gun. Each situation, as we all know, can only be judged from the view of those on the ground."

Murmurs of sympathy and assent.

"I'll be blunt. The good news is that we've cut a lot of balls off of bad guys."

More murmurs, louder, affirming.

"I am going to assume, by the way, that the girls didn't attach the de-nutter to their favorite clients."

Murmurs, not so affirming.

"I know you don't like any of them, but I mean the ones who don't beat you and who tip generously."

"Gearheardt, mi amore, you really don't know what you're talking about, so let's get to the situation discussion?"

"You're absolutely right, Isabella. Absolutely right. But anyway, we got hundreds of balls in traction or chopped off. That's a victory of sorts."

Isabella reached out and took Gearheardt's hand. The kind of gesture which often signals bad news coming. "Señor Gearheardt," she began, "the girls want me to tell you that they appreciate very much what you have tried to do for us." She patted his hand. "Like the times before that men have promised to help us, we may be more worse off than before. In this case, we do not blame you and know that you were sincere. Also, we would like to tell you that we cannot do the intelligence network for longer."

This was probably the bad news. The intelligence network had been a lot of hard work and probably a great leverage for Gearheardt's operation, whatever it was.

Gearheardt took the news calmly.

"I'm sorry to hear that, Isabella." He looked at Daisy. "What do you say, Daisy? You were head of the operation here and in Central America."

Daisy lifted her head and her eyes were full. "Isabella speaks for me, Gearheardt. I am retire."

"Daisy is concerned that the local police and others will not treat her kindly. After they find out. That is why we did not use so many Model 156's in the Las Palomas. It was Daisy's decision, but . . ." She shrugged.

We sat silent for a moment. Downstairs a loud chortling laugh announced the arrival of the late afternoon trade. Isabella let go of Gearheardt's hand and lit a cigarette, offering one to Gearheardt also. It was the new regime.

"The new intelligence network is available for you, Señor Gearheardt," Isabella said with a sly smile. "The fees will be slightly higher, of course. Say, fifty percent higher."

Gearheardt sighed and slumped down in his chair. "I'm not sure I'm interested, but I'll get back to you. You are offering an exclusive of course?"

Isabella just laughed. "My former boss said that exclusive does not make good competition and without competition the fees will be low."

After a moment, Gearheardt drew himself up. "Well friends, I've got an airplane to catch. Jack, you're welcome to come with me." He put on his jacket.

"I think I'll stay and face the music, Gearheardt. Keep in touch though. I don't suppose you'll tell me where you're going."

"I've got about a dozen bastards I need to shoot, Jack. I think I'll head over to India. It's better to be shot like a dog in the street in India. Less embarrassing and hardly noticed. Take care, pal." We both stood and shook hands. "No hugs, Jack, the women are watching."

I walked out into the hall with Gearheardt, passing the women on the way. He took kisses from some of them. He was ignored by others and it seemed to hurt him.

"Nothing quite like the sickening stink of failure, Jack." He sighed. "Don't worry about your job with the agency if you want to stay. What happened this week will never have happened. Too many hands in the boiling pot for this to become a known incident."

I went to the window and after a moment he appeared on the street, joking with the parking valet. A taxi drew up and stopped beside them. Gearheardt walked to the driver's side, opened the door and, after extracting a surprised and frightened cabbie, got in. The taxi roared off in a cloud of burning rubber. As it passed the corner, a black Impala left the curb and accelerated after the taxi. I wanted to yell a warning to Gearheardt, beginning already to feel the loss.

"Gearheardt did not want you to see this, Jack."

Isabella held out the teletype page that Gearheardt had slid under the inkpad on his desk. I had assumed it was personal and he had forgotten it.

"Dear Señor Gearheardt," it read, "this is Sari. I am fine. I will be going to goodbye very soon. I am sorry to do something that has caused you much trouble, Angelica told me. The men here are very angry and will burn my place if I do not let them in. They are also angry because I feed the other parts of the men to the dogs in the street. Maybe this was not nice to do. But I am glad and maybe this is the equal right that you told me of in our conversation. To be angry. Next week I would be thirteen. It is nice in Cuba, yes? Sari."

Isabella seemed friendlier now that Gearheardt was gone. She placed her hand gently on my sleeve. I didn't think I could turn and face her.

"Gearheardt was to be Emperor of Mexico you know, Jack. He wanted to do that very bad. When I asked him why, he says that he likes living in Chapultepec Castle. He likes to be called His Excellency. And he says that when he is Emperor it's goodbye to girls and donkeys. I do not know what he is talking about, but he is crazy, no?"

"He is insane."

"But I like him very much."

"He is insane."

At the far end of the street, I saw the taxi squealing around the glorieta, the Impala close behind. They headed back at us. When the taxi passed, Gearheardt stuck his head out of the window and, grinning like an idiot, gave me a thumbs up.

CHAPTER TWENTY-FIVE

IS THIS THE LAST OF GEARHEARDT?

I t would be an understatement to say I went to my office with trepidation the next morning. My intent was just to gut it out. I still had operations underway (with Rodrigo) that I felt were important. Even though Crenshaw had dismissed me from the agency in the whore's room at Las Palomas, there were even odds that the whole thing would be covered up. Or they could, as the DCI warned, shoot me on sight.

Juanita greeted me warily. As I approached her desk, she shoved her paperwork into a single pile which she dropped in her desk drawer. She rose, which was unusual.

"Buenos dias, Señor Jack."

"Buenos dias, Juanita."

We stood facing one another for a moment. Her eyes, puffy and red-rimmed, avoided me as if I were a too-bright light. She fidgeted with a button on her pink sweater.

"You look nice today, Jaunita."

"Gracias, Señor Jack." Now she looked at me, smiling slightly. "You look like the man who was shoot at and missed but sheet at and hit."

I laughed politely. "Are you still taking English lessons from Corporal Weathers, Juanita?"

Juanita fidgeted with the button faster. I could see the black lacy brassier under her pink sweater where it was tightest. I loved her.

"The ambassador is to meet with you at ten o'clock, Señor Jack. If you need anything, I will get it for you."

I started into what I assumed was still my office. "Thanks, Juanita. I'm fine. Just had a rough week."

When I sat down at my desk, Juanita was at the door. "And Señor Pepe, he is okay?"

"Señor Gearheardt is fine too. Would you close my door please?"

My desk showed obvious signs of "intrusion and invasion." I wasn't surprised but tried to think if I had left behind anything of particular importance and decided I hadn't.

I still had a dial tone, but, after thinking for a moment, realized I had no one to call. Eduardo wouldn't be happy to hear from me. Crenshaw? No. My girlfriend at the Austrian embassy? Not likely. Mom? I didn't feel like explaining the whole thing to her quite yet. Gearheardt? No way to reach him. Unless . . .

"Gearheardt, you rotten bastard, do you still have a tap in my office? Give me a call if you do." I felt foolish talking to the walls.

But I knew when the light on my phone flashed it would be Juanita announcing my pal.

"Señor Pepe is on the line. He is—"

"He is insane, Juanita. I'll take it. You hang up."

Click.

"Gearheardt, are you in India yet?"

"Not yet, Jack. Got waylaid at the airport. The bastards winged me."

"Who?"

"Somebody pissed off at me, I assume. I'm not a detail guy, Jack."

"So are you okay? Where are you? Do you need help?"

"Thanks, Jack. Don't need help right now. I'm still in the city. Some dive near the market. Not the Ritz, I can assure you. Ouch, dammit."

"Gearheardt, let me get over there and give you a hand. I don't want you dying. Mom would never forgive me. How do I get there?" It was rare that Gearheardt really needed help, and I had an appointment with the Ambassador in an hour and a half, but my pal was wounded and holed up in some hovel in a city where he wasn't very popular.

"That was just Isabella pouring scalding water on my leg, Jack. These girls must be able to sit in boiling water. My ass is being cooked and they're just wrestling around like little sea otters."

"Gearheardt, are you in a tub with two or three girls, you rotten shit?"

"One just got out to get some lime for the beer, Jack. So there's only two. Why do you ask?"

I was silent.

"Okay, Jack, if it makes your Boy Scout, Presbyterian heart feel better, I'm lying underneath a shack in mud hut town on dirty hay with cockroaches crawling all over my wounded leg. Feel better, now?"

"Gearheardt, we may have endangered the lives of hundreds or thousands of girls, alienated the Vatican, cut off the nuts of countless worthless men and started down the road to war with Cuba. Not to mention that I am headed into a meeting with a very angry ambassador this morning, where at the very least I will get my ass chewed from here to Sunday. You treat all that as if we had missed the return date on our library books."

I heard Gearheardt speaking to someone. "Yes, it's Jack. No, you can't talk to him. And none of that lesbian crap. I'm trying to concentrate." Splashing and whining sounds. "Okay, Jack. Remember that the men who lost their balls were deserving. The Vatican can take care of itself, and at least the girls know someone tried to do something for them. Believe me, I feel bad."

"How did you get the message to call me?" I asked, wanting to change the subject before I blew up.

"The bug is connected to the com room at Las Palomas. Maria said you were talking to the walls asking me to call. Before you get all pissed off, I was going to call you anyway."

"After you had a bath."

"You're a Puritan, Jack. Yes, after I had a bath. Isn't there something more important we should be discussing?"

"I have no idea what to even ask you."

"Here's what you do. Ask Juanita for the folders I gave her. Take them to the meeting. She'll also have a statement that basically exonerates you from any potential charges. You lay the folders on the table. You pass out the statement, get everyone to sign and then you leave. Take the folders with you after they sign. Clear enough?" He paused and I thought I heard a giggle. "I've been doing some research on our boys. The Ambassador and Daisy. Crenshaw and the donkey—"

"*Crenshaw and the donkey?*"

"Just do what I tell you, Jack. I don't want to cause you trouble."

Heaven forbid that should ever happen.

"I assume the folders contain this information about the Ambassador and Crenshaw."

"You would assume that wouldn't you?"

"So we end up blackmailers?"

"I like to think of it as being extortionists. Blackmailing seems so . . ."

"Tawdry?"

"Yeah, tawdry. This is a non-cash transaction. When you get back from the meeting, tell the wall to call me and I'll ring you back. Good luck, Jack. You're a champ."

I couldn't think of what to say to him. Long ago, in a bar in Vientiane, he had called me a champ and wished me luck. I didn't see him again for three years.

"Gearheardt, why don't you just tell me where you are? Let me at least help you get out of the country."

"All arranged, Jackie. Tomorrow morning I'm off for India. Let's call it a payback for Sari. Then I'm not sure. But I'll call you. You know what they say about the girls in India, Jack—" A loud crash. "—oh shit!"

The line went dead. "Get me Gearheardt!" I yelled at the wall. "Come on, Maria. Get that bastard back on the line." I remembered that I could call Las Palomas. When I finally reached Daisy, she heard me out and then connected me to the com room.

"Maria, can you call Gearheardt? It's urgent!"

Maria sounded shaken. "He is not on the line, Señor Jack. He is not answering."

"Where is he, Maria? Did he tell anyone? Who's with him?"

"He sent the taxi for girls, Señor. I don't think no one knows."

I hung up and sat staring at the communications device Gearheardt had left for me, a wall with a bug in it. I wanted to panic, but couldn't think of a direction to panic in. The feeling I had was Gearheardt slipping away again. So close and probably so totally screwed up.

"Juanita!"

I felt under my desk and extracted a piece of wood lightly glued to the leg brace. Triggering a switch inside that small opening swung the brace aside and let me grasp the butt of a Walther PPK, 9-millimeter, a weapon given to me by my mother after she fell in love with Sean Connery.

"Si, Señor." Juanita stuck just her head into the office.

"Bring me the folders that Señor Gearheardt left with you."

"But Señor Pepe—"

"There is no Señor Pepe. It's Gearheardt. Bring me the folders."

I shoved the pistol into my belt and buttoned my jacket. Meeting Juanita as she came back with the folders, I grabbed her arm and led her back to her desk.

"Call upstairs and tell the Ambassador that I'm on the way up."

"But Jack, it's not ten o'clock."

Jack?

"Call him, Juanita." I started down the hall toward the stairs, then turned and came back to her desk. "Juanita, I'm sorry if I've been angry with you. You may be a very loyal assistant and a friend. But you've been working with Crenshaw, the Ambassador and Gearheardt. I really don't know if I can trust you." I paused and breathed deep. "The black bra trick won't work any more, Juanita. You're not a Mexican bimbo. You're a CIA operative. I just don't . . ." There was really nothing to say. "Just call the Ambassador and tell him I'll be there in two minutes."

"Come in, Jack, come in." The Ambassador sat at the end of the conference table. He had paused a cup of tea heading to his mouth. A cigarette smoldered in the ashtray. On one side of the table sat Crenshaw, a butterfly bandage holding together a nasty gash above his right eye. He nodded and looked back to the window, open to the noisy street below.

"Care for tea, Jack? You can smoke if you want. I enjoy the blasted things." The ambassador pointed toward a seat at the opposite end of the table. "Take that one if you wouldn't mind, Jack. Makes it easier for us all to see one another."

Under different circumstances, the ambassador was a man I would admire. He must have been catching hell from Washington but he was cool and collected and in control.

"Mr. Ambassador, I don't really have time to—"

"Pardon me, Jack." The ambassador looked at Crenshaw. "Major would you please shut that window. And latch it please. The equipment in the room won't activate if the windows are open. Darwin," he nodded to a large man standing by the door, "if you would step outside and close the door I would appreciate it."

I had rushed into the room in such huff that I hadn't noticed the ambassador's bodyguard.

"Good now, Jack. Get's a bit stuffy in here, but the soundproofing doesn't seem to work unless all of the openings are latched. But you were saying you didn't have time . . ."

"Where's the Pygmy? He was supposed to be in this meeting. The issue of blame for the fiasco was to be discussed. You agreed to that."

The Ambassador glanced at Crenshaw. "I'm afraid I don't know his whereabouts, Jack. I've never met the man."

"Then whose booster seat is that?" I pointed to a child's plastic car seat in the chair across from Crenshaw.

Crenshaw stared at it as if it had dropped from the sky. The Ambassador hesitated. "Well it appears that a short person was in the room earlier," he said.

In the silence that followed I heard a scurrying sound from under the table. After resisting the impulse for a moment, I ducked my head to see what (who?) was making the noise. There was nothing but Ambassador and CIA station chief legs and feet but just as I raised my head, the conference room door opened and then closed.

"Was the Pygmy under the table?" It pissed me off that I was being played with.

The Ambassador leaned back in his chair and steepled his hands under his chin, squinting down the table at me.

"I think, Jack, that a more germane issue is a young man in my embassy who would worry about pygmies dwelling under tables. The question 'was the Pygmy under the table' would seem to—"

"I need to find Gearheardt." I needed to get this meeting under control.

The Ambassador smiled and looked to Crenshaw. "Don't we all?" he said.

"I am not going to ask you but once," I said in a voice I hoped was intimidating. "Do you know where Gearheardt is?"

Crenshaw leaned forward and spoke up for the first time. "I'm not even sure *who* Gearheardt is, *Mr.* Armstrong. He certainly doesn't work for us. The rotten bastard is only out for himself. If he hadn't of—"

"That will do, Major. Your opinion of Mr. Gearheardt is not the issue here." He looked back at me. "The answer to your question is 'no,' Mr. Armstrong. We do not know the whereabouts of Mr. Gearheardt."

The Ambassador reached to a credenza behind him and brought back a folder. I wondered if I had been wrong about Ambassador Leahy. He almost seemed to be an ally.

"The purpose of this meeting—which you chose to accelerate rather rudely, Mr. Armstrong—is to examine the charges that various agencies, U.S., Cuban, and Mexican, are bringing against you. Rather serious issues."

The Ambassador began reading the 'charges' against me which ranged from treason to public indecency. Evidently the Mexicans, Cubans and the Vatican all wanted a piece of me. Murder, rape, consorting with prostitutes and non-payment of rent were on the list. Car theft, speeding, conspiracy to commit assassination, and breaking and entering—Chapultepec Castle—were mentioned. The ambassador's face got redder as he itemized the various infractions of embassy procedure that he personally had added to the charge sheet. Crenshaw looked at me with mounting glee, particularly when blasphemy and inciting an insurrection against Rome were mentioned.

So I was to be the scapegoat. Gearheardt mentioning that he 'didn't want to cause me trouble' flashed through my mind—the asshole. The Ambassador was now outlining the process by which I would be escorted to the airport and flown to a federal prison near Washington D.C. to await trial.

"Why don't you just take me to Queretero and shoot me like they did Maximilian?"

"The Mexicans have suggested just that, Mr. Armstrong. But they wouldn't assure us you wouldn't be tortured first." He looked up at me. "We can't be a party to that."

I slipped my hand beneath the table and grasped the handle of the pistol. "Look, you silly bastards, I'm not going to—".

"We have a solution, Mr. Armstrong," the Ambassador said. It was clear he wasn't in favor of it. "There is an opportunity to go to work for the Pygmy. He is contracting his own organization to work for us."

"The Pygmy Intelligence Agency?" I said with as much sarcasm as I could muster." The Pygmy you just denied exists?"

"He is small, but growing. I have been asked by Langley to offer you that chance."

Crenshaw snorted and the Ambassador gave him a stern look.

But Crenshaw couldn't contain himself. "Listen, that freak might think he's taking over the Agency, but just because he's picked up Gearheardt's prostitutes, doesn't mean he'll still have his contract."

"He's picked up Gearheardt's pros—"

"Don't interrupt, Armstrong. You're finished. Done. History. We will not have blasphemers working in the intelligence business!"

The Ambassador sat up straight. "It is you who is finished, *Major* Crenshaw. *I* run the show in Mexico now and I don't need the bible-thumping, donkey loving—"

"It's a *burro*, you whore-mongering—!"

"I thought your expense report said that your burro was eaten," the Ambassador said sarcastically. "I can have that report sent up." I assumed he was grasping for something he could understand. He looked bewildered.

"I have a *new* burro, you sanctimonious dimwit." He dropped his head into his hands, elbows on the table. "Where does the state department *get* you numbskulls? This is not about burros or pygmies or whores! This is about a mission that the Central Intelligence Agency was running that *this* man and his insane cohort screwed up." He raised his head and looked at me. "Now we'll *never* have Cuba." He suddenly slammed his fist on the conference table, hitting his coffee cup and sending it skittering across the highly polished surface.

"Oh my God," the Ambassador said. He tried to gather the broken pieces and ran his hand over a scratch in the table. "This is government property."

It seemed time for me to get to the point. I stood and brandished my pistol so that all could see. "Shut up! Both of you! Crenshaw, get your hands on the table where I can see them! Mr. Ambassador . . . shit, quit crying."

After noticing that I had not inserted a clip into the pistol, I kept my brandishing down to a minimum, but got the desired affect—quiet and attention.

"Gentlemen, here are the new rules. I am not going to be shot, tortured, hung, imprisoned or humiliated. I am not going to join Pygmy

International in order to run the prostitute intelligence network." I placed the folders on the table in front of me, reversed so that the men could read their names. Crenshaw, the Ambassador (I assumed that Gearheardt had never bothered to learn his name), and Armstrong (me?).

I passed a copy of the release and hold harmless document that Gearheardt had prepared to the Ambassador, then copies to the Major.

"It's very simple, gentlemen. You will sign that document and these folders will never reach the press or the respective governments which would have the greatest interest in them. You, Major Crenshaw, can keep your relationship with your burro to yourself. You, Mr. Ambassador, can keep your part ownership of Las Palomas and common-law wife Daisy. There is no negotiation. And finally, I want to know—and I mean right now!—what has happened to Gearheardt. I suspect that he is wounded and needs my help." A small piece of my mind was grateful that he was perhaps actually wounded, otherwise I would have had to argue that he was in a tub with three naked women and needed my help.

"Well, there is not a snowball's chance in hell I'll be signing," the Major said. "For starters, I have not had *relations* with any barnyard animals and specifically not with Caroline, my, uh, current burro."

The Ambassador already had his pen in hand. "That's not the issue, Major. I for one don't want to spend the next decade explaining that I had perfectly valid reasons for investing in Las Palomas (he had the decency to blush and not look at me) and I would think that you would not want to be in the position of always having to deny that you were fucking your donkey. Pardon my French." He handed his pen to Crenshaw.

Who, with a disgusted grunt, signed the last signature block. As he did so, a soft knock on the door caught our attention. Darwin entered, glanced at my pistol on the table and laid a sheet of paper next to the Ambassador's ashtray. The ambassador looked at me then back at Darwin, nodded, and the man left. The exoneration document, probably worthless but which would get me out of town, was slid down the table.

"Now about Gearheardt," I said, "I want every swinging dick in the embassy out trying to find him. Ambassador, you can give that order from here and we'll all just wait for him to be found." I moved the pistol closer, holding the butt, with the gaping hole where a clip should have been, toward my body. "The document you all just signed gives me the right to shoot you as traitors." I was bluffing, but they had only scanned the document and wouldn't know that.

The Ambassador, calm again, smiled and gently shook the message just delivered. "I don't think any shooting will be necessary, Mr. Armstrong. And we won't be waiting for your Mr. Gearheardt. Let me read this to you.

"*Flash: Urgent: Ambassador: Mexico City Airport, eleven hundred hours. White Caucasian male, believed American. Subject appeared to be wounded in arm and upper leg. Subject almost nude (towel around waist) and laughing. Escorted by three Hispanic men in black suits and one Caucasian male in military uniform. Not laughing. Forced onto aircraft roughly, subject greeted stewardesses warmly, tossed towel from airplane saying "I guess I won't be needing this anymore." Again, escorts not amused. Threatening gestures and application of pressure to wounded areas observed. Aircraft left eleven hundred hours and fifteen minutes. Turkish Airlines. Please advise as to action needed.*"

"Does that sound like our boy, Jack?" the Ambassador asked, smiling.

I looked at Crenshaw. "Do your guys know anything about this?"

Crenshaw looked almost sympathetic. "No clue, Jack. But it doesn't sound too good."

The Ambassador shook his head. "Gearheardt pisses off many people," he said.

I rose and gathered the folders. Crenshaw made a move to grab his, but I jerked it away and leveled the bulletless pistol at him. "Don't give me a reason, Major." I blushed at the dramatic statement. I couldn't hate Crenshaw who, it seemed, was doing the job he was asked to do.

"Goodbye, Gents. Give me about fifteen minutes and I'll be out of the building and out of your hair." I had been watching too many movies, but this was an awkward moment. Should I back out? Walk out boldly? I just left.

Juanita stood as I walked by to my office.

"I'm sorry, Señor Jack. To not be a loyal assistant, I mean. I try to work for the Major and for the Ambassador and also for you and Señor Pepe. I work for too many people."

"It happens to a lot of us, Juanita."

In my office I gathered the few remaining personal items and tossed them in a briefcase. I took a deep breath and picked up the folder that had "Armstrong" across the top. Inside was a note.

Jackson,

Fell for it didn't they? I knew that you would open this note only, Boy Scout, so I'll tell you that the other folders have blank pages in them.

I tore the others open. All three were filled with blank sheets of paper.

These suckers have so many secrets they've forgotten who they've screwed. Not that they're bad guys. They have a tuf job. One that I could do with one hand behind my back, but tuf nevertheless. They have congress and all that bureaucratic crap.

You and I did what we did, Jack. Leave it at that. I think it was Teddy Roosevelt who said, 'There are those who never jump into the ring. They just sit in the stands yelling for somebody else to cut the bull's nuts off. The guys who jump in are in deep bullshit and they have sweat on their brows but their eyes are on the bull's nuts and they give their best. And even if the bull wins, he gets his nuts cut off anyway. And the men that never tried jumping into the bullshit' . . . I forget the rest. But you get the idea. Maybe it was Hemingway. Anyway you and I tried, Jacko. God Bless America. God Bless the Marine Corps.

Gearheardt

The word had gotten around by the time I walked to the elevator and started out of the building. No one spoke to me. No one met my eye.

At the entrance, the Marine guard handed me the clipboard for me to sign out. He looked strong, his uniform spotless and crisp.

"Semper fi, sir," he said as I walked toward the door. I could have kissed the corporal right then and there if it wouldn't have ruined his career opportunities.

In Chapultepec Park I found a bench that was catching the afternoon sun. Above me the walls of the castle also caught the sun and somehow made the fortress look impregnable. The Marines had stormed those walls decades ago. Around me the Mexican people laughed and strolled, unchanged and seemingly happy.

I remembered my last conversation with Gearheardt before we headed to the faked assassination.

"You know, Gearheardt, it strikes me that all of the bad guys in this operation were minding their own business until we stirred them up."

"Jack, you know the saying. Defeat is the result of men minding someone else's business. I'm not sure who said it."

"I don't think anybody said it. It doesn't make a damn bit of sense."

Gearheardt had sat twirling his wine in his glass. He tossed it down, broke the glass on the ground and smiled. "What makes sense, Jack, is that we're trying to do something for someone less fortunate than ourselves. We're Americans, Jack. That's what we do. Sometimes we're not successful and the people are even less fortunate. But at least they're people who had a shot at being more fortunate." He paused and lit a cigarette. After picking a speck of tobacco from his tongue, he smiled the Gearheardt smile. "If you want an egg, you've got to squeeze a chicken, Jack."

I looked at him for a moment, wondering which of us was crazy.

"Yes," I said, "there is that I suppose."

I leaned back on the bench and closed my eyes to the smog-muted sun above Mexico City. I missed Gearheardt already. When he left he seemed to take my energy with him.

The plan to take Cuba bloodlessly wasn't a bad one. Giving the prostitutes a decent future, who could argue with that? It all seemed doable. But for the betrayal of Crenshaw, who had his Catholic agenda. And the Pygmy, who had his . . . I guess he just wanted the girls. Was there anyone in the deal looking out for the U.S.?

Sometime in the early morning, the phone rang in my apartment. I climbed over half-packed suitcases and boxes and answered it on the fourth ring.

"Armstrong."

"Sir, this is Corporal Winters. I'm not sure that anyone has called you. I was in the com room just now." He stopped.

"And?"

"A Turkish airliner blew up over the Atlantic, sir."

I didn't say anything.

"There were no reported survivors, sir."

"Thank you, Corporal. If it's possible could you get a copy of the dispatch and send it to my apartment? The drivers will know."

"No problem, sir." He paused again. "Sir, do you think that Mr. Gearheardt . . ."

"I'll drop by and see you tomorrow if you're on duty, Winters. Thanks very much for calling me."

"Better come early, sir. We're supposed to have our gear packed up by noon."

"What's that all about? What do you mean 'have our gear packed up?'" I was in a nightmare and couldn't clear my head.

"The Mexicans have kicked us out, Mr. Armstrong. In forty-eight hours the whole embassy staff is persona non-grata in Mexico."

After a moment I was able to reply.

"Well, at least Gearheardt accomplished *something*."

"The scuttlebutt is that the Ambassador is crediting you with that accomplishment, sir. I hope I'm not talking out of turn here."

I sighed and rubbed my aching head. "Defeat is the result of men minding someone else's business, Corporal." I felt numb, but couldn't help picturing Gearheardt in another flaming aircraft.

"Yessir. That's what Mr. Gearheardt always told us. Semper fi, Mr. Armstrong."

"Semper fi, Corporal Winters."

I hung up and found the bed in the dark. Then I grabbed the phone cord and moved the receiver nearer. I didn't want to chance missing a call from some Godforsaken place where Gearheardt might turn up.